# Praise for *Viking*

**Double RITA nominee, Best First Book and Best Paranormal Romance**

**Winner, HOLT medallion, Best Paranormal**

"Asa Maria Bradley creates a swoon-worthy hero who sizzles across the pages in this tale full of passion and destiny! Sexy, stubborn, and smart lovers clash in a tension-filled race to outwit science and control fate. Bradley is a new force to be reckoned with in the paranormal genre!"

—Rebecca Zanetti, *New York Times* bestselling author of the Dark Protector series

"Bradley has created a fascinating world that merges Norse mythology and modern-day society with plenty of action."

—*RT Book Reviews*, 4 Stars

"A debut novel that breathes fresh air into the overcrowded paranormal romance genre with an exciting tale of modern adventure mixed in with Norse mythology. Vikings are the new vampires!"

—*Night Owl Reviews*, Top Pick!

"*Viking Warrior Rising* is a super fantastic novel that had me wanting more!"

—*Romance Reviews*, 5 Stars, Top Pick!

# VIKING WARRIOR REBEL

# ASA MARIA BRADLEY

sourcebooks
casablanca

*To my dad and my father-in-law, for showing me
what being a good father and a good husband look
like. You are both so very missed.*

*Bengt Arne Harry Larsson
(November 27, 1941–December 19, 2015)
Laurence Frank Bradley
(November 1, 1930–April 10, 2016)*

Published by Sourcebooks Casablanca, an imprint of Sourcebooks, Inc.
P.O. Box 4410, Naperville, Illinois 60567-4410
(630) 961-3900
Fax: (630) 961-2168
www.sourcebooks.com

Printed and bound in Canada.
MBP 10 9 8 7 6 5 4 3 2 1

# Chapter 1

ASTRID ZIPPED HER DUFFEL BAG AND TOOK A LAST LOOK around the sparsely decorated room to see if she'd forgotten anything. She couldn't think of what else to bring. Everything she needed for her mission was neatly packed in her bag. Toiletries and clothes nestled next to weapons and ammunition like pieces of a puzzle. She'd always prided herself on packing light. A true warrior should be able to leave for battle at a moment's notice.

She shrugged into her favorite leather jacket and slipped her cell phone into the pocket. A light knock on the door announced Naya entering the room. The queen wore a traditional Norse sleeveless gray tunic over slim black pants. Although Astrid couldn't see it from her current position, she knew the back of the garment showed an intricately embroidered bear. She knew because she had a tunic just like it in her own closet. The bear was a symbol of their berserker, the inner warrior soul the immortal Vikings and Valkyrie channeled when they went into battle.

Naya flung herself into the armchair next to the bed in a most unqueenly fashion. The slight woman had been handfasted to Leif, the Viking king, for only ten months and still wasn't used to her role as ruling royalty. Although, Astrid doubted Naya would ever put on regal airs. Her new mortal queen and friend was a formidable cybersecurity expert and a master of hand-to-hand combat. Naya wouldn't give up her work or her training to take on a more traditional role. Which was fine with Astrid. Naya's natural tendency to say exactly what was on her mind without any political filtering made it easy to be her friend. And Astrid had too few of those.

"Looks like you're all packed," Naya said. "Are you sure you don't want to take one of the others with you as backup? I'm sure Ulf would go."

Astrid snorted. "Ulf and I would bicker so much that the trip would take twice as long, and one of us would probably mortally wound the other by the time we got back." That was another reason the Norse warriors needed their queen's frank assessments. The fortress hidden deep in the eastern Washington State pine forest held way too much testosterone. Naya and Astrid were two of only three Valkyries trying to educate the immortal Viking warriors about women in the twenty-first century.

A smirk played on Naya's lips. "There is that." She leaned forward in the chair. "But are you sure you will be okay on your own?"

"I'll be fine." Astrid avoided looking at Naya, knowing she'd see deep concern in her friend's eyes. During the last few skirmishes with Loki's creatures, Astrid had struggled to regain control over her berserker after the battle was over. She'd tried to hide it from the others, but the king was connected to all the warriors' berserkers. And Naya felt what was going on with each warrior through her *själsfrände* bond, her soul-mate connection with the king.

"If you say so, it's just that—"

Astrid interrupted. "I am honored that you chose me." She turned to face Naya. "Believe me, I know how much you care about your brother, and I will not screw this up." She couldn't afford to. During her last patrol, she'd gone so far into battle fever that she hadn't paid close enough attention to her surroundings and had almost taken out an innocent bystander. Ulf had been there to witness the near catastrophe, which was another reason she didn't want the warrior with her as backup. He'd just expect her to screw up again. All her battle brothers did. She needed to do this alone to prove to them—and to herself most of all—that she was a worthy warrior.

"We have complete faith in your ability to bring my brother back," Naya answered, her dark-blue eyes serious.

Astrid doubted the king did but chose not to contradict her friend. "I'll be in constant contact. I promise." She'd been chosen for this mission before her last screwup, and she knew Ulf had shared his concern with Leif, and probably with some of the other warriors as well. Astrid suspected she was only still on the mission because the queen had talked the king out of replacing her. Naya's loyalty, once earned, was unwavering.

"Of course you will." Naya waved her hand as if staying in contact was a given. The two of them talked daily, and she didn't know how unusual this new close-ness was for Astrid. "It's just hard for me. I want to bring Scott back on my own."

"You know you can't. Leaving Leif would weaken your bond, and that would weaken all of us." She didn't tell Naya that now that she was queen, it was unlikely she'd ever do major fighting on her own again. Leif allowed her to join regular patrols without him, but anything above that would drive the overprotective king crazy.

"He could come with me." Naya's tone was wistful.

Astrid didn't bother to answer. She just quirked an eyebrow.

Naya sighed. "Yes, fine, I know that's not possible. I have to figure out a new way to monitor the wolverines' activities. The labs have gone completely underground, but I picked up some chatter on the Darknet." The only reason Astrid knew anything about the hidden corners of the Internet was because Naya wouldn't shut up about geeky stuff. Astrid preferred fighting Loki's wolverines to monitoring their online communications. The wolverines were trying to manipulate and dominate the human population into inadvertently triggering Ragnarök, the final battle and the world's' end. Freya and Odin had countered by sending immortal Vikings and Valkyries to battle Loki's minions. With Naya's help, they'd taken down one of the labs used to genetically engineer wolverines, and for a while it had looked like that put a dent in Loki's plans. Recently however, wolverines had started popping up to fight once again.

"I have no doubt you'll be able to find the lab and shut it down."

Naya smiled, but her shoulders slumped. "I just can't get used to being responsible for anyone other than myself and my brother." She suddenly grinned. "I'm pretty sure I'll drive everyone crazy while you are away, especially Leif."

Astrid laughed. "At least Irja will be here to keep you company in this sea of testosterone."

"I may drive her crazy too." Astrid doubted that would happen. The tribe's medical officer seemed to have an endless supply of patience. Astrid had worked with Irja for a century, and the two of them had been friendly but never close. Naya joining the tribe had changed that. Irja was now as much of a confidante to Astrid as Naya was. Of course, surviving multiple attacks and life-threatening diseases tended to make people bond.

The queen stood and pulled her tunic straight. "Are you ready to go?"

Astrid squared her shoulders and nodded. She wasn't looking forward to the *skydd* ritual. Whenever a warrior went on a mission requiring him or her to spend days outside the fortress, the tribe gathered to ask the gods for protection and courage. "As ready as I'll ever be." She hated being the center of attention. Especially now, when her battle brothers second-guessed not only her warrior skills, but also her right to be chosen for this mission.

"Come on then."

Astrid followed Naya out the door and into the hallway, where the sun painted a kaleidoscope of colors as it shone through the stained-glass windows depicting famous scenes from the Norse Sagas. They walked down the stairs side-by-side, the thick carpet runner muffling the sound of their heavy boots. The rest of the Norse warriors had gathered at the bottom of the stairs in the large foyer of the fortress. Each of them had died an honorable death centuries ago and earned their place in Valhalla. The god Odin had trained them—or in the case of the Valkyries, the goddess Freya—and when they returned to Midgard, the human realm, the berserker became a part of them. They all wore the same tunic as Naya's, to symbolize the bond they had with their inner warrior spirit. Since Astrid would set off right after the ceremony, she wore the clothes she'd be traveling in. In the old days, the blessing was believed to permeate what a warrior wore to battle and the weapons he or she carried. Her worn leather jacket was her version of chain mail, and she wore it pretty much everywhere.

The king stepped forward and extended his left hand to help his betrothed descend the last few steps. The Midgard Serpent tattoo spiraling up his arm caught the sunlight streaming through one of the windows and it looked like the snake winked. The king's own ice-blue eyes were focused intently on the queen, and there was so much love and devotion reflected in them that Astrid's heart skipped a beat. "*Älskling*," he said, and Astrid felt a click deep inside her chest as he enveloped Naya's smaller hand in his own. The physical connection reverberated through their *själsfrände* bond and the king's berserker's connection with all of the tribes' inner warriors. Every one of them had a serpent tattoo encircling their biceps, but it was an incomplete image without a tail. When a warrior met their *själsfrände*, the tail formed on the top of their hand, just below their wrist. They then had to complete the bond before the tattoo crept up their arm and met with the main body of the serpent. If they failed to bond before the tattoo completed itself, they'd go into permanent battle fury and be a danger to themselves and their battle brothers and sisters.

A few of the Vikings surreptitiously rubbed their

chests. The king and queen's story had been a rocky one. They'd almost lost Leif to permanent battle fever when Naya had left him to rescue her brother. It was good to see how the royal couple's love for each other kept expanding. In some small part, buried deep in her heart, Astrid wished she would find what they had. But a *själsfrände* bond was a rare occurrence. And it was rarer still between a mortal and a Viking. Astrid looked around the foyer. She wasn't eager to date any of her battle brothers, much less pledge her soul to them.

Leif shifted his gaze to Astrid and nodded, a small smile on his lips. She tilted her head in a small bow and took her position behind the royal couple as they led the warriors out the front door to a clearing in the forest behind the fortress. The king helped his betrothed take her seat on the newly constructed majestic chair that stood next to his own. Both thrones rested on a large flat slab of basalt rock at one of the short ends of the rectangular opening among the trees. Behind the huge piece of volcanic rock, a giant ash tree stretched its branches far above the canopy of evergreens, a physical representation of the mythological holy tree Yggdrasil that reached all realms of the Norse universe. It dwarfed its neighbors, and the lighter-green leaves glittering in the sunshine contrasted with the darker pine needles.

Astrid took a deep breath and stood on the ground in front of the thrones. Her fellow warriors took a knee behind her, the rustling of their tunics a soft whisper through the air.

Leif's eyes were kind as he looked at her. "Astrid Idrisdotter, are you prepared to serve your king and queen?"

"Yes." She was proud of how strong her voice sounded, despite the rapid beating of her heart.

The king stood. "We ask you to retrieve the queen's brother, a valiant warrior who has yet to join our tribe. The queen needs him by her side when she weds me two weeks from this day."

Astrid wasn't sure what to say, so she just nodded.

"Are you prepared to complete this mission?"

"Yes," she said again.

"Will you protect the queen's brother as if he were your battle brother? Will you pledge your life and guarantee his safety?"

"I will." Her heart beat even faster as a wind rustled the ash's branches and pressed through the trees along the clearing. It caressed her cheek and tousled her hair.

"Kneel," the king commanded, reaching for something inside his tunic.

Harald, the king's second-in-command, rose and approached the rock as Astrid sank to her knees and bowed.

"Raise your head, Astrid Idrisdotter," Harald said, standing in front of her. His green eyes met hers, and he held out a cylindrical piece of wood. "May your journey be swift. May your sword be sharp and your enemies' flesh fast to bleed."

Astrid took the stick, and the runes inscribed on the surface glowed. "I will protect the queen's brother with my life. None will harm him on my watch." The runes flared and then the glow slowly died out. Astrid looked up at her king and queen.

Naya stood and joined Leif at his side. "Rise," Leif said, lifting his hands in the air.

The warriors rose as one.

"Chosen by Odin and Freya, we are battle brothers and sisters. As long as we fight together, our enemies will not defeat us. Do you stand with your Valkyrie sister?"

"Yes," the Vikings and Irja said in unison behind Astrid. Their voices vibrated through the air as the wind picked up, whipping the tunics of the king and queen.

"Do you pledge your loyalty to her and to one another with pure hearts?"

"We do," they said in unison again, and Astrid joined them when they thumped their right hands on their chests, right above their hearts.

Leif focused on Astrid. "May Odin and Freya bless your mission, protect your journey, and flood your heart with courage."

Naya took a step forward, looking straight at Astrid. "My brother and I are honored. I have complete faith that you will succeed."

Astrid swallowed the lump in her throat. She wished she could be as certain as her friend.

---

Twenty hours later, Astrid's boots echoed against a shiny marble floor as she crossed the Denver hotel lobby. The male clerk on the other side of the check-in desk watched as she approached, appreciation glinting in his eyes. Despite the tiredness seeping into her bones, she put a little extra swivel in her hips as she strode toward him. After those long hours of driving, she was beyond exhausted and wished only for a cold glass of wine, a hot bath, and a bed with crisp sheets, in that exact order. Still, it would be a shame to let the clerk's attention go to waste.

She smiled flirtatiously and tossed her wavy blond

hair. The travel-limp tresses landed with a flop on her back. She hoped the hotel offered top-of-the-line toiletries, including bubbles for the hot bath. She'd grown up in squalor, and she now used only the best.

The clerk's gaze dipped low and swept up her body before meeting her eyes again. Astrid sighed at the predictability of the human male, but still increased the wattage of her smile.

The man's eyes widened. "Welcome. Are you checking in, Miss...?"

"Idrisdotter, but call me Astrid. It's probably easier." She gently lowered her large duffel bag to the floor. Her smallsword was in its scabbard, wound up in layers of clothing. It wasn't likely to make a sound as the bag hit the floor, but the weapon was her favorite and had been with her for a long time. Plus, the guns might have shifted during travel, and there was no reason to call attention to how armed she was. She straightened and noticed the clerk's gaze had slipped to the V-neck of her plain cotton T-shirt. *Seriously*.

The goddess Freya had blessed her with curly blond hair and curves that seemed to please the male eye. Astrid knew how to use that to her advantage, and her looks could be a great weapon. She quirked an eyebrow at the clerk, fished her driver's license out of her wallet, and threw it on the counter.

The bow tie of his uniform wobbled as his fingers tapped a keyboard. "I see you're with us for only one night." He threw her a quick glance.

"I drove through the night and am really tired." Astrid leaned over the counter, pretending to peek at his screen, while making sure her neckline dipped lower.

The clerk's glance moved to her cleavage as if pulled by a magnetic force. "Ah, let's see what type of rooms we have available." He swallowed loudly.

One free upgrade and a short elevator ride later, Astrid unlocked the door of a luxury suite on the top floor. The expansive windows covered one whole wall and offered a splendid view of the Denver downtown skyline and the Rocky Mountains beyond. Snowcapped peaks rose dramatically against a clear, blue spring sky. It reminded her of the mountains at home, although their tops were more rounded, more worn down. The Scandes, the mountain chain between Sweden and Norway, had been old even when she was a little girl thousands of years ago. And still, they had appeared gigantic to that little orphan thrall girl who had almost no one looking out for her.

She shook her head to get rid of the memories of how powerless she had been when she was a slave. Thanks to excellent fighting skills, she'd earned her freedom and would never again be in a situation where someone else owned any part of her. She yawned. Although she didn't quite feel all the years of her age today, the long drive from Washington State had definitely drained her. Nothing a bath and a nap couldn't fix though.

She strolled into the bathroom, humming appreciatively to herself when she saw the large sunken tub with jets. She immediately turned on the hot faucet and let the steamy water fill the tub. A quick inspection of the sink revealed toiletries that met her approval. She dumped the whole mini bottle of bubbles into the bath. It had been a very long time since she was that dirty, little thrall girl who didn't even own the rags that covered her body.

She didn't go to excess now, but she made sure to appreciate the simple pleasures in life. Pleasures like expensive bubbles and high-thread-count sheets. These little luxuries relaxed her and therefore made her a better warrior. At least, that's what she told herself. There was probably some deep-seated psychological reason why she felt cleaner and prettier if the soap she'd used was expensive, but why waste time figuring that out? It was more efficient just to spend the money.

As the foam swirled and danced on the rising surface of the water, she fished her cell phone out of the back pocket of her jeans and tapped out a text to the queen. Astrid's lips quirked as she imagined how stir-crazy Naya would be by now. Arrived in Denver, she texted. Will head to clinic tomorrow and be back with your brother soon.

She'd pulled off her T-shirt and jeans by the time the phone buzzed an answer. Be careful and thank you.

Astrid's underwear joined the top and jeans on the bathroom floor, and she sank into the hot, fragrant water. A contented sigh escaped her lips as the warmth soothed her travel-worn body, easing the ache in her tense shoulders and stiff back. Driving straight from Washington to Colorado had seemed like a good idea, but now she regretted only stopping for a short nap at a rest stop instead of sleeping in a proper bed. Although, a roadside motel wouldn't have offered the luxury of the suite she was currently in.

She sank in deeper, fully submerging. As she blew out her breath under water, more tension left her body, but a small knot of anxiety remained in her stomach. She couldn't afford to relax fully. Couldn't afford to screw up. She'd seen the look on Ulf's face after their last patrol. Worse, she'd seen the look on her king's face. She knew they tried to hide their worry, but she'd been making too many mistakes lately. Even before that disastrous night, she'd gone too far over the edge into battle fury. Twice, one of the Vikings had to knock some sense into her before she had her rage under control again.

Her lungs ached and she sat up to draw in a deep breath, resting her head against her pulled-up knees. Then there'd been that night where she almost killed a human. It went against everything she stood for. She had been chosen by Freya to protect the people of Midgard. She shook her head. Couldn't think about that night now. Couldn't afford to go down the road of second-guessing herself. It was enough that her battle brothers had lost their faith in her. She had to remain strong.

If she didn't do this mission right and bring back her queen's brother, she might as well not return to the Norse fortress.

Astrid reached for the shampoo, and as she lathered her hair and massaged her scalp, she reviewed tomorrow's plan. She'd drive up to the clinic and pick up Scott. He had endured a long and painful recovery and would probably not be able to do the journey in one stretch, so they'd stop for the night on the way back to Washington. They might have to stop for more than one night, depending on how much the traveling tired Scott, but they would still be back at the Viking fortress in plenty of time for the wedding.

Instead of driving the interstates through Montana and Wyoming as she'd done on the way to Denver,

they'd stick to small roads that would eventually lead
her through Idaho back to the Viking fortress. That
way, they'd be able to stay under the radar of the camp
handlers and Loki's monsters. And if not, it wasn't
like Astrid and her throwing daggers hadn't won fights
where they were outnumbered before. However, she'd
like to avoid a conflict if at all possible. Fighting had a
way of drawing attention.

Thoughts of battle stirred her inner warrior, but she
clamped down on the mental restraints she used to control her berserker. With any luck, it wouldn't surface
during this trip. She finished washing her hair and rinsed
off before reluctantly leaving the bathroom. Wrapped
in a towel with another wound around her still-damp
hair, she crossed the suite toward the bedroom. Sleep
would help her control the berserker. She pulled back
the blinding-white sheets and threw half the pillows on
the floor before crawling into the king-size bed.

—⁓—

A few hours later, Astrid checked her reflection in
the hotel elevator. She'd woken up hungry, but rather
than ordering room service, she planned to visit a well-
reviewed French restaurant a few blocks from the hotel.
When she'd first returned from Valhalla to the human
realm, she'd spent some time in France and still loved
the cuisine. The Viking fortress was unfortunately
located in a part of the United States where people
preferred burgers and barbecue to beef bourguignonne.
The clinic wouldn't open until morning, so she might
as well enjoy to the fullest the hours she had to wait.
Plus, having a meal at an expensive restaurant helped

her cover story of being a wealthy professional woman on a business trip.

She smoothed down the simple black dress she'd brought especially for the restaurant. Made of a clingy knit material, it packed well and didn't take up much room in the bag. She might like dressing appropriately, but weapons would always be a priority and take up the most room in her luggage. The bulk of her arsenal was safely hidden in her hotel room, but she'd made sure she was adequately armed tonight, even for the short walk to the restaurant from the hotel.

She turned sideways to see if the dagger strapped to her thigh would show in profile. The short but full skirt hid her knife sheath perfectly. Twisting a few degrees more, she adjusted the silver belt she wore around her waist. Two throwing blades slid sideways into the back of the custom-made belt, their decorated hilts blending perfectly with the inlays of turquoise and lapis lazuli.

It took only a few minutes to reach the restaurant, and as soon as she stepped inside its doors, Astrid breathed in deeply, appreciating the rich smells of delectable food. The maître d' assured her the table she'd reserved would be available shortly and suggested she wait in the bar.

Astrid took his recommendation and walked the few steps up to the bar, which was raised half a level above the restaurant's main floor. She ordered a glass of her favorite First Growth Bordeaux and inhaled its aroma deeply before savoring her first sip. Sighing contentedly, Astrid perched on a high stool as she let her gaze roam over the patrons enjoying their dinners.

She went for another sip of wine, but froze with the

glass halfway to her lips. One of the men across the room looked familiar. He was in half profile as he spoke with his male dinner companion. It couldn't be Holden. No way *he* would be here in Denver. She'd avoided him and his club ever since that night she'd been high on battle fever and, as a result, had gone down a wide road of poor choices due to lack of impulse control.

The memories of Luke Holden's calloused hands heating her skin had her suddenly blushing.

As if he knew she was looking at him, the man turned and their gazes caught across the room. It was definitely Holden. She'd recognize that blond hair and those steel-gray eyes anywhere. She knew how the one-day stubble of that square jaw felt against her own skin. How those arrogant lips could deliver the most scorching of kisses. Heat spread across her skin as other body parts perked up at the memory of her last encounter with the man across the room.

He quirked an eyebrow and raised his glass to her in a silent greeting, a cocky smile stretched across his lips.

Astrid turned her head away, tipped back her own wineglass, and drained it.

# Chapter 2

LUKE COULDN'T TAKE HIS EYES OFF ASTRID. EVEN though he'd expected her to appear tonight—after all, that was why he was having dinner at this precise location—she still stunned him. The recessed lights around the swanky bar in this pretentious restaurant highlighted her many shades of blond. They ran from palest silver to a rich honey-gold. He remembered what it had been like to wrap his hands in those luxurious waves while he buried himself deep inside her and she clenched around him.

"So that's the mark." Broden whistled appreciatively, forcing Luke's thoughts away from dangerous territory.

He reluctantly tore his gaze away from Astrid and glared at the man across the table. "Yeah, that's Idrisdotter." He'd never worked with this guy before, but his reputation was solid, supposedly the best in the Denver FBI field office. Broden's job tonight was not too taxing. He just had to pretend to be Luke's business associate, which basically meant provide some conversation while they ate their food. Luckily, they were far enough away from the bar and didn't have to fake chatter.

"You're a lucky guy." The way Broden's gaze traveled up and down Astrid's body made Luke want to reach across the table and rip his throat out. Why was he overreacting? Broden was simply sharing the thoughts of every other red-blooded male in the joint.

"It's just a job." The words came out gruffly, and Luke slowly eased the grip on his fork. No need to freak Broden out by bending the silverware.

Broden raised his glass and winked. "Doesn't mean you can't enjoy the additional benefits that may come your way."

Luke ignored the stab of guilt piercing his chest. He hadn't known Astrid was involved in the job when he'd slept with her. And it had only been that one time. Months ago. That he couldn't stop thinking about.

He cleared his throat. "Can we focus on what we came here to do?" Broden thought Luke was a fellow agent, just not from a field office. Luke did have an official special agent FBI badge, but his unit was one that few people knew about, even within the bureau. The Domestic Terrorism Unit, or DTU, specialized in counterterrorism work against citizens who thought violence against their fellow Americans was the best way to create change.

"If I had orders to get close to that chick, I'd get real close." Broden smirked. "Know what I'm saying?"

Did the guy rile him up on purpose, or did being a complete pig just come naturally? "You've made your point. Can we concentrate now?"

"Fine." Broden took a swig from his wineglass and then grimaced. "Fuck, how much are they charging for this shit?"

Luke smiled. "More than either of us can afford in real life." He'd been undercover as Luke Holden, night-club owner with a shady past, for eighteen months now. Knowing expensive wines was one of the many things he'd had to learn as part of his new persona. The real Luke preferred a crisp IPA.

"At least the food is good." Broden took a bite of his entrecôte. "Even if the portions are small as shit." He looked around the expensive restaurant. "And I guess the decor is okay, if you like pretentious paintings and white tablecloths."

"You don't want to know how much the food cost either." Luke tried to catch Astrid's gaze again, but she was not looking their way. Probably on purpose. He hadn't made the connection between her and his mission until she showed up at his club during a business meeting several months ago. He'd managed to become a security client of Naya Brisbane's—although that's not what she'd called herself—and Astrid had shown up to give Naya a message. After that, the only time he'd seen Astrid was when he managed to follow her around Pine Rapids. So far, all he'd seen her do was run errands. Until she all of a sudden headed out of town. He'd been able to track her through traffic cameras across states until it became clear she was going to Colorado. That's when he'd jumped in his own car and got the Denver field office to keep an eye on her until he could catch up.

"So, what's the deal with this woman?" Broden asked, lowering his voice as he kept chewing his very expensive steak. "All I knew was to watch for her name and find where she was staying. When I was told to meet you for a pretend business dinner, I only had enough time to read your cover profile. Why is she a mark?"

Luke would prefer to still be tailing Naya. Astrid messed with his mind too much, but the other woman rarely went out, and he had yet to figure out where either of them lived. The trail just disappeared whenever he tried to follow Astrid home. He couldn't figure out how either of the women managed to evade him. He'd placed trackers on both their vehicles, but the signal was always dropped. "She's more a person of interest."

The smirk was back on Broden's face. "I can see that. You haven't taken your eyes off her since she entered."

"I'm just making sure she doesn't bolt." Luke took another drink of wine to cover the lie. The smooth Rhône slid down his throat, but he still wished it was a cold beer. "She and some of her associates triggered a few red flags." Like not existing in any official databases and probably being part of one massive government cover-up. But he couldn't tell Broden that. The fewer people who knew the details, the less likely it was that the operation would be yanked out of Luke's hands. He'd hate for it to disappear behind men who had security clearance higher than his or, worse, see it buried altogether.

"That's all you're going to share with me." Broden pretended to pout. "Some date you turned out to be. I'm not just some bimbo arm candy, you know. I have a brain."

"Sorry, it's all I can tell you." Luke tried to look apologetic. "Not my call." The lies were coming easier and easier. He hadn't checked in with Whalert for a while. The special agent in charge was Luke's immediate supervisor. The guy probably thought Luke had gone rogue, but DTU agents were allowed more leeway since they were so deeply undercover. And Luke couldn't risk anything standing in his way. He had to find closure for his brother.

"Fine. We locals are used to being kept in the dark." Broden nodded in the direction of the bar. "But since she's already seen us, don't you think you should go and talk to the chick?"

Luke tore his thoughts away from Donovan's lifeless body. "I'm just keeping her in suspense for a little while before I make my move."

Broden glanced over at the bar and quirked an eyebrow. "You may want to hurry up, before that other dude gives her some of his suspense."

Luke's attention snapped back to the bar. Astrid's back was now turned to them as she faced some smarmy dude in an ugly green suit. Who picked out a suit in that color?

The guy was leaning against the bar, his hand on her forearm. Luke pushed his chair out. Swearing under his breath, he strode across the room, struggling to keep his pace at a regular human speed. The chemicals in his blood gave him certain advantages, but they also tended to freak people out. By the time he'd cleared the steps up to the bar, he'd also forced his heart rate to slow down.

The Eurotrash talking to Astrid looked up as Luke approached them. Luke pinned him with a hard stare, and the guy's eyes widened as he quickly removed his hand from Astrid's arm. He mumbled something incoherently and scuttled off. Good riddance to both him and that ugly suit.

Astrid threw a glance over her shoulder and slowly swiveled around in her seat. She crossed her impossibly long legs and leaned up against the bar on her elbows, showing off her sculpted arms and shoulders. A tattoo of a snake head and partial body glimmered on her left bicep.

"Mr. Holden. What on earth are you doing here?"

The tic in her jaw belied her calm voice. As did the flash of anger in her jade-green eyes.

Luke forced his eyes to remain on hers instead of taking in her body. "Surely we are on a first-name basis by now?" He flashed what was supposed to be a disarming smile, but considering how ticked off he still was about the fashion-challenged guy who'd dared put his hands on her, it might have come off more like a predatory grin.

"A one-night stand does not make us close." She turned toward the bar and tapped her glass to signal the bartender for a refill. "Especially when the sex wasn't even that memorable."

What the fuck? That night had been spectacular. And, judging by how she'd screamed when she came, he wasn't the only one who'd enjoyed himself.

He quickly checked his ego and took a silent deep breath. "Is that how we're going to play this?" Sitting down on the stool next to hers, he leaned in to whisper in her ear. "We both know that night was *very* memorable. You voiced your praise quite loudly at the time." She smelled of some flowery soap, and underneath that, he detected a scent he remembered as uniquely hers. It was spicy and sweet at the same time.

Annoyance flashed in Astrid's eyes. She shrugged. "What can I say? I faked it. Didn't want to hurt your feelings."

"There was nothing fake about how hard I made you come that night." She'd milked him to the point where he'd exploded from somewhere so deep inside himself he thought he'd never get hard again. Which he had, only a few minutes after they'd finished the first time.

And for the record, there had been more rounds after that.

Astrid gave him a sideways glance, then turned toward the bartender who'd showed up with a bottle of Bordeaux. "Thank you kindly." She gave him a full-wattage smile. The guy, who was barely old enough to drink himself, blushed to the roots of his hair.

Luke rapped his knuckles on the bar to get the young bartender's attention. It took a few seconds, but eventually the kid turned his way. "I'll have what she's having, and put hers on my bill."

"Certainly." The guy quickly hustled up a stemmed glass and filled it with the rich red wine.

Luke lightly tapped his glass to Astrid's before taking a sip. He closed his eyes, pretending to savor the taste. When he opened them again, Astrid was watching his lips intently. Naked hunger blazed in her eyes until she lowered her lids, shielding her gaze from his view. His groin tightened. She obviously wanted him as much as he wanted her. So why the attitude?

He knew why *he* should stay away from her. Sleeping with her would complicate his mission. But why did *she* resist the strong pull between them? Maybe she was still ticked because he'd bolted the morning following their night together. He should apologize, but he couldn't tell her the real reason he'd had to go. An informant had texted him with a tip. It had turned out to be nothing, and he'd hauled ass back to his apartment. By then, Astrid had already left. She'd even made the bed, as if she wanted to erase all signs of having spent the night.

"So, where's your tall, handsome sidekick tonight?" She sipped her wine, not looking at him.

Luke was busy watching the tip of her tongue catch a wayward drop. It took a little while for her words to register. "Who?"

She threw him a glance and quirked an eyebrow. "Your bodyguard." She put the wineglass back on the bar.

"Oh, you mean Rex." The massive man was actually the head of his club's security team but sometimes acted as bodyguard when Luke's nightclub owner persona had a meeting. "He's managing the club while I'm away. You'll have to be content with just me tonight." Not able to resist her bare skin beckoning to him, he ran his index finger down her arm and watched goose bumps rise in its wake. He barely kept himself from giving in to the powerful urge to press his lips against her warm, sun-kissed skin. He cleared his throat to cover his loss of composure. It was ridiculous how drawn he was to her.

She pulled away and looked at him across her shoulder. "What the hell was that?" she asked.

"I just like touching you." Inside, he cringed. He sounded like a lovestruck teenager.

Her eyes glittered dangerously. "You haven't earned the right to touch without asking permission."

He flashed her a grin, the disarming one he used when questioning unsuspecting females. "May I?"

She closed her eyes briefly, and when she opened them again, she reached for her wineglass. She took a long sip. "That's not a good idea." The tic in her jaw was back.

"I disagree." He leaned forward, careful not to touch her, but close enough to share his body heat. "Come back with me to my hotel. I'm staying at the Warwick."

"That's definitely a bad idea."

"Okay, I'll come to your hotel. Where are you staying?" He already knew she was at the same hotel. That's why he'd booked a room there.

"Does that line ever work?"

"You tell me. I've never used it before."

She shook her head. "I don't have time for your games." She leaned away from him.

He immediately felt cold. "Let's start over." He kept his tone light and friendly. "What brings you to Denver?"

Astrid went unnaturally still. She made a production of drinking the last of her wine and then pushed the glass away from her. "I'm here on business."

"And what is it you do? We didn't have a chance to talk about our jobs during our date." He willed her to look at him, but she kept her gaze straight ahead. From her profile, he couldn't tell her mood. He leaned down and lowered his voice. "Actually, there wasn't much talking at all."

She turned to face him, her eyes flashing. "That was most definitely not a date." Before she had a chance to say anything more, the maître d' approached. "Mademoiselle, your table is ready." The slim man quirked an eyebrow. "Will monsieur be joining you?"

"No." Astrid's answer cracked the air like a whip. She gracefully uncrossed her legs and stood. "Monsieur has already had his dinner." She plastered a fake smile on her lips. "Thank you ever so much for the wine though," she said to Luke before following the maître d' down the steps and into the main part of the restaurant.

All Luke could do was watch her delectable backside as she walked away from him, gracefully navigating her way between the tables. She'd won a small victory, but the battle was far from over.

He returned to his own table and sat down. If Astrid thought this brief interlude would cause him to back off, she was in for a surprise.

Broden pushed a small black folder toward Luke. "Since you asked me out, it's only fair that you pay."

Luke placed his credit card in the holder without looking at the check.

"I take it the lady did not care for your company tonight?" Broden's words dripped with sarcasm.

"She had other plans," Luke said. "We need to hustle back to the hotel so we can search her room before she returns. I want to put a tracker on her car too." The ones he'd placed on her car in Pine Rapids kept disappearing. She must have discovered and removed them.

"Does that mean I don't get dessert?"

Luke gave Broden a hard stare meant to shut him up, but the man had no sense of self-preservation. "Some date you turned out to be," Broden whined. "You leave me alone for most of the night and then won't buy me dessert. No wonder the lady doesn't want you. Do I at least get a good-night kiss when you drop me off at my house?"

Luke closed his eyes. "Shut the fuck up."

"That bad, huh." Broden's voice was now laced with genuine laughter. "This girl really has you in knots. Remind me to buy some popcorn. This is going to be fun to watch."

Luke decided it was safer to remain quiet. If he didn't, he may punctuate his next statement with a fist to Broden's jaw.

Half an hour later, Luke was looking around Astrid's hotel room. It was a mirror image of his own. Same thick, beige carpet offset by gold-and-rust draperies that also contrasted nicely with the white walls. The drapes matched the bedspread, although his bed wasn't rumpled and smelling deliciously of that same combination of a flowery fragrance and Astrid's unique scent that he'd inhaled earlier at the restaurant. He dragged his mind away from the erotic images the unmade bed and Astrid's naked body inspired. She could be heading back to the hotel soon, so he had to hustle if he wanted to do a complete search. Broden had installed a tracker on her car and then headed home. This one was extra hidden.

There wasn't much of Astrid's stuff to look through. A pair of jeans lay perfectly folded on a chair, a leather jacket draped across its back. In one of the dresser drawers, he found a supply of clean underwear in bold satin colors, some clean T-shirts, and a colorful silk scarf. The other drawers were empty. The lady traveled light, but even this small bundle of clothes needed a bag. She hadn't had one with her at the restaurant, not even a purse, so what had she packed in? He searched the room again, but couldn't find any luggage anywhere, not even under the bed.

Returning to the dresser, he pawed through her silky bras and panties and tried not to feel like a pervert when the smooth silk running through his fingers evoked yet another hot memory of his one night with Astrid. She'd worn a hot-pink bra and a matching minuscule thong that had burned images permanently into his mind. He swallowed and adjusted his pants when the crotch started to feel uncomfortably tight.

Between the T-shirts, he felt a hard lump and pulled out a Leatherman multitool. Unfolded, the mini pliers fit comfortably in his hand. He studied its many Swiss Army–like accessories one by one and noticed small specks of white paint on one of the flat screwdriver heads.

The hotel room had several vent covers, but they were fairly small and fastened with Phillips-head screws. Luke went into the bathroom and studied the large vent covering the extractor fan. All six screws were of the flat-head kind. He dragged in a chair, quickly removed the cover, and then pulled out a duffel bag hidden inside the ceiling space.

Astrid did travel with luggage—filled with a sword, several daggers, and two Glock 22s. He copied down the guns' serial numbers and replaced the bag and the multitool where he'd found them. Figuring out what Astrid was doing in Denver moved to the top of his to-do list. What kind of business trip required a small personal armory?

# Chapter 3

ASTRID PACED THE OFFICE OF DR. ROSEN, SCOTT'S personal physician. She briefly paused by the huge picture window and admired the majestic view of the Rocky Mountains. The exclusive clinic was only two hours' drive from Denver but well hidden to protect its famous and well-connected clientele from paparazzi and the media. The only way to reach it was on back roads or by helicopter. She checked her watch. She'd been waiting for fifteen minutes already and really wanted to get back on the road and head for Washington.

The more miles she put between herself and Luke Holden, the better. Her traitorous body had imagined all kinds of delightful activities when he'd suggested they spend the night together. She'd had to give her hormones a stern talking-to, and even then they didn't settle down. Knowing he was spending the night somewhere in the same hotel had made rest hard. She stifled a yawn. Luke was trouble. He saw too much.

The door opened behind her and she turned to watch Dr. Rosen enter, wearing a white lab coat with *Rosen MD* embroidered on the breast pocket. He pushed his rimless glasses higher on his nose and approached her with a cheerful smile. "I'm so sorry to have kept you waiting." He gestured to one of the chairs facing the desk in front of the window, and Astrid sat down while the doctor situated himself in his office chair. "I understand you're here to pick up Scott Driscoll?"

Astrid nodded. Naya had kept her brother's first name on the patient records, but the last name was fake.

Dr. Rosen picked up a folder from his desk and flipped through it. "You must have gotten your signals crossed somehow." He peered at her through his glasses. "Scott checked himself out yesterday."

"I'm sorry, what?" Astrid leaned forward in the chair. She'd been told Scott was better, but not yet completely recovered. The doctor looked down at his folder again. "He left our clinic yesterday."

"How's that possible?" This must be some kind of joke. She must have misheard.

Dr. Rosen smiled. "Thanks to the formula his sister sent us, Scott made an excellent recovery. He's not yet at one hundred percent, but with proper physical therapy—"

Astrid stood. "That's not what I meant. Why did you let him leave? You knew someone was coming to pick him up." This couldn't be happening. Her heart pounded faster, and the berserker paced impatiently inside her, testing the mental barriers Astrid had put in place to cage it. She had to calm down, or this would end in disaster.

"We don't keep our patients against their will." Dr. Rosen frowned. "Scott wanted to leave, so we processed his release."

Astrid forced air into her lungs in deep, slow breaths. "And he just walked out the gate?" She sat down again. "Did someone pick him up?"

Dr. Rosen consulted his notes again. "He called a car service."

"Are you sure you're not mixing him up with a

different patient?" She squeezed her eyes shut while she waited for the doctor's answer. When none came, she opened them again and found Dr. Rosen watching her with sympathy in his eyes.

"Scott is one of my personal favorites. Watching him walk out this door of his own accord was a moment of triumph." He offered a self-deprecating smile.

Astrid slowly shook her head. She was so screwed. "Did he at least leave a message?"

The doctor handed over a yellow sticky note.

*Tell Neyney I'll be in touch.*

Astrid stared at the words. Neyney was Scott's nickname for Naya. The sound of her own heartbeat pounded loudly in her ears. She wanted to hit something. Hard.

She was so screwed. All she had to do was pick up the queen's brother, and she couldn't even do that right. So much for the *skydd* ceremony. Obviously the gods had not listened to the pledge of granting her a successful mission. Odin and Freya had placed a curse on her instead. She turned to Dr. Rosen. "What car service did he use?"

The doctor made a grimace of regret and shook his head. "I'm sorry, but I don't know. Not to mention that if I did, I still couldn't tell you. We have very strict doctor-patient confidentiality rules that I can't violate." He stood. "I'm sure Scott will be in touch soon."

Yep, definitely cursed.

---

Hours later, after many phone calls to car services, Astrid had finally found some useful information. A rather dim clerk had told her they'd had a fare from somewhere "way up in the mountains" to the train station. He'd even given her the driver's cell phone number, and the passenger's description fit Scott. Although "tall and dark, not very talkative" could technically be anyone, she held on to the slim hope that Scott had hired the driver's town car.

The historical Denver Union Station was an impressive light-gray building with an ornate facade and huge arched windows. Astrid stepped inside and admired the tall ceilings created to offset those same windows. The muted light of dusk filtered through their glass, helped by old-fashioned chandeliers illuminating the polished floors with a warm, golden glow. She found the information counter and studied the route map. The station was on the California Zephyr line, which meant Scott could be on his way to any city between Chicago and San Francisco. Mother of Valkyries, why could things never be easy?

A dull headache started to throb between Astrid's temples. She checked the schedule and cheered up a little. The westbound train departed at eight a.m. Unless Scott had spent the night in Denver, he wouldn't have been able to board that route. Most likely, he'd headed east and was now somewhere between here and Chicago. In order to track him down, should she dump the car and board a train, or drive to each city on the route?

Astrid's phone vibrated. She fished it out of her pocket to find a message from Naya. You guys okay? How far did you make it today?

The headache intensified. She needed to buy some time without outright lying to her queen. It's going to take longer than planned to get back, she replied.

No worries. Just stay safe, Naya wrote.

Astrid slipped the phone back into her jacket and wondered if she should just pretend to have lost the device. But worrying Naya by not replying to messages would be worse than not telling the truth. She couldn't do that to her friend. As soon as she caught up with Scott, she needed to haul ass back to Washington. That meant looking for him by car. She headed back to the parking garage.

Dusk had progressed to night by the time she stepped off the elevator on the floor where she'd parked the silver Escalade. A low vibration from the fluorescent lights accompanied the echo her boots made against the concrete floor. Astrid had almost reached the car when two sets of approaching footsteps made her pause. She reached for the throwing dagger she kept in an inside jacket pocket and continued walking but stayed on the balls of her feet to keep her steps silent. Her berserker stirred, alerting her to the fact that her pursuers were not human.

A shadow appeared from around a corner and separated into two distinct shapes. Astrid stopped and cursed under her breath. It didn't look like she'd be able to avoid a fight.

What looked like two human men stepped into the light. Even dormant, Astrid's berserker picked up on the glow of Asgard—the gods' realm—radiating from the creatures. These were Loki's wolverine monsters, hence the otherworldly essence surrounding them. All dressed in black, their faces were narrow with pointed chins. Humans would think they were regular mortals as long as they didn't notice the black voids they had for eyes. As she waited for them to make their move, their nails elongated into claws. The creatures stared at her, arms held loosely at their side, fighting-stance ready.

She gripped her dagger tight and widened her own stance automatically. It would be so much easier if she could just use a gun, but the noise would bring law enforcement, and she couldn't risk getting delayed by answering questions. She had to find Scott. And if she missed, anyone who showed up to investigate the gun shot could get killed by the wolverines.

Her berserker became agitated and growled, now battle ready, but she clamped down on her mental control and willed it to remain dormant. She was in enough trouble already without going into full battle rage. Without her warrior brothers here, she might never be able to recover if she gave her berserker full control.

"Greetings, Valkyrie," one of the creatures snarled. "We've been waiting for you or one of your brothers to show up." He grimaced in what was probably supposed to be a smile. "We'd actually hoped for the queen."

Astrid rolled her shoulders. "Well, doesn't this little welcome committee make me feel all tingly and special."

Apparently, they weren't expecting a smart-ass comment because the smirks disappeared from their faces. "We know you're here all alone," the other wolverine hissed. He took a step forward.

"I don't need any help to send you back to where you belong." Adrenaline surged through Astrid's body, and the berserker pawed at its mental constraints, eager to come out to fight. It was a struggle to remain in control, but she managed to force her inner warrior instinct back down.

The creature who had spoken first rushed her, and she quickly slung her throwing dagger, but he'd anticipated the movement and lunged to the side. The knife clanked down on the floor. Astrid quickly ducked and crouched as the creature lunged through the air and swept out his leg. She blocked the kick with her arm, but his heel made contact with her elbow. The hit vibrated through her humerus bone and up her shoulder, making her teeth rattle. *Mother of Valkyries, that hurt.*

She quickly pivoted to keep track of her other opponent and then took a step back so she wasn't right between them. Instead, they formed a slowly rotating triangle as they circled each other. "Is that all you got?" Astrid taunted, putting a fake smile on her face.

The only answer she got was a low growl. She couldn't tell from which creature it came. Maybe both of them. She crouched slowly, keeping them both in her field of vision as she retrieved another dagger from her boot. Whichever of them attacked next would be the recipient of her fine blade, and this time she wouldn't miss.

"We could do a lot more damage," the one to the left smirked, "but we want you alive to deliver a message."

Astrid frowned. "What message?"

Lefty grimaced that hideous smile again. "Tell your queen we have her brother."

Blood pulsed loudly in her ears, and she wavered as she struggled not to let her berserker out. "That's a big, fat lie," she managed to squeeze out. "Scott is with the queen and king."

"We both know that's not true." The wolverine on the right sounded mighty pleased with himself. "We've wondered why the queen visited Denver several times. We've kept a presence in the city just in case she showed up again. Imagine our surprise when her brother appears instead, all juicy and ripe for the picking. In the train station of all places."

"What do you want?" Astrid scowled.

"We need both siblings. If the queen gives herself up, we'll let both of them live."

This mission was turning shittier and shittier by the minute. She was definitely cursed. "The king will kill you before he allows the queen anywhere near you."

Lefty shrugged. "Then keep the king out of this."

"Good idea," Astrid said, throwing her dagger overhand. "I'll just kill you myself." The knife buried itself just above Lefty's collarbone. She'd gone for the neck, but as if the day wasn't crappy enough, she was now off her aim too. At least she'd hurt the bastard, because he squealed loudly.

The one on her right rushed forward, and she quickly retrieved the knife in her other boot before releasing it in an underhand sideways throw. A wet choking noise told her she'd hit her mark. She barely had time to turn and see the wolverine sink to the ground with her dagger sticking out of his jugular before the one on the left attacked again.

He'd pulled out her knife and came at her with a circular back kick. She blocked with her left arm and countered with an uppercut but only glanced his chin. He flipped backward and landed gracefully, still holding her knife. It was a good thing none of the other warriors were watching. She'd be the laughingstock of the fortress if anyone found out how long it had taken her to down these pests, and she'd never live down the fact that one of them had armed itself with her personal weapon.

Astrid feinted left and ducked down, extending her leg in a sweeping kick when the wolverine stabbed the air where she'd just been. He lost his footing, but twisted midair and somehow landed on his feet again. She'd fought wolverines before, but this guy was different. When did the wolverines become acrobats?

The creature rushed her and she had to retreat a step, wobbling when her foot slipped on some loose rocks on the floor. The wolverine swept the knife down, and Astrid had to block with her left forearm. The knife cut through her muscle. She hissed as white pain radiated through her entire arm. Clenching her teeth, she grabbed the wolverine's wrist before he could pull out the knife and stab her again. Their struggle forced the blade deeper into her flesh, and she bit the inside of her cheek to keep from screaming out in agony.

"You're making it very hard to keep you alive," the wolverine hissed.

She kicked his shin, and when he flinched, she wrenched her arm away, dislodging the knife but keeping her grip on his wrist. Her blood dripped down the blade, coating his skin and making Astrid's grip slippery. She leaned forward, trying to throw him off balance, but the creature matched her body strength and held his own.

Burning pain radiated from her wound, and she had trouble concentrating on keeping his hand and knife away from her. The berserker paced again, howling, wanting to be released, but she couldn't risk it.

The wolverine and she danced clumsily, their feet

scuffing the concrete floor as they jockeyed for dominance. She tried to trip him, but he side shuffled with more fancy footwork, and she just managed to get herself off balance. His shirt had ripped, and she could see that the wound above his collarbone had already closed and was no longer bleeding. Did these suckers regenerate now too? Was there no end to the clusterfuck this mission was fast becoming?

Her strength quickly waned, while the wolverine seemed to regain his. She had to act fast. Leaning her head back, she thrust forward with a burst of energy and crashed her forehead into the bridge of his nose. *Freya's fury, that hurt bad.* But it worked. The wolverine stumbled backward and fell, holding his nose—unfortunately also still holding her dagger, but at least she got a little breathing room. She moved to stomp on the hand holding her knife. Her planned followup would then be a heel kick to his throat, but before she could position herself, a car beeped unlocked and cheerful female chatter approached.

Astrid quickly looked around and spotted three women loaded down with shopping bags walking toward an SUV parked one row over. Freya's mercy, she'd once again been so caught up in a fight that she'd forgotten to check her surroundings. This was how she'd almost killed a bystander. She watched the shoppers, but they were oblivious to her presence and drove off a minute later. That's when she remembered she'd taken her eyes off the wolverine and turned to where he'd last been on the ground.

A sharp stab on the inside of her thigh was the first clue that he'd moved from where he'd fallen. She looked down to find her own dagger buried all the way to the hilt in her leg. Although the wolverine's face was a mess of broken tissue and bone, he still managed to smirk at her. "Gotcha," he hissed.

The effort of bending down was almost too much, but she pulled out the dagger. When blood slushed out of the wound at an alarming rate, she realized she should have left it in. The creature must have hit the femoral artery. She sank to her knees and slowly slumped sideways.

With every slowing heartbeat, her blood pulsed out of her leg. She watched the wolverine struggling to stand. He looked down at her for a minute before slowly limping toward his dead partner. She closed her eyes and listened to the creature's uneven steps and the dragging noise indicating he was taking the body with him as he left.

When she thought they were far enough away, she reached for the silk scarf around her neck. She barely had enough strength left to undo the knot. She was immortal, but only in the sense that her body healed so quickly that injuries never turned mortal. She still bled and this wound was pumping blood so fast that it didn't look like she would be able to heal in time. She wrapped the scarf around her leg and pulled it tight. This was going to be a close one.

# Chapter 4

LUKE DRUMMED HIS FINGERS ON THE STEERING WHEEL. What the hell was Astrid doing at the train station? She'd better not have skipped town. He berated himself for not keeping closer tabs on her. She'd driven into the mountains that morning and he'd followed her for a while, but the roads had become increasingly narrow and more deserted. He'd had to abort, or she would have made him. Maybe he should have sent another agent from the Denver field office, but she'd be suspicious of any car following her for hours on those mountain roads. Instead, he'd kept track of her on his computer through the GPS tracker Broden had attached to her car. He'd been going stir-crazy in his hotel room, pacing back and forth while desperately hoping she'd eventually return to Denver.

She had, and now the little bleep on his screen showed that her vehicle had been stationary in the train-station parking garage for more than two hours. He fidgeted in his seat. This was why he never wanted a desk job. He was a man of action. Sitting on his ass made him squirrelly. Maybe she'd found the tracker and ditched it. He wouldn't put it past her. Besides being one of the most stunning women he'd met, she was also one of the smartest. It wasn't just because her beauty had him tongue-tied that he had to stay on top of his game in their verbal sparring. The lady had an amazingly high

IQ, which was another reason he couldn't stop thinking about her. Intelligent women had always turned him on.

Too bad she was using all those smarts on the wrong side of the law. He couldn't prove it, but every ounce of his intuition screamed that whatever Astrid was up to, it was illegal. And his intuition was rarely wrong. He checked the blinking marker on his screen again. Right now, the uneasy feeling in his stomach told him something wasn't right about Astrid leaving her car in one place for this long.

He'd followed her to the garage and parked in the shadows across the street to keep an eye on the well-lit parking garage exit. From this position, he could also see the two stair exits that would lead to the restaurants in the area. Astrid had not used any of the exits, so he assumed she'd taken the walkway connected to the train station. But why spend hours inside the station? He could see the main exit to that building too, so she hadn't slipped out that way.

Maybe she'd evaded him by jumping on one of the buses that served the station. The uneasiness in his stomach increased to full queasiness, and he hit the heel of his palm on the steering wheel.

Enough sitting around. Time for action.

He grabbed the GPS tracker display and jogged across the street. The device wouldn't show which floor Astrid's car was parked on, but it should indicate that he had gotten closer. If he overshot the right floor, he'd just go back down.

Luke had ascended only a few steps when he saw movement out of the corner of his eye and instinctively hugged the shadows of the stairwell. A lone male figure moved with purpose along the sidewalk in front of the garage. Dressed entirely in black, the man avoided the parts of the sidewalk lit by the streetlamps and kept his chin low, as if to avoid exposing his face to any security cameras. From his higher position, Luke noticed two Band-Aids stretching across the bridge of the guy's nose. A recent break.

The man strode down the sidewalk purposefully but kept his body loose and limber, as if ready for any attack. The dude was either military or law enforcement. Luke would bet his badge on that.

He kept still as the guy jogged soundlessly through the unmanned car entrance, moving as if he knew exactly where he was going. A cold knot formed in Luke's stomach, pushing all the earlier queasiness to the side. This guy had something to do with Astrid, but was he an ally or an enemy? Judging by the guy's covert movements, Luke thought the man was hostile. What the fuck had Astrid gotten herself into?

Luke leaped down the two steps in one motion and followed. The man was moving at a fast clip, too fast to be purely human. Luke quickly scanned the parking garage, but nobody else was around. No need for himself to keep to a human-only speed. Making sure his footfalls landed on the balls of his feet, he soundlessly followed his prey. If the man led him to Astrid, Luke might have another connection between her and the covert bio labs. He already knew Naya was somehow connected. It might just be a coincidence that the guy appeared near Astrid's car, but he definitely had received some of the same treatments that Luke and his brother had. Nobody could move like that without some kind of bio enhancement. And Luke didn't believe in coincidences.

Ice-cold determination trickled through his veins. He was so focused on following the man undetected that the rest of the parking garage blurred as he used his inhuman speed to keep up. The man kept circling up the floors until he reached the third level, where he headed in a straight path down one of the rows of cars. Luke could make out Astrid's silver SUV farther down the row and wasn't surprised when the man headed straight for it.

The guy paused in front of the car and checked the surrounding area before putting his face up against the side window to look inside. His smile was feral as he focused on whatever he saw. Luke held his breath. Was Astrid in there? Seeing a trail of blood leading to or from the car—he couldn't tell at that distance—he took a deep breath to keep his heart from jackhammering out of his chest.

Grabbing the door handle, the man yanked it hard. The motion turned more violent when the car door didn't cooperate. Relief flooded through Luke, and he exhaled. The guy was so intent on his task that he still hadn't noticed Luke. He yanked the car handle again and growled low in the back of his throat when it still didn't budge. His fist hit the window. Whatever or whoever was inside that car, this guy wanted to get inside badly. A trickle of fear made the hairs on Luke's neck stand up. Whatever illegal shit Astrid had gotten herself into, this guy was out to physically harm her. If she was inside that car, Luke had to protect her.

*Shit.* Where did that thought come from? Astrid was

the most capable woman he knew. She needed protection like he needed a manicure. Still, this guy wasn't human. Maybe that's why she wasn't reacting to him breaking into the car. Or maybe she was hurt. *Double shit*.

The man took a half-turning step back and raised his elbow into the perfect position to bust the window open. Luke closed the distance between them soundlessly and sidled up to the guy. He plastered a how-you-doing smile on his face. "Hey, need some help there, buddy? Lock your keys in the car?"

The other man startled and jumped back to face Luke. His eyes had no irises or whites. They were a void of continuous black. So much for pretending this would be a normal interaction.

Freaky Eye's lips furled. "This doesn't concern you," he hissed. "Move along."

Luke widened his stance. "Oh, but it definitely does."

In addition to the bandages arched over his nose, deep purple rings shone beneath the guy's unsettling eyes. Definitely a broken nose. He stared at Luke for a heartbeat and sniffed the air. "What are you?" he asked. "I don't know your scent."

Luke kept his face blank to keep from showing how creeped out he was. The guy was *scenting* him? "All you need to know is I'm the guy who's going to kick your ass." He kept his eyes on the guy's hands. Normally he'd look into his opponent's eyes to catch the flicker of eye movement that betrayed an attack an instant before the body acted on the thought. But this freak had no eye movement. Just that dull, dark void with an occasional sinister glitter. That, combined with the whole sniffing thing, had Luke officially wigged out.

"Don't get involved in this, human. It will only get you killed." Freaky bared his teeth in what was probably supposed to be a smile but looked more like an animal snarl.

Luke forced himself to ignore all the creepy stuff and focus on kicking the freak's ass. "We'll see." He slowed down his breathing, and the dead calm that always flooded his body before a fight covered him like a familiar, favorite warm blanket. He offered a smile of his own. Something of Luke's feral nature must have shone through, because the guy blanched and stepped back.

Not waiting for his opponent to recover, Luke advanced and delivered a rising-knee kick. He aimed for the guy's already broken nose, but Freaky rotated his body in time and instead got the back of Luke's foot in his throat. The guy went down sputtering and coughing.

Luke didn't wait for him to get up, aiming another kick to the head, but Freaky was quick again and rolled out of the way. Instead of the face stomp he'd planned, Luke modified the arc of his heel and thumped the guy's collarbone with a solid downward kick. Bones crunched as Luke leaned in with all of his weight.

Freaky screeched and grabbed Luke's leg, struggling to wrench it off his body.

Luke's jaw clenched as he braced his other foot on the ground, adjusted his contact position slightly, and increased the pressure on his opponent's shoulder and neck. A satisfying pop sounded as Freaky's shoulder slipped out of its socket. *Try to fight with that, asshole.*

The guy writhed on the floor beneath Luke's foot and then stilled, as if reaching inward to find the strength to pull himself together.

Luke wished him luck with that. A dislocated shoulder hurt like crazy, and the pain was almost impossible to press through. He knew from personal experience.

Freaky seemed to be making progress though, and Luke's brow furrowed as he increased pressure on the mangled shoulder. His opponent just hissed and turned his head to meet Luke's gaze head-on. A chilling smile stretched the man's thin lips.

The guy tightened his grip around Luke's calf, and alarm bells sounded in Luke's head. He quickly pulled back his leg, barely missing getting shredded by the claws elongating from Freaky's fingers.

*What the fuck?* Talk about needing a manicure.

Luke had to scramble backward to avoid being stabbed. Everything happened much faster than any fight he had been in before. He'd used inhuman speed to track and attack opponents since he had escaped the lab as a teenager, but he hadn't fought someone who could match his agility. Luckily, the guy was still groggy, which gave Luke the advantage he needed. He quickly stomped on the guy's hand and used his other foot to aim another kick to Freaky's face.

The guy caught the foot and uttered a guttural groan as he pushed Luke back. Inhuman speed combined with abnormal strength. A trickle of fear slithered through Luke, and the hairs on his neck stood again. He quickly dismissed his reaction and centered himself into fight mode again, but by the time he found his footing, Freaky was standing. His left arm hung uselessly by his side, and the shoulder drooped low at an abnormal angle. Luke couldn't help but grin. The guy might be some kind of genetically modified monster, but so was Luke.

And this was the first time as an adult that he got to test his abnormal abilities with a matched opponent. Despite the fear still clinging to the edges of his mind, the soldier in him rose to the challenge. Worthy opponent or not, no need to give Freaky any time to recover. Luke stayed on the offensive and kept an eye on those claws. He attacked with a right uppercut to the chin, and when his opponent's head snapped back, Luke delivered a left cross to the guy's shoulder. For the finale, he followed up with an axe kick.

Freaky grunted and swiped at Luke with his vicious claws, almost shredding Luke's shirt. The guy tried to regain his balance, but the injured shoulder threw him off axis and he hit the ground like falling timber. His head bounced off the concrete floor, and his eyes rolled back into his head, finally displaying some white. Freaky was out for the count.

Luke let out a big breath of relief. That had been exhilarating but close. After his brother Donovan's suicide, the only thing that had kept Luke going was the need to avenge his twin brother. That had been almost twenty years ago, and now finally, after living on the street, military training, and then the FBI academy—where he'd been recruited into the clandestine DTU—he had the skills and the opportunity to make that happen. He was not going to get himself killed. Not when he was so close.

Freaky was still out, resting with his shoulder at an uncomfortable angle. Luke strode up to the car and peeked inside to see what the creature wanted so badly. The pale form of unconscious Astrid made Luke's heart skip a beat. He rubbed his chest and told himself the reaction had nothing to do with caring about the blond Amazon. It was only due to her being an important link to the lab that had held him and his brother captive so many years ago.

A quick check revealed all the doors locked, so Luke took a page from Freaky's game book and used his elbow to bust in one of the windows. He chose the passenger-side front window to spare Astrid from as much of the spraying glass as possible. Once inside, he checked her vitals, mostly by touch since the garage's fluorescent lights didn't penetrate to the depths of the back of the car. Her pulse was weaker than he'd like, but regular. She breathed unhindered. He patted her down, checking for any injuries that would explain the blood trail, and found her car keys in the front pocket of her jeans.

As he moved down her legs, his hands became coated in blood. Astrid's jeans were covered in it, as was the backseat. A strip of cloth had been tied around her leg like a tourniquet. He debated loosening the makeshift bandage, but she'd obviously tied it after the jeans got soaked, so it must have stopped her bleeding. Her steady breathing and pulse were good indications that she hadn't bled out.

He fished the car keys from Astrid's pocket and adjusted her position so she was resting more comfortably and more securely. Outside the car again, he spared Freaky another look. Ideally, he'd like to bring the unconscious creature with him so he could interrogate him, but he didn't have anything strong enough to tie Freaky up. If he wasn't working undercover, Luke would have had useful equipment with him. Anything less than regulation handcuffs would probably break as soon as Freaky woke up and decided to exert some force on his bindings. Luke couldn't risk that happening while driving, especially not with Astrid in the car.

There was that chest tweak again. He rubbed the skin above his heart. Something he ate must have given him heartburn.

He stepped into the silver SUV and started it. His first priority was to keep Astrid alive, to get her to medical care before any of Freaky's friends showed up. If that involved leaving a potential source of information unsecured, so be it. Life was full of bitter choices.

He put the car in Drive and took off toward the hotel.

—⁓—

Luke parked as close to the hotel's service elevator as he could. By some stroke of luck, he managed to get unconscious Astrid up to his floor and in his room without running into anyone. He'd considered taking her to the emergency room, but he preferred not having his undercover name in any official records, not even on ER intake forms. Showing up at a clinic with a woman who'd been stabbed would lead to all kinds of questions and probably a visit from more than one law enforcement officer. Luke had field medic training. If her injuries weren't too severe, he'd save time and paperwork by taking care of her himself.

He grabbed a towel from the bathroom and spread it on the bed before lowering Astrid onto it. He wouldn't know the extent of her injuries until he removed her clothes. Feeling slightly uneasy about undressing her while she was unconscious, he forced his mind into clinical mode and scanned her exposed skin for wounds as he peeled off her jacket, some kind of knife harness, and her T-shirt. He found plenty of bruises on her upper body and a knife injury on her left forearm. It appeared only superficial, so he moved lower.

The fabric tied around her thigh was soaked, but no new blood trickled through as he loosened it. He couldn't get the jeans to cooperate. He finally reached for his utility tool and cut through the denim so he wouldn't aggravate her injury more than necessary. Then he returned to the bathroom for soap and to fill the ice bucket with warm water. As he cleaned the injury with a soft washcloth, he checked for infection. The skin around the gash was red and irritated, but there was no discolored discharge.

Breathing a sigh of relief, Luke continued wiping Astrid clean of blood. He didn't find any other injuries except for a few minor abrasions on her legs. They would heal on their own. In the first aid kit that he never traveled without—once a Marine, always a Marine—he found a suture-and-needle package. After irrigating the gash with alcohol, he broke the sterile package and retrieved the pre-threaded needle. He applied small, precise stitches to close the wound. She'd hopefully not have too much of a scar. Stitching up your own injury sucked balls big time and hurt too much to pay attention to scarring, which was why part of his shoulder looked like Frankenstein had stitched it together.

He cut the last piece of suture and put some antibacterial gel on her wound before placing a large sterile dressing to stop the small trickle of blood his stitches had caused. Astrid's heart rate and breathing were still steady, even if he wished her pulse was a little stronger. He tucked her under the covers and gathered the bloody towel, jeans, scarf, and discarded medical supplies. The metal trash can seemed like the perfect fireproof receptacle, so he went out on the balcony to burn it all. No reason to leave DNA evidence behind, although he kept one small blood-soaked square of the scarf. He'd run a match search through some of the FBI's databases.

He'd just returned inside when his work cell phone rang. A quick glance on the display revealed it was Special Agent in Charge Whalert. Luke hesitated. He hadn't reported in for weeks and had known eventually the boss would track him down. He'd just hoped the guy would have so much on his plate that Luke would have a little longer before he had to explain being out of touch. The phone stopped ringing but immediately started again. Whalert again. As impossible as Luke knew it was, this time the ringtone seemed more insistent.

Luke took a deep breath before stepping out onto the balcony again. He hit the button on the phone that would connect him with his probably very irate boss. Before he had a chance to even squeeze out his name, Whalert was barking in his ear.

"What the hell, Hager? Almost a month and you don't check in?" Whalert's voice was so loud that Luke wouldn't be surprised if Astrid could hear the guy, despite the patio door and her unconscious state. Yep, definitely pissed off.

Luke's ears rang from hearing his real name at such a loud volume. "In my defense, I've been a little busy running a nightclub while also handling my mission and maintaining cover."

"Do we really need to have the talk about why you need to follow procedures? We have some leeway within the DTU since we're mostly off radar, but even I demand some sort of protocol."

Luke felt like a little kid being reprimanded. His body was actually squirming. He reminded himself that it'd been some time since he hit puberty, and he manned up. "Procedure or no procedure, have I ever let you down before?" When in the wrong, going on the defensive usually worked.

Some grumbling traveled down the line. Luke couldn't make out all the words, but one was definitely "asshole." He didn't mind not hearing the rest.

"What progress have you made?" Whalert asked in an almost normal tone of voice.

"I've made contact with the target."

"Yeah, Broden shared that in his report. You know, those things most agents fill out on a regular basis."

*Fuck Broden and his reports. Why did he have to be such a brownnose?* "That's correct. We saw her at dinner last night and I spoke with her, but I had continued contact with her tonight." He had to give his boss something but would keep the details to himself. Until Luke could figure out exactly what Astrid was up to, there was no reason to involve people higher up the chain of command. The longer someone sat behind a desk, the more complicated they tended to make things.

"What kind of contact?"

"I followed her tonight and pretended a chance meeting." That wasn't exactly a lie. Even if Astrid was unaware of his presence in the parking garage, they had kind of met.

"You don't think she'll find that suspicious?"

"Not at all. She has no clue I followed her." The only full truth he'd said during this conversation.

His boss chuckled. "You've already managed to get her into bed, haven't you?"

Luke glanced at Astrid asleep under his covers. "Something like that." He ignored the stab of guilty conscience and refused to explore if it was because he was misleading Astrid or his boss. "We've flirted."

Another chuckle traveled down the line. "I just bet you have. I've seen how you flirt."

Luke pushed down the irritation he felt at his boss' insinuation. He wasn't that bad. Women found him attractive, but that didn't mean he jumped into bed with everyone who gave him a clear signal. Most of them maybe, but not all of them. "Let's move on," he muttered.

"I understand, no kiss and tell. I like that about you." Another chuckle. "Okay, down to business then. Have you set up a meeting with Kraus?"

"Yes, but he's not available until two days from now." Luke was meeting with the German businessman under the pretense of offering money-laundering services through the nightclub. In reality, he wanted to check if the man had a connection with the covert government labs. Before the North Dakota lab closed down, Kraus had met with the head scientist of the facility. It had taken weeks to set up the meeting. "I'm not sure if he'll take me up on my offer though. He seems a little skittish."

"Most criminals turn paranoid a few years into their careers. And with good reason." Whalert sighed. "I'm actually calling for more reasons than just finding out why the hell I haven't heard from you." *Uh-oh*. Luke had heard that tone of voice before. It always delivered bad news. He braced himself for what was coming. "There's been some chatter in cyberspace," his boss continued. The bureau monitored several regions of cyberspace, including the off-the-grid corners that were usually referred to as the Darknet. Conversations that seemed related to the covert labs often popped up, but so far DTU hadn't been able to pinpoint who was taking part in the discussions.

"What can you tell me?" Luke asked. The information gathered was often sensitive enough that only people several security levels above him were allowed access.

"I don't know much." Whalert sounded apologetic. "But there is a lot of talk about a 'live package' arriving."

Luke sighed. "That could mean anything."

"I know, but in this case we think it has something to do with a person or persons. Maybe someone with sensitive information."

"Arriving where?"

"That's the problem." It was his boss's turn to sigh. "We don't know the location. Hell, we don't even know if this person is coming voluntarily or has somehow been coerced."

Luke's intuition tingled, and cold tendrils trailed across his scalp. He glanced at Astrid through the glass door. Somehow she was involved in this. What the fuck had she gotten herself into?

# Chapter 5

THE FIRST THING ASTRID NOTICED AS SHE FOUGHT TO wake up was that a weight around her waist had her trapped. She opened her eyes and saw a male arm draped over her middle. A solid, warm body spooned her from behind.

Holy Mother of Valkyries, she had no memory of going to bed with anyone. Who was he? Light-headed and disoriented, she tried to remember the events that had led to this situation. Her head throbbed as if she had a hangover, but she didn't remember drinking alcohol. Slowly she lifted the arm trapping her and slipped out from underneath it and the covers.

Once safely out of the bed, she turned and found Luke Holden looking at her, leaning on his elbow, head propped up with his palm. His hair was tousled and his smile sleepy as he stared at her. "Hey," he said, his voice husky.

The vision of maleness melted her insides, and hearing that throaty voice pulled at something in her chest. Lounging on top of the covers in a gray T-shirt and black boxer briefs that hugged his assets tightly, he was pretty much irresistible. Wait, on top of the covers?

"What?" she croaked and looked down to see if she was naked. She had on both bra and panties. Maybe they hadn't slept together.

Yeah, right. As if she would get into bed with Holden and keep from jumping him. The man was sex incarnate.

As if he knew what she was thinking, he grinned.

She swallowed a few times to get her throat to work. "What's going on?" she managed to squeeze out, marginally clearer.

Holden's gaze dipped low and then slowly traveled upward before meeting her eyes again. Heat flashed in his gray eyes and his pupils dilated.

Her nipples tightened in response to his blatant appreciation, and she swore under her breath. She crossed her arms to hide the evidence of her attraction. How was she supposed to stay away from this man when her body didn't listen to her brain? She tossed her hair and then stumbled when the gesture made her dizzy.

Holden shot up from the bed and caught her before she did a face-plant. He put his arm around her shoulders, supporting her as he gently lowered her to sit on the bed. "Easy there, hothead," he mumbled, his lips buried in her hair. "You lost a lot of blood last night. For a while there, I wasn't sure you'd wake up." His Adam's apple trembled as he swallowed.

"I was hurt?" Astrid blinked several times to clear the white spots dancing in front of her eyes. Disjointed memories flittered through her mind. She'd fought wolverines in a parking garage. "They attacked me," she mumbled, enjoying the heat radiating off his body.

She couldn't help herself. She snuggled closer into his embrace. The small shift of her legs made her wince. The skin on the inside of her thigh throbbed and pulled. She angled her leg and looked closer. A neat row of sutures held a knife gash together. Had she gone to the hospital? But why wasn't she still there? "Did you stitch me up?"

Holden slid down on the floor and kneeled in front of her. Gently, he traced the stitches with his fingertip. "Shit, Astrid, you almost bled out. I didn't know if I had time to get you to an ER, and the hotel was closer. I've had some medical training, so when I saw that your bleeding had slowed, I took care of it myself."

She swallowed loudly. Who the hell traveled around with a suture kit? Who exactly was Holden? The vision of him kneeling between her thighs distracted her from her thoughts. More than just the wound throbbed now. Her inner warrior responded to the heightened emotions. Astrid clamped down on their connection, willing the berserker to calm down and resume its slumber. The beast inside her had other ideas though.

*Mine*, it whispered in her mind.

Astrid jerked. *What the hell?* The berserker had never spoken to her before.

Holden looked up. "I'm sorry. I didn't mean to hurt you."

"You didn't." She forced a mental command through the connection with her berserker, and finally the beast settled down. "I'm ticklish," she said to Holden. Hopefully he wouldn't notice her internal struggle.

She felt beads of sweat breaking out on her forehead. Her blood loss must be why she imagined her inner warrior speaking to her. The weakened state had caused some sort of hallucination. She cleared her throat. "How did you find me?"

He looked away and withdrew his hand from her thigh. "You were in the back of your car in the train-station parking garage. At first I thought—" He rubbed his face. "You were unconscious."

"No, not *where* did you find me. How?" She narrowed her eyes.

His gaze darted to hers before flitting away again. "I followed you," he mumbled.

*Bullshit*. She'd have noticed if anyone followed her down from the mountains. Those twisty roads would have shown someone in pursuit immediately. Even if she'd been upset, she'd have known to check for someone tailing her.

Naya didn't usually talk about her clients or their security plans, but she'd once let it slip that Holden liked high technology and spy equipment. His business often crossed over to the shadier side of the law, and he needed to keep himself and his club patrons safe. Astrid would bet a fair amount of money that he had trackers in his little arsenal of gadgets and had placed one on her car. Which would explain the trackers she'd often found on her car back in Pine Rapids. But that was something they could discuss later, when she'd also get the details about his "medical training." Right now, she needed to find out how much he'd figured out about the wolverines.

She touched the stitches, and his gaze returned to the wound as if pulled by magic. Astrid deliberately trailed her fingers higher up her leg.

His Adam's apple wobbled.

She allowed a small smile of victory to grace her lips. So, she wasn't the only one affected by this near-naked proximity. "These look great. I'll probably only have a small scar." She remembered making a tourniquet with her scarf because the wolverine had nicked her femoral artery. Her rapid healing abilities had fixed the damage before she bled out, just as she'd hoped. But that wound wouldn't have closed without Holden's stitches.

Did Holden notice that the injury looked more healed than it should for just one day? She looked up and caught him scrutinizing her face, as if searching for a sign of something.

Holden rocked back on his heels and stood. He walked over to the minibar and pulled out a bottle of orange juice, which he threw to her. She caught it before it bounced on the bed. The room was almost identical to her own. She'd checked out before she'd gone to pick up Scott and stashed all her weapons in a hidden compartment in her car. Hopefully, they were still there.

"Drink," he said without looking at her. "I got some fluids in you during the night, but you need more." He walked toward the adjoining bathroom. "I'm grabbing a shower, and then we'll talk."

She watched his retreating back while hazily remembering someone rousing her and forcing her to drink. She'd wanted to sleep, but that someone had nudged and cajoled until she'd swallowed the liquids. The voice had whispered endearments and called her things like "sweetie" and "darling." Holden's voice, she now realized.

The shower turned on in the bathroom. Astrid scooted up in the bed and reclined against the headboard. Cracking the juice bottle open, she lifted it to her lips while deep in thought. This was going to be complicated and messy.

By the time Holden sauntered out of the bathroom with a fluffy, white towel draped around his waist, Astrid had finished the juice and crawled back under the covers. She couldn't find her clothes and wanted a shield between all that maleness and her own semi-nakedness.

Holden's towel hung low on his hips, threatening to fall down at any minute as he crossed the room to dig through a small carry-on case. She both hoped and dreaded that gravity would win. He fished out some underwear and another T-shirt. This one was dark blue. It would make his eyes look like the ocean at dusk. She knew, because he'd worn a shirt the same color the night they'd... Best not to go there with just the two of them in a room with a bed.

Holden grabbed a pair of jeans and returned to the bathroom, shutting the door behind him. Less than a minute later, he returned fully dressed except for bare feet. Even though he was fully clothed, he still exuded sex as he walked toward her. Her mind flashed back to what it had been like to have the fullness of that hard body pressed against her. That one night in the club when she'd listened to what her body wanted. Holden. Hard. Inside her.

It had been fantastic.

So fantastic she hadn't been able to stop thinking about it for months. That scared the crap out of her. She forced the carnal thoughts away and watched him as he pulled up a chair beside the bed. "Okay," he said, sitting down in the chair. "Tell me what the hell is going on. What is that creature I saw in the parking garage?"

Freya's cats. One of the wolverines must have come back for her. How was she going to spin this? She'd never had to explain to a regular person that weird creatures walked among them, able to kill them with a single blow. It wasn't knowledge people would take well. How badly would Holden freak out?

Possible explanations for the wolverine's claws and black-void eyes flittered through her mind. None of them was plausible. "What creature?"

Holden leaned forward, bracing himself with his elbows against his knees. "Don't play dumb with me. You know exactly what I am talking about."

She wasn't playing dumb. "I really don't." She was stalling.

He laced his fingers together, looked down at the floor, and sighed heavily. "Astrid," he growled. "I don't have time for this." He looked up and the storm of emotions swirling in his eyes made her breath catch. "He almost killed you." He blinked, schooling his features into a familiar blank expression. The professional blandness Holden had greeted her with only a few days after they'd had the most intense sex she'd experienced had hurt more than she'd ever admit. She should have expected it, considering he'd disappeared in the middle of the night. She'd woken up in an empty bed in a strange, empty apartment. That blank look on Holden's face had hurt then, and it did now.

She couldn't afford to go there. She inhaled deeply and dropped her shoulders as she breathed out. "Fine, what do you want to know?" After all, the man had probably saved her life. The least she could do was to tell him about the creatures he'd fought to keep her alive. No matter how badly he'd freak out.

Her stomach growled loudly.

Holden shot her a look and stood. "You need food." He walked over to the dresser and grabbed a binder. Returning to the chair, he handed it to her as he sat down again. "Room service menu is on page ten."

Astrid held the folder in her lap but didn't open it. "We could just go out for something." Eating a meal while still in bed—and with him sitting beside her— would be too intimate. And going out would give her more time to figure out what to tell him.

He shook his head. "Nope, we'll eat here. You need some food in you now." He tapped the folder. "Pick what you want."

She sighed but did what he asked. While he used the phone on the bedside table to call in her order of a double burger and fries, she studied his profile. He'd shaved while in the bathroom. The smooth skin of his jaw had a small nick just below the earlobe. She wanted to touch the spot to soothe it and had to curl her fingers to stop from reaching out. The berserker stirred again, but Astrid quickly lulled it back into sleep. Her attraction to Holden was freaky.

When she and Holden had hooked up all those months ago, her inner warrior had been enthusiastic. More so than it usually was when Astrid had sex with someone. She'd thought it was because she'd overindulged a little when she fed off the sexual energy from the people on the dance floor. But could it be that the berserker wanted Holden?

Nonsense. Astrid didn't even like the man.

Unaware of her mental analysis of their sexual history, or more accurately their one night together, Holden added his own food selection to their order and hung up. "Talk," he demanded and sat back down in the chair.

She didn't know where to start. "How about you ask me what you want to know, and I'll see if I can answer?"

He quirked an eyebrow. "Okay. What is that creature I saw in the parking garage, and why was it trying to kill you?"

Astrid's mind spun. She couldn't endanger her warrior brothers and sisters, but she could probably spin the truth into something palatable for Holden. "I don't know exactly what those creatures are, but I call them wolverines."

A tic pulsed in his jaws. "You're using the plural. There are more of these freaks?"

"I've seen a few." As in, she used to see them all the time when she went on patrol outside the fortress. Then they disappeared for a while but came back in smaller numbers. And now they seemed to have remarkable healing ability and new acrobatic skills. Like they were wolverines, version 2.0. She really needed to get in touch with the warriors back home so she could tell them.

Without somehow revealing that she'd lost Scott.

She was so screwed.

Holden sighed, got up, and retrieved another bottle of juice from the minibar. He handed it to her without comment and sat back down. This one was cranberry. "Look, I get that there are loads of information you don't want to share. But can we cut the crap? Just share what you know."

Astrid cracked the juice bottle open. "I am sharing." She took a swig of the bright-red liquid, hoping she wouldn't spill any on the nice white sheets. How had Holden kept her from bleeding all over the linens? "Just ask me what you want to know." That way she could censor each chunk of information more easily, and maybe his questions would show a pattern. Holden definitely had an agenda. His body betrayed him. He was too tense, too probing. This felt more like a debriefing than just him wanting to know about the creature he'd fought. Why would a nightclub owner interrogate her?

"Fine." Holden ran his hand through his hair. "Answer the second part of my question. Why are they trying to kill you?"

This one would be a little trickier. A long explanation about the power struggles in the Norse gods' council and Loki's circumvention of the rule about not taking the gods' battle to the human realm by instead sending wolverines seemed like a lot to lay on Holden all in one go. Plus, describing herself as an immortal sentinel fighting for Odin and Freya to keep humanity safe from Loki and his deranged plans might make Holden put her in a straitjacket.

She drank from the juice bottle again and took her time swallowing. The tic in Holden's jaw pulsed faster. Maybe he was able to control his physical reaction to her—which she so obviously struggled with, her nipples still hard—but she definitely got to him on some level.

She looked down and fiddled with the cap on the bottle to hide the small smile tugging at her lips. "That's a complicated story. I'm not sure if they wanted to kill me as much as capture me. I'm just good at fighting back." She looked up.

Holden met her gaze with an intense stare. He didn't blink before firing the next question. "Why do they want to capture you?"

"They want information." She held up her hand when it looked like he was about to explode out of the chair.

"Information I can't give them and I can't give you. It would endanger people I care about."

He sat back and studied her. "If these people are so concerned about keeping their secrets, why are you here on your own? Why aren't they protecting you?"

Good question. Although a better question would be: Why was she such a stubborn dumbass that she didn't take someone with her instead of endangering herself and the queen's brother? "They wanted to, but I... screwed up a few weeks ago, and I had to prove to them and myself that I could do this on my own."

His eyebrows shot up. Obviously he hadn't expected her to admit to that weakness. She hadn't expected to either, but it slipped out before she could stop it, and it was very much the truth. Somehow it was easier to admit this flaw to Holden than to her Norse brothers and sisters. Although she was pretty sure they were aware not only of her stubbornness, but also of how tightly she held on to her pride.

"Is Daisy Driscoll one of those people?" He used the name of Naya's fake identity. The one he'd known her by when she worked as his security consultant.

"She's a friend. That's all you need to know." Astrid kept her voice flat so no emotion would slip out. Let him interpret that statement as he wanted to. She would not betray her queen.

He seemed to sense that questions about Naya were off-limits because he nodded. "Fair enough. But then tell me what your business here in Denver is." She hesitated, and he leaned forward, putting his hand on top of hers. "Astrid, they almost killed you. Let me help you."

She shook her head and looked away in case the

sudden burst of tears welling up in her eyes escaped. The blood loss had made her into an emotional mess.

*Trust* whispered through her mind. The berserker again, but it didn't come out of its slumber.

"I have great resources." Holden squeezed her hand. "Please, let me help you."

Could she risk taking him up on his offer? He seemed awfully eager to help. "What's in it for you?" she asked.

He looked away. "What do you mean?"

"Why do you want to help so badly? What do you get out of this?"

Holden stood and paced the room. "I care about you."

Her heart fluttered, but she ignored it. She already knew she couldn't trust her hormones around Holden. Apparently other parts of her body were now betraying her too. "Bullshit. You hardly know me."

He turned, a wicked smile on his lips. "I would say I know you quite intimately."

Her whole body tingled, and heat pooled in her stomach before moving lower. She was glad she was under the covers so she could hide her body's reaction. She forced her breathing to remain steady and quirked an eyebrow. "Can we keep this conversation serious?"

His grin widened, but he nodded. "Alright, let's just say that I have an interest in this since you're a friend of Daisy's." Naya had worked with Holden before she met the king. Had there been something more than just a professional relationship between the two humans? The thought disturbed Astrid more than it should.

The berserker suddenly woke fully from its slumber.

*Mine*, it growled. An intense burst of anger flooded Astrid's senses. Images of her fighting the queen invaded her mind. She struggled to keep her face from betraying the horrific thoughts flittering through her mind and the rage spreading through her body.

She must not have been successful, because Holden frowned and took a step toward her. She held up her hand to stop him.

A knocked sounded on the door. Saved by room service.

As Holden turned, Astrid bolted out of the bed and slipped into the bathroom. She locked the door behind her and leaned her forehead against its cool wooden surface. What the fuck was going on?

# Chapter 6

LUKE CHECKED THE TRAY OF FOOD. EVERYTHING WAS exactly what they'd ordered, so he tipped the room-service guy and sent him on his way. Astrid was still in the bathroom, and he debated knocking on the door to see if she was okay.

He replayed their conversation in his head to figure out what had upset her. He'd teased her about how close they actually were, at least physically. That's when Astrid's eyes had widened and all the color had drained out of her face. Did she feel sick all of a sudden? Hopefully it was the cranberry juice that didn't agree with her. He'd hate to think the memory of them in bed made her physically ill.

They'd also talked about Daisy Driscoll—Naya— but was that before or after Astrid's strange reaction? If they were close friends, talking about the other woman shouldn't upset her.

He sighed. He'd probably never figure this out.

Astrid kept so much information hidden from him that he didn't even know how to start unraveling her secrets. If he wanted her to share, first he had to gain her trust, and Astrid didn't seem to trust anybody. Maybe if their night together had ended better, they'd have a chance. As it was, that little fuckup would cost him. Instead of starting at zero and building from there, he was now setting off from a position of negative infinity.

The shower turned on in the bathroom. He considered waiting for Astrid before eating, but he had no idea how long she'd be in there and his scrambled eggs would taste awful cold. He put Astrid's burger plate on the dresser and took the tray and his two cell phones with him out onto the balcony. There were no new messages on his work phone, so he slipped that into his jeans' pocket and tucked into his breakfast while scrolling through the emails on his alter ego's phone.

He'd been undercover so long that he felt like the two personas were starting to merge. It didn't help that he'd kept his real first name, but that had been a conscious decision since he'd just come out of a different assumed identity. He'd react authentically to someone using his real first name in much less time than having to absorb a new persona with a new first name.

He scrolled through the list of emails on Holden's phone. None seemed urgent. Rex, the head of security at his club and his occasional bodyguard, had some problems with one of the liquor deliveries, but it had been taken care of and now everything was fine. Not that Luke had ever doubted it would be. Rex was responsible and efficient. In a different situation, the two of them would have been great friends. Rex probably thought they were, but he was friends with Luke Holden, not Luke Hager.

Luke put the phone down and doused his eggs with more hot sauce. Out of the corner of his eye, he noticed the bathroom door open and glanced up to watch Astrid through the sliding glass doors.

She glided into the room swathed in one of the hotel bathrobes. The white, fluffy terry-cloth should make her shapeless, but instead she looked like a sexy Amazon queen draped in royal cloth. Her hair flowed down past her shoulders in wet waves.

She turned her head and locked gazes with him out on the balcony. That finally broke the trance he'd apparently succumbed to. He cleared his throat and put down the Tabasco bottle he was still holding midair. Gesturing toward her plate inside the room, he motioned that she should grab it and join him outside.

Astrid cocked her head and gave him an odd look, but then headed toward her food. The robe flowed around her, and he wondered if she was naked underneath or had put underwear back on after the shower. The idea of the robe sliding unhindered against her smooth skin made his cock throb, and he had to adjust himself before sitting back down. Since the table was made of wrought iron, he positioned his napkin so it hid the evidence of his attraction. This mission was going to give him a bad case of blue balls.

Astrid joined him at the table and dug into her burger. She looked up and caught him staring. "What?" she asked. Wearing no makeup and with a glob of ketchup smeared in the corner of her mouth, she was still the sexiest thing he'd seen. He was in big trouble.

Luke adjusted the napkin on his lap and then forced out a slow grin to hide his reaction. "Looks like you were hungry. You've got ketchup on your face."

"Thanks." She wiped her mouth with the napkin and kept eating.

He reclined in his chair. "Let's continue our earlier conversation."

Astrid took a big bite out of the burger and chewed

demonstratively, pointing at her cheek to show her mouth was full.

"It's okay," Luke said. "You eat and I'll talk. Just nod or shake your head if I ask you a question." She frowned at him, but he pretended not to see her irritation. "These creatures obviously want very badly to capture you. They're not going to give up." He paused.

Astrid nodded.

"Let's talk strategy then. You basically have two options." There were probably more, but not if she wanted to resolve this quickly. He'd thought it through. His Marine instincts would be right in this situation.

She paused mid-chew and raised her eyebrows.

Luke leaned forward and snagged a fry from her plate. He chewed slowly, dragging it out to see how long she would hold out before speaking. He didn't have to wait long.

Astrid finished chewing her bite too quickly and started coughing. "What two options?" she choked out. He pushed his glass of water toward her. She took a deep swallow. "What options?" she insisted.

Luke reached for another fry, but she slapped his hand away. "It's basic battle strategy," he said as he pretended to nurse the hand she'd hit. "Either you wait for them to come to you, in which case you set an ambush. Or, you go on the offensive and attack them at their home base."

A fleeting shadow passed across her face. "I don't know where they hang out."

He'd love to know what she was thinking right now. "Find out."

She cocked her head, studying him like he was a

new species she'd never seen before. "How?" Her voice trembled a little.

He waited a breath longer than necessary. "Let me help you."

Astrid just kept looking at him. "How will you find out where their home base is?" Skepticism practically dripped from her words. Did she really have that little faith in him? He would enjoy proving her wrong. If he could get her to partner up with him, that was. And that was a big "if." But he could tell she wanted this badly. She was holding herself too still and trying hard to keep her voice steady.

Luke shrugged. "I've got resources." He grabbed several fries from her plate. Whalert would shit ducklings when Luke requested to use DTU's computers and databases, but he'd come around eventually. He wanted to flush out these covert labs as badly as Luke did, just not for the same reasons. Whalert wanted to put a stop to the domestic terrorists they brewed up through their illegal genetics program. Luke's reason was personal. He wanted revenge for Donovan.

Astrid didn't seem to notice the theft of the fries this time. "What kind of resources?"

"I can't tell you that," Luke said. "Let's just say I've got a way to find things." Well, the government did. Big Brother was watching and listening intently everywhere.

Astrid picked up her burger again, but put it back down before taking a bite. "Okay, let's say we find where the wolverines hang out. Then what?" She looked up, her green eyes as clear as a forest lake.

"What do you want to do? Blow them up? Capture them?" He almost held his breath. What she chose would tell him a lot about why the creatures were after her.

She looked away. "They have something I need."

Money? Guns? Drugs? Luke's mind reeled with possibilities. "I need more than that if I'm going to help you with this." His pushed some authority into his tone of voice. This game they were playing was taking too long.

"Okay," she nodded. "I came to Denver to retrieve something—someone." She was finally sharing. But who had she come to pick up? A boyfriend? The thought bothered him more than it should, and he pushed aside the alpha instinct to demand answers. Instead, he waited for her to continue. "The wolverines somehow kidnapped him before I could pick him up."

So it was a *he*. Luke forced his voice to remain even. "Someone important to you?"

She traced the table's lattice iron pattern with a fingertip. "Someone important to…Daisy." She looked up, studying him closely.

The relief he felt was immediate. "Daisy's boyfriend?"

"Would that bother you?" she asked in a dry voice.

Why the hell would he care who Daisy—Naya, whatever the hell her name was—dated? "Why would it?" He frowned. What crazy tangential path had they gone down now?

Astrid looked him straight in the eye, as if his next answer would be very important. "I thought the two of you had a thing while you worked together."

Was that what had made her bolt into the bathroom earlier? "Ms. Driscoll and I had a strictly professional relationship." Naya was attractive, but he'd never been drawn to her. Not like with Astrid. She'd practically shone like a beacon on the dance floor the first time he saw her. He had spent the whole night staring at her. Plus, he'd always known that Naya was involved with the covert labs. A brief glimpse of her was on the security tapes from the North Dakota explosions. What was left of the footage, which wasn't much. Naya had been his mark from the beginning.

Astrid muttered under her breath, but he couldn't make out the words. Before he had a chance to ask, she spoke again. "Daisy's engaged to someone else."

"The guy who was upset with her when you came to find her at the club?"

She nodded. "The guy I was supposed to pick up is her brother." She looked away. "I should never have lost him."

Luke grabbed her hand and was ridiculously pleased when she didn't pull away. "Don't beat yourself up. You couldn't have known." He still wanted to know what this guy meant to her.

She looked him straight in the eye. "But I should have known. I should have been more careful." Pain filled her gaze. "He's not well." She swallowed. "What if they're hurting him? Daisy will never forgive me."

Was she talking about torture? So, this brother knew whatever Astrid was keeping from these creatures. And Naya was connected to all of this, as well as to a lab like the one that had destroyed Donovan's life. Excitement rose in Luke's chest. He was so close. After all these years, would he finally get revenge for *his* brother? He forced himself to concentrate and not let his emotions trip him up. He couldn't give anything away now. "We'll find him."

Astrid nodded. "We'll get him out." Her voice dropped lower. "And then we'll kill all of those miserable wolverine bastards." Chills ran down Luke's spine. She must have noticed, because she looked at him, a cold smile on her lips. "Sorry, I can get a little bloodthirsty."

*A little?*

---

Luke found Broden in his office on the second floor of the Denver FBI field office. The modern building was made largely of glass and located in the east part of the city, where the old airport had been. Broden's office had large windows, but for some reason he had the blinds drawn. "It's too bright and freaking hot when the sun shines straight in," he explained when asked. "Plus, I don't like the view of Walmart and Sam's Club across the street."

Luke took a seat. He'd called Whalert before heading over. The special agent in charge had grumbled for a while but finally given his consent to Luke using the Denver office's resources. "I need your help," Luke told Broden.

The field agent watched him from across the desk. "So I've heard. Your boss called my boss, and here we are." His tone wasn't exactly unfriendly, but his body language said he wasn't too thrilled about the request. Great, another person Luke was going to have to cajole into trusting him. When he'd left Astrid back in the hotel, she'd worn exactly the same skeptical expression that Broden's face bore right now.

"My mark had a run-in with some bad...people.

I need to check last night's security footage from the parking garage at the train station."

Broden quirked an eyebrow and picked up his phone receiver. He punched a button, and when someone picked up on the other end, he issued a few short commands. Slipping the receiver back in its cradle, he nodded to Luke. "They're pulling the feed and preparing a viewing room for us."

*Oh shit.* No way he could watch that creature with Broden in the room. Talk about freak-out in the FBI. "Some of the information on there could be of a sensitive nature. I'm not sure you have the security—"

Broden slammed his hand down on the desk. "Don't give me that shit about security clearance. Unless your girl has her top off and is blowing the president while he's reciting secret missile codes, I'm watching that footage with you." He took a breath. "And even then, I'd just watch it after you left. Maybe with the sound off, but I'd watch."

Luke's mind raced. He had to keep Broden from seeing that fight. "Look, I've been working this case for eighteen months. I can't risk it falling apart just because you have your panties in a twist and want to watch a movie with me."

"How would me seeing security footage from a parking garage make your case fall apart?"

Well, he had Luke there. Maybe he'd just have to knock out the agent before the wolverines showed up on the video. "I don't know, but it could happen." He sounded like a petulant teenager.

Broden raised an eyebrow. "Are you doing something illegal in that garage?"

Luke shook his head. "No." Technically, he had attacked first, but considering the creature had claws, he didn't think anyone would hold that against him. They'd be too busy freaking out about the monsters walking among them.

The phone on the desk buzzed. A tinny male voice announced that viewing room two was set up for them. Broden stood and motioned for Luke to proceed out the office door.

They walked down a corridor where skylights brightly illuminated walls painted in yellow and blue. Broden squinted against the light. Maybe he was a vampire. Or maybe he was just hungover. At the end of the corridor, they took two flights of stairs down to a narrower hallway. Green and red lamps hung over closed doors. Broden opened one where the green light was on and ushered Luke inside. He entered a small room with two executive office chairs placed in front of a wide desk with oversize screens resting on top.

Broden sat in one of the chairs and typed on a keyboard on the desk. The screens came alive, displaying a numbered list with columns of dates and times. "Alright," the agent mumbled as he tapped the keys. "Let's see if I remember how to do this."

Luke took the chair next to Broden's and watched as the data scrolled past on the screen. Broden selected several rows, right-clicked, and selected "map" from the drop-down menu. A 3-D model of the parking garage showed up on the screen.

"What floor do you want to view?" Broden asked.

"Three," Luke answered, fascinated by how the agent

rotated the image of the garage. He pointed at some blinking circles on the screen. "Are those the cameras?"

"Yep. Which location on third?"

Luke peered closer on the screen, not sure if he was relieved or disappointed when he discovered Astrid's parking spot was in a dead zone. He pointed at the screen. "This is where her car was."

Broden swore under his breath. "The city did a piss-poor job of covering this garage. There aren't enough cameras. Probably wanted to save money on the setup."

Luke silently agreed. Even the cameras that were there seemed poorly placed. Naya would have done a much better job. His club had no corners to hide in after she'd placed cameras according to her security plan. The absurdity of asking Naya to come up with a plan for Denver so he could spy on Astrid made him smile. "What about entrances and exits?"

A few more taps on the keyboard, and Broden had split the screen between the double entrance and exit drive-ups Luke had used when chasing after the wolverine creature and a lone exit ramp on the side of the building. They watched the footage on triple speed. The cars zoomed in and out of the garage like angry, yet slightly confused insects, stopping and going with jerky movements.

Luke's subconscious recognized something on the footage from the camera displaying the lone entrance. "There." He pointed. "Go back and let's watch that again." On the film, a white van exited the garage, and Luke saw what his instincts had picked up on before his mind could catch up. The driver of the van tried to keep his face from being captured on camera, but even in profile there was no mistaking his broken nose. Swollen and misshapen, it stood out even in the grainy resolution of the security footage. "That's the guy. Zoom in on the license plate."

Broden did as asked and then cursed. "The thing is so dirty I can't make out the numbers."

"Can you get someone to clean up the picture for us?" Luke leaned forward in the chair, peering closer on the plate even though he knew there was no use.

"I doubt it," Broden said. "Not only did they save money on the number of cameras, but with this resolution, the picture would just get blurrier if we tried to zoom in on the plate."

Luke sighed and thought for a moment. "The guy comes back later, but he's on foot."

Broden turned toward him. "You're thinking he might have parked on the street?"

Luke nodded.

"It's not a bad idea." Broden faced the screen again. "He would have parked off-site to not to draw attention to himself, but not so far that he couldn't reach the vehicle if he needed a quick getaway."

They fast-forwarded a few hours until they saw the creature enter the garage again. The camera picked up the butterfly bandages across his nose as white bright spots on the grainy gray footage. Broden returned to map mode and zoomed out the image so the three-dimensional model now included streets and structures outside the garage. His fingers tapped on the keys and switched between several street-view cameras in quick sequencing, all displaying the same time stamp as when the creature walked up to the parking garage.

They both noticed the parked white van at the same time and scooted forward in their seats. Broden enlarged the image and then grunted triumphantly when the camera caught the rear license plate and the registration number showed up clear as could be. "Got ya," he exclaimed and reached for the phone. After he'd asked for a BOLO alert on the registration, he turned toward Luke. "Shall we see if we can do some more sleuthing and figure out where it came from?" His eyes glittered.

Luke sat back in the chair. "Go for it." He watched as Broden's agile typing manipulated the software to quickly search through footage via a street-by-street view in ever-expanding circles radiating out from the parked white van. As the time stamps counted down, they were able to trace the van's route backward from the parking garage to wherever it had started out.

Broden muttered under his breath the entire time, but he obviously knew the software tool well and was enjoying himself. Luke's respect for the field office agent grudgingly grew. At the same time, he felt slightly creeped out by the idea that Broden had such an excellent view of Denver's citizens from this small room and seemed to excel in voyeuring. At least when it came to traffic patterns and parking. Hopefully, Broden only used his powers for good.

# Chapter 7

THE INSIDE OF ASTRID'S THIGH ITCHED LIKE CRAZY, and she tried not to fidget in the passenger seat of Holden's car. She'd pulled out the stitches that morning, using nail clippers and tweezers. Not the ideal tools for removing sutures, but they were all she had and she couldn't afford to wait any longer. Her skin regenerated too quickly and had started to absorb the thread. It was either remove them or have them become a permanent part of her.

Holden yawned widely as he drove and took another sip out of the paper cup of coffee he'd insisted they buy at a drive-through coffee place. She wondered how much sleep he'd gotten. Before they left, Astrid had booked another hotel room for herself using the phone in Luke's room. She'd then strolled through the hallways and the lobby wearing only the hotel robe, but nobody had so much as raised an eyebrow. They must have thought she was on her way back from the spa or the pool.

Once she got to her room, she'd sent a quick text to Naya so she wouldn't worry. Astrid had felt guilty then, and a quick pang of unease hit her now too. Although the guilt hadn't kept her from sleep. As soon as she hit Send on the message, she'd crashed and been out for straight twelve hours. She felt remarkably rejuvenated after that. Even the berserker seemed more alert and yet calmer. It hadn't spoken again and wasn't restlessly pacing like it had for the last few days. Since the train-station garage allowed overnight parking, she wasn't too worried about having left the car there. The locked weapons compartment was well hidden in the floor of the chassis. And the car had an inline fuel shut-off valve. If someone tried to steal the car, they'd only be able to drive it a few feet. The fuel supply was shut off unless the engine was started with a key.

"It's not much farther now." Holden put his cup back in the holder. "Golden is just twenty minutes from Denver, and the building I think the freaky creatures are in is only a few miles past town."

Astrid studied her phone. According to her Internet search, Golden had been founded in the late 1850s when gold was discovered in the mountains surrounding the town. Only a decade or two later, Adolph Coors had shown up and started his famous brewery. Miners and beer, a winning combination. She figured Adolph had ended up with more gold in his pocket than the men who'd dug it out of the mountain and panned the streams.

She returned her thoughts to current times and wondered how Holden had discovered where the wolverines were hiding out. When she'd asked him about it, he'd just shrugged and said he had reliable sources. She hadn't pushed for more information, but that didn't mean she wouldn't do so later. There was a lot more to him than he let on. The average nightclub owner did not have medical training or know interrogation techniques. "What's the plan once we get there?"

He glanced her way. "I figured we'd do some recon and then lie low until dark. Maybe find a bed and get some rest, unless you have other ideas." He shot her one of those cocky grins he doled out so frequently. It infuriated her and turned her on at the same time. She was in so much trouble with this guy.

Astrid pretended to ignore the cocky smile and the innuendo. "Any ideas about how many wolverines we may encounter, or where they're holding Scott?" Crap. She hadn't meant to use his name.

Holden concentrated on the road and didn't look her way, but from the stillness seeping into his body, she could tell he'd noticed her slip. "My intel couldn't give me that detailed information. I'm hoping we'll figure that out once we do some surveillance."

She nodded and then realized he couldn't see her answer. "Okay," she added.

They drove through town, passed Colorado School of Mines, and turned left onto a smaller highway that took them into the mountains west of town. The road turned narrower and more twisty. Not that different from the road to the medical clinic where Scott had been treated. She didn't want to think about that trip and how discouraged she'd been when she returned to Denver. She also didn't want to reflect on how much better it felt to have Holden by her side. At least during the reconnaissance. When it came to taking down the wolverines, she would have to somehow ditch Holden and go up against the nasty creatures on her own. She couldn't afford to have a regular mortal killed during her mission. Although Holden might not be as regular as he wanted her to think.

A few miles later, Holden turned off the highway and followed a dirt road through a narrow gap between the mountains. He squinted up at the walls of granite surrounding them. "There," he said, pointing toward a smaller ridge and slowing the car. "If we hike up to the top, we'll have a great viewpoint of the freaky creature place. According to the intel I got, they should be in the valley next to us." He turned toward her. "Will your leg be up for this? You can stay in the car if you don't think it can take the excursion."

"Not on your life," Astrid answered. "I'm coming with." She never stayed behind. Not during recon and not during battle.

They got out and closed the doors with only soft clicks to prevent the sound from carrying. It might not reach as far as the next valley over, but there was no reason to alert anyone to their location. Holden opened the trunk and took out binoculars, water bottles, and a small day pack. Had he been a Boy Scout when younger? He seemed awfully well prepared and used military words like *recon* and *surveillance*. He also seemed way more comfortable in the outdoors than you'd expect your average city nightclub owner to be.

He handed Astrid one set of binoculars and started off up the ridge. She looped the strap around her neck and followed closely behind him. Increasing her stride, she enjoyed the loosening of her tendons and muscles, the flow of strength back into her body. Birds chirped in the trees around them, and the sun shone from a clear blue sky as they ascended the ridge. Astrid enjoyed the view around her, as well as the one right in front of her. Back in Pine Rapids, Holden always wore impeccably tailored suits. This was the first time she'd seen him in casual wear. The soft denim of his well-worn jeans cupped and outlined his trim ass. There was nothing sexier than a great butt in a pair of jeans. And Holden's was a fine specimen.

As if he could hear her thoughts, he turned around. "Are you okay?" He grinned as he caught her ogling his behind.

She looked away, cheeks heating. "Yep, no problems here."

They crested the ridge and looked down into a wide, green valley. A creek glittered in the sunshine as it snaked through the length of the valley. A dirt road, not unlike the one they'd left their car on, followed the water until it forked and one path went across a bridge and up to a group of buildings nestled against the ridge.

Holden pointed at the cluster of houses "That's where they should be holed up."

Astrid lifted the binoculars to her eyes. "There is no movement outside or inside any of the buildings."

"Someone's there though." Holden peered through his own lenses. "There's smoke coming from one of the chimneys."

Astrid turned slightly to the left and focused on the white tendril floating toward the sky. "But how many of them are there?" This far away, her berserker couldn't pick out individual creatures.

"How many attacked you in the parking garage?"

"Two." An image of sinking her knife into the jugular of the wolverine rose in her mind. "But I probably killed one."

His eyebrows rose. "Probably?"

She tried to remember details, but her memory after being cut in the thigh was hazy. "I remember sinking my knife into his neck and later hearing the other creature drag the body away, but I can't be sure."

Holden studied her for a moment. Some emotion flickered through his gray eyes, but it was gone before she could identify it. "Better to plan for many than be surprised by extra enemies." He looked back at the house. "Let's say there are at least two of these creatures, and if they're in any kind of battle unit, we should plan for maybe a team of four."

His analysis was along the same tracks she'd follow, but how did a nightclub owner know so much about battle preparation? "They may have another team for backup."

He nodded, still studying the buildings below. "You're right. They may even have enough soldiers down there for a full squad."

Astrid waited to see if he would catch himself using precise military vocabulary, but Holden just kept watching the buildings. She followed his gaze. Other than smoke still streaming up from the chimney, nothing was going on below them.

Holden suddenly turned toward her. "I brought some food. Let's eat while we wait." He grabbed the small backpack, walked toward a small grove of aspens, and sat down on a rock. Astrid followed and sank down on a rock next to his. Holden handed her a sandwich and a bottle of water.

His leg brushed against hers, triggering an immediate response from her overactive hormones. Just being near him turned her on. She busied herself with unwrapping the food but kept an eye on him. He held himself differently now than at the club. Although he sat in a casual pose with one leg slightly bent and an elbow resting on his knee, there was tension coiled in his muscles. A warrior watching over enemy territory and prepared for an imminent attack. "You seem very familiar with military terminology," Astrid said, keeping her tone casual.

He shrugged and finished chewing his sandwich before answering. "I served for a while."

She'd bet it was for more than "a while," judging by how quickly his mind had snapped into strategic planning. It would have been a career. "What unit?"

"The Marines, of course. There is no other branch worth joining." Holden fired one of his grins at her. She wasn't overly familiar with the different branches of the U.S. military, but she did know that the Marines were elite soldiers. She and her battle brothers and sisters were *einherjar*, Odin's and Freya's elite soldiers. She wondered if Holden's training had been similar to theirs but doubted his had included how to kill supernatural creatures like Loki's wolverines. Although he had neutralized one of them when he saved her, so he had obviously been trained well. "What about you?" Holden asked.

Startled from her thoughts, she didn't know what he meant. "What about me?"

"You obviously know something about the military if you figured out that's my background." He took a sip of water. "Did you serve?"

Talk about a loaded question. She'd been born a thrall but earned her freedom as a shield maiden. "I did." Her skills on the battlefield had earned her respect, and she'd participated in many raids. In a way she'd "served," even if it hadn't been in an organized army of modern times. She still served as a soldier. She served her gods and her fellow warriors.

"And in what branch?"

She didn't even have to think about it. "Navy," she said with a small smile on her lips. The Viking ships she'd sailed on were a far cry from the modern ships he'd associate with that term, but it was close enough.

"So we're both sailors," Holden said. "I never asked where you're from, but did you serve here in the States?"

Astrid shook her head. "I was born in Sweden." Almost a thousand years ago, but a woman didn't discuss her age.

Luke opened his mouth as if to ask something else, but then quickly picked up his binoculars and aimed them down the hill. "Something's happening." He stood.

She joined him and peered down at the buildings through her own eyepieces. A wolverine walked across the courtyard to one of the buildings that looked more like a barn. He carried a tray in his hands, and she could see steam rising from one of the plates. "I don't think that's one of the ones who attacked me." It was hard to tell because the creatures looked so much alike, but she was pretty sure she hadn't seen this one before.

"What do you want to bet that's food for their prisoner?"

Astrid fought the worry rising in her chest. "That's a fair assumption." Some of her distress must have come through in her tone of voice, because Holden lowered his lenses and shot her a look.

He reached for her hand and squeezed it. "You okay?"

She had to look away to not reveal how much that small gesture comforted her. "I'm good." Why was she so emotional around him? She needed to get a grip and warrior up.

He gave her hand another squeeze and turned back to the buildings. She did the same. After about twenty minutes, the door on the barn opened and the wolverine came out again. The tray was empty.

"At least we know they're feeding him," Holden said.

The thought of the wolverines mistreating Naya's brother overwhelmed her. She shouldn't have been so cocky. Despair welled up so fast in her throat that she choked. She knew she should have asked for backup, but the only way she could trust herself to be a worthy warrior to the others again was if she brought Scott back on her own.

Dropping his binoculars back around his neck, Holden turned and reached for her. He enveloped her in his arms. "Hey, this is going to be okay. We'll get him out."

"This is all my fault," Astrid forced out through her constricted throat. His body heat was both comforting and disturbing.

He rubbed his hand up and down her back. "You didn't know they planned on taking him."

She rested her head against his broad chest, reveling in the strength she found there. She'd fucked up so badly on this mission. If she didn't get this right, she'd never be able to look her queen—her friend—in the eye again. She'd never be able to fight among her Norse brothers and sisters again. They would not trust her to have their back, and she'd be a liability in battle. And fighting was the only thing Astrid had ever been good at. It was what had changed her from a slave to a person of worth.

Holden's nearness inundated her senses. She needed

some distance so she could think clearly again. She flattened her palm against his chest to push him away, but paused when he hissed in a breath at the contact. She could feel his muscles contract underneath her hand. Slowly she raised her head to look up at him.

His gaze smoldered and zoomed in her lips. They parted of their own accord, and her breath hitched. His hand on her back pulled her closer, while the other cupped the back of her neck. "Fuck it," he whispered and descended on her lips.

The kiss seared her senses, firing through every nerve of her body. Heat pooled at the junction of her thighs. She moaned and he slanted his head, deepening the kiss. His tongue explored her mouth, sending darts of pleasure zinging through her body.

She laced her hands behind his neck and pressed into his warm, solid body. His hard shaft rubbed against her stomach, and he growled into her mouth. Holden backed her up against one of the aspens. He grabbed the back of her knee and hooked her leg over his hip, angling down so all that male hardness pressed in just the right spot. Liquid heat shot from her core through her limbs. She groaned her approval and buried her hands in his hair. A powerful need built inside her, and she wanted to get closer to his solid body.

*More. Mine*, whispered the berserker, feeding on the sexual energy radiating off Holden. Horrified, Astrid froze in place, panting heavily. *What the fuck*. Her berserker could not be claiming Holden.

He immediately stopped, leaning back to gaze into her eyes. "You okay?" he asked, a frown marring his face.

She looked away and slid her leg out of his grip until

she stood on solid ground with two feet again. "This is not right," she managed to whisper.

He leaned his forehead against hers, and she closed her eyes to savor the sensation, while desperately forcing the berserker back into slumber. "This is the most right I've felt in a long time," Holden countered. "We need to stop kidding ourselves about how badly we both want this."

She did want him, but she wanted to complete this mission more and to break this weird connection her berserker seemed to think it had with him. "I can't risk losing focus. I have to get Scott back to his sister."

He pushed her hair behind her ear and turned the motion into a caress of her jaw. "We're going to make that happen."

He stood too close, the heat from his body distracting her. She stepped out of his embrace. The temptation to become lovers was too strong. She needed to think this through. "Then let's concentrate on coming up with a plan." She took another step back.

Holden reached for her but then dropped his arms. "Alright." His jaw clenched. "My suggestion is that we rest until darkness falls. Then we return here and hit them hard."

"Okay." Astrid watched him warily, but he didn't look at her. Instead, he picked up the backpack and headed down the ridge the way they'd come up. She paused for a moment and then followed, catching up with him halfway down. He shot her a quick sideways look and then grabbed her hand in his. Her first instinct was to pull it back, but then she relented. Maybe getting this sexual sizzle out of their system would make it easier to concentrate on the mission. Freya's wagon, it's not like it could get any harder. Her mind scrambled whenever she was near Holden.

She lengthened her stride to match his. They walked hand in hand the rest of the way to the car and got in without any further talk. Holden drove them back out to the main highway and headed for Golden. Halfway there, a sign advertised a motel, and Holden steered the car into the parking lot. He turned sideways and looked at her. "This okay?"

Astrid peered through the windshield at the building in front of them. Someone had gone to a lot of trouble to make wood carvings look like gingerbread. The facade of the building seemed to be straight out of Hansel and Gretel, complete with colored lights standing in for candy decorations. "It definitely looks festive," she said.

Holden opened the door and got out. "Let's see what crazy stuff they did to the interior." He grabbed her hand again when she got out of the car, and they walked up to a set of double doors with an entrance sign above. Holden held the door open and motioned for her to precede him. A gentleman-like gesture, but it also meant she'd encounter any potential danger first. She clutched her hand around the knife in her pocket but needn't have bothered.

The woman on the other side of the reception desk greeted her with a cheerful smile. Her tight gray curls and big, red plastic glasses made her look like Red Riding Hood's grandmother. Hopefully, the wolf was not around today. "Hello," she called. "What can I do for you?"

Holden stepped up from behind Astrid. "Do you have rooms available?" He smiled, oozing charm and goodwill.

The woman immediately responded to his flirty ways. "Why, yes, you are in luck. I just had a cancellation." She consulted a ledger on the desk. "A king."

Astrid cleared her throat. "Is that your only room?" Sharing a room would be temptation enough. Sharing a bed would mean the inevitable, and she wasn't sure she'd yet made up her mind about taking Holden as a lover—again.

The grandmother frowned. "We have only the one. And it may be your only chance of a room tonight. We're hosting a big family reunion, so I am all full up."

Luke threw a credit card on the counter. "We'll take it." He turned to Astrid. "I don't want to drive all the way back to Denver. The added distance will put us more than an hour out from where we need to go tonight."

Astrid decided to interpret the only one room available situation as a sign from the gods. Now she just had to make up her mind about whether the gods had made a good or bad choice for her.

# Chapter 8

LUKE LOOKED AROUND THE GINGERBREAD HOTEL ROOM and shuddered. The wood carvings and lights on the outside of the hotel had been cute, but the room decoration was taking the theme too far. Painted gingerbread men and women danced from floor to ceiling on off-white walls. The bedspread was made to look like a huge birthday cake. Basically, the decor looked like a five-year-old had been the interior designer. Astrid seemed unaffected. She sat down in one of the armchairs by the window and removed her boots. Stretching her long legs out before her, she wiggled her toes and sighed contentedly.

As usual, he only had to look at her to grow hard. Although, his dick had been erect since the kiss on top of the ridge. For the first time, he'd been distracted on a mission. His Marine team had called him Hyper because of his ability to become hyper-focused. That intensity had carried over into his work in the DTU. Sometimes he didn't sleep because his brain just wouldn't stop processing case details. But a few hours with Astrid on a mountain ridge had made him completely forget why he was on top of that hill in the first place. The kiss had seared his brain, and all he could think about was getting her naked and then getting inside her. He forgot all about the wolverines, their hostage, or his own mission.

He'd forgotten about Donovan. Unforgivable.

He bent down to unlace his own boots and to hide how angry he was with himself.

At least Astrid had managed to keep her head in the game and stop him from making a complete fool of himself. What had he been thinking?

He hadn't. He'd been listening to his dick, and that damn fool had almost talked him into getting naked with Astrid. Outside. With enemies just below them.

She'd been unusually quiet on the ride over to the hotel. Did she regret the kiss? Even while he was back focusing on the mission, he still wanted her. Even though the bed was draped in that monstrosity of a blanket, his mind kept picturing her naked between the sheets. "The pizza should be here soon," he heard himself say. Lame, but at least he'd broken the silence. There was no food service in the area other than a pizza carryout place. There was also no cell phone service, so the nice lady at reception had called in the order for them.

Astrid nodded. "Yep."

Well, so much for trying to break the awkward silence and distract himself from the sexual tension practically crackling between them. He tried again. "Are you hungry?"

This time she looked up at him, her eyes dark and stormy. "Starving." She might not have meant the double entendre, but her words went straight to his dick. He inhaled sharply as his crotch tightened.

Astrid must have picked up on his attraction. Her pupils dilated, and she leaned forward as if pulled by an invisible force. He felt his own body move toward her chair and reminded himself of why he was on this case. It was about Donovan, about his brother.

But they were stuck in this candy room for a few hours until they could get the hostage out under cover of darkness. And he needed Astrid. Needed her like he needed his next breath.

Luke kneeled by the chair and buried a hand in her luscious blond waves. She looked at him, her eyes deep pools of green. She stilled for a heartbeat but then moved in for a kiss, a sigh escaping as her body turned soft in his arms. He angled his head for better access and deepened the kiss, pulling her closer to him. It wasn't enough. He needed to feel her whole body.

He stood and pulled her up with him out of the chair. Her breasts pressed against his chest, and he could feel her nipples grow hard through the cotton fabric of her shirt. A growl escaped from his throat. Trailing kisses down her jawline, he caressed her hip through her jeans and steered her backward toward the bed. All he wanted was to throw her down and pound into her, but he reeled himself in just enough to be able to carefully lower her onto the hideous bedcover.

Taking a deep breath, he sat back and looked down on Astrid lying below him. Her lips were red and swollen from his kiss, which stirred up deep alpha male pleasure inside him. Her glorious green eyes were slightly glazed over, and her blond hair fanned out around her head. She looked like a Norse goddess of seduction, if there was one. His dick ached with the need to be inside her, but he had to slow this down or he'd blow his load before he got out of his jeans.

A knock on the door and a muffled "pizza delivery" had Luke cursing out loud. He'd forgotten all about their food and was tempted to tell the guy to just fuck off.

Astrid giggled. He shot her a stern look meant to intimidate her, but she only smiled back. "Don't you dare move," he growled and went to get the door.

The pizza delivery guy's welcoming smile at the two twenties Luke shoved his way turned into shock when Luke grabbed the box out of his hands just before slamming the door in his face. Luke tossed the pizza on the dresser and returned to the bed.

Pulling his T-shirt over his head, he lowered himself over Astrid, seeking her lips with his own. She moaned softly as he caressed the side of her face and increased the pressure of the kiss, exploring her mouth thoroughly. Her tongue darted out, dancing with his, and this time she deepened the kiss, turning it into a frantic mating thrust.

He couldn't get enough of her. Needed to feel her hot skin against his own. Using both hands, he grabbed her hips and then slid his palms up under her shirt, caressing her breasts. She inhaled sharply, and he growled his approval when she arched against his palms. In one quick swoop, he pulled her shirt off over her head. He leaned back briefly to take in the lovely view of her bare skin before planting his hands on both sides of her. He braced himself against the bed as he traced the edge of her lacy bra with his mouth. She was perfection.

He nuzzled the thin fabric away from her breast and lightly bit her nipple before taking the whole juicy confection into his mouth. Astrid arched beneath him, a growl escaping from her throat. She reached for the button on his jeans, and as her fingertips brushed the swollen head of his dick, his abs clenched and his balls ached from the effort of not coming right then and there. She quickly unbuttoned him and pulled down the zipper.

When she reached in and grabbed him, he covered her hand with his own. "Sweetheart, if you don't slow down, I'm not going to last long," he mumbled against her chest.

She grabbed his hair and kissed him, nipping his lips and then tracing his jaw with her tongue. "Then you better find some protection. I need you hard and throbbing inside me right now," she whispered, her voice dark and raw. It was the hottest thing he'd ever heard.

Luke pulled his hair out of her grip, and she growled deep in her throat as he left the bed to find the condom he'd put in his wallet as soon as he knew he'd be chasing Astrid to Denver. His brain had insisted he shouldn't bring it, since sleeping with her would make it difficult to stay objective. His dick had celebrated and told him to put the rest of the pack in his carry-on.

Pulling the foil package out of the wallet, he headed back to the bed, chucking his jeans and socks on the way. Astrid half sat up and reached for him, but he gently pushed her back down. Leaning over her, he kissed her again as he reached behind her to unsnap her bra. He congratulated himself on getting it done in one try. Not a small feat considering how badly his hands trembled with the effort of not grabbing her and pushing himself inside her in one deep stroke.

He slid the shoulder straps down her arms and let his gaze caress her skin. She moved restlessly and reached for him again, but he evaded her hands. "I want to look at you. You are so beautiful."

She snorted. "You don't have to use pretty words on me. Besides, you've already seen what's on offer." The time before, in his apartment, had been a frantic tangle of arms and legs, her lips hot on his. They hadn't taken the time to remove their clothes completely, never mind turning on the lights before he'd pushed inside her. Just like now, she'd driven him mad with need, but this time he wanted to see her. To taste her.

"We were in the dark." He lifted his head to lock gazes with her. "And I only use pretty words when I mean them." The reluctant smile on her lips touched something deep inside him. He pushed the feeling aside and concentrated on the feast in front of him.

Cupping her breasts, he licked and nipped, biting a little harder when his teeth grazing her nipple had her arching high off the bed. Her hands caressed the back of his head and then buried themselves in his hair as he trailed his mouth lower.

He found a spot just above her hip that had her moaning out loud, so he spent extra time tasting her golden skin before moving over to see if the other side was as sensitive. Judging from how her fingers grasped his scalp, it was. Her sounds of pleasure drove him further toward the brink. He needed to taste her.

He pulled her jeans and panties down, and then starting from her knee, he kissed his way up toward the sweet spot at the junction of her thighs. As his fingers mimicked his lips' movements on the opposite leg, he took extra care with the area around her stitches. The wound was almost healed. She'd removed the sutures already. Something in the back of his mind nagged him about that, but he was distracted by Astrid's sweet moans as his breath fanned her core. All he could think of was tasting her. To suck and nip her in the most intimate spot, to really make her his this time.

Easing a finger inside her, Luke slipped his tongue between her folds. Astrid's response was a guttural groan that made him want to beat his chest and congratulate himself on his prowess. He slid another finger inside her and curled both fingers forward as his tongue searched out her clit. Thrusting the tip of his tongue on the sensitive nub repeatedly, he matched the rhythm with his fingers, curling and uncurling.

Astrid's hands pounded against the ridiculous cake bedcover, her thighs clenching. She pulled her legs up, bracing her heels on the bed as she arched against him, pushing her core closer to his mouth. "More," she demanded in that deep, sexy voice.

He obliged by sucking hard on her clit, and she clenched around his fingers before shattering beneath his mouth, crying out as the orgasm claimed her.

When her body stopped convulsing, he had to cover his mouth to hide the triumphant grin on his face. He wasn't successful. "You're pretty pleased with yourself, aren't you?" she asked, arching an eyebrow.

"Shouldn't I be?" He lay down beside her. "I didn't hear any complaints." He angled his hips away from her so he wouldn't bump his throbbing dick. It ached with the need to be inside her, but he could wait a millisecond longer.

Astrid had other ideas. She grabbed his shoulder and pushed him on his back. "No complaints here, but let's see what you can do with other parts of your anatomy." She reached for the foil package he'd dumped on the bed. In no time, she'd ripped it open and covered him with one long sweep of her hand. The cold latex and the pressure of her hand made him gasp with pleasure. "Hold on," Astrid whispered, straddling him.

She slowly lowered herself onto his cock. Her hair created a curtain around their faces, the tips of her strands brushing against his collarbone. The hotness of her clenching around him—in contrast with the whisper caress of her hair on his skin—was the most erotic thing he'd experienced. He grabbed her hips and arched against her as he pulled her down.

Astrid moaned when he was fully sheathed and then sat back, taking him even deeper. She cupped her breasts, tweaking her nipples as she looked down at him. Her eyes glittered, unfocused. He had to grit his teeth to not immediately come inside her. He wanted her to come again.

Luke lifted her hips and bent his knees so he could ram deep inside her. He repeated the motion, each time going faster. He angled his thumbs inward and massaged her pubic bone. Astrid sucked in a deep breath and then moaned loudly. He felt her sheath tremble around him, and he pushed into her and then held still, his thumbs pressing down hard just above her core. She screamed, her orgasm milking him.

His balls clenched and he shouted her name as he came with her, blowing his load so hard he forgot to breathe. Stars flittered in front of his eyes, and he thought he might pass out.

Luke crashed back into his body and tried to remember how to force his lungs to take in air. He was dimly aware of Astrid slipping off him. She lay down beside him, curling into his chest. He wrapped an arm around her shoulders. "Any complaints?" she asked.

He turned toward her and found an impish grin stretched across her lips. Her eyes glittered with mirth.

"None," he said. "Except for maybe having to eat the pizza cold."

She laughed, a light sound that slipped inside his chest and warmed places that had no business being warmed. No matter how irresistible she was, Astrid was still a job. This would make the case difficult to handle objectively, but he would somehow manage. He owed it to Donovan to take down the genetic lab and the men behind it who had fucked up both his own and his brother's childhoods.

She didn't seem to notice the dark turn his thoughts had taken, because she laughed again. "Let's hope it's at least lukewarm." She got off the bed. "I hate it when the cheese loses it gooeyness." She went into the bathroom.

He'd just disposed of the condom when she came back out, a towel wrapped around her body. "Don't cover up on my account," he said, already missing the view of her curves and warm skin.

Astrid blushed a pretty pink. "I'm not shy, but even I draw the line at eating naked." She grabbed the pizza box and returned to bed.

"We'll have to explore food and nakedness some other time then," Luke joked as he got out of bed and headed to the bathroom. The silence behind him made him turn around. Astrid looked at him, a slice of pizza halfway to her mouth. Her eyes looked troubled. "What?" he asked.

"I like going to bed with you, but I'm not in a place where I can promise any kind of relationship." She took a bite of the pizza and chewed while watching him carefully, as if gauging his reaction.

Her words pissed him off more than they should.

Of course they couldn't have any kind of relationship, but did she have to state it so bluntly? What was wrong with just enjoying the sex but still planning for the next occasion they'd get together? He turned around and kept walking toward the bathroom, pretending to be indifferent when inside he seethed with anger. An anger he had no right to feel.

"We'll keep it casual," he threw over his shoulder. He closed the bathroom door behind him and leaned against the sink. Shit, there was nothing casual about what happened between him and Astrid in bed. *Explosive* was a better word for it.

He turned on the faucets, washed his hands, and rinsed his face. As he reached for the hand towel, a thought struck him and he stared his reflection in the mirror, water dripping down his face. *How the fuck had her gash healed already?* It had only been two days since the injury.

The only way she could undergo such rapid healing was if she'd been given some kind of accelerant, or if she'd been genetically altered. And the only place either of those things happened was in labs like the one where he and his brother had been raised.

# Chapter 9

THE ALMOST-FULL MOON ILLUMINATED THE FARM buildings but still allowed plenty of shadows in which to hide. Astrid glanced at Holden, who was crouched five meters to the side of her. Just like her face, his had been darkened with camouflage paint, another surprise Holden had dug out of his trunk. That's also where he'd found the communication sets currently hooked over their ears. Technically, his eyes glittering in the darkness could betray their position, but she noticed them only because she knew where to look. His body radiated tension, a supercharged mass of muscles ready to spring into action. How had she never noticed his warrior nature before? Out here it was so obvious.

Of course, she'd never seen him naked before. If she had, she'd have noticed that his muscular body had been shaped by fighting and weapons training, not by running on a treadmill or using resistance machines. The letters *USMC* tattooed above his heart were also a big clue. She hadn't noticed his United States Marine Corps brand during their hookup in his apartment months ago. That had been a desperate, hurried affair. Not like this afternoon, when they'd explored each other's bodies completely. The memory of how thoroughly he had explored every inch of her skin with his hands and mouth caused heat to flood through her entire body.

Holden had been quiet as they ate their pizza and

insisted on rest after. Satiated by sex, she didn't complain, but she was surprised when he'd lain down on the edge of the bed, as far away from her as possible. Maybe she'd somehow offended him with her comment about a relationship between them not being possible, but when the alarm on her phone woke them up, Holden's body had been curled around hers. He'd been terse as they prepared for their operation, but she didn't think anything of it. She didn't like chitchatting while preparing for a mission either.

Astrid focused her attention back on the buildings. They'd crossed the ridge before the moon rose and found a surveillance spot high enough up that it offered a clear view of the courtyard between the buildings while keeping them hidden in the shadows. They still didn't know how many wolverines were in the main house or the buildings surrounding it, but their plan was to get Scott out before any of the creatures were alerted to their presence. And if they did notice, Holden had a surprise for them in the form of the long-range Remington sniper rifle slung over his shoulder.

She'd worried about how to keep him out of the immediate action, but Holden's plan had taken care of that for her. He'd dug the rifle out of the treasure trove that was his trunk and said he'd find a spot close enough to cover her but far enough to keep an eye on every building. The rifle had a range of 1,500 meters. She was secretly pleased that he trusted her to take care of the close-range fighting, but also pissed that he thought he was in charge. It made sense that she would be the one to go in though. She knew what Scott looked like.

Holden set up the rifle and checked the scope. It

pointed straight at the door of the main house from which the wolverine with the food tray had appeared. He signaled for her to move out, and she took off in a wide-arced path that would eventually end at the back of the barn. She hugged the shadows created by the trees, her eyes focused on the large building while she kept her footsteps quiet.

When she reached the barn, Astrid clicked her mic twice to signal Holden that she'd arrived. Double doors high up on the wall probably led to a hayloft. The only other opening was a small door at ground level. There were no windows. She smeared Vaseline on the hinges of the door, just in case they hadn't been opened for a while. The door handle twisted easily in her hand, and she swung the door open with minimal squeaking. Slipping inside, she paused while she listened for movement and allowed her eyes to adjust to the darker interior.

Slivers of moonlight filtered in between the wooden slats of the wall, painting everything in stripes. Large shadows of abandoned farm equipment loomed around her. None of it looked like it had been used in the last fifty years. Dust and grit covered the outdated machinery. She moved deeper into the barn, checking the ground carefully so she wouldn't step on anything that could make a noise and give her away.

After ten meters, the building opened up into a large space with a high ceiling. A cloud moved in front of the moon, but she could still see the man sitting in a chair close to one of the roof's support poles. His hands were tied to the arms of the chair, his feet twisted and fastened to the chair's legs. A rag stuffed in his mouth and tied around his head served as a gag. His face was dirty and streaked with sweat, but she didn't see any bruises or blood. She'd seen a picture of him, but even without it she'd recognize Scott. His curly hair was the same midnight black as Naya's and the eyes staring straight at Astrid had the same dark-indigo hue as his sister's.

Astrid sidestepped to get a better view of the closed front door. The man watched her without blinking. She approached him with caution, keeping a hand on one of the throwing knives stored in her over-the-shoulder harness. Although she was certain it was the queen's brother sitting before her, he could be bait for an ambush.

Suddenly, he shook his head quickly and dipped his head toward a spot right in front of her feet.

Astrid looked down but couldn't immediately see what he was warning her about. The cloud obscuring the moon moved away, and pale light illuminated a glittering thin thread of fishing wire by her foot. She gingerly stepped over the almost-invisible trip wire and proceeded to Scott. He flinched when she unsheathed her knife, and his eyes widened as she brought it close to his head. In one quick draw, she severed the gag.

He spit it out on the floor, and she crouched in front of him, holding out an opened water bottle. He raised his eyebrows and nodded toward his bound wrists. Astrid shook her head. She wiggled the bottle in a silent question. The man nodded and she tipped the bottle to his lips. He drank several long draws before tilting his head back down. "Who are you?" he asked in a low voice.

"Your sister sent me." Astrid watched his eyes carefully, but all she saw in them was surprise.

"Neyney knew I was here?" He used the childhood nickname Naya had told Astrid about.

"No, she doesn't know you were taken," Astrid said, ignoring the stab of guilt she felt over not telling Naya about her brother's disappearance. "It was a hell of a thing to find you. Why did you leave the clinic?"

A shadow crossed his face. "I saw a monster outside the clinic grounds and thought I was going crazy. There is so much darkness in me. I couldn't bear to go to my sister with a broken mind. I've put her through so much already."

Astrid frowned. "What kind of monster?" She cut the restraints fettering him to the chair.

Scott rubbed his wrists. "I thought it was all in my imagination, but then when I got to the Denver train station, there were several more monsters. They drugged me with something, and I woke up here."

Two rapid clicks sounded in Astrid's earpiece. Holden was silently listening to their conversation through her mic and had just signaled for her to hurry things up. She'd have to ask Scott what he meant about the darkness inside him when they weren't under immediate threat. "They're real, all right," she said. One of the wolverines must have scouted the clinic but somehow not discovered Scott. "Do you know how many of your captors there are?" She ushered him toward the back door, careful to help him step over the fishing wire.

He stumbled along. His legs and arms were probably on pins and needles after being in one position so long. It would be a while before his blood circulation returned to normal. "I don't know exactly. Two different ones bring me food, and I've counted another four voices outside the barn."

Holden clicked once in Astrid's ear to show he'd heard

the number. They were almost at the back door of the barn when his voice crackled in the earpiece. "Incoming. Unfriendlies," he said. Four rapid pops from the Remington transmitted clearly as well, and then Holden cursed. "Lost track of two. I can't tell where they went."

Astrid opened the door and darted a quick look outside. "Clear here," she said for Holden's benefit. She grabbed Scott's arm and hurried outside. He stumbled behind her but didn't complain. They rounded the corner of the building and ran straight into one of the wolverines Holden had missed. The creature hissed.

Astrid shoved Scott behind her to shield him from the monster's view. Its nostrils flared, and it sniffed the air. "Valkyrie," it sneered. "Do you think you can save the queen's brother? Such a fool. Now we'll have two prisoners. Two bargaining chips."

"You'll have to catch me first," Astrid said. She widened her stance and unsheathed a second knife.

The creature's claws popped out.

"Fuck," Scott whispered behind Astrid. That was pretty much what she thought every time she had to put up with one of these nightmares. Not letting the talons distract her, she kept her focus on the creature's torso. A split second before he charged her, his body leaned left. She pushed Scott in that direction and parried to the other side, correctly judging that the creature was trying to fake her out.

She raised her right knife and arched it downward. The creature ducked out of the way at the last minute, but she made contact with his shoulder. A large gash appeared in his shirt and skin. Astrid grinned and the wolverine snarled back.

When another shot from the Remington echoed through the trees, the wolverine's head turned toward the sound. Astrid immediately charged and thrust her knife upward just below the rib. Her blade slid in easily, its steel long enough to pierce the heart.

The creature's eyes widened in surprise as its vital muscle stopped pumping blood. He sank to the ground, and Astrid's knife automatically slid out of him with a wet sound. She leaned down and wiped it on his shirt.

"Are you okay?" she asked Scott.

He pushed himself off the ground and stood. "Yeah," he said. "I see why you and Neyney are friends. Same bloodthirsty nature and mad fighting skills."

Astrid smiled. "I'll take that as a compliment."

He brushed off his pants. "I should know your name."

"Astrid," she said.

A rustle in the bushes behind him had her stepping between him and the potential threat.

Holden stepped out, holding the rifle with the barrel pointing upward. "You okay?" he asked Astrid, eyes roaming over her body as if searching for injuries.

"Just fine." She gestured toward Scott. "Meet Daisy's brother."

Scott shot her a look but didn't say anything about her using his sister's alter ego. He took a step forward and shook hands with Holden. "A pleasure," he said. "I'm an immediate fan of anyone coming to my rescue."

Holden returned the shake and nodded once before turning to Astrid again. "That's six dead. I searched the main house and had a quick peek in the other buildings. There's no one else here."

"Did you find anything else in the house?" Astrid asked.

"Some food, but no weapons." Luke looked around the buildings. "It's as if this was a temporary camp."

Scott nodded. "That's what I got from the way they talked. They were waiting for someone to arrive and tell them where to go next."

Who were the wolverines waiting for? Astrid shook her head. She'd worry about that later. Right now, she needed to get Scott back to his sister. "Phones?" she asked Holden.

"Two burner phones, but no outgoing calls on them. Incoming calls were all from blocked numbers."

"I'd still like to collect them, just in case I can get something from them," Astrid said.

Holden grinned and threw her a small plastic bag. "Figured you'd say that. I've disabled the GPS and removed the batteries. Nobody will be able to track them."

She caught the bag and turned to Scott. "We'll analyze all of this later. Right now, I need to let your sister know you're okay and that we'll be heading her way soon."

Scott frowned. "I'm not sure this is a good idea. I know she wants me there for the wedding, but—" He stopped when Astrid held up a hand to keep him from spilling more in front of Holden.

"No buts," she said, covering up the real reason she wanted him to stop talking. "Your sister sent me to retrieve you, and that's what I'm going to do. I'm taking you to see her. What happens after that is up to you and her." Scott shot her an obstinate look but didn't say anything.

Holden paid close attention to their exchange, his eyes gleaming with interest. That man was too observant and his mind way too sharp. Astrid worried about what he was thinking or, worse, what he might ask her. She had trouble outright lying to him, which was not a problem she'd ever had with mortal men before. "Let's head out," Holden said. "We have a way to drive before we get back to Denver, and we should probably wash some of this camo paint off before we return to the hotel." He looked at the wolverine body on the ground. "But we need to do some clean up before we head back."

"This is going to sound strange," Astrid said, "but the bodies will disintegrate as soon as sunlight hits them."

Holden's eyes widened. "If you say so. You're the expert on these freaks."

They dragged the bodies to the southwest side of the main house to maximize the sun exposure and then made their way back to the car. Astrid kept the pace slower to accommodate Scott. He stumbled a few times as they descended the ridge, but in general kept up fairly well. At least she wouldn't be bringing back her queen's brother injured. She still didn't want to think about how much shit she was in by not telling Naya and Leif about the abduction.

Holden dug a container of baby wipes out of his magic trunk and pulled out a few before handing the box over to Astrid. She used the wet squares to clear her face of the greasy paint they'd smeared on earlier.

Scott whistled softly when she'd finished. "Beautiful," he said.

Holden shoved his shoulder into Scott's as he moved around him to open one of the doors to the backseat. "Get in," he growled.

Scott's lips stretched in a lazy smile as he crawled

into the car. Holden closed the door and shot Astrid a sour look. She rolled her eyes at his machismo. Seriously, she was so happy she'd been born with two X chromosomes.

Once they were on the road, she steeled herself for the interrogation bound to come from Holden. He fired the first question as they turned onto the paved highway.

"Why did the wolverine call you 'Valkyrie'?" He kept his eyes on the road, but the deliberate stillness with which he held himself betrayed that this was anything but a casual question.

"I get that a lot." She pretended to study the scenery out the side window. "Must be the hair and my height. I've been called Amazon too."

"All compliments, I'm sure," Scott said from the backseat.

Holden shot him an irritated look through the rearview mirror. "And why would the creature call your sister a queen?"

"I have no idea, but she sure bosses me around like she thinks she's royal." Scott exaggerated a yawn and stretched his arms. "Think I'll nap for the rest of the way." He leaned back in the seat and shut his eyes.

Holden snorted. He turned to Astrid. "We'll see each other when we get back to Pine Rapids." His voice was low, and heat flared in his eyes before he looked back on the road again.

Her body immediately responded to that heat. "That's not a good idea." She couldn't control herself around Holden. Plus, the man saw too much. He'd likely figure out her secrets without her even noticing she'd given them away.

"I wasn't asking."

She sighed and welcomed the anger and indignation seeping into her body. It distracted her from the guilt she felt over lying to Holden. Why did men think they could start ordering her around once they'd slept with her? This was exactly why she kept her sex casual. Although, if she was being honest with herself—always an unpleasant sensation—there was nothing casual about sex with Holden. And he'd come through. Holden had saved her ass in a major way. She'd still have to apologize to her queen and king for losing Scott and not telling them about it, but at least she was returning with him. That should soften her punishment. "We'll see," she finally said, instead of the harsh words that had first entered her mind.

Holden glared at her. "You owe me one honest conversation."

She did. The problem was that she owed her battle brothers and sisters so much more, and being honest with Holden would jeopardize their safety. Besides, if he wanted a completely truthful conversation, it would have to go two ways. "Honest as in you explain how come your trunk seems to be an all-inclusive kidnapping rescue kit?"

He kept his eyes on the road. "Rex and I go paint-balling. We use the headsets and the camo paint."

Convenient, but she'd bet it wasn't anywhere close to the truth. Holden was holding himself unnaturally still again, which was obviously his tell for when something was important and he pretended it wasn't. "And you just happen to carry a Remington sniper rifle with you?"

"You're a little suspicious, aren't you?" He shot her

a grin. "I bought the rifle used and wanted a complete overhaul. One of the best gunsmiths I know lives here in Denver. That was one of the reasons for my trip."

She wasn't buying the grin or the casual tone, but there was no use badgering him. He had an answer for everything, another sign there was a lot more to his club-owner persona. Naya said the guests at the club weren't always on the right side of the law. If Holden was involved in some shady business deals, that might explain the contents of the trunk.

"And why do you need a rifle?" She smiled as if this was all a casual chat.

He shrugged, not taking his eyes off the road. "I was a sniper in the Marines. I like to keep up my skills." They continued the rest of the drive in silence. Apparently Mr. We-Need-An-Honest-Talk wasn't all that chatty when he was the one responsible for sticking to the truth. They pulled into the hotel parking garage, and Holden surprised her by handing over some car keys. "I had your car cleaned and the window repaired while we were away."

She twisted the keys in her hand, keeping her gaze lowered to hide how much the gesture touched her. He obviously hadn't found the hidden weapons compartment. "Thanks. We'll probably get on the road early tomorrow." Awkward silence stretched between them.

Scott yawned loudly in the backseat and stretched his arms. "Finally here." He opened the door and exited the car.

She got out and Holden followed. "Thanks for everything," she said, not knowing whether she should hug him or shake his hand. What was the etiquette for saying farewell to the man who gave a girl the best orgasm ever and then helped said girl rescue her queen's brother?

Holden nodded. "Anytime."

"You coming?" Scott shouted from halfway to the hotel door. "I don't know what room I'm going to."

Astrid looked at Holden again, not sure what to say. His face was closed off, and she couldn't read what he was thinking or feeling. She gave him a nod of her own and followed Scott.

---

Later that night, or more like very early the next morning, Luke sat on his bed staring at the tablet he'd found under a loose kitchen floor tile at the farm. It had been a fluke that he'd stepped on it and felt it wiggle under his foot. At first, he thought he'd stepped on an explosives detonating device, and his heart had leaped into his throat. He'd stood there like an idiot for a few seconds before realizing that the tile was not in the direct path of an intruder, so why would they rig it? When he bent down to examine the floor, he'd found the tablet.

It was password protected, and he'd been running an encryption breaker application on it for the last hour. Blurry-eyed, he stared at the numbers blinking on the screen and ignored the stab of guilt he felt whenever he remembered that he'd outright lied to Astrid about not finding anything in the house. At least he'd given her the phones—after he copied their drives himself. Using FBI technology, he'd only needed a few seconds to upload their content to a secure server. There wasn't really a reason to feel guilty about his actions; she hadn't been all that forthcoming with the truth either. The answers she'd given him in the car had all been bullshit. Their conversation about the things he'd overheard through the communication device tonight was far from over.

She might think they wouldn't have any kind of relationship other than casual hookups, but she was wrong. There would be a lot of talking involved as well. Hopefully he'd be able to cover his tracks better than he'd done in the car. She'd surprised him with her questions about the gear and the rifle. He should have known she'd notice that the average nightclub owner did not travel with a full rescue-mission kit.

At least he hoped she wanted to hook up again. He'd had ugly thoughts about Scott replacing him in her bed ever since he'd watched them walk off together.

The screen brightened, and the encryption app beeped. Luke held his breath as the input boxes stopped scrolling, one by one displaying a five-digit code. He touched the Okay button, and the home screen displayed. There was only one icon, and when he touched it, a map of Pine Rapids popped up. Question marks circled in red marked three different locations. None of them were of anything he recognized. One was in the middle of the farmlands southeast of town, close to the Idaho border. Another was in the warehouse district near the railroad tracks, and the third was right in the middle of the forest north of town.

What the fuck did this mean? And how was it connected to Astrid?

# Chapter 10

THE NORSE WARRIORS' ARMORY HAD ALWAYS BEEN A place where Astrid could find peace and tranquility, but this time the repetitive motions of cleaning and polishing did nothing to soothe her agitation. She'd been restless ever since they left Denver two days ago. Her berserker paced endlessly, and her body ached as if she was running a low fever. Which was unusual, since the immortal Vikings and Valkyries didn't succumb to regular human diseases. She wiped her forehead with the back of her hand and slid the whetstone along the edge of her smallsword once more. A perfectly sharpened sword needed to be sharp enough to pierce flesh, but if she overdid it, the too-thin edge would dull quickly during a fight.

The door opened, and Ulf walked in. "So this is where you're hiding." His blond crew cut's lines were as sharp as ever, and his blue eyes glittered with mischief. Although it was only April, his face was already tanned.

"I'm not hiding." She was just avoiding certain individuals. Smart-ass Ulf included.

"The king wants to speak with you."

And the king was definitely another person on her to-avoid list. "What does he want?" Astrid asked.

Ulf raised one eyebrow. "You really have to ask?"

She sighed. No, she didn't have to ask. The king

wanted to discuss disciplinary actions for going rogue while retrieving Scott from Denver. Actually, *discuss* was not the right word. *Declare* fit better. "What time?"

"He said to give him about an hour to finish up some emails, but then you better have your ass in one of the chairs in front of his desk."

Astrid wiped off the blade of her smallsword with a soft cloth. "How angry is he?" She regretted the words as soon as they left her mouth and couldn't look at Ulf. She didn't want to see the gloating in his eyes.

Instead of the flippant comment she expected, Ulf put his hand on her shoulder and squeezed. "Hey," he said. "Are you okay?"

Startled, she looked up. "I'm fine." She could tell from his eye roll that he didn't believe her any more than she did herself. Ulf and she were not friends though, more like competitors. They never had heart-to-hearts where they shared their feelings. More like fist-to-fists with shared blows.

He pulled his hand back. "You can talk to me, you know." His eyes were solemn. "I know we're not close, but you're one of my battle sisters. I worry about you."

"Okay," she hedged. This was weird. Did he mean he worried that she wouldn't be able to hold her own in a fight? Or, was he actually concerned about her mental and physical health? "But there is no reason to worry. I'll be fine." Provided the king's punishment wasn't too severe. They'd never had a warrior breach protocol as badly as she had. She had no idea what to expect. She debated asking Ulf what he thought the king might do, but changed the topic instead. "Are Naya and Scott still catching up?" When Astrid and Scott arrived a few hours ago, the queen had immediately pulled her brother away for a private talk.

Ulf rolled his eyes again. "They are. And there's some crying too, mostly from Naya. They're in the game room. I had to leave the computer room because I could hear the queen sobbing through the door." The computer room door was at the back of the large game room, which was filled with big-screen TVs and every game console imaginable. Astrid wasn't much into gaming, but the male warriors spent hours killing pixelated soldiers and mythical creatures. She thought fighting creatures in the real world was thrilling enough.

"Is the queen going to be at my meeting with the king?" Eventually she'd have to sit down with her friend and apologize for her behavior. But she wasn't ready to explain why she hadn't called the fortress for help when she couldn't find Scott. Wasn't ready to explain that it was easier to trust Holden than to admit defeat to her fellow warriors. Wasn't ready to talk about Holden at all.

"I have no idea," Ulf answered. "You look like you could work off some energy though. Care to spar while you wait to see the king?"

His abrupt change of topic confused her at first, but exercise would help her with the restlessness she didn't seem to be able to shake. "Swords?" she asked. Ulf wasn't likely to go for her suggestion. Her former fencing master and lover, Henri, had been one of the very best. He had shown her how the smallsword was a weapon perfectly suited to her natural fighting skills. The sword was a cousin to the more famous rapier, but shorter and lighter. Henri had taught Astrid to use it during its most popular time in history, and she'd had two hundred years since then to practice her skills.

Ulf cocked his head, a slow smile stretching his lips. "Sure, but only if we pick broadswords this time." Last time they'd fenced with smallswords, Astrid had beaten him soundly, and he'd lost a bet in the process. Apparently he'd learned his lesson.

The heavier two-edged broadsword was not one of Astrid's favorites. She'd rather fight with fists or knives, but Ulf's challenging tone of voice made it impossible to back down. "No problem," she said and put the sharpened and polished smallsword away. Each of the warriors had their own weapons cabinet, and Astrid had three Viking broadswords in her arsenal. Even if she preferred not to use them in a real fight, she used them in training. The heavy blade built up arm and wrist muscles in no time. She retrieved her favorite broadsword from its stand.

The sword had a hilt large enough for a two-handed grip, and she swung it through the air to test its weight.

Ulf's eyes widened. "Are you serious? You want to fight with real swords?"

Astrid hid a smile and shrugged. "If you're not man enough, we can use training swords. Do you want wooden bokkens or synthetic ones?"

"Synthetic," Ulf threw over his shoulder as he strode to the communal cabinet that held a wide variety of practice weapons. He pulled out a black sword made out of heavy polypropylene. About two-thirds of the weight of a regular sword, the weapon still simulated a good approximation of the heft of a regular sword because its center of mass was close to the handle. Although it didn't cause as much damage on contact, it still hurt. Astrid had received more than a few bruises during sparring, but at least the weapon wouldn't maim or kill.

She took the sword Ulf handed her but shook her head when he held up a padded vest. The garment would protect her but also slow her down and make quick maneuvers harder. She did pull on some gloves though. Wielded with enough speed, the practice swords could crush knuckles and fingers.

The armory connected to a large barn used as the training arena and gym. Half of the area was covered in floor mats and designed for combat sparring. The other half contained punching bags, a boxing ring, and treadmills for use when the track outside was covered in snow.

Astrid followed Ulf to the floor mats and took her position across from him. They bowed to show their respect for each other and their weapons. Astrid then held back to see what Ulf would do next. Ulf had died back in the mid-1000s and trained with the rest of Odin's warriors in Valhalla until he'd been returned to the human realm only eighty years past.

Although he'd picked up additional weapon skills and hand-to-hand combat techniques since entering the mortal realm, his swordsmanship was the same as when he'd been a marauding Viking. Basically, he had very little technique and relied mostly on brute strength. The problem with training in Valhalla was that time passed differently there. Centuries could feel like only a few weeks, and each of the Vikings and Valkyries who trained together had died in the same century, so they reinforced only the fighting skills they already knew.

Even before she died and became one of Freya's Valkyries, Astrid had relied on speed and agility to win against more massive opponents. And since her opponents were mostly male, she always had to be faster and more agile. She swung the sword in a circle, switching her grip from hand to hand. Even if the heavy blade wasn't her first choice of weapon, it still felt familiar in her hands. She was confident she could match Ulf's skills and even beat him.

Henri's training had enhanced her natural skills, no matter which blade she fought with. Thinking about Henri always made her angry, and she swung the sword with more power. She'd felt deeply for the French fencing master, and when he chose war and glory over their relationship, the betrayal had cut deep. Henri had been a soldier through and through. Maybe that was why she'd recognized the warrior nature in Holden so quickly during their rescue mission. He had the same intense focus as Henri. Would Luke also choose duty over her?

Wait, where did that thought come from? She and Luke didn't have a relationship. There would be no choices.

She forced thoughts of both Henri and Luke out of her mind. She needed to concentrate on only one male at the moment, and he was standing right in front of her.

Ulf held his sword loosely in his left hand, which was his dominant and another reason it was tricky to fight him. It was like fighting a mirror image of what she expected from an opponent.

Astrid held the hilt of her weapon in both hands by her right hip, the blade raised at a thirty degree angle. She'd placed her left hand below the right so that her dominant right could control the power of the sword while the left could twist and steer.

"You're different since you returned from Denver," Ulf said.

She kept her gaze on his eyes, watching for the tiny flicker that would broadcast an attack. "How so?"

"Your berserker has been intense, close to the surface, for several months." He cocked his head and sidestepped to his left. "I can still feel her, but she's not as erratic."

Astrid moved with him and briefly checked the mental connection she had with her berserker. "My inner warrior is focused on its opponent and the upcoming fight. That always calms it."

Ulf shook his head. "No, it's more than being battle ready. I can't quite describe it, but it's as if she is more present."

"You're just trying to distract me. And stop calling it 'she.'"

He slowly twirled his sword by rotating his wrist. "What gender do you think your berserker is?"

"I don't care." She hadn't actually thought about it that much. Her inner warrior had always been an "it" to her. She knew it was technically part of her person, but it felt more like a burden. Like she had a beast inside that wanted to get out. Her own Dr. Jekyll and Mr. Hyde. She mentally shook herself. Now was not the time to philosophize about the weird dual nature of her personality. She needed to concentrate on her opponent instead.

"The only other time I've experienced the same intense presence of a berserker was when our king first met his *själsfrände*." Ulf kept twirling his sword in slow circles, a lazy smile on his lips. "His inner warrior recognized his destined soul mate before he himself did. Is there something you're not telling me, sweet Astrid?"

His words made her skin feel cold and clammy all over. Her berserker couldn't possibly have honed in on Astrid's soul mate. It supposedly happened the first time the people destined to be together made physical contact. And she hadn't met anyone she didn't know from before. Unless Scott… No, Ulf was just trying to distract her. Besides, the berserker had first talked to her before she met Scott. She had been with Holden—she cut off that train of thought quickly and shook off her unease. "Stop yapping and concentrate on the fight."

He quirked an eyebrow. "Sounds like you don't want to face the truth, but if you say so." Ulf leaned forward, holding his sword in front of his torso with a slightly bent elbow.

Astrid watched his eyes carefully and caught the exact moment their focus became more intense. Ulf lunged, thrusting his sword at her torso. She easily parried right, blocking his blade, and then counterattacked with a downward thrust.

He sidestepped but wasn't quick enough, and the point of her blade hit his right hip. "Fuck," he hissed as he took a step back.

Astrid smiled as they circled each other again. Ulf would have a nice bruise where she'd made contact by tomorrow morning. She planned on giving him a few more.

He lunged again with a center thrust, but then feinted at the last minute and turned it into a cross. She swept her sword up to parry center and protect her stomach, but his strike had too much force. Although she slowed it down, the flat side of his heavy rubber blade hit her, and a thud of pain reverberated through her body. She hissed in a breath but kept her brain from acknowledging the hurt. She'd been hurt much worse in combat, and the adrenaline rushing through her body made it easier to ignore the pain.

Ulf attacked again, this time with a thrust toward her heart. She parried again but moved her sword outward, forcing his blade to slide down the length of hers instead of making contact with her body.

His momentum carried him forward while she sidestepped, quickly turned, and immediately counterattacked. Ulf had managed almost to twist around so he was facing her again, but he was slightly off balance. She used that to her advantage and executed a cross to his neck.

He threw his body back, and although she made contact, her sword hit his collarbone instead. Ulf stumbled and she attacked again. This time, she used a basic lunge to his center of gravity, and when he parried center, she twisted her hands so she could trap his blade. The two hilts tangled, and with a flick of her wrist, his sword flew off to the side.

Ulf swore under his breath but quickly stepped backward and widened his stance. Balanced on the balls of his feet, his arms hanging loosely by his sides, he was ready to fight her with only his fists as weapons.

"Want me to lose my sword?" she asked.

He smiled slightly, intently watching her eyes. "Wouldn't want you to give up your only advantage. After all, you're just a woman."

As always, he knew exactly how to push her buttons. Anger quickly welled up inside her, and her first instinct was to immediately throw her blade to the side.

*Punish*, whispered her berserker, startling Astrid so badly she stumbled back.

Ulf's nostrils flared, a sign his berserker was awake and alert. "She's surfaced. Just like I knew she would." Triumph laced his voice.

Astrid shook herself and raised her sword in front of her, grip steady and feet far enough apart to give her balance but close enough for fast footwork. "My inner warrior is awake and alert, alright." And the beast was absolutely right. Ulf needed to be punished. He'd manipulated her enough for one fight. Any other time, his verbal challenge would have made her ditch the sword, but not this time. This time, he'd get to know her training sword really well. Especially what it felt like to be hit with it repeatedly.

She feinted left and then sideswiped from the right instead. Hitting his waist with the sharp edge of her sword, she made sure she put extra strength into the cut as she pulled the blade toward her. It would burn his skin even if it didn't draw blood.

Ulf groaned and gripped his side. She quickly struck at his knuckles with the edge of her sword. Although he yelped, the gloves protected his hand and he was quickly back in his fighting stance.

Astrid grinned. "You're such a gentleman. Thank you for allowing a weak girlie like me to keep her weapon. I do enjoy using it. Hopefully I won't break a nail as I kick your ass."

"Shut up," he forced out through clenched jaws.

She cocked her head. "You ready for another beating, courtesy of me and my berserker?"

Ulf straightened. "Bring it."

She raised her sword and lunged as if she'd execute a downward swing. When he raised his fists to block, she adjusted her balance to her back foot, brought back her sword, and instead hook kicked his chin. Ulf fell and landed on his back. Before he could jump back up, she pressed the tip of her blade into his Adam's apple. "Are we done yet?" she asked.

His blue eyes blazed with so much anger it startled her. "Not yet," he said, gripping her blade with gloved hands. He pushed it sideways away from her, and before she could let go of the hilt, the motion had her off balance. Ulf swiped out with his leg and toppled her.

She landed on her back, the air knocked out of her lungs. As she struggled for breath, Ulf quickly twisted his body so he straddled her hips. He placed his hands on her biceps, pushing them back into the mat and trapping her with his body weight.

*Wrong*, the berserker yelled, and Astrid had to close her eyes to shut out the noise in her head. She forced her body to relax.

"I do like sparring with you, Astrid," Ulf said.

She opened her eyes to find him grinning down at her. She so wanted to wipe that grin off his face. She widened her eyes. "Are we done, then?"

He frowned as if he didn't understand the question, and in his confusion, he eased his grip on her arms.

Astrid bucked her hips, and as he slid forward, she raised her knees and dug her heels into the mat. Using her new leverage, she quickly twisted her body and pressed with her shoulder to throw Ulf off her.

He landed on his side and twisted to raise himself on all fours.

Already on her feet, Astrid kicked him in the stomach as if she were hitting a soccer penalty kick.

Ulf went down again with a loud groan. She pushed on his shoulder with her foot until he was lying on his back, panting with pain. Putting her foot back on the mat, she crouched down beside him and pocked his chest with one gloved finger. "I like sparring with you too, but we're definitely done now."

He glared at her, shaking his head.

She laughed at his obstinacy, but the sound turned into a curse as Ulf grabbed the back of her neck. She tried to twist free, but he'd startled her and his grip was strong.

Before she could escape, he pulled her face down and pressed his lips to hers. She opened her mouth to protest, and he deepened the kiss. His tongue delved deep inside her mouth, and she pushed against his shoulders, sputtering in outrage.

He quickly released her, a self-satisfied grin on his face. "Now, we're done."

She almost couldn't hear the words because of the berserker screaming in her head.

*No! Wrong!* It repeated over and over again. It clawed at the mental barriers Astrid had quickly raised to keep it from completely taking over her body. She had to exude great willpower to control the inner warrior and calm it enough that she could think clearly again.

Once the berserker stopped screaming, Astrid did what any self-respecting Valkyrie would do. She punched Ulf in the nose and exited the training facility.

# Chapter 11

ASTRID TOOK A DEEP BREATH BEFORE KNOCKING ON the king's office door. She'd taken a quick shower and changed her clothes after her fight with Ulf, but nerves had sweat beading on her skin again.

"Come," rumbled from inside the office. She grabbed the door handle, squared her shoulders, and entered. This meeting would be hard. She knew she deserved to get punished. But the unknown had her heart beating faster and made her hands clammy.

Leif sat behind his desk, leaning back in the chair with one boot resting on top of the other knee. His six-foot-four body appeared relaxed, but the intense gaze in his ice-blue eyes and his serious face showed he was anything but.

If this was any other meeting, Astrid would have lowered her head in a short bow before taking one of the chairs in front of the desk. But she was in deep shit here. She'd disrespected her king, her queen, and her fellow warriors. There was much atonement to be done. Much guilt to deal with.

She walked around the desk and kneeled in front of her king, touching her forehead to the knuckles of his hand resting on the armrest closest to her. "*Min kung*, I am sorry," she said.

The hand under her forehead jerked as if startled, and she felt Leif's other hand briefly touching the back of her head. "Stand," he said. "Go sit."

She rose but kept her head bowed as she made her way to one of the visitor chairs and sat down. Despair welled in her chest as she anticipated her punishment. Would Leif exile her from the fortress? She'd been a lone soldier in the human realm for a hundred years. Freya and Odin had used her as a scout to look for places where Loki's creatures popped up. When they did, the god and goddess would send a band of warriors to deal with them. Sometimes Astrid would join the warriors, but most often she'd move on to continue her lone mission. And then Freya had sent her to join these Vikings in the early nineteen hundreds.

She hadn't realized how much she needed the fellowship of the others until this very moment, when she might lose not only their camaraderie but, worse, their respect. She swallowed the lump in her throat and raised her head. There were other Viking kings with permanent tribes in the human world, two others in North America. Maybe she could join one of them. It wouldn't be the same though. This tribe had become her family.

She'd expected Leif to look at her with anger or disappointment, maybe even both. Instead, he studied her as if she was a problem he couldn't figure out. He stroked the stubble on his chin. "Let's talk about what happened in Denver."

His simple request stalled Astrid's brain for a moment. So much had happened in Denver. She didn't know where to begin. She stared wide-eyed at the king.

Leif dropped his leg on the floor with a thud and rested his elbows on the desk. "Just start from the beginning. You got to the clinic…and then what?"

She cleared her throat. "Scott had checked himself out,

and because of patient confidentially, Dr. Rosen wouldn't tell me how Scott left the clinic or where he went."

Leif frowned. "Why in the Allfather's name would Scott not wait for you? He knew someone was coming to get him."

"He said he saw a wolverine scouting the clinic and thought he was hallucinating. He wanted to spare Naya the pain of watching her brother go crazy."

"That would have been painful for her, but not knowing why her brother disappeared would have been even more painful." He scratched his chin again. "Do I need to worry about Scott's mental state?"

Astrid shrugged. "He seemed fine during our drive back here. He slept a lot, but when we talked, I didn't notice anything amiss."

"Good." Leif nodded. "Now tell me why you didn't report Scott's disappearance as soon as you found out."

Astrid folded her hands in her lap and studied the interlaced fingers. "My pride wouldn't let me. The queen gave me a chance to redeem myself by bringing her brother back. I couldn't bear hearing the disappointment in her voice when I told her I screwed up. And I couldn't face my fellow warriors after messing up another mission. They'd never trust me in battle again."

"Astrid," the king barked, and she looked up startled. "How did you use your normally smart—yet stubborn—mind to come to the conclusion that Scott checking himself out was your fault?"

She opened her mouth to answer, but no sound came out, so she closed it again. What Leif asked sounded so reasonable now, but back in Denver, it had made perfect sense to go looking for Scott on her own. She'd been so confused, so tired. And her berserker had been so out of control. "I decided to see if I could find him before I reported in." She leaned forward slightly. "And I did find him."

The king waved his hand as if to dismiss her claim. "You found him two days later and decided on some harebrained rescue scheme." His gaze pierced into her eyes. "Without backup."

"I did have backup," Astrid mumbled, lowering her gaze back to her lap.

"Who?"

"Luke Holden."

"Fucking Holden again." The king cursed some more under his breath. "Tell me everything that happened," he demanded, "starting from when you left the clinic, and include all the details about how Holden got involved."

Astrid recited how she'd ended up at the train station and described her fight with the wolverines.

"Hold up," the king interrupted. "What do you mean, they have accelerated healing and fight like acrobats?"

Astrid thought for a minute. The wolverines the warriors had encountered on their patrols were worthy adversaries but possible to defeat. In the parking garage in Denver, she'd been genuinely scared. The reason she was still alive was because the wolverines had wanted her that way. "It's like they've been enhanced somehow."

The king cursed again. "Irja is so close to developing an antidote to their poison, but now they've become fucking circus artists." Leif and Naya had both been poisoned by the wolverines using a chemically altered version of wolfsbane. Although it took a few days, their bodies had purged the poison. "How exactly are they different?" Leif asked.

Astrid had to think again. The fight in the train-station parking garage had become a blur after she was stabbed in the thigh. And she did not plan on telling Leif how close she'd been to not making it back at all. Thanks to Holden—

*Mine*, the berserker suddenly whispered in her head.

Astrid took in a deep breath and gripped the arm-rests of her chair to center herself. Damn her horny internal beast.

She thought she'd calmed the bitch down after she'd gone haywire when Ulf kissed them.

And now she was using female pronouns thanks to Ulf. Damn him too.

Astrid closed her eyes and forced a mental block between herself and the berserker. She had to get it together. She couldn't freak out in front of the king.

"Astrid," Leif said, concern deepening his tone.

"I'm fine," she said and opened her eyes.

"I don't think you are." The king's nostrils flared. "The presence of your berserker is so strong it's almost like having another person in the room with us."

Astrid's eyes widened. "What does that mean?"

"I don't know." Leif shook his head. "Your inner warrior has always been close to the surface and quick to enter battle fever. But I can't tell if it's because you've been in the human realm longer than most of us, or just part of your personality." He smiled. "You're quick to jump into confrontations, whether your berserker has surfaced or not."

Astrid swallowed the retort on the tip of her tongue.

She knew she had a quick temper, but it wasn't a product of her berserker or how long she'd wandered with humans. She'd been born with a short fuse and a quick tongue. She'd basically been in constant trouble from the time she learned to talk. An uppity thrall, especially a female thrall, was not tolerated by most owners. "But now it's different?" Cold trickled down her spine. Should she tell the king her inner warrior sometimes spoke to her? What had changed her berserker's behavior? Had the wolverines slipped her something without her noticing? Had Holden?

"Yes. Naya's berserker's presence is as strong, but this feels different."

"How?"

"Well, for one, you're not my *själsfrände*." The king smiled again, but then his face became drawn, tired. "Let's get back to the wolverines. If they're back and stronger than before, we need to know what we're up against."

Astrid nodded, but his words about his *själsfrände*, his soul mate, stayed with her. She couldn't help envying the connection that the king and queen shared. "Sure," she said and took a quick peek at Leif's left hand. Although he was wearing a long-sleeved shirt, the tip of his snake tattoo could be seen under the cuff. Naya had a completed serpent tattoo as well, although hers were more of an intricate Celtic knot-like design than traced out runes, like the king's and like the snake heads of his warriors. Naya had received her tattoo when Freya claimed her as a Valkyrie.

At least she didn't have to worry about having to complete a soul-mate bond. If she and Holden were destined to be together, the serpent tail would have showed up the first time they hooked up.

Freya, Mother of Valkyries. Why was she obsessed about Holden now? Astrid shook herself and concentrated on the conversation. "I was injured and couldn't concentrate as well as I would have liked, but the wolverines' quick reflexes were mainly what threw me. These creatures reacted and anticipated my moves much quicker than the ones we fought ten months ago. They moved out of the way too quickly for me to do any real damage."

She and Holden would never be anything more than casual. She didn't do long-term with regular humans. Henri had cured her of that. The berserker stirred again, but Astrid clamped down on her mental shields and forced it back to sleep. Sweat beaded on her forehead from the effort.

Leif gave her a curious look but didn't say anything about her odd behavior. "Go on with the report. What happened after the fight?"

Astrid continued her story, describing how Holden had found her and patched her up before offering to help find Scott. She glossed over the night in the gingerbread house, but she had to look away during that part or she'd have blushed redder than the apple clenched between the jaws of a roasted Yule pig.

The king grunted a few times but kept mostly quiet until she'd finished. "Where are the phones you found?" he asked.

"Ulf is investigating them." She had to look away again. This time because of anger bubbling up inside her. Why had Ulf kissed her? To show that as a woman, she would always be a sexual object first and a warrior second? She'd punch him harder when she saw him next.

The door flew open, and Naya strode into the room. She gave the king a quick kiss and then perched on the arm of his chair so she too faced Astrid.

The king's face lit up, and he grabbed Naya's hand. The tiredness disappeared from his face, and his eyes filled with love as his gaze caressed her face. That click and hum Astrid always felt when the royal couple was together reverberated through her chest. It was as if the two completed a network and automatically pulled every warrior in their vicinity into that web through their berserkers.

Naya smiled briefly at Leif, the same powerful love mirrored in her own eyes. Then she turned to Astrid, and her gaze hardened. "Scott tells me Luke Holden helped rescue him," she said in a brisk, businesslike tone.

"Yes." Astrid nodded. A stab of irritation shot through her. Why was the queen so interested in Holden? Had there been something between the two of them, even though Holden denied it? "He used his resources to track down Scott and offered to be my backup during the rescue." Her tone came out snippy, and Naya leaned back. Her eyebrows rose toward her hairline.

"Wow. Touchy much?" A small smile played at the corners of Naya's mouth.

Freya's meadow. She'd just insulted her queen. "I'm so sorry, *min drottning*." Astrid bowed her head. "I meant no disrespect." Shit. She was here to grovel, not to make the situation worse.

"None taken." Naya waved her hand in the air. "But why was Holden in Denver?"

"He had some business deal going on."

Leif snorted. "Likely story. I never trusted that guy."

"That's because you're both alpha males." Naya dismissed the king's words with another hand wave. "You don't trust anyone with as much testosterone overload as you. Your brain short-circuits and all you can think of is challenging the other man." Astrid had to look down again, this time to hide a grin. She glanced up through her lowered lashes. The king frowned at his queen, but all Naya did was blow her fiancé a kiss. "Look, Holden helped save my brother. We owe him."

Leif grumbled some more. "What do you want me to do? Send him flowers?"

"I want to invite him to the wedding." Naya dropped her verbal bomb while staring intently at Leif.

"Not possible," the king barked. "Put that idea out of your head right now."

Naya turned to Astrid as if she hadn't heard her fiancé's command. "And I want Astrid to invite him for me."

"Not going to happen," Astrid and Leif said in unison.

Naya just smiled serenely. "He helped save my brother. I want him at the wedding. Plus, Scott wants Holden there. It will make him feel better if there's another familiar face."

Astrid shook her head. "This is not a good idea." She was one of the bridesmaids and on display throughout the ceremony and reception. It would be impossible to avoid Holden.

"Listen to her, *älskling*," Leif said. "Having humans at the wedding is not a good idea."

Naya whirled around to look at her fiancé. "I'm human."

"You know what I mean." Leif reach out a hand, but she ignored it. "Regular humans, not enhanced."

"Like my brother?" The queen's words were laced with ice.

Astrid frantically searched her mind for an excuse to leave the room. This was definitely leading up to a fight, and as much as the royal couple loved each other, that passion also spilled into their disagreements. It was not a good idea to be in the fallout zone during one of their nuclear meltdowns.

Leif pulled Naya into his lap, putting his arm around her. "You love your brother. I love you, and so I love your brother."

The queen's shoulders relaxed, and she curled into her fiancé's embrace. "Okay, but I still want Holden at the wedding." Astrid took a breath to protest again, but the queen pinned her down with her gaze. "And you owe me for not telling me that Scott was lost." She stood. "For two days, you were sending me texts as if everything was okay. When you didn't even know where he was. You lied to me." Naya's voice rose and broke a little on those last words.

Astrid felt lower than the slimiest slug. She looked down at her lap. "I'm so sorry, my queen. Pride and stubbornness got in the way. I wasn't thinking clearly." She raised her head and felt moisture in her eyes. "I didn't outright lie, but I lied by omission, and for that I apologize most deeply."

"Don't you trust me?" Naya's brow furrowed. "Is our friendship so unworthy you can't ask for help when you need it?"

Oh shit. Those words caused a stab of guilt to pierce

Astrid's heart. "Our friendship means everything. I was weak from blood loss and confused. All I could think was that I would disappoint you and the king again."

The king had kept very quiet, but now he cleared his voice. "I should gather the others so we can discuss a new strategy for these enhanced wolverines. If they are in Denver, it won't be long before they show up here in Pine Rapids. Especially if they're tracking Scott." He stood and briefly kissed Naya on her forehead before walking toward the door.

"Holden's coming to the wedding," the queen shouted after him.

"Never," the king shot back before the door closed behind him.

Naya turned back to Astrid. "You will invite him for me, since Leif won't let me leave the fortress." It wasn't a question.

"Why can't you leave the fortress?"

"Leif thinks I might be in danger. There is a lot of chatter on the Darknet. These new wolverines are super-intelligent. They are organized and communicating in ways we haven't seen before. Their efforts to get to me and Scott have ramped up." The wolverines were created on order from Loki by the covert organization behind the lab the siblings grew up in. As an extra bonus of having the creatures, the lab handlers used them to hunt Naya and Scott. They wanted to use the siblings in a breeding program of super soldiers.

The Darknet information was disturbing, but that wasn't what Astrid had meant to ask. She shook her head. "No, I mean why do you want me to deliver the invitation?"

Naya frowned. "Because you know him already," she said as if that was an obvious reason.

"Don't you think he will find it odd that Daisy is marrying under the name Naya in a pagan Norse ritual?"

The queen paused for a moment, but then dismissed the words with a wave. "Nah, he'll understand why I used an assumed name. I bet a lot of his customers and business associates do the same." Astrid wanted to ask Naya more questions, but she didn't want to give away her interest. Especially when she didn't know herself why she was so hung up on Holden. "Besides," Naya continued, "when someone rescues your brother, you thank them in person and you invite them to your wedding. And since I can't go, you'll have to be my proxy."

Freya's crazy wagon-pulling cats. This was such a bad idea, but Astrid couldn't think of the words necessary to stop it from happening. "Leif is not going to like this," she tried, already knowing the protest was futile.

"He doesn't like a lot of things I do, but that doesn't mean he won't see reason eventually." The queen opened the door, but then turned toward Astrid. "Thank you, Astrid, for saving my brother and for bringing him back to me." She tipped her head in a quick bow. "I owe you for this." She raised her head and paused for a moment, her eyes dark. "Make this happen. Scott wants Holden at the wedding, which means Holden *will* be at my ceremony. I've made an appointment for you to see him at lunchtime tomorrow." She strode out into the hallway before Astrid had a chance to say anything else.

Her punishment was to invite Holden to the wedding—in person. That was so not what she had expected. It didn't seem as dire as some of the outcomes she had imagined, and yet cold sweat broke out all over her body at the thought of being near Holden again.

*Mine*, whispered the berserker.

*Shut up*. Astrid willed the command down her mental connection with the beast, but she could have sworn her inner warrior laughed in response.

Why did this man have such pull over both her and her berserker? Even if she ignored her vow not to fall for another mortal, her battle brothers would despise her dating a human. And the king had already shown how much he disliked Holden.

She had to be strong. She would meet with Holden and invite him to the wedding without as much as touching or kissing him. Surviving a whole wedding without giving away how her body reacted to his would be a challenge, but somehow she would make it through.

A snicker echoed inside Astrid's mind. "Shut up," she said out loud, but her berserker wasn't listening.

# Chapter 12

LUKE LOOKED UP FROM HIS LAPTOP WHEN REX entered the office. He'd been going over accounts and was more than happy to be interrupted. The feds took their undercover operations seriously, and he was expected to not only balance his budgets, but to make it look as if he was running at least a semi-legit business.

The tall African American head of security smiled broadly as he approached the desk. "Your favorite well-armed blond is here to see you."

"Astrid?" She was Luke's favorite blond, period, but the last time Rex had met her, she'd carried a small arsenal of knives inside her jacket and a large sword strapped to her back. Luke had been talking to Naya about updating his security system when Astrid crashed their meeting. For months after, Rex had talked about how long it took to disarm Astrid before she could enter the club.

"WWA, the one and only," Rex said. He'd given her the nickname Walking Weapon Arsenal. "You okay seeing her?"

Something suspiciously close to happy anticipation bubbled up inside Luke. He rubbed his chest. "How does she seem?" Naya had left a phone message that someone would meet with him, but she hadn't said who or about what.

The question seemed to puzzle Rex. He frowned

and cocked his head to the side. "What do you mean? She appears healthy and strong. Runs her mouth as fast as ever."

"Does she seem pissed off?" He'd made Astrid give him her cell phone number before they parted ways in Denver. Every day since, he'd had to force himself not to call. He couldn't think of a reason why she'd be here. She'd made it clear she didn't think it was a good idea for them to see each other again. Had Naya and Astrid found out he took the tablet? But how? It took sixteen hours of straight driving time to get to Pine Rapids from Denver. Astrid had been back in town only a day, two tops.

"Oh, so it's like that." Understanding glinted in Rex's eyes. "You hooked up with the girl and left her hanging."

"That's not what happened." That was exactly what had happened the first time they'd met, but then they'd had Denver and a hot night in a gingerbread hotel. And *she'd* left *him* hanging. Luke cleared his throat. "Did she say why she's here?"

"Nope." Rex grinned. "Just that she needed to see you in person."

Luke rubbed suddenly damp palms on his pants. "Okay, show her in." This was ridiculous. There was no reason the woman should make him feel nervous.

Rex threw him a strange look and went to open the door. He paused with his hand on the handle and turned toward Luke. "Want me to stay?"

And witness Astrid asking him about things he couldn't explain? "No, I'll be fine." He forced a smile.

"She surrendered four throwing knives when I asked for weapons. I frisked her and found two more tucked away in a secret pocket in her jacket. She also had a dagger in her boot." Rex raised his eyebrows.

"What are you saying?" Luke's words came out harsher than he'd meant them to, but the idea of the other man's hands roaming over Astrid's body brought out dark thoughts. Thoughts like needing to punch his head of security in the face.

"I'm saying, I think she's unarmed." Rex shrugged. "But with this lady, you never know."

Luke nodded. "Thanks for the warning, but I think I'll be okay."

Rex grinned. "I warned you, Boss. Now it's on your head if she stabs you." He opened the door and spoke to someone—presumably Astrid. "You can go in now."

Luke stood as the gorgeous blond strode toward him. She walked with the loose limbs of an athlete, lithe and graceful, yet there was power in her movements. He couldn't take his eyes off her. He gestured with his hand toward the couch and chairs set up at one end of the room. "Let's sit over here," he said.

She quirked an eyebrow but didn't say anything as she changed direction and took a seat in one of the armchairs. Dressed in blue jeans and a plain T-shirt, she should look anything but seductive, and yet she was. She ran a hand through her hair and licked her lips.

His throat ran dry at the sight, and he desperately needed some liquid. He walked over to a sideboard and poured himself a glass of water. "Anything to drink?" Luke asked, holding up the pitcher.

"Sure," Astrid said, her throaty voice washing over him and waking up his dick. "I'll have a Coke. Regular, not any of that diet crap."

The lady had strong opinions about soft drinks, it seemed.

Shit, Astrid had strong opinions about everything.

Luke just hoped she wasn't here because she thought ill of him. Her opinion shouldn't matter, but it did. That was one of the perils of working undercover. When he started to like people, what they thought about him mattered, and the closer he got to them, the harder it was to separate his own feelings from those of his undercover persona. Harder to keep the secrets necessary to get the job done.

He retrieved her drink from the fridge next to the sideboard and schooled his face before turning toward her by forcing himself to think of Donovan. This was all for his brother. He couldn't afford to think about anyone else's feelings.

Luke placed the red can on the table in front of Astrid and took the chair next to her, scooting it closer in the process. She frowned as he crowded her but didn't move back. Instead, she squared her shoulders as he invaded her personal space. Standing her ground looked sexy on her. Actually, he found everything about her sexy. Just thinking her name turned him on. He brushed an invisible piece of lint off his pants leg and straightened the crease. "What can I do for you?" he asked as he turned back toward her.

A smirk graced her lips. She apparently found his grooming amusing. "I'm here because Daisy made me come."

The usage of Naya's assumed identity threw him for a moment, but he nodded and waited for her to continue.

She opened the can of soda and took a deep sip. Watching her swallow made him hard in an instant, and he had to adjust his seat to allow for the extra bulge in his pants. Astrid didn't appear to notice, but she took her time putting the can back on the table. "Her name isn't really Daisy. She uses that as extra protection when she works with clients."

Luke made a noncommittal sound. He had no idea where Astrid was going with this, which made him feel queasy. If he couldn't predict what was coming next, he couldn't plan for the desired outcome.

"Her real name is Naya." Astrid's green eyes searched his.

He didn't know what she was looking for, so he made sure his face was neutral as he kept eye contact. "Okay, but why are you telling me this?"

"She's getting married." Again she scrutinized him, as if looking for some kind of reaction to the news.

"I already knew that. That's why you were in Denver to pick up Scott. To bring him to the wedding."

She looked down on her lap. "Yes, Naya wants her brother there when she marries Leif."

"I'm still confused about what this has to do with me."

"Naya also wants you to come to the wedding."

Another completely unexpected turn in the conversation. His thoughts pinged in a thousand different directions as he desperately tried to figure out what the catch was. What Naya and Astrid hoped to gain by inviting him. "Why?" he finally asked.

Astrid shrugged but didn't look at him. "She wants to thank you for helping to rescue her brother. And Scott seems to want you there."

Luke took a measured sip of his water. He hadn't considered Scott in the equation. What game was the brother playing? And what was his relationship with Astrid now? Had the drive from Denver been a cozy one? "Did you have a good trip back from Colorado?" His voice came out louder than necessary.

Her hand stopped midway in reaching for the Coke, and she gave him a startled look. "What?" He couldn't tell if she was surprised by the abrupt change of topic or if she looked guilty. Had she slept with Scott so soon after leaving Luke's bed?

"The drive," he clarified. "Did you have any trouble? How long were you on the road?"

She grabbed the can and held it in both hands. Her brow furrowed. "No trouble, and we made it back in a little over two days."

That meant at least one night on the road. "Where did you stay overnight?" He forced his tone to sound casual.

Astrid's frown hadn't let up. "In Bozeman, Montana." She looked at him like he'd turned crazy. "Why do you want to know?"

He did sound crazy. But it was her fault. She drove him loony. "Just making conversation."

"Can we get back to whether you'll come to the wedding?"

"Two rooms?" The words slipped out before he could stop them.

Astrid leaned back in the chair and turned slightly toward him. "One room, two beds. I didn't want Scott to bolt again." Heat blazed in her eyes, but not the good kind. "Why don't you ask what you really want to know?" Anger laced her voice.

Fine. He'd just come right out and say it. "I don't want you sleeping with him." He had no right to claim her, and yet some caveman part of him couldn't help it. He shouldn't care who she spent her time with. She'd be better off with someone other than him, yet it killed him to think of her in the arms of anyone but him.

She held herself very still. "I sleep wherever and with whomever I want." Her voice lowered, an edge of darkness slipping in. "You don't own me just because we had sex. Nobody owns me." Tension crackled between them.

Fine. She refused to acknowledge anything beyond the physical between them. Two could play at that game. "This wedding, when is it? Can I bring a date?"

A tic pulsed in Astrid's jaw. "Five days from now," she bit out almost in a growl. Her nostrils flared, and something feral glared in her gaze.

Mesmerized, Luke couldn't stop staring at the untamed creature looking at him through Astrid's eyes. Something wild and dangerous deep down in him responded. He felt like howling and beating his chest. He had a raging hard-on, and his breathing grew short and shallow.

Astrid blinked and looked away, breaking whatever crazy, wild connection they'd just shared. "You'll have to ask Naya about bringing a date," she said without meeting his gaze.

He envied how calm she sounded. He still hadn't caught his breath. "I may be busy," he stalled, testing to see how much his presence at the wedding meant to Astrid or whatever agenda she and Naya had cooked up, but also to get his breathing under control.

"Unbusy yourself," she barked out. "Naya and Scott want you there."

Apparently, it *was* important that he come. "What about you?"

She looked up at him, her green eyes still as a forest lake. "Why would I care if you come to the wedding?"

"Naya's happiness seems to be important to you." He watched her carefully.

"She's a good friend, and I want her wedding day to be perfect." A small smile played at the corner of her mouth, as if thinking about her friendship with Naya made her happy.

Luke felt like a creep for taking advantage of that happiness, but the wild part of him that she had awakened wanted more than just being her hookup buddy. He forced himself to think of Donovan, but even that didn't help. Getting closer to Astrid would be good for the mission, he told himself. He couldn't make himself truly believe the words, but mostly he didn't care. He wanted this woman any way he could get her. "I'll go to the wedding if you go out with me."

Her eyes widened in shock. "You're blackmailing me?" She shook her head and muttered something that sounded like "asshole" under her breath. "Two minutes ago, you were asking if you could bring a date to the wedding."

Okay, so she had him there. His behavior was not what anyone would call consistent, but that was her fault, damn it. He couldn't think when she was around. All the blood left his brain and rushed straight downstairs. "It was just a request for information. I didn't have anyone specific in mind."

She rolled her eyes. "When?"

The heat in her eyes had him losing track of the conversation. "What?"

She sighed. "When do I have to go out with you?" She made it sound as though a date with him would be the most unpleasant thing she could imagine.

He grinned. "We don't have much time if the wedding is in five days." Astrid didn't smile back. She just stared at him, anger still swirling in her eyes, and that feral look was back too. "Tomorrow," he said and mentioned an upscale restaurant in downtown Pine Rapids.

"Fine." She stood. "I'll meet you there."

"Oh no." Luke stood as well, and heat flared between them. "This is a real date. I come and pick you up."

Astrid shook her head. "You won't find the...my house. It's in the middle of nowhere."

Exactly. That's why he needed her to tell him where it was. He'd tried several times to track both her and Naya back to where they lived. Each time, he'd lost the trail in the same vicinity. They lived close to each other, maybe even in the same place. And the area where he'd lost the trail was close to one of the locations marked on the tablet map he'd confiscated from the wolverines. Even if he hadn't known about the creatures targeting Naya and her brother, there were just too many coincidences. "My car navigation system is excellent. All I need is the address to your house."

A peculiar smile brightened her face, as if she was laughing at an inside joke. "GPS doesn't work where I live. It's too rural."

He didn't use regular GPS. He used top-secret technology, and the maps he could access had been created using Department of Defense satellites. His trackers should work everywhere. The only way to interfere with them was to use some kind of signal-blocking device, but he could tell from the stubborn tilt of her head that he wasn't going to win the argument. At least not this time. "We'll compromise. Meet me here, and we'll go to the restaurant together."

She opened her mouth as if to protest but closed it again. "Fine," she bit out between clenched teeth, but the heat in her eyes wasn't from anger.

"That wasn't so hard." He wanted to touch her face, but instead, he stood and caught a strand of her hair. He wrapped it around his index finger as he took a step closer, his eyes on her mouth. "I promise you'll like the date."

Her breath caught and her lips opened.

Lowering his head, he caught her mouth in his. The kiss seared his lips, heat radiating through his body and stirring the wildness inside him again.

Astrid moaned, a sweet sound that made liquid fire rush straight to his groin. He deepened the kiss and pulled her body closer. The soft mounds of her breasts crushed against his chest, and he groaned when he felt her nipples hardening through the fabric of both their shirts. Luke grabbed her hands, pulled them up behind his neck, and caressed her arms as he moved his own hands down to her shoulders and then cradled her face. She complied with a soft sigh, laced her hands at the nape of his neck, and pressed herself even closer to his body.

Undone by her surrender, he wrapped one arm around her back and threaded the other in her hair, tilting her head for a better angle. He delved his tongue into her mouth, savoring the sweet taste of her. Her chest rose in rapid breaths.

He trailed kisses along her jaw, nipped her earlobe, and then moved his lips lower. She gasped when he reached the base of her throat and paused to explore that sensitive spot.

Luke bent Astrid backward, supporting her with an arm behind her back as he pulled down the collar of her shirt and nipped at her clavicle. He was heading lower, but a loud knock on the door made him pause.

Cursing under his breath, he straightened. "What?" he yelled toward the door.

Astrid swayed, and he steadied her by grabbing her hips. Her eyes had a dazed look, and her lips were swollen from his kisses. He couldn't help the satisfied grin that spread across his face.

"Mr. Walter is on the line." Rex's voice sounded muffled through the door. Luke wondered why his head of security didn't just open the door, but then realized he was being tactful. He and Astrid must have been louder than he thought. "He insists on speaking with you," Rex said.

"Walter" was the code name Special Agent in Charge Whalert used. Something serious was going down if he insisted on speaking with Luke now instead of just leaving a message. Since Luke kept his FBI-issued phone on silent at all times, Whalert posed as a business associate when he needed to get in touch immediately.

"Are you okay?" Luke asked Astrid. He grinned again when she had to breathe a few times before she could answer.

She glared at him. "I'm fine," she said, her voice throaty. "I need to go." She released her hands from the back of his neck and took a step back. Reluctantly, Luke let go of her hips.

"I'll see you tomorrow," he said and kissed her lips lightly.

Her nose crinkled. "I'm going to order something very expensive to eat."

He chuckled. "Of course you are." He watched her tempting ass as she strode to the door and noticed she put on some extra hip action. Vixen. "Wear something pretty for me," he threw after her.

Her answer was holding up a middle finger. Without as much as a glance his way, she exited the room.

Luke wondered how much of a hassle she'd give Rex as she rearmed herself.

He sat down at his desk and adjusted the raging hard-on in his pants before he punched the blinking button on the landline. "Yo," he said into the receiver.

"What the fuck took so you long?" His boss sounded angry and impatient at the same time. "Your obnoxious hold music is giving me a migraine."

Luke smiled. Whalert was obviously not a fan of house music. "Bathroom," he lied.

"TMI," Whalert growled.

"Then don't ask," Luke shot back.

Some grumbling traveled down the line, and then Whalert took a deep breath. "Is this a secure line?"

"It is." Luke's club owner persona didn't always walk on the right side of the law, so he made a point of having all his office lines in permanent secure.

"There's increased chatter on the Darknet. Pine Rapids has been mentioned several times."

Cold spread through Luke's stomach. "Any details?"

"No, but something heavy is going down. Troops are being assembled. We don't know by whom yet." Luke bet the wolverines were responsible, but disclosing that would mean describing the paranormal traits of the creatures. And that would get him pulled out of the field for sure. Straight to a mental health evaluation. "I'm sending you backup from the official divisions of FBI," Whalert said.

"Not yet," Luke implored. "Let's figure out the extent of the threat and who's posing it before we spook these bastards and they go underground again."

Whalert sighed, which told Luke he'd won this round of the argument. "No backup right now, but I'm keeping the men on alert standby."

"Fair enough," Luke said.

"Any progress with the map?"

"The southeast location is an abandoned farm. The fields are cleared of crops, and the buildings haven't been used for several months, maybe a year. Another marked area is in the middle of the forest." Whalert didn't need to know yet about that place's connection with Naya and Astrid. Luke had to figure out how the women and Naya's fiancé and brother fit into the picture before he put them in an official report. He knew the immediate people up the chain from Whalert, but a few links further up, the titles and names grew vague.

Until he knew exactly who was receiving the information he reported, he was keeping a lot of it to himself. He didn't want to unknowingly disclose something that could trigger extra interest or drop just the right name that would cause him to be replaced by someone with higher security clearance. Or worse, someone who wanted this case buried for the wrong reasons. "The marked area in the warehouse district is just that—a warehouse," he continued. "It doesn't look abandoned as much as just unused. I have a tap on some security cameras in the area in case any activity flares up."

"Good," Whalert said. "Anything else I should know?"

Luke hesitated, but then decided it would be in his best interest to mention Astrid's invitation now. If something came of it, he didn't want to be reprimanded later for not keeping his boss in the loop. Besides, Astrid was already in official reports, thanks to Broden. "I'm making progress with the target. She's invited me to a wedding." Okay, so technically Astrid was just the messenger. The invitation came from Naya. And Luke knew he made it sound as if the wedding was a date, but...

What if Astrid had a date for the wedding? The thought raced through his head, leaving a lump of burning anger in his stomach. He banged his fist hard on the desk. If Astrid went to the wedding with another man, he'd—

"What the fuck, Luke," Whalert shouted down the line. "Am I having this conversation with myself now?"

Luke had completely zoned out. He raked his fingers through his hair and took a deep breath. "I knocked over a glass on the desk," he fibbed. "There's water everywhere."

"Fine. I'll let you go," Whalert said. "Keep me posted and remember, I'm sending backup as soon as we can assess the situation better."

"Roger that." Luke saluted with two fingers.

Whalert sighed and then hung up.

Luke returned the receiver to its cradle with more force than necessary. He was still thinking about Astrid's potential date to the wedding. When he saw her tomorrow, he'd make it clear that he'd be the only one by her side at the wedding. An image of him and Astrid facing the preacher together at the altar flashed through his mind. Instead of scaring the shit out of him—like it should—it felt strangely right.

Luke leaned forward and banged his forehead on the desk several times. The woman had him so mixed up, and he saw no way out of this mess. There was no way not to hurt Astrid. Eventually she'd figure out he'd lied to her. The worst possible outcome was Astrid finding out he'd deceived her before he solved the case. If that happened, he had no doubt of the outcome.

She'd kill him.

The only question was how much she'd make it hurt.

# Chapter 13

ASTRID WAS TRYING ON DRESSES WHEN NAYA BURST into her room. The queen's fists were clenched at her sides. "He makes me so mad," she said and sat down among a pile of discarded dress candidates on the bed. Distracted, she looked at the carnage beside her. "What's this?" she asked, holding up a pink-and-yellow-flowered dress. The pattern was way too girlie. Astrid didn't know why she'd bought it in the first place.

"You want it?" she asked, looking at Naya through the mirror on her closet door. She smoothed down the skirt of the emerald-green knit dress she was currently trying on. Even with three-quarter-length sleeves, it looked too wintry.

Naya frowned. "I so don't have the curves to pull off flowers. I'm all sharp edges and jutting bones. I'd look like a twelve-year-old girl pretending to be a grown-up." Astrid disagreed but didn't bother saying so. The queen had a slight but muscular frame, and there were plenty of curves on her body. "What I meant was," Naya continued, "why are you trying on all these clothes?"

"I'm cleaning out my closet." Heat crept into Astrid's cheeks at the lie, and she could see Naya noticing the blush. Her friend opened her mouth as if to speak. "What did Leif do this time?" Astrid quickly interjected.

The distraction worked, and the speculative glint in

Naya's eyes disappeared. "Not Leif. Scott," she said. "My brother insists on leaving the fortress."

"Why?" Astrid turned around and shoved the pile of dresses toward the headboard so she could sit down next to Naya.

"He says this is my life, and he needs his own." She fiddled with the dress she was still holding. "I can't make him see that he *is* part of my life."

"Give him some time to settle in. Once he gets used to all of us, he'll change his mind."

Naya shook her head. "We've had this argument ever since you got back from Denver. He won't see reason. Just tells me to stop bossing him around."

"It's going to be hard for him. Now that you're a full Valkyrie, he'll be the only regular human around here." Naya had been a genetically enhanced human when she met Leif, but Freya had claimed her as a Valkyrie. Just before the royal couple completed their handfasting ceremony—their betrothal—Irja and Astrid had performed a private Valkyrie initiation with Naya. They still didn't know if the queen had become immortal through her bond with Leif, but she now had a full-fledged berserker. Her fighting skills were even more honed than they had been when she first came to live with the Norse warriors. She trained longer and harder than all of them. Usually sparring with the king, verbally and physically.

Naya stilled. "I didn't think of it that way." She plucked at the bedspread. "But I didn't feel like an outsider just because I wasn't one of you at first."

Astrid made a rude noise. "You said you'd always felt like an outsider."

Naya dismissed her comment with a wave of her hand. "But not because I wasn't like you. Because I'd never learned how to connect with other people. Except for Scott."

"Maybe your brother needs some time to figure out how to do that too."

"That's why I want Holden at the wedding. So that Scott has someone else to relate to. Someone who isn't one of the warriors."

At the mention of Holden's name, Astrid had to look away. "That's a good plan," she said.

"What did he say when you asked him?"

"He'll be there." Astrid still couldn't look at her friend. "Has Leif come around to the idea of Holden as one of the wedding guests?"

"Not exactly. We just don't talk about it." Naya stood, holding the flowered dress up against her body and turning in front of the mirror. "I get that it's a big security risk, but I screened Holden before I took the contract to redesign his security system." She lowered the dress, holding the bunched fabric in both hands. "Besides, he helped you rescue Scott."

Astrid shrugged. Holden may not be a physical threat, but he was definitely a threat to her sanity. The kiss in his office shouldn't have happened, but heat had crackled between them as soon as she stepped through the door. She couldn't control her emotions or her libido when he was around. When he'd touched his lips to hers, her berserker had gone wild. It had taken an enormous amount of willpower to leave the room after Rex interrupted them. Thank Freya he had. Her skin felt flushed just thinking about the kiss again. She needed another topic of discussion. "Is Scott well enough to leave the fortress?"

Naya turned her back toward the mirror and threw the dress on the pile on the bed. "Irja says he's improving steadily, but she recommends several months of physical therapy."

"Maybe you should also bring up the escalated threat of the wolverines and how we think they're on their way here for an attack."

"I did. I told him it wasn't safe for him to be out on his own." Naya rubbed her forehead. "But Scott said that was another reason for him not to stick around." She fell facedown onto the bed. "I don't know what to do," she said into the comforter. She turned her face sideways. "There's more chatter on the Darknet message boards. The wolverines are assembling large troops and moving this way. They specifically mentioned Pine Rapids several times."

Cold shivered down Astrid's spine. Troops of enhanced wolverines threatening the population of Pine Rapids were a nightmare come true. How was their band of warriors going to defeat the creatures? "Do you still want to go through with the wedding?"

Naya's eyes turned solemn as she watched Astrid. "Yes. Leif and I need to complete our bond now more than ever. The stronger our connection, the stronger the warriors are." It was true. Ever since the handfasting, the intricate connection the warriors' berserkers created with each other and the royal couple had become more powerful.

They still didn't know all the advantages of their increased awareness of each other, but so far it was working out great during fights. Without having to think about it, Astrid knew exactly where each of her battle brothers and sisters were. If an enemy entered their field of vision, she could feel the physical location of the opponent. It had been overwhelming and distracting at first, but the more the warriors trained together, the more they knew how to use this new skill to their advantage.

Astrid rubbed Naya's back. "I wish you could have a wedding only for joyous reasons."

Naya smiled. "The main reason is all about joy. I love Leif. I want to pledge myself fully to him. And to his people."

"To your people," Astrid corrected.

"All our people," Naya replied, moisture gathering in her eyes. "Ah, this is getting all sappy. Let's talk about how to change my stubborn brother's mind instead."

Astrid refrained from pointing out that stubbornness was a family trait. "You're approaching the problem wrong."

Her friend looked at Astrid through ink-black bangs. "What do you mean?"

"Instead of telling him how dangerous it is for him to be without protection, play on his pride and manhood. Tell him you don't feel safe unless he's here with you."

Naya snorted. "He'd never go for that. Why would I need my brother to protect me when I fight better than him and have a gang of burly Viking guards around twenty-four-seven?"

"If you lay it on thick enough, it may work." Astrid tucked a lock of hair behind her ear. "The testosterone-filled half of the human species is not known for thinking logically and is definitely not immune to flattery."

Actually, Holden seemed to be. She could flatter and flirt with him the whole night, and he still wouldn't cave in to her demands. Unless she demanded things in bed. She pushed the thought out of her mind, but it was too late. Heat crept up her neck and into her cheeks. Astrid cleared her throat. "But that's not what I was talking about."

"Go on," Naya said. "What are you talking about?"

"Emotional security." Astrid scratched her nose. "Tell Scott you need him here for your mental well-being. Explain how you are connected to us through the bond with Leif and your berserker. Tell him that worrying about him would make you a liability to all of us. No man would want the responsibility of that."

Naya's eyes went round. "You're a genius." She grabbed Astrid's face and planted a kiss on her forehead. "Freaking brilliant idea," she shouted.

Astrid smiled at her friend's enthusiasm, but then turned serious. "I don't know your brother very well, but during the car trip from Denver he talked about how much he admired you." She grabbed Naya's hands. "He may not understand how much you need him. Plus, it's always been just the two of you, and now there's this whole tribe of people who support you and love you. He may feel like Leif and the rest of us have replaced him in your heart."

Naya nodded. "I've been selfish. I haven't looked at the situation from Scott's point of view." She flashed a mischievous grin. "But that doesn't mean I'm not going to majorly guilt trip him into staying." She rushed out the door at the same reckless speed with which she'd entered.

—∽∽—

Astrid arrived at Holden's club ten minutes after their agreed-upon time. She hated being late, but she couldn't leave before she'd hung the outfits back in her closet. Leaving them in a wrinkled heap on the bed would have bugged her all night. She'd had so little for so long that she cherished every possession she now owned.

In the end, she'd settled on black skintight jeans and a sleeveless tunic. The top was covered in intricate, black pearl embroidery that sparkled when she moved. It also hid the throwing knives tucked into special sheaths around her waist. The tunic was both beautiful and practical. A Valkyrie couldn't ask for more.

She adjusted the daggers in her boots before she strode up to the club's entrance. It was still early in the evening, and the usual long line of people eager to be seen at the exclusive club hadn't yet formed. The berserker stirred, projecting into Astrid's mind an image of writhing bodies on the dance floor. She clamped down on her mental connection with the beast and soothed it back into rest. Her inner warrior had never before been that explicit in her demand to *feberandas*. The process of absorbing the sexual energy that generated on a dance floor. The berserker had projected hunger before, but it had always been a feeling, never a clear picture or actual words.

Astrid breathed deeply several times to calm herself and her inner warrior. Although Holden had blackmailed her into the situation, she was secretly thrilled to go on a date with him. Even if the flowery dress back at the fortress wasn't her style, she still had girlie feelings.

And sharing a meal with a handsome man to whom she was attracted physically and intellectually didn't happen often. She never went through with the courting part because she knew she'd only spend one night with a man. A date meant slow sexual buildup. Handling the berserker tonight would be like trying to keep the lid on a pressure cooker.

She took one more deep breath and then pushed open the door to the club. Astrid passed through the foyer and continued. Rex was standing by the bar, discussing something with one of the bartenders. The circular bar was a giant glass aquarium with fish swimming around and around. The bright lights filtering through the water and the glass cast the club in shades of blue and turquoise. There was no sign of Holden.

Rex turned and walked toward her. "Astrid," he said, holding out his hand.

"I'm not surrendering my weapons tonight." She batted her lashes. "Besides, you should know that if I wanted to hurt your boss, I could do so with my bare hands."

Rex chuckled. "I have no doubt you can, but you can keep your knives tonight." Instead of frisking her, he took her by the elbow and led her to the bar. "You are always stunning, but you look especially beautiful tonight."

"Thank you," Astrid said, wondering why all the flattery.

"Mr. Holden is a little delayed, but he will be down shortly." Ah, so that was why Rex was laying on the compliments so thickly. He was covering for his boss. "How about a drink while you wait?" Rex asked.

Astrid asked for a gin and tonic and settled on one of the barstools. She was deep in a discussion with the bartender and Rex about soccer when Holden appeared by her side. In the gloom of the club, she hadn't noticed him walk up.

He kissed her temple. "Sorry I'm late."

She shrugged, hiding how much the small gesture pleased her. "No problem." She nodded toward Rex and the bartender. "These guys have kept me entertained with their faulty logic on why they root for the English players in the UEFA Champions League."

Holden's smile crinkled his eyes. "Let me guess. You support the Scandinavians."

She swung the barstool around, freeing her legs from underneath the bar. "But of course. They're superior players. Why else does every self-respecting professional team recruit at least a few of them?"

Both Rex and the bartender protested loudly, but she was too mesmerized by Holden to pay them any attention. He was wearing a charcoal shirt over indigo denim jeans. The fabric of the shirt looked impossibly expensive and draped his shoulders in a perfect fit, obviously tailored. The dark-gray color perfectly matched his eyes, and it was hard not to lose herself in the heat she saw smoldering in their depths.

Great Freya, she was in trouble and their date hadn't even started yet. She took a breath to steady herself and slid down from the barstool.

"Shall we?" Holden swept his hand out toward the door.

Not trusting her voice, she waved good-bye to the other two men and walked toward the club exit.

Holden's hand applied a comforting pressure on the small of her back. "You look great," he said.

"You're not so bad yourself, Holden," she said with a smile.

He returned her smile. "Okay, so I'm going to only say this once: It annoys me that you won't call me by my first name."

"I'll work on that," Astrid answered.

"On annoying me, or on using my first name?"

She didn't answer, just gave him a smile. He shook his head.

Once outside, Holden grabbed her hand and strode down the sidewalk. "It's only a few blocks. I thought we could walk."

"Good idea." The night temperature was pleasant but had a little bite. Maybe it would cool down her libido.

Holden asked her about her day. She didn't want to admit she'd spent most of it primping for their date. Instead she mumbled something about working out, which was true. In the early afternoon, she'd sparred for a few hours with Sten and Per, the two youngest Vikings. Per was working on his strength after barely surviving one of the wolverine's altered wolfsbane injections. A transfusion of the queen's genetically modified white blood cells had pulled him back from the brink of death.

Ulf had watched the sparring for a little while but left without saying anything. Astrid had been glad. She was still pissed off about the kiss and pretty sure she would deck him if he tried to speak to her.

She and Holden walked down one of the main streets where closed shops displayed their offerings in well-lit windows. Holden steered them down one of the pedestrians-only streets that connected two main thoroughfares. During the day, it would have been filled with people visiting the lunch places lining both sides of the wide street. This late after closing time, the pavement was cast mostly in darkness, illuminated in spots by decorative streetlights.

Halfway down the street, Astrid's berserker went on high alert. The otherworldly essence of Asgard rose from behind one of the tall metal sculptures displayed next to some huge flower pots. She tugged on Holden's hand. "Incoming," she said. "I hope you're armed."

He lifted an eyebrow in a silent question and looked in the direction she nodded.

Four wolverines stepped out from behind the artwork. Their claws were already extended, and their eyes glittered with dark menace.

Holden swore under his breath.

# Chapter 14

LUKE REACHED FOR THE GLOCK HE CARRIED IN A shoulder holster underneath his jacket, but Astrid put her hand on his arm. "The noise of a gunshot this close to people will attract cops."

He nodded that he'd understood. Normally, he'd love to have the men and women in blue backing him up, but the wolverines would literally shred his law enforcement comrades. "How do you want to handle this?"

Her eyes widened, as if she was surprised he'd asked. He didn't understand why. She'd taken these guys down in hand-to-hand combat several times. Other than looking at their ugly faces down the scope of a rifle, he'd only fought one of them up close and personal. She was definitely the expert here. "They're going to try to separate us," she said in a low voice. "We should stay back-to-back as much as we can, but that may be hard because they're fast and very limber."

"Yeah, I noticed." He widened his stance and kept his eye on the creatures. They were still just standing by the ugly metal statue. The creatures watched them and they watched back. It was as if they were in a Western movie standoff. The music from the final showdown in *The Good, The Bad, and The Ugly* played in Luke's head.

"Watch out for their claws," Astrid said. "They also use blowguns with poisonous darts, but I don't see them carrying one tonight."

Luke squinted toward the wolverines and counted four sets of clawed hands, but it didn't look like any of them carried a weapon. "They could have a whole arsenal stashed behind that ugly sculpture," he said. "What is that thing supposed to look like?"

"An abstract representation of the human experience through a lifetime," Astrid said.

"For real?" Luke shot her a sideways look. The artwork looked like a heap of sheet metal that someone who failed Welding 101 had put together.

She gave a half shrug. "I read it on the Pine Rapids Chamber of Commerce website. They have a self-guided art walk you can print out."

The lady was full of surprises, but Luke needed to focus on the fight before them. "What else should I know about the wolverines?"

"They're much faster than your average human." She paused and half turned toward him. "How did you manage to defeat the one in the parking garage?"

"I probably just got lucky," Luke hedged. "How did you survive your fight with them?"

Astrid paused for several moments. "I almost didn't," she finally muttered.

Luke knew there was a ton of information that she wasn't sharing in that one small sentence, but now was not the time to press. Eventually he'd get Astrid to share how she'd become such an excellent fighter and why she healed faster than humanly possible. After they'd put down the ugly fuckers glaring at them from across the street. "I don't think we'll make our restaurant reservation," Luke said and smiled when Astrid chuckled.

The wolverines took a few steps closer, fanning out

in a semicircle. In unison, Luke and Astrid adjusted their stances so his right shoulder almost touched her left, their bodies positioned like an arrow pointing toward the center of the wolverine crescent.

The four creatures raised their heads and sniffed the air. "Valkyrie," one of them growled. Slow, evil smiles spread across each of their faces. There was that word again. Luke was not dumb enough to believe they called Astrid by the name of the Norse warrior women just because she was tall and blond. *Valkyrie* was code for something he did not yet understand. But again, a conversation for after they'd declawed these monsters.

The creature who had spoken focused on Luke, and a small shiver of dread slid down his spine when he looked into the freaky eyes. All that black was like looking into two eye sockets filled with pure evil.

The wolverine sniffed the air again. "What are you?" he asked as his three companions also raised their noses to smell. They cocked their heads, watching him with those weird dead eyes.

"Nobody important," Luke said. "Just on my way to have a lovely date with a beautiful woman."

The wolverines snickered as if he were a complete moron. Luke was okay with that. Being underestimated meant he'd have the advantage. And he could really use that. Although he was fast, he wasn't sure he could handle multiple supernatural freaks. Beside him, Astrid muttered under her breath. It sounded like she was counting, but he didn't dare take his eyes off the monsters.

The creatures took a few steps closer, fanning out further. Luke couldn't keep all four in his field of vision without turning his head.

"You got eyes on the two closest to you?" he asked Astrid in a low voice.

"Yep," she answered, also keeping her tone on the quiet side. "Just need them a little closer for a true aim."

He was about to ask her what she meant when she reached underneath the hem of her sparkly top and pulled out two shiny throwing blades. In one smooth motion, her hands continued their momentum and the knives left her grip in perfect arcs. They tumbled hilt over blade, reflecting the light from the streetlamp closest to them, and buried tip first in the necks of the wolverines closest to Astrid. Both went down with a wet gurgling noise. The whole choreography had taken no more than a few seconds. It was glorious.

Astrid was glorious.

Right then and there, Luke fell just a little bit more in love with her. *Fuck, wait no*. Where had that thought come from? He couldn't afford deep feelings for Astrid.

He shook himself mentally and concentrated on the other two monsters. They appeared as shocked as he was and stood staring at their fallen comrades.

Astrid palmed two more blades and threw them, but the wolverines knew what was coming and moved quicker than Luke's eyes could track. The knives clanked to the ground.

Luke swiveled his head to see where the two fuckers had leaped to, but he didn't lay eyes on either of them before a swift kick to his head had him down on one knee. Ears ringing, he stayed down.

Astrid stayed near, slashing with yet two more blades in her hands. How many knives could one woman carry? She had definitely earned the nickname Rex gave her.

Luke felt inadequately prepared with his lone switch-blade tucked into his shoe, but it would have to do. He retrieved the weapon and stood.

Both the remaining wolverines faced Astrid. Instead of making the rookie mistake of standing next to her, Luke remained in a position where he could defend her back. He felt blood trickling down the side of his face, but no immediate pain other than a dull throbbing where the wolverine's foot had made contact. Of course, the adrenaline rushing through his body kept the pain at bay. But unless he got woozy from blood loss, he'd worry later about how injured he was.

The two creatures attacked again. Just as Astrid had predicted, they flared out in a pattern that would have separated him from her if they had been less experienced fighters.

One of the creatures disappeared in another blur, and Luke received a hard side-kick in his stomach. *Shit*, he thought he'd covered his upper body. This was like fighting one of the characters from *The Matrix*. Hunched over and gasping for breath, he stopped trying to track the creatures by sight. Instead, he used sound and tried to predict where his opponent would be, based on the air moving against his skin. Most soldiers and cops knew to act purely on instinct and intuition. Luke's battalion used to tease him that he had more Spidey sense than others. Tonight he would really need it.

A low flurry to the right made him react instinctively with a side kick. His foot made contact with the shoulder of the wolverine in a low thud. The creature twisted backward from the impact, and Luke immediately delivered a semicircular kick to the head.

The monster ducked at the last minute, and Luke's foot hit its bicep instead of the intended target. Claws swiped out and ripped Luke's pants, piercing the skin of his calf. He hissed in pain but planted a front kick in the creature's face. Luke was rewarded by the sweet sound of crunched cartilage. He buried his switchblade in the creature's jugular and turned to see if Astrid was okay.

She had shoved a blade underneath the ribs of her opponent and then pulled it out impossibly fast to sink it into the creature's temple. She turned and caught Luke watching her. "He has some kind of collar protecting his neck. I couldn't go for the jugular." Blood splattered her face, and her hair was in complete disarray. Her beauty stunned his senses.

Hopped up on adrenaline, he closed the gap between them and kissed her once. Hard.

Astrid's nostril's flared. Her eyes went wild. She reached for him and pulled his head back down to hers. He let her take the lead as her tongue plundered his mouth. All he could think about was having her, right there and then.

She groaned as he pulled her toward him, caressing his head. All of a sudden she stopped and pushed against his shoulders. He reluctantly released her mouth. "What?" he asked.

Her eyes were enormous deep-green pools of desire. "You're hurt," she said, showing him her hand. Fresh blood coated her palm.

"I got kicked in the head."

"We need to bandage that wound." She took a step away from him.

"Later," he growled, reaching for her again.

She shook her head, but there was a smile on her face. "Zip it up, lover. Right now we have to get rid of these bodies before someone decides to investigate what all the noise was about."

Reluctantly, Luke went back to the creature he'd downed with the switchblade. He made sure there was no pulse before he pulled the weapon out and wiped it on the creature's shirt.

Astrid retrieved her weapons—the sheer number of knives taking a while—and together they dragged the bodies to a nearby alley. An open Dumpster served as a burial site for the creatures.

"They'll take longer to decompose with limited sunlight," Astrid said. "But by the time these are emptied, there shouldn't be any traces left of the wolverines." She turned to face him. "Let's get you home so I can take a look at that wound." She grabbed his hand, and together they walked back to his apartment.

—⁓—

One of Luke's favorite amenities in his apartment was the large dual-head shower. As he watched Astrid's magnificent body under the stream of water, he decided it was now his absolute favorite feature. Most likely, he would never again be able to get clean without busting a hard-on.

His head wound had stopped bleeding by the time they got to his apartment. The parallel furrows on his calf stung a little, but he'd had worse. He'd slap some antibacterial gel on it after the shower, and in the morning he'd be as good as new.

He had better things to think about, like the blond

arching her back in front of him. He grabbed the soap, lathered up his hands, and then reached for her.

Astrid moaned as he slid his hands across her slick skin, tracing a path from her flared hips and up the sides before cupping her breasts. He rubbed his thumbs across her nipples, enjoying the feeling of them hardening against his skin. The water rinsed away his lather. Leaning in, he lifted her breasts up and closer together, capturing both her areolas in his mouth.

Alternately sucking and biting, he kept pleasuring her until Astrid pulled his head up to her mouth with a growl. He met her demanding tongue thrusts, matching them with his own.

"I need you inside me. Now." Astrid groaned against his lips.

He slid his hands under her ass, squeezing the taut globes and lifting her up. She wrapped her legs around his waist, and he pressed her into the wall. The shower pounded his back as he slid his dick deep inside her, overloading his senses. She clenched tightly and warmly around him, and his balls pulled up. He had to fight hard to not come right then and there. "You feel incredible," he whispered to her.

"Harder," she moaned and he obliged by withdrawing and thrusting harder and deeper inside her. Her moans increased in frequency, matching the rhythm of his breathing.

The moment he felt her first tremor, he couldn't hold back any longer. He thrust into her one final time, his dick pulsing as her strong muscles milked him.

The release was so powerful that Luke had to brace himself against the shower wall to keep standing. Stars glimmered behind his closed eyelids, and he felt like he had soared out of his body. The bathroom disappeared as a peaceful darkness surrounded him. A warm and balmy wind blew against his skin. Across the void, a dark-haired man beckoned to him. An eye patch covered one of his eyes, and he had what looked like two large crows, one sitting on each of his shoulders.

Luke had obviously gone insane from adrenaline and sex overload. The best orgasm of his life would do that to a guy. He opened his mouth to ask the one-eyed dude how to get back to his body, when the sound of a great waterfall rushed toward him and a strong wind blew him backward. He closed his eyes, and when he opened them again, he was back with Astrid in the shower.

Her face was pale and her eyes enormous as she watched him with a shocked expression.

"You okay?" he managed to squeeze out as he caught his breath.

She nodded and unhooked her legs from behind his back. When she tried to slip away, he held her in place, resting his forehead against his. She exhaled a long breath, and he hugged her close. "Stay the night," he whispered against her hair.

She tensed and he waited for her to protest, but then she relaxed and snuggled closer. "Okay," she whispered, her lips hot against his neck.

He turned off the shower heads and slid open the door. Astrid wrapped herself in an oversize bath towel, securing it over her breasts. He dried himself off but didn't bother covering up before he grabbed her hand and led her into the bedroom.

She slipped under the covers and he joined her,

spooning her from behind. From her even breathing, he knew she was asleep within moments of her head hitting the pillow. She felt so right in his arms. It scared the crap out of him.

To distract himself, he thought about the night's fight. Astrid had taken down three of the creatures on her own. Granted, she'd neutralized two of them with throwing knives, but still. She moved faster than an average human, and then there was how quickly she healed.

Had she received the same magical cocktails that gave Luke his enhanced abilities? Somehow she was connected to the covert labs, and he was starting to believe the wolverines were too. They looked like weird human-animal hybrids.

He shuddered. Truly warped minds had thought up that experiment. At least Luke's injections had only enhanced him, not made him into a monster.

In the lab, both he and Donovan had trained relentlessly to become perfect soldiers. They excelled in combat and weapons techniques. Luke also responded well to the chemicals they pumped him full of, his body beefing up, his speed increasing. But Donovan hated the injections. They gave him horrible migraines and vivid nightmares. That was why they'd decided to escape. Donovan had begged Luke to help him, and he couldn't say no to his twin brother. There had been only the two of them for as long as he could remember. They had no memories of parents, only the lab with the scientists and their instructors. And now there was only Luke left.

Luke forced the bitter memories away. If he could just figure out who the people responsible for the main lab operations were, he'd be able to shut them down. The FBI Domestic Terrorist Unit had the same goal, but they had to deal with internal power struggles. If the wrong powerful name ended up on a list of the guilty, the whole undercover operation would be stopped. And there must be someone high up in the government working with the labs. How else were the labs always one step ahead of the law enforcement chasing them?

Luke couldn't risk the operation shutting down. He needed to see this through for his brother, which was why he couldn't stop until he had the kind of evidence that no one could sweep under the rug, no matter how powerful they were. Donovan deserved to be avenged. They'd been thirteen when they finally got out. At first, they'd survived on the streets with other runaways. Eventually, they'd gotten menial jobs under assumed names and scraped together just enough to cover rent. But the nightmares wouldn't leave Donovan alone, and he started having hallucinations. He self-medicated with whatever drugs he could get his hands on, but nothing worked. One day, he'd overdosed on purpose. He'd left a note begging Luke for forgiveness.

It was Luke who needed to be forgiven. He'd didn't do enough to ease his brother's pain. He didn't get him off the illegal drugs.

He finally drifted off to sleep, dreaming of Donovan and a one-eyed man with pet crows.

———

Someone shook Luke's shoulder. "Wake up." The voice sounded worried. He tried to do as he was told, but his eyelids were too heavy. His skin was on fire, and something was gnawing on his calf. Fever raged through his body.

The voice sounded like Astrid and he tried to answer, but his mouth was dry and his lips cracked.

"Freya have mercy," she said. "Your leg is infected. The fuckers must have laced their claws with poison."

He drifted in and out of consciousness. There were more voices, more people. Someone put a cold towel on his face. It felt wonderful.

He recognized another female voice but couldn't place it.

Astrid told him he would be okay, but he could hear panic in her voice. He tried to tell her not to worry, but darkness claimed him and the voices faded away.

# Chapter 15

ASTRID PACED OUTSIDE THE GUEST ROOM LUKE WAS IN. Irja had told her to get out when she couldn't sit still. The medical officer was busy taking care of Holden's— Luke's wound. Astrid should have known something was wrong with the claw marks on his leg, but she'd been distracted by his clever tongue and hands, not to mention his dick.

The gashes hadn't looked bad when they got back to the apartment. She thought they just needed to be cleaned and bandaged. She hadn't even done that. The intense orgasm Luke had given her had completely drained her. She'd come so hard, she saw stars and a vision of Freya. As soon as she had gotten into bed, she'd fallen asleep. How could she have been so selfish?

She knocked lightly on the closed door.

"You can only come in if you sit still and keep quiet," Irja said from the other side.

Not moving wasn't possible. Her emotions were all over the place, and the berserker wasn't listening to reason. It roared constantly inside Astrid's mind, and she couldn't think. She placed her hands over her ears in a futile attempt to quiet the beast.

Harald, the king's second-in-command, appeared at the end of the hallway. He walked toward her carrying a medical kit. "You alright?" He creased his forehead.

"Yeah," she lied and lowered her hands.

"You look like crap," Harald declared. "Here." He held out the kit. "Irja needs more bandages and saline to irrigate the wound."

Grateful for an excuse to enter the room again, Astrid grabbed the kit.

"Not so fast." Harald grabbed her elbow. "What happened?"

Astrid summarized the fight with the wolverines and Luke waking up feverish. "I didn't know what to do other than bringing him to Irja," she finished.

"I'm not even going to ask why you were with him, but Leif is going to want a recap."

Astrid bristled. "Would you ask one of the men why they were spending the night with a woman?"

Harald shrugged. "If they brought her here for medical attention, yes I would." He released her arm. "Now get in there."

Astrid nodded and opened the door without knocking.

Irja turned as Astrid entered. She held up the kit before the medical officer could tell her to get out. "Harald sent me in with this."

"Okay," Irja said, beckoning with her hand. "Put it here on the bed."

Astrid moved closer and did as she was told. "How is he?" Her voice broke. Luke lay on top of the covers, wearing only a pair of boxers. A towel was spread underneath his legs. His skin was pale and his breathing rapid.

*Mine*, the berserker wailed. Astrid tried to tune it out, and a throbbing headache spread from her temples through the rest of her head.

"I think he's going to be fine." Irja held up her hands covered in surgical gloves. "Can you open the new kit for me?" Once Astrid had snapped off the lid, Irja retrieved the saline irrigation bottle and some bandages. "The wound is shallow, and I gave him a small dose of the antidote I'm working on. It looks like it's helping him purge the poison."

Astrid exhaled with a whoosh of relief, her shoulders lowering. "What about his fever?"

"It broke already. That's why he's sweating so much. We just have to keep giving him fluids while we wait for his temperature to return to normal." She watched Astrid for a moment, her dark eyes gleaming. "Who is he?"

"Luke Holden." The headache intensified. Astrid had to close her eyes, even though the room was only dimly lit.

"Naya's friend."

"Client," Astrid corrected, opening her eyes again.

*Mine*, the berserker roared.

Irja's nostrils flared. "What's going on with your berserker?"

"I'm just tired," Astrid lied.

Irja raised a brow. "Sit here." She patted a spot on the bed close to Luke.

Astrid walked around the bed and sat down. She looked at Irja with furrowed brows. "Now what?"

"Touch him." Irja watched her closely.

Astrid hesitated, the intense look on Irja's face holding her back. Finally she reached out and placed her hand on Luke's uninjured leg. As soon as she touched his skin, an intense calm spread through her body, sweeping her anxiety and the headache out of the way.

*Yes*, the berserker whispered, stretching like a contented cat. *Mine*.

*What the hell?* Startled, Astrid turned to Irja. "I–I don't understand," she stuttered.

The other Valkyrie watched her with solemn eyes and reached for Astrid's left wrist. She pulled the cuff of the shirt up and lifted the hand so it was illuminated by the lamp on the nightstand. The pale yellow light revealed faint black lines shaped like the tail of a serpent. The tip curved delicately toward Astrid's little finger. "That's what I thought," Irja mumbled.

"No," Astrid protested. A million thoughts raced through her head, only to dissipate into nothing. She snatched her hand back from Irja's grip and removed her hold on Luke's leg. The berserker immediately snarled. Astrid told it to shut up, and after some grumbling, the beast calmed down again. "This can't be right. Luke's human."

Amusement flashed in Irja's eyes. "That's what Leif said when he bonded with Naya, and yet she is his *själsfrände*."

Astrid pressed a hand to her throat. "No, you don't understand. This isn't the first—" She looked up at Irja, willing her to understand what a magnificent fuckup this was. "You have to fix this."

Irja laughed. "There's nothing to fix. You've found your true mate."

Astrid swallowed the lump growing in her throat. She'd have to tell Irja everything in order to make her understand. "I met Luke a long time ago. We had sex several months ago." She gestured to the faint lines on her hand. "So this can't be real. This is a mistake." She looked at Luke. Sweat beaded on his forehead and his breath was shallow, but he seemed to be resting peacefully.

She curled her fingers to keep from touching him. Luke couldn't be her *själsfrände*, no matter how much the thought brought on an impossible longing deep inside her. According to the old Norse stories—the Sagas—the sign appeared when a Valkyrie or Viking first touched their true mate. She looked at Irja. "What do I do?" To her horror, moisture gathered in her eyes.

Irja grabbed her hand. "This is a good thing." Astrid shook her head, but Irja squeezed her hand. "I've done a lot of research on the *själsfrände* bond since Leif met Naya. The bond isn't always triggered the first time a Norse warrior meets their potential mate. In some of the stories I've found, two people developed the bond even if they'd known each other for a while."

"How?"

Irja shrugged. "You know the Sagas. They aren't big on scientific details. From what I've been able to piece together, I think you have to have physical—maybe even sexual—contact with your potential mate, but your berserker also has to recognize that person as a *själsfrände*." She chuckled. "Leif can be rash and impulsive, especially on the battlefield. It makes sense that his berserker would make up its mind about Naya after one kiss." She tugged on Astrid's hand.

"As opposed to you, who are extremely independent and stubborn to a fault. It would take a while for your berserker to decide whether a *själsfrände* was worthy. In one of the stories I read, a couple was married for five years before the serpent tail appeared. It was an arranged marriage between a thrall and a wealthy landowner. They had to gain each other's trust before their berserkers would bond."

"Figures," Astrid said. "Some rich guy buys a much younger bride and then makes her fall in love with him."

Amusement gleamed in Irja's eyes again. "Actually, it was a spinster who purchased a good-looking younger male, married him, and then had five children."

Astrid couldn't help but smile a little. As much as any stories about thralls brought back bad memories of her own time as a slave, she liked the idea of a woman who'd been put on the shelf buying herself a handsome stud. "But Luke doesn't have a berserker," she said. The headache came back, throbbing behind Astrid's closed eyes. Without thinking, she reached out and touched Luke with her free hand. The pain immediately subsided. She opened her eyes again. "It's going to take a while to process this."

Irja nodded. "I imagine so. You have some time before you're in danger." She smiled. "But you do need to complete the bond."

"How?" Astrid pulled her hands from Irja and Luke and instead buried them in her hair. "I've already slept with him. The bond should be completed." The orgasm-induced vision of Freya from the night before popped back in her mind. Had that triggered the bond? She had no choice but to commit to him now. If they didn't complete the bond, her berserker would enter permanent battle fury, eventually taking complete control over Astrid. She would be a danger to all the other warriors, and Leif would have to send her back to Valhalla, where Odin would make her sleep for eternity. What if Luke didn't want to be tied to her? Had he been affected by the bond? Did he have visions of Odin when he came?

"Don't worry so much right now." Irja put two fingers

on Luke's pulse and held up her other hand while she counted. She nodded, satisfied. "I'm sure it will work out somehow." She popped her surgical gloves off. "It did for Leif and Naya. If they can make a relationship work, I have high hopes for you." She smiled.

Astrid didn't feel as confident, but before she had a chance to answer, there was a knock on the door and Harald stepped inside. She quickly pulled down her sleeve to cover the serpent tail and turned to Irja, a silent plea in her eyes.

The other Valkyrie nodded. She would keep quiet. For now.

Harald didn't seem to have noticed the exchange. "I'm sorry to bother you," he said and then paused for a moment. "Is he okay?" he added, nodding toward Luke.

"He will be," Irja said. "What's on your mind?"

"I need Astrid," he said. "I could use both of you, but I understand if you need to stay with Holden, Irja."

"What's going on?" the medical officer asked.

Harald scratched his beard, worry making the lines on his face more pronounced. "The king wants all warriors ready for battle."

Astrid stood. "What's happened? Are we under attack?"

"No, but there have been some bad things happening at the farm southeast of here." Norse warriors had been monitoring the farmhouse for almost a year, after destroying a wolfsbane crop grown there. "So the newly arrived wolverines are moving into the farm?" Astrid asked.

"Yes," Harald said, his fists clenching. "And they've brought prisoners."

"Who?" Irja frowned.

Harald focused on her, pain reflected in his eyes. "We don't know," he said, his voice dark. "But it looks like they've captured mortals."

Astrid inhaled sharply. The wolverines were Loki's minions, but this was bold even for that half-god son of a sow.

"Freya protect us all," Irja whispered. "What would they want with mortals?"

"I don't know," Harald said. "But I don't think it's anything good."

"I'll get my sword," Astrid said.

Harald nodded. "I'll see you downstairs." He left the room.

Astrid stood and took one more look at Luke. She stroked his chin. Stubble had already started to grow along his strong jawline.

"I'll take good care of him," Irja promised.

Astrid gave her a grateful look, nodded once, and then went to fetch her weapons. If the wolverines were taking mortal captives, something big was going on. Which meant the stakes were high, and most likely the wolverines would fight hard to keep their hostages.

The berserker stirred and stretched. *Fight*, it whispered inside Astrid's mind, and then smiled.

Astrid answered the smile with one of her own. When things got complicated, there was nothing like a good fight to clear her mind. Battle was easy and straightforward. Kill your enemy. Avoid dying.

She went to the armory and collected one of her broadswords before joining the other Norse warriors on the training grounds. They lined up shoulder to shoulder, facing the king and the queen, sword hands on the hilts of the weapons hanging in scabbards on their belts. In these modern times, the swords weren't practical. They were not effective against guns, and they were hard to conceal. But the swords tied the Viking team to a shared history and culture. They still used them in training and in ceremonies like this one, aimed at strengthening their bonds with one another before heading into battle. Astrid also used her smallsword as an anchor to Freya, the guardian of Valkyries. Her prayers to the goddess felt more genuine when she made them while holding her favorite Norse sword.

Leif pulled his blade out of its scabbard. The sound of steel brushing against leather resonated through the air. The king held his sword up high. Naya repeated the gesture, looking small but fierce as she stood next to her soon-to-be husband.

The warriors drew their weapons, and Harald led them in a war cry. Although Astrid preferred her small-sword, the broadsword felt right in her hand as part of bonding with her battle brothers and sister. She felt a ping deep in her chest as her berserker connected with the Vikings' and the royal couple's inner warriors.

Harald took a deep breath and stepped forward. "Will you join your king and queen in victory?"

"*Ja!*" Their shouts echoed in unison through the building, vibrating deep in Astrid's body.

"On Odin's and Freya's order, our duty is to protect the mortals and their realm. Loki's monsters have captured a group of humans. They need our help. What shall we do?"

"Fight," Ulf shouted, and the others' voices joined his.

"What will be the outcome?" Harald bellowed.

"Victory, victory, victory," Sten chanted, and everyone joined in.

Astrid's berserker threw its head back and howled. She could feel the others' inner warriors doing the same. Battle fever swept through the Vikings, and they stood taller with wild eyes and flared nostrils.

Fight.

It was what they were meant to do.

What their god and goddess required them to do.

---

Outside the farm on the Idaho border, Astrid laid flat on her stomach in the tall grass. She was grateful it was spring and the ground still held some moisture. In another month, the grass would be prickly and itchy. She peered through her binoculars. The farm buildings looked exactly as they had when their team had been on that previous mission to rescue Per from here.

"What do you think?" she asked Ulf, who was hiding next to her. The surrounding fields were flat and open. There wasn't much cover to use as they approached the buildings, so they were waiting for dusk to turn into early evening. Astrid was tired of waiting. It made her wonder how Luke was doing.

"I think you're an idiot for bringing Holden to the fortress." Ulf lowered his own binoculars and looked at her directly. "What were you thinking? Do you have any idea what kind of danger you exposed us all to?"

Astrid sighed. She had known this would happen when Harald paired her with Ulf. At first she thought about asking for a change of partner, but with Irja staying behind, this was really the only choice. Sten and Per were natural battle brothers. They had that special bond that two warriors often developed after fighting side-by-side for a while. They communicated without words and always knew where the other was without having to see each other. Through the king and the queen's bond with their berserkers, all the warriors had this ability to a certain degree, but having a true battle brother—or sister—increased a warrior's skill.

Leif and Naya were paired, their berserkers strongest when the couple fought together. And tonight the warriors needed all the advantage they could get. Rescuing human hostages was a new situation and not one they'd trained for.

"Shut up," Astrid told Ulf while she looked for Pekka and Torvald through her binoculars. Having been assigned the position farthest from the cars they drove to the farm, the two men were still moving into their hiding spot. Once they were in place, the Vikings would have all sides of the farm covered. Torvald and Pekka were new to fighting with each other but had found in training that their similar styles were well suited.

Harald was running technical command from where they'd left the vehicles. Naya had hacked him into a surveillance satellite, and he was monitoring the whole scene on the infrared spectrum. And that left Astrid with grumpy Ulf as company. "I don't have to explain myself to you, but if I were to do so, I'd tell you that Holden is a friend of Naya's and invited to the wedding."

Ulf's eyes widened. "You're lying."

"Just ask the queen yourself." Astrid turned to watch the farm again.

Ulf stirred next to her, adjusting his position. "But what is he to you?"

"None of your business."

Her headset crackled, and Harald's voice broke through the static. "Could you two drama queens keep it down? I'm sure the wolverines would be riveted by the soap opera playing out between you. But since it looks like they haven't yet picked up on our radio frequency, let's just keep our chatter to a minimum, shall we?"

A chuckle followed Harald's announcement—probably Pekka—and then a giggle that was definitely Naya's. Heat creeped into Astrid's cheeks as she realized that everyone on the team had followed her and Ulf's exchange. She gave him a cold stare, which he countered with one of his own.

"In position," Pekka's voice said over the headset.

The evening slowly turned darker, and the illuminated windows in the main house appeared as beacons in the gloom. The light made the farmhouse look homey, as if it were a safe and welcoming place. Looks were deceiving indeed.

"How many wolverines?" Leif's voice asked over the headset.

Harald's voice answered. "The satellite footage shows five shapes huddled in a back room. I assume those are the prisoners, but Loki's damned creatures have the same heat signature as mortals. There are eight shapes moving around in the building. Two of them are close to the huddled cluster, probably guards."

"What about the other buildings?" Naya's voice cut in.

"Two shapes in the outbuilding closest to the main

house. They're not moving, maybe sleeping in some sort of bunkhouse."

"Time for a distraction," Sten's voice declared.

Astrid held her breath while through the binoculars she watched the shadow that was Sten streak across the field and close in on one of the outlying smaller buildings. A flame briefly illuminated his face, and he then swiftly returned to his original position next to Per. A large boom sounded, and bright, tall flames shot up from the building, licking their way toward the sky.

The door to the main house flew open, and two wolverines ran outside. The door closed behind them.

"Wait for more," Harald's voice commanded.

"Got it," Pekka answered. He had the best position for the long-range rifle they'd brought.

But no more creatures left the house. Instead, the two outside cleared some debris next to the burning building and then made their way back to the main house. The flames from the burning building illuminated them as they walked at a fast clip.

"They'll be out of my sight soon," Pekka's voice warned.

A muffled curse from Harald came down the line. "Take them out," he commanded.

Two short pops later, the two wolverines were sprawled just in front of the door of the main house. There was no indication that anyone would leave the bunkhouse or the main house to investigate.

"Fuck, these guys are smarter than the ones we've dealt with before. Maybe even combat trained." Leif's voice sounded angry.

"What do you see, Harald?" Naya's voice asked.

"They're taking positions by the window, and the two in the bunkhouse are up and on alert."

"Let me try smoking them out," Naya's voice said.

Astrid waited for a protest from the king, but it never came. It had taken a lot of convincing to get Leif to agree to Naya joining patrols and missions with the rest of the warriors. He still preferred that she stay by his side while fighting, but it looked like he was coming around to letting her operate on her own when she was the best person suited.

A small, dark shape darted across the field. If Astrid didn't know where to look, she would have missed it. For a brief moment, Naya appeared clearly as she had to cross a lighted area of the courtyard. A shot rang out, and then another.

"Naya," Leif's voice barked, anger and concern evident in his tone.

Astrid held her breath, waiting for the queen, her friend, to answer.

# Chapter 16

NAYA'S VOICE CAME THROUGH THE HEADSET STRONG and clear. "I'm good. Both shots missed."

Astrid felt more than heard the collective sigh of relief. She tapped into her mental connection with her inner warrior and found it on high alert. Strengthening the bond and making the connection wider, she sensed the others' berserkers in similar ready states. Naya's warrior spirit distinguished itself from the others in the web of interconnected warrior spirits. It didn't feel strange but had a different signature. Astrid could easily pick out her fellow Vikings' berserkers because they felt like home, like they spoke the same dialect as Astrid's warrior spirit. Naya's spirit felt like home too, but as if it spoke with a different accent. Leif's berserker was also clearly distinguishable. His berserker felt more intense, more powerful.

Through the mental connection, Astrid sensed Naya climbing up on the roof and making her way to the chimney. She dropped something down the chute and then shimmied down at double speed. Instead of returning to her position by Leif, she waited by the house, tucked up against the wall.

Smoke billowed inside the house, and one by one, the windows flew open.

"Move in," Harald's voice commanded. "Sten, you take care of the two in the bunkhouse."

"Got it," Sten's voice confirmed.

Astrid tucked her binoculars away and kept the Glock in her right hand ready. Taking a deep breath, she secured her mental connection to provide a map of her battle brothers' and sister's locations. She turned to Ulf and found him watching her, his eyes sparkling with excitement. She imagined her own eyes mirrored what he felt, the beginning of a battle high. They nodded to each other and then jogged across the field shoulder to shoulder, staying low in the tall grass.

As they got closer, she heard coughing and screaming from inside the house. The hostages must be scared out of their minds, but soon they'd be freed.

Harald's voice crackled through the headset, temporarily drowning out the rifle shots coming from the windows of the house. "The guards outside the captives' room are not leaving their position, but they are low to the floor, so the smoke must be bothering them. Every window has a warm body next to it, ready to shoot."

"Bunkhouse cleared," Sten's voice announced. "Moving to main house." He must have snuck up on the two creatures if he'd cleared the house that fast. It didn't surprise Astrid. It was as if Sten had a switch inside that allowed him to operate in ninja stealth mode.

She and Ulf were almost at the house. "We're going in the front," Ulf announced, and Astrid moved to cover him as he sidled up to the door, gun ready.

Directions and announcements from the other warriors sounded in Astrid's earpiece, but she zoned them out as she concentrated on backing up Ulf. He grabbed the door handle and looked over his shoulder, a question in his eyes.

She switched to a double-hand grip of her gun and nodded that she was ready. "Go."

Ulf swung the door open, swiftly moving to the side.

Astrid didn't wait for the wolverines to change their aims from out the windows to the door. She somersaulted low across the floor and twisted so she landed ready to shoot. She took out one creature on her left and wounded another. That monster dropped its gun and scuttled behind a sofa.

At the same time, Ulf stepped in low through the open door and shot at the wolverines on Astrid's left. One creature cried out in pain, but the other disappeared into the back of the house. Ulf shot again. "Two neutralized, one's wounded behind a couch, and another fled to the back of the house," he said into his mic.

Leif and Naya stepped into the doorway. "We'll take care of the ones down here. You head upstairs," Leif said.

A shot rang out from the back of the house.

"Fuck, I've been hit in the leg." Torvald's voice sounded more angry than in pain.

"Looks superficial," Pekka's voice interjected. "I can handle it."

Astrid headed around the corner and up the stairwell. She felt Ulf moving in behind her. "What can you tell me, Harald?" she said into her mic.

"The guards are now in the room with the prisoners. I can't tell their heat signature from the others."

"Shit," Ulf said. "I've never dealt with a hostage situation before."

They'd cleared the last step of the stairs, and Astrid darted a glance down the hallway for a quick look.

"Clear," she said to Ulf and moved slowly toward the closed doors.

"You're close," Harald's voice directed her. "The next door on your left should be it."

Astrid moved past the door and turned to face Ulf so the door was now between them.

Crying and wailing could be heard on the other side. "Shut the fuck up," someone shouted, and the sound changed to whimpering.

Astrid paused and listened. She heard only female voices besides the wolverines. "They're women speaking Spanish," she whispered to Ulf.

"How do you know?"

"It's not that different from French. I've picked up a few Spanish words."

"More like picked up a few Spanish dudes," Ulf muttered.

Astrid rolled her eyes. "Really, you want to go there? Right now, in the middle of this?"

Ulf gave her a half shrug.

"Odin's missing eye," Harald's voice barked in the headset. "Will you get your heads out of your asses and concentrate? We don't have time for your soap opera."

Astrid grimaced at Ulf, who smirked right back. She got her mind back on the mission. "We go in on three," she said to Ulf.

He nodded.

She put her ear close to the door but could now only hear low murmurs, no individual words. She took a deep breath and relaxed her shoulders. "*Estamos aquí para ayudar. Cuando abro la puerta, acuestate en el suelo*," she shouted through the door. Looking back at Ulf, she silently mouthed a count of three. On the last count, Ulf kicked in the door and went inside low with his gun drawn. Astrid followed, sending a silent prayer to Freya for the goddess to help their gamble to pay off.

Complete mayhem met Astrid as she entered the room. Women shrieked and cried out in Spanish, but they lay on the floor as she'd requested.

The wolverines hovered over them, shouting in English for them to shut up.

Bullets flew everywhere as the wolverines turned and aimed at Astrid and Ulf.

"*Quédate abajo*," Astrid told the women and hoped she'd gotten "stay down" correct. Her Spanish was rudimentary at best.

Ulf shot one of the wolverines in the leg, and it went down screaming while returning fire. The shot went wide and took out the ceiling lamp. The only illumination in the room now came from the light trickling in from the hallway.

The remaining wolverine grabbed one of the women on the floor and dragged her up in front of him as a human shield. The coward was closer to Astrid than he was to Ulf.

She looked down her raised gunsight at the monster, but wasn't sure she could take the shot without hitting the woman. She looked so young, maybe in her midteens. Her long, brown hair hung in tangles around her pale face, and her brown eyes were enormous. Tears flowed down her cheeks.

Astrid took aim, but she couldn't do it. "I don't have the shot," she said.

"Talk to me," Harald implored through the headset. "I can't tell what's going on."

"One monster down," Ulf answered. "The other is using a prisoner as his shield."

"Fuckin' coward," Harald's voice muttered.

"Stay back," the wolverine hissed and slowly moved toward the door. It kept its gun pointed toward Ulf and Astrid, sweeping the aim from one to the other. "You move and she dies." The fingers gripping the young girl's neck twitched as his claws emerged. Blood trickled out where the horrendous talons broke the girl's skin. She screamed.

Astrid and Ulf slowly followed the wolverine, widening the distance between them with every step they took. "*Como se llama*?" Astrid asked the girl.

"Camila," she whimpered through her tears.

The wolverine shook her. "Shut up." He glared at Astrid, panic in his eyes. "Don't talk to her, or I'll shoot her." He put the gun to Camila's temple. She closed her eyes, feverishly whispering something that sounded like a prayer.

The women on the floor were whispering too. They lay on their stomachs with their hands covering their heads, except for one girl who looked even younger than Camila. She was curled up in a fetal position, hands covering her ears and slowly rocking back and forth.

"Help is coming up the stairs," Harald's voice announced quietly. "Keep the fucker busy."

The wolverine kept moving toward the door. Astrid and Ulf followed. "Stay back," he hissed.

Astrid and Ulf stopped at the same time but kept the monster in their sights.

When the creature got to the doorway, he looked over his shoulder to navigate the opening.

*Bam.*

A rifle stock hit him between the eyes, and he went down.

"Take that, shithead," Pekka shouted.

Camila screamed and sank onto her knees, her hands covering her ears. Astrid sat down beside her and hugged the girl close. She rocked them both, mumbling into the girl's hair. Camila curled up against her, sobbing and trembling.

Over the girl's shoulder, Astrid saw the wolverine come to and reach for its gun. She tried to move her arm, but Camila was clinging to her, and she couldn't clear her gun. "Watch out," Astrid shouted.

Naya cleared the stairwell just in time and leaned around Pekka to place a bullet neatly between the eyes of the monster. Leif joined her and Pekka in the doorway. "Freya's mercy," Leif whispered.

He and Ulf moved to help the women up, but they shied away, scooting deeper into the room. The men looked at Astrid and Naya. "What did we do?" Ulf asked, despair shining in his eyes. Leif had the same look.

Naya took a step into the room. "It's not what you did. It's who you are," she said, her voice grim. "They're afraid because you are male."

Pekka inhaled and cursed under his breath.

Astrid tried to untangle herself from Camila, but the girl held on tight. "Call Irja and let her know we have five mortals who need medical attention," she said. "Go back to Harald and bring back the vehicles. Naya and I will move the women out. We'll take them back as one group in the van."

Leif hesitated. "Are you sure we should bring them back to the fortress?"

Naya looked up from where she was kneeling on the floor. She was stroking the very young girl's back. "They're coming back with us," she said in a low, dark voice.

Leif nodded once and indicated to Ulf and Pekka that they should leave with him.

Naya turned to Astrid. "I want to kill these wolverine fuckers all over again."

Astrid nodded. "I don't think they're the only ones who've mistreated these women."

Naya's mouth turned grim as she turned back to the girl on the floor and whispered in her ear while stroking her back again.

——◊◊◊——

Astrid lay next to Luke. She'd tried to get some rest in her own room, but her restless berserker wouldn't settle down. Not until she touched Luke would the beast finally let her rest, but even with the inner warrior quiet, she couldn't sleep. She kept thinking about the girls. Irja had examined them all. In addition to scrapes and bruises, two of them showed signs of sexual assault. Physically and emotionally, they would need a long time to heal.

Astrid and Naya had helped Irja to care for the women. Camila spoke English fluently, and two of the other women knew some words. Irja turned out to be fluent in Spanish. Slowly they'd pieced together their story.

The five young women were from different areas of Mexico. Some from rural areas, others from cities, but they had all been abducted and then smuggled across the border. They had no idea where they were or how much time had passed since they'd left Mexico. They said a man had bought them at an auction and then given them to the wolverines. They couldn't give much of a description of the man, just that he was tall, had light-brown hair, and spoke English with an accent that wasn't Spanish.

Nausea rose in Astrid's stomach when she pictured the auction. Once upon a time, she'd stood on the selling block. At least she'd lucked out in who bought her. Her new master had been strict, but fair. His weapons master had trained her when he discovered her interest in fighting. Or, maybe he'd just humored her. But she'd excelled. So much so that she'd become a shield maiden, and eventually her master had granted her freedom. No one would ever own her again.

Luke stirred next to her, and she turned to face him. His temperature was down to normal, and Irja said his body had purged all of the poison. Astrid had asked the medical officer how Luke had been able to recover so quickly, in just twenty-four hours. Irja thought her antidote may have contributed to the accelerated healing, but she was running more tests on Luke's blood.

Astrid caressed his forehead and then trailed her fingers down the side of his face. He looked younger when he slept, more relaxed. She followed the strong line of his stubble-covered jaw and then traced the outline of his lips. The memory of those lips against hers heated her blood, and she blushed.

Luke startled her by opening his eyes. "Hi," he whispered against her fingers, his voice hoarse.

"Hi back," she said and rose. "Let me get you some water."

He reached for her wrist. "Please don't go," he said.

Astrid leaned down and kissed him lightly. "I'll be right back." She got out of the bed and poured a glass of water.

Luke pushed himself up to half sitting against the headboard. "What happened?"

"What's the last thing you remember?" Astrid handed him the water.

A slow grin spread over Luke's face as he drank, and he looked down at her boobs.

Fantastic. Another male who hadn't progressed past the emotional state of a twelve-year-old boy. "That's not what I meant," she said but couldn't help returning his grin. "Do you remember waking up with a fever?"

Luke shook his head. "I'm not sure. I heard voices, but it's all blurry."

"I had to call my...friends. The wolverine claws must have been poisoned, and I brought you here to get an antidote."

He frowned. "How long have I been out?"

"Almost twenty-four hours."

He patted the mattress. "Come sit next to me again. You look exhausted. Have you been awake this whole time?"

Astrid leaned against the headboard next to Luke. He put his arm around her and she sank into him, her head resting on his chest. "There was another fight." She ignored how good it felt to be this close to him or how the berserker curled up and purred.

Luke's body stilled beneath her. "Are you hurt?"

"No. Torvald got shot, but it's superficial. He'll limp for a while and complain about it, but he'll be fine."

"I have no idea who you're talking about, but I'm glad the guy's going to be okay. What happened?" He caressed her hair. "By the way, where the hell am I?"

Astrid sat up so she could see Luke's face. She decided to start with the easier of the two questions. "You're at my house, which is also where my friend who has the antidote to the poison lives. Naya and my... other friends live here too. It's where we all live..." On second thought, maybe this was not the easy question. She shook her head. "I'm not sure I can explain this."

"Okay. Take a deep breath." Luke captured her hands in his. "So you have a lot of roommates."

"You already know Naya. Her fiancé, Leif, lives here, as does Irja, our medical officer."

"Officer? You are some kind of military unit?"

Shit, she shouldn't have let that slip out. Why hadn't she just called Irja a doctor? "This is a little hard to explain, but basically there are a whole bunch of Scandinavians living here. Well, plus Naya. And Irja, she's from Finland and technically that's not part of Scandinavia. Maybe I should have said the Nordic countries." She stopped her rambling and took a deep breath. "We do operate kind of like a military unit, with Leif as our leader."

"I'm not sure I understand. Are you in some kind of law enforcement?"

*Yes*, she wanted to say. They enforced the law of Odin and Freya, but how would she phrase that without sounding like a religious nut? "Not in any official capacity. We basically fight the wolverines—and other creatures like them—but stay under the radar and try not to attract the attention of the actual police." She searched for the words to explain their off-grid status. "We're like a sovereign nation with diplomatic immunity." The diplomatic immunity was recognized only by the Norse warriors themselves, but hopefully Luke wouldn't pick up on that.

He pinched the bridge of his nose. "This is a little much to take in." He lowered his hand and looked at her, his eyes shining with concern. "Could we go back to why you were in another fight? Are you sure you're okay?"

Astrid nodded. "I really am fine. Not a scratch on me." She thought about the bruises on the women they'd rescued, and the more permanent scars they were hiding on the inside. "It was just a tough mission. It brought up some bad memories."

"Tell me."

"The wolverines had taken hostages. Five women from Mexico were kept at a farmhouse on the Idaho border. The monsters are now involved in human trafficking."

Luke reared back. "You have proof of this?" He gripped her hand hard, his eyes intense.

"Yes. We brought the women back here."

His jaw set. "This is much bigger than I thought," he mumbled.

"What's bigger than you thought?" Unease spread through Astrid's body. Luke's reaction showed an interest level she didn't expect from him, even after fighting the wolverines twice.

He startled and then caught himself, his eyes changing from troubled to guileless. "I'm just thinking out loud." He caressed her cheek. "Tell me about the hard memories that resurfaced."

Astrid wasn't buying it. What wasn't Luke telling

her? "It's nothing I like to talk about." She pulled away to create some distance between them and tried to pull her hand out of his.

Luke held on. "Hey, don't shut me out." He squeezed her fingers. "We may have skipped a few steps before ending up in bed together, and I still owe you a proper date." He grinned. "But you can trust me with anything from your past. It won't change the way I feel about you."

He had feelings for her? Warmth spread through her chest as alarm bells still rang in her mind. Talk about conflicted. What was his agenda? How much of what he was saying could she trust? Astrid hesitated, but if the *själsfrände* bond was real, she might as well find out now if her past repulsed him. That way, she could prepare for never being able to complete the bond. "I was once in the girls' situation."

Luke tried to pull her closer, but she resisted. "You were kidnapped?" he asked.

"No," she said. "But I grew up in a situation where a man had complete power over me. He owned me." She had to look away. "Owned my body."

Luke's jaw clenched, but he cradled her face and made her look at him. "Hey, none of that was your fault."

Astrid nodded. "I know that now, but it took a long time to get to a point where I didn't think I had somehow caused some of the things that happened to me."

His jaw tightened further. "Were you…" He swallowed. "Did this man hurt you?" His eyes burned with anger.

"I had a benevolent master. He didn't abuse his property, human or cattle." She realized Luke thought she was talking about sexual slavery and didn't have the historical context. But revealing her true age—close to a thousand years old—would probably be too overwhelming for him right now. That conversation would have to wait until later, and maybe then she could explain that having thralls—slaves captured during raids and later sold to landowners—was a common practice during the Viking era.

"It wasn't that he cared for me, but I was an investment." Astrid looked away again. "He didn't abuse me, but some of his men could get over-familiar. I learned how to fight, and after I cracked a few ribs and broke a few noses, they left me alone."

"Are these men still around?" Luke's voice burned with a dark intensity.

She shook her head. "No, they've been dead a long time."

He raised his eyebrows.

"I didn't do it," she said in answer to his silent question. "Some of them died a natural death, but most of them were killed while fighting." Her master had been a rich landowner, and many other Viking chieftains had tried to gain his lands by warfare. She'd left as soon as she earned her freedom and never did find out what happened to her former owner. The only person she'd cared about was the weapons master, and he'd passed away in his sleep by then. The man had lived to a very old age, which by that century's standard was into his fifties.

Luke tucked a strand of her hair behind her ear and placed a light kiss on her lips. "You're so amazingly strong, both mentally and physically." He paused and traced her lips with his thumb. "You're a true warrior. I would have been honored to serve with you in my unit. I am honored to have fought with you."

Tears welled up in Astrid's eyes. She'd had many compliments in her life, but always about her looks. Luke's words warmed corners of her heart that had been cold for a long time. And of course the berserker was purring with pleasure, firing up Astrid's libido. She told the beast and her hormones to stand down, but it was no use. The berserker howled its approval as Astrid reached for Luke and claimed his mouth with her own. He growled, grabbed her shoulders, and pulled her closer.

A knock on the door startled them both. Astrid cleared her throat. "Come in," she said, straightening her shirt and hair.

Naya poked her head around the door. "You guys decent?" She grinned and entered the room holding a phone. "Mr. Holden, Rex has been trying to get ahold of you. When you and Astrid didn't answer your phones, he tried mine."

"I didn't think to bring your phone on the way over here," Astrid said to Luke. "And mine is charging in my bedroom. Sorry."

"No apology necessary. I care more about my life than my phone." Luke smiled and gestured for Naya to hand over the phone.

"How did he know to call me?" Naya asked.

"He knows Astrid and I were going on a date. And he knows you know Astrid."

As Luke talked with his head of security, Naya turned to Astrid. "Everything okay?"

How much had Irja told the queen? Astrid pulled on the cuff of her shirt. An unfortunate gesture, since it drew

Naya's eyes exactly where Astrid did not want them. The small woman moved lightning quick and sat down on the bed next to Astrid. Naya grabbed Astrid's hand and pulled up the sleeve. Her eyes widened. "Him?" she asked in a low voice, slanting her eyes toward Luke.

Astrid nodded, watching the queen carefully to see what her reaction would be.

To her surprise, the queen grinned widely and shook her head. "Oh, Leif is going to love this." She gave Luke's bare chest a slow once-over and hummed her approval.

The berserker growled, but Astrid told it to stand down. She grabbed Naya's hand. "Don't tell him. Not yet."

"Okay, but I can't keep it a secret for long."

Luke hung up and looked between Astrid and Naya. "What did I miss?"

"Girl talk," Naya said and jumped up from the bed. She held out her hand for her phone.

Luke handed it over and turned to Astrid. "I have to go."

"I'll find you some pants and drive you back into town," Astrid said as she scooted off the bed and stood.

"Actually," Naya said. "Leif wants to drive Luke home. Irja and I could use your help with the young women."

Oh shit. Luke and the king in the same car. "Did you just now decide that Leif would be the chauffeur?" Astrid asked her friend but kept her voice respectful. Naya was, after all, also her queen.

The smaller woman practically bounced with excitement. "Nope. Leif made that request before I came in here."

Astrid grimaced.

"What am I missing?" Luke asked. "You two look like there's something going on beyond just a ride home."

Naya walked toward the door. "Nothing going on here except an opportunity for you and Leif to get to know each other better. It's going to be great." She grinned and then left the room.

Yeah, super great. Not awkward at all to have the king interrogate Astrid's *själsfrände*.

# Chapter 17

THE SILENCE IN THE ESCALADE WAS THICK WITH tension. Luke fidgeted in his borrowed clothes. He sat in the front passenger seat next to Leif, who was driving. Naya's fiancé didn't have to try hard to be intimidating. At six foot four and with broad shoulders, the dude appeared threatening just by sheer presence. A sphere of danger surrounded him, as if it slowly seeped out of his pores. Add a square jaw, cold, ice-blue eyes, and blond hair tied back with a scrap of leather, and the alpha male picture was complete.

The other guy in the car had joined them at the last minute and worked much harder on his aggressive vibe. Ulf—weird name—sat in the back. Luke could feel the dude's gaze trying to burn a hole in his neck. He was the same height as Luke, but his shoulders and biceps were massive. His blond hair was sheared into a crew cut, and he held himself with the posture of a soldier.

So did Leif.

Every instinct Luke had honed while in the service screamed at him to get out of the car. And yet the alpha in him wanted to fight the two guys to see how they would measure up. He was pretty sure he could take Ulf. Fighting Leif would mean bruises and pain, but he'd probably be able to get in a few good punches and leave his mark before he was crushed to death by those massive arms.

He shook himself. He should be concentrating on his

mission, not on picking a fight just because he needed to prove himself. Rex had called because Whalert had tried to reach Luke. His boss had left a message to get back to him ASAP.

As they'd left Astrid's house, Luke had tried to pay attention to his surroundings. With the two guys flanking him, he'd only glimpsed the huge mansion's interior of wood panels and old paintings. The outside had been equally impressive. Basalt rocks were incorporated into the landscaping, and the house itself was covered in rocks that made it blend in with the surrounding nature. Now, he concentrated on learning where the road joined the main arterial so he'd be able to find it again.

It was so hard to concentrate though. His head swirled with what Astrid had told him. He couldn't get a grip on what she meant by a sovereign nation and fighting wolverines. And her description of how she grew up made him want to punch someone.

Ulf would do. The guy's silent glowering was getting on Luke's nerves.

Ten minutes in, the forest thinned out and Luke figured the turn onto the main road would soon appear. He paid attention to the landmarks, creating a mental map.

"Let's talk about you and Astrid." Leif's voice was like a sonic boom in the uncomfortable silence. Luke jerked, hitting his elbow on the side window.

Ulf sniggered. Luke wanted to smash his other elbow in the dude's face.

Instead, he turned to Leif. "Astrid and I are not your business." He rubbed the sore spot on his arm.

Leif shot him a chilly look. "Anything or anyone interacting with my people is my business."

What the fuck? *His people?* "Well, I'm the exception."

Leif laughed, but not in a good way. The sound sent chills down Luke's spine. "You've been my business ever since you worked with Naya. I know a lot about you already, Luke Holden." He bared his teeth in what was probably supposed to be a smile but looked more like what lions did before they attacked. "And now that you've hooked up with Astrid, I intend to find out a lot more."

Ulf growled.

*Enough.* Luke turned around and glared at the dude in the backseat. "What the fuck is your problem?"

"You're my problem. Have been ever since you decided to stick your dick where it doesn't belong." So that was what this was all about. Ulf wanted Astrid. The thought brought out something ugly and possessive in Luke. Did the two have a history? They'd make a striking couple, both tall and fair.

Luke plastered his most condescending smile on his face. "I see now. You made a move but struck out. You're pouting because she obviously figured out I'm the better man."

Ulf lunged forward, placing his face a fraction of an inch from Luke's. "I'll show you who's the better man."

"Looking forward to it," Luke hissed, refusing to move his head.

Suddenly, the car swerved and he hit the window again, striking the same tender spot on the elbow. Ulf fared worse. His head smacked into the back side door.

"Knock it off," Leif said as he straightened the steering wheel. "If Astrid finds out you're having this pissing contest, she'll beat the shit out of both of you." He paused. "And then she'll come after me for putting you both in a small enclosed space together," he mumbled.

Luke turned around for another glare at Ulf. The other man returned one of his own but didn't say anything. Luke faced forward again and then cursed under his breath. They were on the main road, and there was no sign of where they'd turned from the smaller country road. He'd missed it. He slanted a look Leif's way. Had the guy distracted him on purpose? From the pleased smile on Leif's face, it was very possible.

"Look," Leif said. "Let's try to talk like adults." He looked at Luke for a second before focusing on the road again. "What's going on with you and Astrid? I'm asking because I care about her."

Luke wanted to tell the guy to fuck off again, but Leif obviously was looking out for Astrid. "We're still figuring that out," he offered instead, ignoring the hitch in his chest that reminded him their relationship had a predestined ending.

Ulf muttered something from the backseat, but both Leif and Luke ignored him.

"She's family," Leif said. "If you hurt her, I'll kill you." He smiled as if they were talking about the weather or some equally benign shit.

"You don't have to worry about that, my king," Ulf said. "If he hurts Astrid, she'll kill him herself."

Luke ignored the guffaw from the other two and focused on the peculiar way Ulf had addressed Leif. "Why did he just call you *king*?"

Leif shot Ulf a warning look through the rearview mirror. "Because that is what I am."

"Is your title related to this whole sovereign nation status?"

"So Astrid told you about that." Leif made it a statement. "We operate within U.S. laws as much as we possibly can, but sometimes we have to step outside those limits." He looked at Luke again. "You've seen what the wolverines can do. We can't just call the cops to come and stop them."

Okay, that made sense in a really warped way. Luke's own division was created so its agents could work outside the limits of the FBI, but he was a U.S. citizen. "But how can you operate within our country's borders if you're from a different country? What international agency oversees your operations, and how do they work with U.S. law enforcement?"

"None of your business—"

Leif interrupted Ulf's outburst with a small shake of his head. "Our superiors have global jurisdiction," he said. "It allows us to operate under a kind of diplomatic immunity."

"What is the name of your agency?"

"I can't tell you that." Leif turned to look at him and cocked his head. "Why so interested in who we work with in your government?"

*Fuck.* The cop in Luke had automatically tried to work out the web of jurisdiction. Leif would figure out Luke's true identity if he wasn't careful. He couldn't blow his cover. "I'm just interested in who I should look out for. Hazard of the trade, I guess. The club attracts people from the shady side of the law sometimes."

"From what I've heard, you walk the shady side too," Ulf interjected.

Luke ignored him but filed away that they'd obviously researched both him and his business. "Let's talk about these wolverines. What are they?"

A line appeared between Leif's brows. "We don't know for sure, but Irja's figured out they're made through genetic manipulation and cross breeding."

"By whom?"

Leif paused for a while. "We don't have concrete evidence."

"But you have a suspect?" Shit, he sounded like a cop again. For that matter, so did Leif. Was it possible that Astrid and everyone else at the big house in the forest were part of some kind of international policing effort?

Leif just nodded.

Luke waited for more details, but the silence stretched on. He changed tack. "And why did they kidnap the women?"

Ulf leaned forward. "Astrid told you about them?" Leif shot him a surprised look too.

Luke frowned. "Yeah. She was pretty shook up. Seeing them so powerless brought up bad memories."

Leif's eyebrows shot up, and Ulf made a noise of surprise.

Shit, they hadn't known about Astrid's background. "Don't tell her I said anything," he begged, but two others weren't paying attention.

"It makes sense," Ulf said. "She was a shield maiden. If she was born a thrall, that could be how she earned her freedom. I had battle brothers who became free men that way. Sign up for a few years of raiding without pay, and you'd be your own man eventually."

"Shut up," Leif warned him. "We'll talk about this later."

Luke stored away the words they'd used. He'd figure out what *shield maiden* and *thrall* meant later. "I thought you already knew," he said.

Ulf smirked, but Leif nodded. "If Astrid wanted us to know her history, she would have told us." He shot another warning look Ulf's way through the rearview mirror.

The guy grumbled but finally nodded his head. "I'll keep quiet."

Luke let out a breath he didn't know he'd been holding. "I owe you guys."

Leif's feral grin made Luke regret the words as soon as they left his lips. "I'm sure I'll collect at some point," Leif said. "Meanwhile, brush off your formal wear. Naya wants you at our wedding."

"You can't be serious," Ulf stuttered, but Leif interrupted him by holding up his hand.

"I'm not pleased about it, but my *själsfrände* wants him there so her brother won't feel like the only outsider." He pulled up in front of Luke's apartment building and turned halfway in his seat, facing Luke full-on. "Naya says I still have a lot to learn about the art of compromise, which is the only reason you are allowed at my wedding. I and the rest of my warriors will be monitoring you carefully. Not just at the wedding."

"Understood." Luke got out of the car. At the same time, Ulf opened the back door and exited. He made sure to bump Luke with his shoulder as he moved to take the front seat.

"Not here and not now," Ulf hissed. "But soon."

"Looking forward to it," Luke said in the same low voice as he walked toward the building entrance.

—◦◦◦—

Back in his apartment, Luke took a quick shower and dressed in his own clothes before he called Whalert. The number in Rex's message was not one Luke had used before. His boss answered on the first ring.

"That you, Holden?" Whalert asked. There were myriad voices in the background, and someone laughed loudly.

"Where are you?" Luke asked.

"I can't use the office anymore. We've been compromised."

Luke straightened. "Okay."

"The fucked-up part is that I triggered it myself." Frustration laced his boss's tone. "I should have known better. You've warned me several times. Instead, I acted like an overconfident rookie."

Luke interrupted the self-flagellation. "Slow down and tell me what's going on."

Whalert swallowed loudly. "This morning, I checked to see if the lab had finished the analysis of the blood sample you had me enter." Luke had sent Astrid's blood-soaked scarf to his boss so his own identity wouldn't be associated with any records. It was standard when an operative was undercover, but also a way for Luke to be extra careful. "I couldn't even see the lab request entry," his boss continued.

"It's been locked for higher clearance?" Luke had suspected the case would trigger something like this, but he'd thought it might only move beyond his own security clearance. He'd never imagined it would get ripped out of Whalert's hands. The guy was way above Luke's pay grade.

"No, the record is completely gone. It's as if I never sent the request. Even the confirmation email has been deleted from my inbox. Someone really wants that sample to disappear."

Luke pinched the bridge of his nose. This was way worse than he'd thought. What the fuck were Astrid and her band of Scandinavians involved in? "Are you safe?" he asked his boss.

"For now. I grabbed my files and got the hell out of the office. Luckily it was early and not many people had arrived yet. No one saw me there, so the cleanup crew will probably go to my house first." *Cleanup crew* was code for the assassins used when an agent went rogue.

"This is bad," Luke said. "Do you have a safe house?"

Whalert paused. "Nice try, but you know I won't tell you." A hint of suspicion had crept into his voice.

"Fuck, man. You're thinking I'm out to get you now?"

"I think I've earned the right to be paranoid."

He was right. Luke apologized. "What do we do next?"

"I'm going off grid. It will take me a little while to get situated. Once I know I'm safe, I'll work on figuring out how far up the chain this corruption goes. I think I know some people I can trust to look into this, but I need to make sure they're not susceptible to manipulation before I contact them."

"Makes sense. I'll cover my tracks as well."

"No need."

"What do you mean?"

Whalert paused for a moment. "Look, I should apologize for not taking you seriously when you were trying to tell me something weird was going on with this case."

"I never said it straight out." Luke had hinted to his

boss that he suspected an unusual number of their super-visors were invested in the case, but he'd never actually told him he thought the covert labs had been operating as long as they had because someone within the agency—shit, within the government—was supporting them.

"You were clear enough." Whalert cleared his throat. "I owe you an apology, but maybe the fact that I listened on some level will make up for that. I started separating your cover identity from a lot of the official records. It didn't take much, since DTU operates under the radar anyway and is on a separate IT infrastructure. But I did enough so that this morning I only had to run a few com-puter routines to separate your undercover identity from your real identity. Luke Holden no longer exists in any bureau records, but his official paperwork is still valid."

"I don't know what to say." He was stunned both by the audacity of his boss's action—who knew how many laws he had just broken—and the brilliance of his plan-ning. What had happened to the stuffy office guy who insisted on the wisdom of following procedures?

"You don't have to say anything. It's not a foolproof plan, but it should buy us enough time so we don't have to worry about anyone coming after you immediately. I even doctored Broden's report in the Denver office's records."

"That makes things easier on this end. Do you still want me to meet up with Kraus tomorrow to see what that connection is?"

"Yes, dig around in whatever that shithead is up to. I have a hunch he's the key to a lot of this." Whalert paused. "I'm heading closer your way."

"Okay." If his boss had shared that much about his new location, he must trust Luke at least a little.

"Ditch this phone," Whalert continued. "We'll communicate in safe areas online until I can set up a safe phone connection again. Use DTU code modification." The Domestic Terrorist Unit had developed code words no other agencies were aware of. No electronic or written records of the encryption key were stored. Each new agent learned and memorized the code when a senior agent taught it to them.

"How will I know where on the Net to find you?"

"You'll get an invitation you can't miss." Whalert chuckled. "Anything new with your target?"

Luke hesitated. Talking about Astrid somehow seemed disloyal. A completely irrational feeling, but there it was. "I found the connection between her and Naya Brisbane."

"Spill."

Luke summarized how Naya's fiancé was the leader of the group and how they all lived in the same mansion.

"Sounds like a cult," Whalert said.

"They function more like law enforcement than a cult." Luke paused for a breath. "Actually, they're very much like soldiers. I definitely get the warrior vibe from all of them."

"If they're operating within our borders, they must work with some branch of the U.S. military."

"That's just it. Leif says they're a sovereign nation and have diplomatic immunity."

"What, like some sort of Native American ambassadors? That doesn't even make sense."

"I know. I'll have to do some more digging. I'm invited to Naya and Leif's wedding the day after tomorrow."

"Weddings are excellent opportunities to make friends."

Luke doubted he'd become friends with any of the other guys if they were at all like Ulf and Leif. It was more likely they'd all get drunk and brawl. "I'll try my best. There's more." He told Whalert about the women kidnapped by the wolverines.

"If there's a human-trafficking connection and someone within our government is involved, they will want this covered up." He cursed under his breath. "And why haven't you told me about these wolverine freaks before?"

"I figured you'd have me committed to a room with padded walls."

Whalert laughed, but it was more bitter than joyful. "Probably. But at this point, my eyes are opened to all kinds of depravities and weird shit. So you think these creatures are genetically engineered."

Luke nodded and then realized his boss couldn't see. "Yes." He almost told Whalert about growing up in one of the covert labs and what it had done to his brother, but keeping quiet about that part of his life was too ingrained.

"We need to stop this. You find out more about what the Scandinavians are doing and how they are connected to these creatures. See if Kraus is somehow involved. I'll work on flushing out who in the government is covering for these fuckers." He paused. "Could we use Leif and his troops as allies? If they're fighting the wolverines, it seems like we have a common enemy."

"I don't know enough about them to be able to answer that yet." Although, there was no way Astrid would be an ally once she figured out how much he'd kept from her. Ulf had pointed out that Astrid was quite capable of killing him. She'd probably choose a very slow and painful method.

They ended the conversation, and Luke destroyed the phone he'd used. That would be his last link to Luke Hager for a while. He'd only have to worry about being Holden now. At this point, he wasn't sure how separate the two identities actually were. Meeting Astrid had a lot to do with why he preferred being Luke Holden.

His other phone dinged the signal for incoming email, and he checked his inbox. A message welcomed him to his new membership in the Hair Club for Men.

Whalert had a sick sense of humor.

# Chapter 18

FLOWER GARLANDS WERE STUPID, ASTRID DECIDED AS she tried to get the stalk of a rose to bend and attach to some twine. She'd never been into girlie stuff, other than her love of luxury bath products and lotions. Why did Naya need flowers all the way down the aisle? Just a few at the front by the altar would have been plenty. The wedding was tomorrow, and there was no way Astrid would get all these freaking roses to cooperate in time for the ceremony. The florist had told them they could put up the flowers the day before, since they would keep in the cool temperatures of the spring nights. She'd been miffed Leif wouldn't let her and her crew on the premises but reluctantly gave the Vikings the instructions.

A large tent had been erected in the meadow behind the fortress, and by keeping it closed, they'd protect the flowers from any late-spring frost. The flowers had to be sprayed with water this evening and then again in the morning to look fresh and dewy. A lot of effort for a bunch of prickly weeds. Luckily, Astrid didn't need to be involved beyond trying to wrestle the stems into garlands. Irja and Torvald would be on water-spraying duty. Torvald loved flowers. Who would have guessed?

Leif and Naya would say their vows on Walpurgis Night, the traditional Norse celebration of spring and the beginning of new life. Astrid had always loved the celebration, especially the giant bonfires that were lit at dusk. After a long winter, seeing nature wake up to spring made everything seem possible. What better timing for the king and queen to celebrate their new life together as a married couple? All the warriors had enjoyed collecting wood into a giant pile in the meadow behind the fortress. Astrid looked forward to lighting it. Maybe Naya would let her throw some of the rose garlands into the flames. The thought made her smile, and she twisted the rose stem one last time and forced it in place.

Thinking about marriage made Astrid's thoughts stray to Luke. The *själsfrände* bond had forced them together, but were their feelings strong enough to sustain a relationship? Somewhere deep inside, no matter how disappointed she'd been in love in the past, she'd always wanted what Naya and Leif had. Though their relationship had been rocky in the beginning. At one point, Naya had run away from Leif and the warriors because the pressure of the forced connection was too much. That damn bond.

Astrid had been furious and hurt when Naya left, but now she understood better. Were her own feelings for Luke real, or was the bond manipulating her into a relationship—a marriage—she wasn't emotionally ready for? This must be what brides of arranged marriages felt like. And she still had to explain to Luke that the Norse handfasting ritual needed to be completed or Astrid's life in the human realm would be over. No biggie.

A rose thorn pricked her finger, jarring her thoughts off the depressing path they'd been heading down. She sucked her finger and looked up to find Scott standing in front of her, a crooked smile on his face. Freya's fury, either he had ninja stealth like Sten, or she'd been so wrapped up in her own head that she'd actually allowed him to sneak up on her. That hadn't happened in centuries.

Damn the *själsfrände* bond and damn Luke.

One or both would be the death of her.

"You take these flowers seriously," Scott said. "I had to say your name twice before you looked up."

She grimaced. "Sorry, I have a lot on my mind." If the rose hadn't pricked her finger, he may still be standing there hollering at her.

"I can tell." He looked at her hand, where the lines outlining the serpent's tail were contrasting more and more against her skin.

She frowned. Did Scott know about the bond? Naya must have told him when she explained her relationship with Leif. Astrid lowered her hand and pulled her sleeve down to cover the markings. "What can I do for you?" She liked the queen's brother. Their time together in the car had been pleasant. Scott explained he had passed his time in the clinic catching up on pop culture, so they'd chatted about movies and TV shows. He'd also had a lot of questions about Naya and how she fit in with the Vikings and Valkyries. Compared to that lively conversation, he seemed more subdued and maybe a little sad today.

"I'm trying to find something to do." He smiled that crooked smile again. "I'm not very useful around here. It's taking a toll on my ego."

Astrid laughed. "I imagine most of the men in the house feel that way right now. There doesn't seem to be much need for brawn now that we've finished the woodpile for the bonfire." She looked him over. He had

Naya's coloring, that midnight black hair and eyes so dark they were almost violet. But he was much taller than his sister, at least six foot two, and his hair was a mess of curls while Naya's fell straight as a cascading waterfall. With broad shoulders and sinewy muscles, his body didn't show any of the sickness that had kept him bedridden for years.

Something sad passed in Scott's eyes. "It's more than that. I truly don't belong here."

"Of course you do. You're Naya's brother. You're the queen's blood. How could you not belong?"

"But that doesn't describe me, just my function. How do you truly know what kind of man I am? You only know the circumstances of my birth. How do you know you can trust me?"

Astrid knew better than most that the role into which you were born didn't dictate who you chose to be. "It's more than that," she hedged, not finding the exact words to describe why he was automatically accepted. "You mean everything to Naya and she means everything to us, so you are one of us automatically."

Scott picked up one of the roses and fingered its petals. "Maybe my sister doesn't know me as well as she thinks." He flung the rose on the floor. "I don't know who I am. I've never lived outside an institution. I don't know what real life is."

Astrid looked down at the flower and then up at Scott. "If you're going to mangle the decorations, at least you can do so by helping me attach the little suckers to these garlands." She smiled to soften her words. Scott was having some sort of existential crisis, but she wasn't great at giving advice or comfort.

"Sorry." He gave her a sheepish grin, collected another flower from one of the buckets, and added it to the garland in just a few seconds.

"How did you do that so quickly?"

Scott gave her a puzzled look. "I just used the little fasteners." He pointed to some plastic clips hanging off the twine.

Astrid muttered a few choice swear words under her breath. The section she'd started on didn't have fasteners. She moved some over to her part of the twine and started to add flowers. Now that she didn't have to bend the stems into figure eights, the job went much quicker.

They worked in silence for a few moments. "I understand what you're dealing with," Astrid said.

Scott looked up. "How so?"

She avoided looking at him. "I grew up in a very controlled environment." She stopped, searching for words. "I couldn't decide my own schedule. Someone else was in charge of when I ate, when I trained, when I slept." She shot him a look.

Scott nodded. "You felt powerless, like you weren't your own person, just a function of someone else's life."

"Exactly." It had been much worse than that. She'd also felt worthless, as if she deserved the degrading treatment. For a while, she'd believed her low status gave the others the right to treat her like shit. But she wasn't going to share that with Scott. She didn't share that with anyone.

"How did you reclaim your life? How did you figure out who you truly are?"

"I didn't." Astrid shrugged. "I was so messed up there wasn't a chance in Valhalla I'd be able to do that."

Scott's eyes widened. "This is not helping. Please tell me you figured out how to deal with that situation without having to spend years in therapy."

She laughed. "I didn't see a shrink, but after some time I figured out who I *wanted* to be. Once that was clear, I set out to become that person." A succinct summary that skipped over years of self-destructive behavior and bad choices, but Scott didn't need to know that. He had Naya to help him through. Hopefully, his journey would not include the truly fucked-up episodes that had been on Astrid's path to self-awareness.

Scott smiled and moved as if to answer, but then focused on something behind her. His face displayed such naked yearning that Astrid's breath caught. She turned and saw Irja walking toward them. Well, wasn't that an interesting development. Scott and Irja.

"The garlands look great," the dark-haired Valkyrie said when she caught up with them.

"Thanks, I had some help." Astrid snuck a quick peek at Scott, but his facial expression had gone completely blank.

"I didn't do much," he offered. "Mostly chatted her ear off."

Irja turned to Scott. "I've come to steal you away for physical therapy."

Scott dropped the flowers he was holding back into their bucket with more force than necessary. "Of course you have. I'm the invalid whose body doesn't work right."

Irja took a step back. "Your doctor said to continue the physical therapy you'd started in the clinic. I didn't mean to—"

"I know. You mean well and are just helping." Scott

stomped off in the direction of the fortress. "Everybody is just helping and wants what's best for me."

Irja turned to Astrid. Hurt flickered in her eyes. "What was that about?"

"Don't worry about it." Astrid squeezed her shoulder. "His Y chromosome is making him feel inadequate because he's not out marauding." She watched Scott as he walked away from them. "The guy has more in common with our Norse men than he thinks."

"What?" Irja shook her head. "Never mind, I don't think I want to know." She looked around the tent. "This is going to be beautiful."

"Sure." Astrid shrugged.

Irja smiled. "I forgot that you're not into flowers." She turned serious again. "Your Holden sent an email, recommending a safe house for the women we rescued."

"He's not mine."

Irja quirked an eyebrow and looked pointedly at Astrid's left hand. "I would argue he is."

Astrid sighed but decided not to get into it. "Fine. What safe house? Why is he emailing you?" That last question came out more petulant than she'd intended, but Irja just smiled.

"He sent it to all three of us—you, me, and Naya. He knows of an organization that works with refugees who have experienced trauma. I called them, and they said they have space for all five of our guests."

Astrid hesitated. She recognized that the women couldn't stay at the fortress, but after what they'd been through, she didn't want to move them so soon, didn't want them to feel abandoned. They needed to be seen as people, not victims or property. The assholes who had

abducted them had microchipped them. As if they were
pets. Astrid had helped Irja remove the trackers from
under their skin. She swallowed the anger rising in her
chest. "What do we know about this organization?"

"Naya checked them out, and they do good work.
They can offer counseling and other services we're not
qualified to give and do not have experience with." If the
queen had screened them, that meant she'd done an extensive review through official and not-so-official channels.

"At least let me say good-bye to them." Astrid had
spent a lot of time with Camila. Although the young
woman still wouldn't—probably couldn't—share the
details of what had happened during her captivity,
they'd talked about other things. Camila was older than
she looked. She'd been a senior in college, studying
prelaw. She'd been abducted one night as she walked
across campus from the library to her dorm.

"You'll definitely have that chance. Naya wants you
to drive them there. She's busy with wedding stuff, and
I'm supposed to work with Scott." She looked toward
the fortress, a frown marring her forehead. "Unless he's
decided to skip today's session."

Astrid would much rather drive the women into town
than deal with whatever complicated situation Scott and
Irja had landed themselves in. Although Irja seemed
clueless, so maybe Scott was the only one who had to
come to terms with his feelings. Whatever. As long as
she didn't have to deal with it, she was happy.

Driving. Women. Clear and uncomplicated, just the
way Astrid preferred her life to be.

"Oh," Irja said. "Leif doesn't want any of us out on
our own, so you're to take Ulf with you."

Mother of Valkyries. That threw uncomplicated way out the window.

———·∿∿∿·———

Astrid was impressed. Ulf had managed not to utter a single sarcastic or nasty word to her during their entire outbound trip. That was mostly because he hadn't actually said anything while he drove the black Escalade through the streets of Pine Rapids. Not that Astrid blamed him.

He'd already been in the driver's seat when the women entered the car. In an attempt to lessen their anxiety, he'd said a few words in Spanish and given them a gentle smile. They'd shrunk back in terror. After that he'd kept his silence, his jaw clenching tighter and tighter as he drove. He'd stayed in the car while Astrid escorted the women to their rooms and spoke with the organization's personnel. She'd given each of the women a prepaid cell phone with hers, Irja's, and Naya's numbers preprogrammed. Camila especially had promised to stay in touch.

Now that Astrid and Ulf were on their way back, she braced herself for the eruption of anger that was bound to happen in five, four, three…

"I'm glad we killed those fucking monsters at the farm, but I want to get the fuckers in charge." Ulf turned to her briefly before focusing on the road again. "They don't deserve to live after treating women like that."

She murmured her agreement. It didn't matter what she said. Ulf was on a rant, so he wasn't really looking for input.

His hand hit the steering wheel. "They treated them like cattle. Like they were worth nothing."

She swallowed the lump forming in her throat. Ulf's words hit a little bit too close to home. As if he knew she'd become emotional, he quieted down for a moment. "Nobody deserves that," he said in a lower voice. He didn't look at her, and they continued their car ride in silence.

The silence grew denser and more loaded as Astrid slowly realized that Ulf wasn't looking at her because he *knew* this was personal for her. But that was impossible. She hadn't even told Naya or Irja. "How did you find out and what do you know?"

Ulf ran his hand across his close-cropped hair. "I don't know details. When we drove him home, Holden said the abducted women hit you hard because you'd been in a similar situation in the past." He turned to her, his eyes kind. "Knowing you'd been a shield maiden, Leif and I put two and two together. We figured you'd been a thrall and earned your freedom by fighting."

Great, now the king knew about her screwed-up beginnings too. She swallowed. "I'd appreciate it if you kept this to yourself."

Ulf frowned. "There's no shame in who you were, and even less in who you became. I've fought with plenty of warriors who started out as property and became freemen by fighting for their master."

She could only nod. The lump in her throat blocked any words from passing her lips.

He hit the steering wheel again. "But none of them had to put up with the abuse the women we rescued did. You have to be a sick fucker to do that to another person. Why would anyone do that?"

Astrid cleared her throat. "There is a lot of money to be made in human trafficking. And if the scum get caught, the law punishes them less than if they were running drugs or guns."

"That blows. We need to—" Ulf stomped on the brake and threw the car in reverse.

"What the hell are you doing?" Astrid held on to the dashboard with both hands.

"There are wolverines in that alley." He threw her a manic grin. "Feel like kicking some ass?"

"Hell yeah." After the journey down memory lane and seeing once again the emotional scars the Mexican women were struggling with, Astrid had all kinds of aggression she'd like to work out. And what better way than to unleash some of that anger on Loki's minions?

Ulf slowly steered the SUV down the alley with the headlights turned off. "This is a dead end. If we park, we can corral them on foot."

They closed the car doors soundlessly and headed down the alley. The lights on the buildings surrounding them were placed too high to light the ground properly. Astrid concentrated on avoiding stumbling on cracks in the asphalt. She tapped into the connection with her berserker, asking the beast to look for the Asgard glow that always surrounded the wolverines. There was more than one presence up ahead.

Past a large brick building, the alley expanded into a parking lot. Ulf and Astrid crouched by the alley wall, surveying the open space. Two wolverines hoisted a large box onto a loading dock. A nondescript sedan with an open trunk was parked close by.

Astrid tapped Ulf's shoulder and put a finger up to her mouth. They both had guns, but the noise might attract people or cops. Plus, shooting the bastards wouldn't let her work out her issues. She palmed two knives from the special sheaths underneath her coat. Ulf picked up a piece of rebar from the ground and whistled.

The two wolverines turned around, and their eerie black eyes caught the weak light filtering down from an overhead lamp. Astrid shuddered. No matter how many times she saw their dead eyes, they still freaked her out.

"Come here, little wolvies," she said.

The wolverines hissed, and their claws popped out. They looked at each other for a brief moment and then nodded.

Astrid balanced on the balls of her feet, ready for their attack. She didn't have to wait long. The creatures rushed them, and she released her daggers. But instead of coming straight at them as she had anticipated, the monsters split up and ran up half the height of the walls. Her blades missed, and the creatures ran past her and Ulf before they continued down the alley at an inhuman speed.

"Come on," Ulf shouted and ran after them, gripping the rebar in his left hand.

"Wait," Astrid said. "Something isn't right about this. They want us to chase them."

Ulf stopped and jogged back toward her. "You're right. Let's check out what's in the building."

They crossed the parking lot and made their way up the stairs. It didn't take them long to disable the lock on the metal door at the end of the loading dock. Astrid fell into the familiar pattern of backing up Ulf as he entered ahead of her. On the other side was a long, narrow hallway. Nighttime low lighting cast ghostly green shadows as they moved down the corridor. Both of them drew their guns.

The building had an abandoned feeling, but Astrid still scanned for more of Loki's creatures by again tapping into the connection with her berserker. The beast stirred, but didn't go into battle alert the way it would if any of the monsters had been around.

*Safe*, it whispered and Astrid shuddered. She still wasn't used to that part of her speaking. "You detect any Asgard essence?" she asked Ulf.

"No," he answered in a low voice. "But there could be human unfriendlies. We have no idea who the wolverines are working with."

Astrid nodded and then realized he probably couldn't see her well in the low light. "True."

The hallway ended at two double doors. Ulf slowly twisted one handle and found it unlocked. The door swung open on quiet hinges, revealing a cavernous darkness. A low electrical humming reached Astrid's ears. She looked closer and could make out large darker shapes.

"What the hell is this place?" Ulf asked.

"I have no idea." Astrid felt along the wall. Her fingers found a light switch, and she flipped it. Bright overhead spotlights illuminated a big warehouse. A group of large cages were clustered in the middle, and weird-looking refrigerators lined one of the walls. Hospital gurneys waited outside the cages, and further into the room, curtains divided sections into what looked like ER examination areas. Astrid walked up to one of them and pulled apart the curtains. She found a gynecological examination chair, complete with stirrups. She turned to Ulf. "I have a really bad feeling about this."

"No kidding." He looked at the cage and then the

chair. "Let's take some pictures and then get the hell out of here. Irja will know what all this stuff is for."

Astrid didn't argue, but she had a pretty good idea what this creepy place was. All that was missing was Doctor Frankenstein. She kept the grip on her gun and pulled out her phone with the other hand to snap several pictures of the chair, the weird refrigerators, and the cages.

"What the fuck?" Ulf growled.

Astrid looked up. He was staring at her left hand.

Mother of Valkyries, she'd forgotten all about the serpent tail. There was nothing she could say, so she braced herself and returned Ulf's hard gaze as it shifted from her hand to her face. Anger blazed in his eyes, and something else. Hurt? She swallowed.

"Holden," Ulf spit out.

She nodded even though he hadn't phrased it as a question.

"Why?" He took a step toward her. "How could you?" His nostrils flared as his berserker rose to the surface.

She stood her ground, but her inner warrior wanted to answer the challenge.

*Fight*, it growled.

"It's not like I had a choice," Astrid said. "The bond happened on its own. Ask Leif or Naya."

"Don't you dare compare your sordid affair to their relationship," Ulf hissed. "And you did have a choice. You should have stayed out of his bed." He spit on the floor, threw down the rebar, and walked toward the door. As he reached the exit, he flipped off the lights and slammed the door behind him.

Astrid stared at the small beam of light the screen

of her phone provided. That could have gone so much better. And now that Ulf knew about the *själsfrände* bond, it was only a matter of time before he told the rest of the warriors. She'd thought dealing with their pent-up testosterone before was a challenge, but this would make things so much worse.

Mother of Valkyries, the wedding was the next day.

The queen really didn't need Astrid's messed-up situation ruining her day. Somehow Astrid needed to convince Ulf to keep quiet for another twenty-four hours.

Using her phone as a light, she ran after him, only to reach an empty parking lot. The shithead had taken the Escalade and left her stranded.

He was going to pay for that.

She debated calling one of the other warriors for a ride, but then she'd have to explain why she needed one. And either way, she wouldn't catch up with Ulf before he blabbered the news all over the fortress. Better to stay low for a while.

They still needed to get what they discovered to Irja though. Astrid typed out an email on her phone and attached the pictures before sending them to the Finnish Valkyrie.

Her next step was to find Holden. It was way past time for the two of them to talk.

She needed to prepare him for the testosterone overload he would now face at the wedding.

# Chapter 19

LUKE POURED HIMSELF TWO FINGERS OF LAGAVULIN and sipped the smoky single-malt whiskey as he walked to the windows to watch the nighttime view. His apartment was on the top floor. It was a converted loft, all open plan, with one entire wall made out of windows. He was strangely proud of the fact that as his alter ego Holden, he made enough completely legal money to pay for the place. None of the money-laundering profits were spent on his living expenses. All that currency went into a special bank account. The plan had been for the Domestic Terrorist Unit to claim the funds eventually, but now that Whalert was in hiding, Luke had no idea what would happen.

He watched the streets below and felt far removed from the busy traffic. The apartment was a sanctuary. Here he could relax and just be himself, whoever that was. Astrid had him all confused about how much of himself he wanted to share with her.

He focused on his own reflection in the window as he took another sip of the single malt. He might have to remain in Holden's persona forever, unless Whalert found a way to flush out the corruption within the DTU. There had been no word from his boss—his former boss. Luke had spent hours trolling discussion forums on the Hair Club for Men website. He now knew way too much about male pattern baldness, but there had been no messages from Whalert. And he really needed to get in touch with the guy.

Luke had met with Kraus earlier in the day under the pretext of offering money-laundering services through the nightclub. The FBI/DTU file on Kraus revealed him to be one sick dude who basically did anything, no matter how illegal or how despicable, as long as there was a big payout in the end. There were several indicators that he was involved in human trafficking, but no concrete proof. Luke's instincts told him there was no way that Kraus showing up in Pine Rapids at the same time as the abducted Mexican nationals was a coincidence.

He thought back to the conversation he'd had with Astrid. She'd tried to cover up how upset she was, but he could tell the women's situation got to her. Luke had to nail Kraus for Astrid's sake.

Christ.

The woman had him so twisted up that he couldn't even remember the main goal of his mission. He downed the rest of the whiskey.

He wasn't doing this job to please a woman. He was doing it for Donovan. He needed to remember that. His dick needed to remember that.

The problem was, he couldn't stop thinking about Astrid. It hadn't even been twenty-four hours since he last saw her, and he already missed her. And it wasn't just the physical aspect. He missed their verbal sparring. Her quick mind forced him to up his game. He raked his fingers through his hair.

The only way he'd navigate this without losing his mind was to come up with a way to avenge Donovan while protecting Astrid. He wasn't deluding himself into thinking there would be a happily ever after for him, but when the shit finally came down, she needed to be spared as much hurt as he could manage. He owed her that.

He turned from the view and walked back to the whiskey bottle. It would take more than one glass of the amber liquid to get to sleep tonight.

A knock on the door made him pause as he was about to pour. He put the bottle down and reached for his gun. The doorman was not supposed to let anyone up without notifying Luke first. He undid the weapon's safety and placed himself to the side of the door frame. A quick dart-and-look through the peephole showed him his visitor was no threat. To his sanity maybe, but hopefully she wouldn't shoot him. He opened the door. "This is a pleasant surprise." He kept his tone neutral.

Astrid strode in. Her eyebrows shot up when she noticed the gun in his hand. "Paranoid much?"

"The doorman is supposed to notify me of guests." He tucked the gun into the back of his pants. "Is he still alive?"

She tsked. "I didn't touch your precious doorman. He was in the back looking for an umbrella when I snuck by."

"It's not raining."

"I may have told him I left an umbrella in your lobby the other day." She moved past him. "This is nice. I like the view." The moon shining through the windows highlighted her glorious hair. Luke's fingers curled as he remembered running them through the silky strands.

"Are you here for a reason?" His voice came out gruffer than he'd intended.

She turned around, her eyes wide with pretend innocence. "Can't a girl visit her…lover without an ulterior motive?" On the word *lover* she blushed, and his groin tightened. Astrid was an enigma. Would she ever trust him enough for him to figure out who she really was?

He put the thought out of his mind immediately. Their relationship was short term. There would be no figuring out. "A different girl maybe. With you, there's always a hidden agenda." Hurt flashed briefly in her eyes before she blinked and looked away.

He felt like scum.

She turned her back to him, once again looking out the windows. "Yeah, you're right." Her shoulders slumped. The gesture of defeat made him feel even lower. Astrid pushed a curl of hair behind her ear. She had a new tattoo on the back of her hand, but he couldn't make out the design. "We need to talk," she said.

Luke sighed. Those were his least favorite words. He walked back to the still-open bottle and finished pouring his drink. "Can I get you one?"

"Sure."

He retrieved another glass and poured her drink. As he handed it to her, her fingers briefly touched his. A great calm flooded his senses. It startled him to the point of fumbling the glass. Astrid's quick reflexes saved it from dropping to the floor.

What the hell was that? Some sort of psychic connection? To hide his discomfort, he gestured toward the pair of brown leather couches in front of the flat-screen TV. "Sit?" He didn't wait for her answer before heading over.

She sat down across from him, looking down at the

drink she was cradling in both hands. "This is going to sound very crazy." She took a sip of whiskey and looked out the windows again. He admired her profile. She was beautiful, but what made her irresistible was the incredible inner strength she possessed.

"Try me," he said gently. His phone rang, and he fished it out of his pocket. Kraus's name showed up on the display. He'd deal with that lowlife later. He hit Ignore and threw the phone on the table. "Sorry about that. Just business. It can wait."

She threw him a weak smile and took another drink. Squaring her shoulders, she held out her left hand. He looked down at the new tattoo, admiring the intricate ink shaped like a large V with the tip curved toward her little finger. "So, this happens when someone in my culture is handfasted—or engaged, I guess you'd call it."

The bolt of jealousy striking his chest rendered him speechless. She'd gotten engaged.

Fuck that.

He stood. And then paced, his anger a tangible thing between them. He had to distance himself from her. He walked over to the kitchen area again and held on to the counter.

Three days ago, she'd fucked him in the shower like he was the only man in the world for her. And then she got engaged to someone else? She'd even stopped off to celebrate the event with some kind of traditional Scandinavian tattoo?

He ran a palm across his face. She must have been seeing this guy while she was fucking Luke. "Who?" he forced out between clenched jaws.

She frowned. "What?"

"Who the fuck are you engaged to? Ulf?" He turned around to face her and lowered his voice to a growl. "I knew that asswipe was trouble." He walked toward her. "Does he know how good I make you feel in bed?" He clenched his fists to keep from reaching out for her. To haul her up against him and show her who she should be with.

"Holy Mother of Valkyries." She put the glass down on the coffee table and shoved her hair away from her face. "I'm not handfasted to Ulf."

"Then who?"

She stood, her mane of blond hair cascading down her back, her green eyes blazing. "You," she shouted. "I'm handfasted to you."

Luke completely deflated. His knees buckled, and he had to grab the back of the couch to keep from hitting the floor. "What? How?" he gasped.

Astrid cursed under her breath. "Sit down," she ordered. He sank back down on the couch. It was apparently her turn to pace. "I knew this was going to be impossible to explain," she muttered. She stopped suddenly and took a deep breath. "When one of us—when one of my people—meets the person they are destined to be with, this freaking tattoo shows up on the back of the hand. Eventually, it will work its way up the arm to meet the serpent head."

His brain was trying to switch to a channel that would help him understand what she was saying. "When did you get this new tattoo?" He cringed at the stupid question, but being engaged without realizing it was a shock. The fact that he'd even been able to form proper words was a fucking miracle.

"I didn't *get* the tattoo. The lines appear automatically." She sunk down on the couch across from him again. "Look, this is weird. I get that." Her eyes pleaded with him. "But if you think about it, it's not that much weirder than human wolverine hybrids."

The creatures they'd fought he could deal with. Those were nothing but genetically manipulated freaks. A self-generating engagement tattoo was way worse. "How do you know I'm the guy and not one of the dudes you live with?"

She jerked back, hurt flashing in her eyes again. "Because I'm not sleeping with any of them." As much as he felt like a jerk—again—her words released some of the tension in his chest. And that was just beyond fucked up. Astrid stood. "This was a bad idea. I should leave."

Luke leaned forward and grabbed her wrist. That same eerie calm flooded through him. He pulled her down next to him. "Don't go." He looked into her eyes. The feral creature he'd seen peeking out from behind her gaze before was back. This time, it took its time looking him over before Astrid blinked and it was gone. Somehow the encounter didn't disturb him. It was just another one of the many facets that made up Astrid. "I reacted badly, but this is a bit of a shock. I wasn't planning on getting engaged."

She pulled her hand back, a bitter smile on her lips. "Yeah, I get that." She studied her fingernails. "This is not exactly what I planned for either, but there's nothing I can do about it. When it happens, you can't stop it."

Okay, that made no sense. "Do you want to stop it?" And that question made even less sense.

Startled, she looked up. "What are you asking?"

Fuck if he knew, but his addled brain kept on trekking in the same direction. "Do you *want* to be with me?"

Lines appeared between her eyes as she looked at him. "I don't know. Do you want to be with me?"

Hell yes, but that wasn't a choice. He grabbed her hand. "I can't guarantee any kind of stability or offer any long-term commitment." She tried to pull her hand back, but he held on. "But yes, there is no one I want to be with as much as I want to be with you." Luke gazed into her eyes again, trying to convey all the things he didn't have the right to say. "I can't get enough of you. Astrid, I crave you when you're not next to me."

Her breath hitched, and the hand he was holding clenched around his fingers. With her other hand, she traced his jaw. Instead of the calming effect from before, her fingers left a blazing hot trail on his skin. He groaned, which made her smile. "I can't get enough of you either," she whispered.

Luke grabbed her roaming hand and brought both to his chest. She fell forward, and he leaned in to claim her lips. With a soft sigh, she parted hers and he traced the bottom part of her mouth with his tongue. She groaned, sinking into the kiss, but he held back and continued exploring her lips with soft licks and nips. She tasted like honey and home.

Astrid moaned and tugged on her hands, but he held on. This was his show. After the tumult she'd put him through, he needed to be in control. He tortured her for a few moments longer. Not until she growled and caught his lip between her teeth did he deepen the kiss. She met him thrust for thrust, and he let go of her hands to bury his fingers in her hair. The strands were as soft as he remembered. He fucking loved her hair. Pushing it back from her face, he positioned her head at a better angle and took complete control.

She was his now. She'd said so. This handfasting thing meant she belonged to him, and he wanted— needed—her to show him it was true.

Without removing his lips from hers, Luke pushed her back until she was lying on the couch. He trapped her beneath him, using the weight of his body to immobilize her. He wasn't sure what he wanted to prove, just knew he needed to be the one who took the lead, needed his body to touch all of hers.

Astrid freed her hands from where they'd been trapped between them. One palmed the back of his neck, while the other traveled lower and grabbed just below his ass. Her fingers dug into his inner thigh as she pulled on his leg so that his dick pressed right at the junction of her thighs. He came close to shooting his load early when her softness pushed against his hard ridge.

Luke growled, capturing both her hands in his again and pushing them up above her head. "My rules," he rasped in her ear and trailed his tongue down her neck to just above her collarbone.

She sighed, her whole body sinking back into the couch. He shifted her wrists to his left hand and used the right to unbutton her black cotton shirt. As each button popped open, revealing more delicious skin, he trailed his tongue lower.

Her bra was a front-closure, praise the powers, and he released her breasts so he could taste them too. Her golden skin was warm to the touch, and he took his time sucking and biting each areola. Astrid writhed beneath him.

"Let me touch you," she whimpered.

He didn't bother answering, just tightened his grip on her wrists and used his other hand to unbutton her jeans. Luke struggled with the zipper but was finally able to slip his hand inside her panties. She inhaled sharply as his fingers found her wet folds. He pushed his finger deeper while continuing his tongue's worship of her breasts. Her legs moved apart, and a moan escaped her lips.

Luke set a steady rhythm, matching what his fingers did with kisses and nips on her nipples. He caught one of them between his teeth while he curled his fingers inside her, pressing down on her mound with the heel of his hand.

Astrid shattered beneath him. She shouted his name—his first name—and her core clenched around his fingers. He felt ridiculously pleased.

She went limp and he scooped her up in his arms, carrying her to his bed. She put one hand behind his neck while her head fell against his shoulder. "Dang, Luke, you have very talented hands." Her voice was several octaves deeper than usual.

He chuckled and put her down on top of his covers. "We're not done yet. That was just the appetizer," he whispered against her ear, taking great delight in how she shuddered when his breath caressed her skin. He quickly shucked his clothes. Astrid leaned back on her elbows, watching him while he undressed. She bit her lower lip. It was sexy as hell, and Luke's already rod-straight shaft hardened even more. "Lose the clothes," he ordered.

She gave him a coy look, but shrugged out of the shirt and bra. He pulled off her boots and tugged on her jeans. She wiggled her hips to help him. As she lay naked on his bed, he paused to admire her strong body. She had the muscular definition of a fighter, a warrior, but with curves in all the right places. "Beautiful," he whispered.

She sat up and scooted toward the edge of the bed where he was standing. Grabbing his hips, she pulled him closer. The tip of her tongue shot out, tasting the tip of his dick. His breath hitched.

Astrid encircled the base of his shaft with her hand and lowered her mouth over the head. He'd never seen anything as erotic as her hot, wet lips gliding down the length of his dick as she swallowed him whole. She sucked hard and cupped his balls.

He had to concentrate to not expire on the spot. His head fell back, and he grabbed a handful of her blond curls to hold on as she slowly pulled her mouth back to release him, only to swallow him again and again. His balls pulled up and she squeezed them gently.

He growled and broke out in a sweat from the effort of not blowing his load in her mouth. He tugged her head back by her hair.

The vixen grinned at him, eyes glittering from behind her lowered lashes.

He vowed payback and grabbed her arms to push her back on the bed. Astrid had other ideas and rolled over on her stomach, looking at him across her shoulder. She kept eye contact as she slowly pushed herself up on knees and elbows. Her sultry gaze and that glorious ass in the air had him hyperventilating.

He rushed to the nightstand and grabbed a foil package,

which he ripped open using his teeth. The silicon glided
down his dick in a weak echo of where Astrid's lips had
been. As soon as he had sheathed himself, he kneeled
behind her. He grabbed her hips and paused, waiting for
a sign that this was still okay with her. She touched the
top of her lip with her tongue and nodded.

With one deep thrust, he buried himself fully inside
her gloriously wet sheath.

She groaned as he pulled out and then moaned his
name when he pushed in again. He tried to keep a slow
pace, but she pushed back against him, meeting his
thrusts. Astrid arched her back and he couldn't hold back.

He plunged into her over and over again, reaching
around to find her clit. He pinched it and she shattered,
screaming out her pleasure. As she convulsed around
him, he thrust one final time. The power of his release
floored him. He collapsed on the bed, taking her with
him cradled in his arms.

Like last time, he blacked out and felt as if he somehow left his body. The warm darkness engulfed him
until the dude with the crows showed up again, his body
somehow lit from within.

The guy smiled, but it wasn't a joyful expression.
"Trust the bond," he said. The crows cawed.

Luke wanted to ask him what the hell he meant, but
he was pulled by an invisible force and shoved back
into his body. He came to with a gasp and opened his
eyes to find Astrid watching him with a worried look
on her face.

"You okay?" she asked. He could only nod as he tried
to catch his breath. She rubbed the back of her hand and
frowned as she looked down. "Look," she whispered

and held up her arm. The lines on the back of her hand extended and spiraled up around her wrist, continuing over her forearm and elbow until they met the snake on her bicep. When the whole body was complete, the lines glowed in gold and then faded back to black.

Luke would have freaked out if he wasn't so exhausted. "We'll figure it out in the morning," he said, pulling Astrid closer and folding the comforter around them.

"I can't stay," she protested.

He silenced her with a kiss and tightened his embrace as sleep claimed him.

# Chapter 20

ASTRID QUIETLY CLOSED THE DOOR OF THE FORTRESS behind her. She'd caught a cab from Luke's house to the main road outside the Norse compound and then jogged through the forest. She hadn't meant to fall asleep at Luke's, but after their session in bed she'd been exhausted, and snuggling in his arms had felt safe. He felt like home. She'd never had a place she'd thought of as home. Even after living for more than a century in this mansion, she had no personal effects on the walls of her room or knickknacks on her shelves. A warrior was always ready to head out at a moment's notice. She could see herself creating a home together with Luke.

She was so screwed.

Shaking her head, she walked across the entryway to the stairs that would take her up to her bedroom. The sun's rays were barely touching the sky. She'd still be able to help Naya get ready for her big day. Maybe she'd even be able to get some sleep and grab a shower before the queen got up. She'd only made it up a few steps when she heard her name quietly spoken and turned.

The king regarded her with solemn eyes. "We need to talk."

"Yes, *min kung*." On heavy feet, she descended the stairs and followed him down the hallway to his office. She always managed to screw up a good situation. Henri had left her when she issued the ultimatum of choosing between duty or her. And now she'd messed up her relationship with the Norse warriors.

She was actually surprised it had taken this long. Leif had been lenient when she screwed up the mission to retrieve Scott, and he'd been kind when she almost got that bystander killed. She wouldn't survive this third strike though. The king would see her bond with an outsider as a betrayal.

The only thing she could hope for was that Leif would let her attend the wedding before he told her to leave. She wanted to be there for the queen and to have a chance to say good-bye. She swallowed the lump forming in her throat. She would miss Naya and Irja. They were the closest she'd ever had to sisters, to family.

Astrid followed the king into his office and then frowned when she saw Ulf, Irja, and Harald sitting in front of the king's desk. She hesitated as the king took a seat in his usual chair. She preferred no witnesses to her dismissal.

Harald jumped up and fetched another chair for her, which he plunked down between his and Irja's. Astrid thanked him and sat down. Ulf gave her a sour look, which she returned with one of her own. She'd deal with him later.

"I looked at the pictures you emailed me," Irja said.

Astrid startled. "Okay," she hedged. She shot a quick look at Ulf, but he ignored her.

"The warehouse has all the equipment needed for in vitro fertilization," Irja continued.

"Test tube babies," Harald barked.

Irja gave him an impatient look. "Yes, although that's a very outdated term. Judging by the large incubators and the gynecological examination chairs, this warehouse is going to be used as a fertilization clinic."

"Incubators?" Astrid asked. Maybe this conversation wasn't about her bond.

"The large refrigerator-looking appliances along the wall," Leif injected. "What worries me the most are the cages." He clicked the mouse in front of him and swiveled his computer monitor toward them. "These are designed for very large animals."

"Or humans," Harald said. The king looked up and nodded.

A chill spread through Astrid's body as she realized the fears that had surfaced as soon as she'd seen the examination chair in the warehouse were true. "The women from Mexico," she said. "They were going to use them as surrogates."

Irja nodded. "That's what I think. All the women were in their early twenties or younger. Those are prime years for conception."

Bile rose in Astrid's throat. She swallowed loudly. Those cages had been meant for Camila and the others. As poorly treated as Astrid had been when she was a thrall, she'd never been kept in a cage. "What kind of babies are they making?"

"That's the big question," Leif said. "We've talked it over." He gestured to include the other three. "Based on how quickly these new wolverines have evolved in terms of fighting skills, they're most likely created through new methods of gene manipulation. I've been chatting online with some of the other kings to see if they've encountered similar creatures." He closed the image and brought up a map. "The Vikings in Taos,

New Mexico, have fought creatures with similar inhuman speeds and acrobatic skills, who also seem to heal abnormally fast."

Astrid sat back in her chair. Freya have mercy. It shouldn't be that big a surprise, since she'd encountered them in Colorado, which bordered New Mexico. "But we shut down the lab in North Dakota ten months ago. Wouldn't it take at least nine months to make a wolverine hybrid baby? And then they would have to grow up. These wolverines are definitely full grown."

Harald muttered something about "science shit." Irja glared at him and then turned to Astrid. "If I had a blood sample of the new wolverines, the ones we call 2.0, I'd know more. But based on the genetic makeup of the wolverines we fought ten months ago, they undergo accelerated growth at some point." She shifted some papers in her lap, which was a complete ruse. If Irja had read it, the information was logged in her head forever. "But I don't think they came from human ova. If these new wolverines do, that may be one of the factors that give them enhanced skills, at least enhanced intelligence."

"English, please," Harald said. "What the heck is an ova?"

Even Astrid knew that. "It's the term for women's eggs," she answered.

Harald blushed beet red. "Oh."

"Maybe this lab is for an even more advanced model," Ulf said. "Maybe they're making wolverines 3.0."

Alarmed, Astrid turned to Leif. "I barely held my own against two of the 2.0 models when they ambushed me. Anything more enhanced than that, and we're totally screwed."

Leif nodded. "I know. We have to destroy that lab." He rubbed his forehead. "And the New Mexico king has also asked for our help."

"Would the gods…" Ulf hesitated. "Can we take this to Odin and Freya? There must be a way we can convince the gods' council that Loki is behind this."

Leif shook his head. "Odin hasn't come to me in dreams for a while, but the power struggle in the council had worsened the last time we spoke. The demise of a few humans is of no consequence to the gods at the moment."

"What about the demise of a few immortal Vikings?" Harald muttered.

"The council prefers to pretend that we don't exist," Leif countered. "We're a pet project of Odin's and Freya's. We're not supposed to call attention to ourselves." His shoulders slumped.

"You should get some sleep," Astrid said. "Today is going to be a long day for you."

The king smiled. It transformed his face, melting away the early tiredness. "It's going to be a joyous day," he said.

Harald slammed his fist on the table. "These fucking wolverines. They're ruining our royal wedding day. Our celebration of love."

Astrid exchanged a look with Irja. Since when had Harald become a fan of weddings and love? Irja shrugged.

Leif stood. "You're right. Today is for my bride. Tomorrow we regroup and decide on a plan of action to shut down the fertility lab here in Pine Rapids. How we'll help New Mexico will be an action item for a different day completely."

"I'll see what chatter I can pick up on the Darknet before tomorrow," Ulf offered.

Leif nodded and the others stood to leave. "Not you, Astrid," he said as she headed for the door. The king sat back down in his chair.

Irja squeezed Astrid's shoulder and headed out with Ulf and Harald. The door clicked closed behind them. Astrid studied her folded hands in her lap. This was it, the moment she would be told she didn't belong and had to leave.

"Ulf will apologize to you for leaving you stranded during a mission," the king said. Once again, Astrid startled. She looked up and found Leif's ice-blue eyes studying her. "Are you alright?" the king asked. "We didn't send anyone to get you because Irja said you'd emailed that you were staying with a friend in town."

"I'm fine." She tried to look away, but his piercing gaze had her trapped. "I stayed with Luke Holden," she blurted out.

Leif closed his eyes briefly. A pained grimace twisted his face. "Of course you did. I'll never get rid of that guy." He schooled his features and captures her gaze again. "Ulf says Holden is your *själsfrände*."

Astrid nodded.

"Have you completed the bond?"

Astrid shifted in her seat and nodded again.

Leif sighed. "This is going to be challenging for you. The others accepted Naya, even though she was a mortal, but she's a woman and is handfasted to a king." Not quite sure where he was going with this, Astrid made a noncommittal noise. The queen had also saved the life of Per, one of the younger Vikings, which went a long way toward earning the respect and acceptance of the warriors. "As much as I respect and admire my warriors, they are very territorial," Leif continued and then paused for a breath. "I can be very territorial. You are our sister. It's not going to be easy accepting another man as part of your life." He smiled.

Astrid had lost all ability to speak. This was so not how she had imagined this conversation. Where was the reprimand? The blame? She mumbled something incomprehensible again.

"Have you decided where you are going to live?" Leif asked.

"Live?" she croaked.

He frowned. "It's going to take some getting used to having Holden live here at the fortress, but if that's what you want, the warriors will adjust." He sighed. "I'll adjust."

Astrid finally found her voice. "You are taking this very well. Better than I am. I'm not sure how to feel about being bonded to someone I don't really know."

Leif smiled. "Believe me, I know that feeling, but you can't plan for the bond. It's the gods' choice." He turned serious. "The important thing is whether or not it makes you happy. Are you happy, Astrid?"

A huge lump formed in Astrid's throat, and to her mortification, tears welled up in her eyes. "I'm getting there," she croaked out.

The king stood and came around the desk to sit in the chair next to hers. He grabbed her hands. "The bond can be confusing. If you need to talk, find me or Naya."

Astrid blinked to keep the tears from falling. "I will."

"Let me know what you decide about the living

situation. I'd prefer you to be here with your battle brothers and sisters, but it may be easier for the others if you lived at Holden's for a little while. Come here for meals and other social gatherings. Once the men…and I"—he shot her a quick smile—"are used to him, you two can decide if you want to live here."

She couldn't look at him. If she did, she'd be reduced to a sniveling mess. "Sure," she said. "Luke doesn't quite understand the bond or the handfasting. Making him live with a bunch of burly Vikings is probably not the best idea." She didn't even know if he wanted to move in with her, but he did seem to want some kind of commitment. He'd said he needed her, that he craved her. Warmth filled her chest.

Leif snorted. "I don't know how mortal men react when they are first bonded, but I was insanely jealous if another male as much as looked at Naya." Astrid hid her smile. The king was still insanely jealous. He'd learned to hide it better on the outside, but he usually got so caught up in the emotion that he forgot to shield his berserker's reaction. The warriors always knew when he was jealous. "What about your inner warrior?" Leif asked. "Has she calmed down?" Apparently, the king also used pronouns for the beasts.

Astrid paused for a moment and checked in with her berserker. "Yes, the berserker is easier to control. And whenever I'm close to Luke, it's almost docile."

"Good." Leif stood, pulling her up with him. "What do you say we go and get ready for a royal wedding, Valkyrie?"

"I say that sounds like an excellent plan, my king." The joy she saw on his face made her happy for him and her queen. Maybe one day, she would have what they had.

Leif pulled her in for a bear hug. "If he doesn't make you happy, you let me know," he whispered in her ear. "I'll make him sorry."

—◆◆◆—

Astrid had a big problem.

She stared at her bridesmaid's dress on the bed.

She'd managed an hour of sleep and a long shower before she started getting ready for the wedding. Irja had braided her hair, which was now kept from her face with small twists coiled around the rest of her curls to keep them in place while allowing most of them to cascade freely down her back. She felt very feminine and pretty in the hairstyle. The dress, however, was a disaster.

The flared skirt reached midthigh, and the bodice draped over only her right shoulder, leaving the left one completely bare. And she happened to have a very eye-catching tattoo swirling all down her left arm.

She sighed. The dress was the same one she'd worn to Naya's and Leif's handfasting ceremony. That's what Naya wanted. As a bride, she would wear the same white dress she'd worn too, but with the addition of a bridal crown and veil.

Astrid gnawed her bottom lip. The other warriors would take the blatant display of her tattoo as a challenge. She sank down on the bed next to the dress, trailing her fingers along the rose-colored weightless chiffon. Why did testosterone always complicate things?

She shrugged out of the robe she was wearing. The completed serpent tattoo contrasted sharply with her skin.

She twisted her arm to better see its design. Two parallel lines outlined the serpent. In between the two lines, runes and symbols formed the body. Astrid read runes better than anyone in the fortress, but these she couldn't interpret. They were either of a Norse dialect so old it had been forgotten or a language that was not Scandinavian.

The night before, when she had found her release with Luke, her spirit had left her body and traveled through a vast darkness until she'd encountered a circle of pinprick lights. Freya had appeared as a silver-haired woman in a long, white dress. Astrid had tried to speak to her, but the goddess had just smiled cryptically and stroked her cheek.

A quick knock sounded on the door, and Irja stuck her head in. "You're not dressed," she exclaimed. She wore a dress in the same color and material as the one on Astrid's bed, but it covered both shoulders and reached her midcalf.

Irja's dark hair was twisted into an elegant updo, and small wild roses of the same color as her dress were sprinkled through her hair. "We're supposed to be helping Naya by now."

"I can't wear my dress," Astrid explained.

Irja frowned. "I don't understand."

Astrid gestured to her left arm. "This is going to stand out too much."

Irja came closer and bent down to study the tattoo. "It's so beautiful." She traced the shape with her index finger. When she looked up, her eyes gleamed. "Two of our warriors have found their *själsfrände*. The odds of that are not very high."

"I didn't want this to happen."

"But now that it has, are you happy?"

Astrid smiled at Irja's unintended echo of the king's words. "I am." At least she thought she would be once Luke and she figured out what their relationship would be like. The bond required two soul mates to remain geographically close to each other. That shouldn't be too hard as long as they lived in the same city. She could keep her room here at the fortress and continue her warrior duties. Whenever possible, she'd stay at Luke's place. Maybe eventually, when they knew each other better...

She shook her head. This was too complicated to think about now.

She needed to concentrate on the wedding and then on taking down the fertility clinic. "Screw it." She stood and grabbed the dress. "Naya wants us to wear these, so that's what I'm going to do. The men are just going to have to deal."

Irja chuckled. "I think they'll be too busy glowering at Luke to notice your tattoo. How's he getting here?" Unless one of the Viking team was in the car with him, Luke wouldn't find the road to the mansion. Enchantments kept the whole place cloaked.

"I wanted to pick him up, but Leif told me to stay with Naya until the ceremony. He's sending Harald instead." She shimmied into the dress.

"That's going to be interesting." Irja smiled. "This wedding is going to be explosive one way or the other." She gestured for Astrid to turn around and then zipped up the dress.

Astrid silently agreed with her. She just hoped that the bloodshed wouldn't be blamed on her. "Let's go help Naya," she said.

Irja grabbed her hand and squeezed it as they walked out the door. "Don't worry. Everything will work out okay." She chuckled again. "Leif will keep death and dismemberment at a minimum on his wedding day. Naya would never forgive him if anyone got hurt."

That's exactly what Astrid was worried about.

# Chapter 21

LUKE ESCAPED THE SILVER SUV THAT HAD BROUGHT him to the mansion as soon as the vehicle pulled to a stop. A red-haired guy named Harald had shown up at Luke's office and informed him that he was Luke's ride to the wedding. Those had been the only civil words out of the guy's mouth. The whole ride he'd done nothing but berate Luke for taking advantage of Astrid and forcing this freaking handfasting bond on her. Had the dude met Astrid?

Nobody forced her to do anything.

Harald revved the Escalade's engine and drove off, almost crushing Luke's foot. He headed for the front door, but a dark-haired dude slipped out of the building and held up a hand. Did these Norse men come any shorter than six foot two? That was Luke's height, and except for Ulf, every one of these men looked down on him. He studied the man. He actually didn't look Scandinavian. His skin was pale, but he had eyes so dark that it was hard to see the border between the iris and the pupil. His black, straight hair was tied at the nape of his neck. His face was a more masculine version of the woman who had taken care of Luke when he was poisoned: Irja. The clothes he wore were a riot and belonged at a renaissance fair, and yet somehow the dude made them look manly.

"I'm Pekka." The guy held out a hand.

"Luke." He shook the offered hand, expecting an attempt to crush his bones, but Pekka countered with just a regular firm grip.

"I'm going to be your bodyguard since Scott is in the wedding party." Pekka smiled, but it wasn't reassuring. He looked like he would quite enjoy someone attacking Luke.

"I wasn't aware I'd need a bodyguard. I'm used to taking care of myself." Luke studied the outfit the guy wore. A gray tunic reached his mid-thigh. Under that, he wore leather pants tucked into boots. Some sort of cape was slung over one shoulder. "Am I underdressed?" Luke asked, gesturing to his charcoal suit. He'd Googled what to wear to a daytime wedding.

That's how screwed up he was over Astrid. He looked up fashion on the Internet because he wanted to fit in with her people, but none of the sites had mentioned a cape.

Pekka grinned. "After I strip-search you, you can decide whether you want to keep the suit or put on more traditional clothing. I should let you know that this is easier to fight in."

Luke could fight just fine in what he was wearing. If it got extra rowdy, he'd shed the jacket, but there was no way he was putting on a tunic and a cape. "Strip-search? If I'd known we were going to get kinky, I'd have brought you flowers."

That earned him a lazy grin. "I may grow to like you, Luke Holden, even though many think you stole Astrid to your bed unfairly."

"I'd tell 'many' to mind their own damn business."

Pekka studied him for a moment, a slow smile

building on his lips. "I think I'll enjoy today's wedding more than I thought." He turned all business again. "Hold out your hands. I'm going to pat you down."

Luke tolerated the search and didn't even flinch when Pekka reached under his jacket and removed the Glock from his shoulder holster. "Can we at least do the stripping inside?" He'd have a hard time saving his dignity if one of the other men saw him in his skivvies out in the courtyard.

Pekka looked up from removing Luke's ankle backup piece. "How about you just tell me what you're hiding in your shoes, and I'll let you keep your clothes on?" Luke cursed softly but wiggled his foot so that his switchblade fell out. Pekka chuckled. "Any weapons in your underwear?"

"Not that you'd be interested in."

"I walked straight into that one." Pekka flashed a smile. "Follow me." Instead of going inside the house as Luke expected, Pekka led him around the building and down a trail in the back.

"Are you related to Irja?" Luke asked.

"She's my twin sister."

That explained it.

They trudged on for a few minutes until the trail ended at a large clearing. A big, white tent had been erected in the middle. Underneath, chairs had been placed on two sides of a central aisle, which was flanked by rose garlands and ended with an arch covered with the same flowers. On the far side of the clearing, a large, flat rock dominated the landscape. It had some kind of thrones placed on it. Behind the rock, a huge ash tree extended its branches, reaching far over the rock and casting another smaller tent in shadow. That tent contained long tables that bowed from platters of food.

A cluster of those freakishly tall men stood just outside the food tent, drinking from tankards. Their conversation stopped as soon as Luke stepped into the clearing. Each of them threw him a hostile glare.

Yeah, this was going to be one fun party. Instead of wasting his time on fashion, he should have Googled what to do in case of an attack by giants.

"Beer or mead?" Pekka asked.

Luke didn't know what the hell mead was. "Beer," he bit out and followed the other man as he made his way toward the cluster. Ulf stood in the middle of the group, his glare promising death.

Pekka shook his head when they reached the men. "I sense a lot of tension, gentlemen. You know both Astrid and Naya would skin your hides if you let anything happen to my new friend." He clamped a hand on Luke's shoulder.

Before the men had a chance to answer, Harald approached from across the clearing. He'd changed into the same kind of getup the rest of them were wearing. "There will be no fighting at this wedding," he ordered.

Ulf's nostrils flared. "Holden will head home eventually. No telling what could happen once he's left the property."

Harald took a step forward, fists clenched. "You can't hurt him without hurting Astrid."

"Maybe Astrid wouldn't mind being released from her bond," Ulf sneered.

Something dark and primitive awoke in Luke. His

vision narrowed as he took a step toward Ulf. "She's made her choice, and you are not it. Why don't you find yourself a woman who welcomes your advances? If there is one."

A rumble passed through the rest of the men.

Harald held up his hand and gave Luke a pissy look before facing Ulf. "I dislike her choice as much as you do, but he's right. It is her choice, and if you don't like it, take it up with her."

"Ulf has a better chance against Luke than he does Astrid," a young blond guy said. "She's already beaten his ass several times."

"*Ja*, Ulf," an older guy said. "You're not going to impress her by beating up her *själsfrände*. She can do that by herself."

Laughter broke out among the men, but Ulf's face turned an ugly red. "We're not done," he hissed at Luke.

"You name the time and place, and I'll be there." He shot the other men a nasty glare for having a laugh at Astrid's expense.

Pekka shoved a mug of beer in his hand. "Let's go find our seats."

"Good idea," Harald said. "The rest of you should do the same."

Luke made his way to the ceremony tent. "Bride's or groom's side?" he asked.

"The fuck if I know," Pekka answered. "I've only known them ten months."

Harald came up behind them. "You're sitting on that side." He pointed to the side farthest from the food tent. "Everyone else is sitting on the other side."

Luke picked a chair as ordered, and Pekka chose

one next to his. "Are the men always that disrespectful toward Astrid?"

Pekka frowned. "That was not disrespect. Astrid is one of the most respected warriors in the group." He sat back in his chair. "She's one of them. They treat her exactly the way they treat one another."

Luke mulled that over. He didn't like any man claiming Astrid as one of his own, no matter the intention. The he-man in him wanted to stake his claim and keep her hidden away. The rational side of him realized Astrid would never tolerate that. And if these men were her family, they'd be there for her when he no longer could. "You keep saying 'them.' Are you not one of these Norse warriors?" he asked Pekka.

The other man paused for a moment. "I'm from Finland," he said as if that would explain everything.

"I don't follow."

"I shouldn't have ended up in Valhalla, but I did, and then Odin sent me back here. I don't consider myself a Viking. Those are Swedes, Danes, Norwegians, or Icelandic—not Finnish."

"I have no idea what you're talking about."

Pekka leaned back and scrutinized Luke. "Astrid hasn't told you about her time in Valhalla?"

Luke shrugged. "Nope. I know Valhalla is some kind of heaven in Norse mythology, but that's about it."

"You and Astrid have a lot to talk about."

No shit. "Why don't you fill me in on some of it?" Luke took a drink from his beer. It tasted like a regular crisp Pacific Northwest IPA.

"Astrid should really give you the details. I'll give you the short and concise version."

"Fine. I promise I'll ask her for specifics." Luke faked a casual tone. He doubted Pekka would give away any state secrets, but maybe he'd finally be able to figure out why these Scandinavians were here and what their mission was.

"When you do, make sure you've got some time." Pekka grinned as if that was an inside joke. "All of us here died about a thousand years ago."

Luke stared at him, trying to figure out what metaphor the guy was reaching for. "I don't get it."

Pekka shook his head. "This will also require some time."

"Just tell me what you know, and I'll figure it out later with Astrid."

"Everyone who lives in this house—well, except for Naya—was alive during the Viking age. We all died what's considered a heroic death and were sent to Valhalla to train as Odin's warriors. He calls us *einherjar*. The men, that is. The women go to some magic meadow where Freya is in charge. No man knows what goes on there. The women become the goddess's Valkyries."

Luke's head was spinning. Odin, Freya, Valkyrie—what the fuck? The wolverines had referred to Astrid as Valkyrie. Was that in recognition of her being some kind of otherworld creature? Was she like them? "Why are you here?" he asked. "Why are you not still in Valhalla?"

"Ah, that's the clincher." Pekka grimaced. "The half god Loki is a bit of a bad boy. He's sending wolverines to the mortal plane, what we call Midgard, and hiding that from the Norse gods' council. Freya and Odin are very keen on protecting humanity, but they can't prove to the council that Loki is behind these creatures. And gods are not allowed to bring their conflicts to Midgard."

"So they send you here to fight the wolverines instead." Luke couldn't believe he was having this conversation. Astrid seemed so normal. She had superior fighting skills, but he figured she'd received treatment similar to what he and Donovan had.

Pekka thumbed his nose. "You got it."

This was crazy, and yet Luke couldn't stop himself from continuing the conversation. On some ludicrous level, this explained a lot about Astrid and Leif and the rest of the men. "Are you going back to Valhalla?" The thought of losing Astrid made his chest ache, but Luke ignored it. It would happen eventually, no matter what he did.

"Nobody knows," Pekka answered. "The king was worried for a while that he would have to send Astrid back. Her berserker—her inner warrior—was growing too strong and fighting her for control. Now that you are bonded, she'll be okay." He chucked Luke's shoulder. "Just don't die on her. Then she'll trip into permanent battle fever, and she'd be a danger to all of us. Leif would have to send her back to Freya's meadow."

"Berserker?" Luke asked, but he already suspected he'd seen Astrid's "inner warrior." That must be the feral creature that sometimes showed from behind her eyes.

"You seriously know nothing about this? What do you and Astrid do when you spend time together?" Pekka held up his hand. "Never mind, I don't want to know." He took a sip of beer. "The berserker is the reason why Vikings and Valkyries are undefeatable. It whips them into battle frenzy so fierce they feel no pain and never tire."

Astrid would go into permanent battle fever if he

died. She'd have to leave her warrior brothers and sisters. Would there be any consequences when he left, hopefully still alive? He opened his mouth to ask, but Leif entered the tent. Dressed entirely in black, the tall man walked up the aisle and stood next to Harald by the flower arch. From somewhere, music started playing and the guests stood.

Luke followed their lead.

After a few moments, Irja strode down the aisle. She looked great, but Luke's attention was captivated by the woman following behind her. Astrid's short dress hugged her curves and showed off her spectacularly long legs. One shoulder was bare, proudly displaying the serpent tattoo on her arm. She wore knee-high leather boots in the same pinkish color as her dress. Images of her in bed wearing nothing but those boots flooded his mind, giving him an instant hard-on. She gave him a smile and a wink as she passed by, and he had to shuffle his feet to adjust the tightness of his pants.

Irja and Astrid took their places on the other side of the flower arch. Luke noticed Ulf watching Astrid and must have made a move toward him, because Pekka caught his sleeve. "She'll kill you if you mess up this wedding," he hissed.

Luke glanced toward Astrid, and sure enough, she glared at him. He gave her a reassuring smile, but her forehead didn't smooth out until the music changed and Naya came down the aisle on the arm of her brother. She wore a white dress and some kind of crown with a veil on her head.

Leif stepped forward. The dude had a grin as large as the Grand Canyon on his face as he held out his hand to his bride. Scott placed his sister's hand in her groom's. Her slight frame next to Leif's would have looked weird if it wasn't for the smile she wore when she gazed at her groom. It made her radiant, and as she grasped his hand, no one could have had any doubt that these two belonged together.

Astrid watched the couple, her eyes glistening. Luke felt intensely happy for the couple, which seemed odd, and yet watching their smiles for each other made him uncomfortable.

He wanted that. He wanted happily ever after. And he wanted it with Astrid.

Fuck.

Leif tilted down and claimed Naya's lips, the kiss turning into a deep one, and the audience cheered. Harald stepped up in front of the couple. "We had this same problem at the handfasting ceremony. Haven't you two gotten this out of your system yet?"

Leif ended the kiss. "Never," he said, steadying Naya, who swayed a little and then blushed furiously.

Handfasting ceremony? Luke's mind spun as everyone sat down again. Would *they* have to have some sort of engagement ceremony? He widened his eyes in an unspoken question aimed at Astrid. She must have understood, because she shook her head. Or maybe she just wanted him to stop staring at her.

That was impossible.

Except for the bare arm and the short hemline, her dress was kind of modest. There was no cleavage to speak of and the skirt flared, but something about the fabric showed off her curves to perfection. Or, maybe it was just that he knew exactly how those curves looked and felt when she was naked underneath him. His pants grew uncomfortably tight again.

Astrid shot him a look. How had she known?

Harald was talking, but Luke hadn't heard a word. He'd been too busy picturing Astrid out of her dress. They must be nearing the end of the ceremony because Leif had Naya's hand in his and was sliding a ring onto her finger.

"This ring is a token of my undying devotion and affection," he said. "Like the circle of this ring, my love for you will never end. You are my wife, my queen, my everything."

Naya repeated the words about the circle as she placed a ring on Leif's finger. She clasped his hand in hers and lifted her face. "You are my king, my husband, my world."

A rush of wind bore down on the glen. The branches on the tall ash rustled furiously. It swept through the clearing and whipped Naya's veil around her face. Leif's long hair was caught in the same breeze. He tilted his head back, his whole face lit up in bliss. A deep growl escaped from his throat.

Something clicked deep inside Luke's chest and his senses sharpened. The scent of the roses became stronger. The wind touching his skin ignited every nerve ending. The sounds of the wedding guests amplified. He heard their murmur as clearly as if they stood right next to him. Their clothing rustled so loud it hurt his ears.

He hyperventilated. Was he having a panic attack? He loosened his tie and collar.

The weird sensations left as quickly as they had come over him. He watched as Harald spoke over the couple's intertwined hands but couldn't concentrate on the words. He leaned back in the chair, rubbing his chest. Everyone else appeared completely unfazed. Was he the only one who had noticed the wind?

Astrid stared at him. *Okay?* she mouthed. He nodded in response.

Pekka shot him a concerned look. "You're sweating. Drink your beer."

Luke took a long pull from his now lukewarm draft, trying to collect his jumbled thoughts.

Harald declared the couple husband and wife, and Leif planted another deep kiss on his bride's lips. She didn't seem to mind. Neither did the guests, judging by the loud cheering. They didn't wait for the couple to walk back down the aisle, instead joining them up front. The old guy who earlier had made fun of Ulf slapped Leif's back.

The kiss finally ended. Leif released Naya with another smile. She headed for her bridesmaids, and the three women hugged.

"Am I allowed to get up now?" Luke asked Pekka sarcastically.

"Sure. Just stay out of Ulf's way."

"As long as he keeps away from Astrid, that shouldn't be a problem." Luke strode up to his fiancée. She frowned as he got closer.

"Are you okay?" she asked. "You looked like you were going to pass out."

His heart rate had finally slowed down. "I'm fine. Maybe it was the beer." He held up his empty mug.

"I need a drink," Astrid said. "And food. I'm starving."

Luke grabbed her hand, and they sidestepped the

crowd to walk over to the food tent. He could feel Ulf's eyes following them, but ignored him. "Pekka's been telling me a little bit about your background," he said when they reached the keg inside the tent.

Astrid stilled. "What did he tell you?"

He kept his eyes focused on her face as he repeated Pekka's tale. A part of him desperately looked for any sign of this being one big joke. A setup to make fun of the new boyfriend. Another part knew that Pekka had told the truth. The wolverines, the mansion that couldn't be found via GPS, the feral nature inside Astrid, they all fit.

Astrid poured herself a glass from a pitcher filled with deep golden liquid. She drank a large swallow. "Yes," she said. "That is who I am."

"Who you are?" Luke frowned, but she wouldn't look at him. He nudged her chin until her green eyes gazed into his. "Pekka told me how you ended up here and what your job is. That's not who you are, which is what I want to know."

Astrid nodded slowly, as if she'd made a decision. "Okay, let's grab a plate of food and find somewhere more private."

He grinned. Interesting things happened whenever they found themselves in "more private" places.

"To talk," she said firmly. "Somewhere private to talk."

As he moved down the buffet, Luke loaded up on pickled herring, eggs, paté, and ham. He filled his mug with more beer and then followed Astrid into the trees, where she sat down on a felled log. Luke sat on the ground in front of her so he could see her face. She took another sip of her drink before putting it down on the log.

She looked at him, her eyes serious and a little apprehensive. "I was born to a thrall, a slave, so my mother's master became my master. He wasn't always kind, but he was decent to us. We were his property, so he protected his investment. He clothed us and fed us. We didn't have an actual home—he didn't think we needed one since we worked all day—but he made sure we had shelter for the night."

Luke grabbed her hand. "Astrid, I had no idea. When you said a man had been in control of your life, I thought—"

"I know what you thought. I wasn't ready to tell you the whole story then." She pulled her hand away. "If you touch me, I'll have a hard time telling it now." A sad smile graced her lips.

Life in the lab had sometimes made him feel like someone's property, but at least he'd had his own room. He'd shared it with Donovan, and since they'd never known anything different, they thought of it as home. "I understand," he told Astrid. "Go on."

She took a deep breath and continued. "My mother died when I was ten, and my master didn't want to raise an orphan. He sold me on the auction block, and I was lucky to get another owner who treated his thralls well. As long as I obeyed orders and kept in line, I received food, clothes, and shelter."

"Was there a time when you didn't obey?" Luke asked. Christ, he couldn't imagine Astrid following anyone's orders but her own.

"I only talked back once. And I got the whip for it," she said. "After that, I was a very obedient child. I taught myself to read and write runes, and that's how I spent my time whenever I wasn't working. I scratched symbols in the yard." She smiled at the memory, and his heart ached for the lonely little girl she must have been. "When I hit puberty, things changed." She looked away.

Luke's jaw clenched. He reached out for her again, but she shook her head. Resigned, he sat back down.

"The master never touched me, but his men would often grope me as I walked by and some tried to get me alone. One night, one of the worst offenders caught me alone in the stable."

Luke's fists trembled from the effort not to touch her.

Astrid seemed to withdraw into herself. Her voice became distant. "It could have ended badly, but I fought him. When I bit his arm, he let me go."

Luke wanted to kill the bastard,

As if she could read his thoughts, she looked up and smiled. "He's been dead many, many years now. In a way, it was a good experience."

"How could attempted rape be good?" Luke growled.

"It showed me that I needed to learn to fight. I talked the master of arms into teaching me, and it turned out I had an affinity for swords. When I was old enough, I became a shield maiden—a female warrior—and eventually earned enough loot to buy my freedom."

He forced himself to keep still. He wanted to crush her to him and tell her that he'd take care of her. Tell her that nothing bad would ever happen to her again, but he wasn't in a position to promise that.

The strength within Astrid floored him. Every day she'd shown him courage, but nothing like what she did now by telling him her story. "What you had to overcome is nothing short of amazing." He felt like complete scum for not telling her his story. But he couldn't. Too much depended on him keeping his secret, including Whalert's life. "How did you die? Pekka said that the men and women who end up in Valhalla die an honorable death."

Astrid smirked. "Honorable by old Norse standards. I died in battle, of course. I was a wizard with the sword, but an arrow got me in the end." She rubbed her chest as if she could still feel the wound.

"Was Irja a shield maiden too? Did she die in battle?" He could see Leif's brawny male warriors getting their heads bashed in on the battlefield, but the doctor seemed too gentle.

"Irja is very secretive. She hasn't shared many details about her life before or after Valhalla. We were all surprised when Naya found Irja's twin brother in the—"

Luke frowned. "Where did she find Pekka?" His instincts tingled.

Astrid hesitated. "It's not exactly a secret, and you already know how weird we all are." Luke felt even lower for manipulating her this way, but he needed to know everything. For Donovan's sake.

She sunk down on her knees in the grass next to him. "Naya and Scott were raised in a genetic lab." Luke held his breath. "They were taken from their parents and then genetically manipulated into becoming super soldiers. Their dad had been a first generation of the same kind of soldier, but he escaped and then met their mother. The parents were both killed when the lab scientists caught up with them again. In the lab, the treatments worked on Naya but made Scott weak. She escaped the lab and later rescued her brother." Astrid rubbed her forehead.

"That's the short version. You'll have to ask Naya for any other specifics."

Luke had a million questions but forced himself to appear calm. "What happened to the lab? Where is it?" Some of his urgency must have reflected in his voice.

Astrid gave him a worried look. "The lab was in North Dakota. Naya killed the lead scientist when she broke in to find an antidote for her brother's condition. Scott was in a vegetative state by then. That's also when she found Pekka. He was a prisoner in the lab."

Luke forced himself to calm down. That's why the North Dakota lab was abandoned. And Pekka was somehow involved. He'd been sitting next to the person who might know everything he wanted about the lab's operation. "How long was Pekka there?"

"He doesn't know, but he doesn't think it was long. He was knocked out and woke up in a cage, where they kept him for the duration of his time there." Shit, that ruined his plan of pumping Pekka for information.

"You seem awfully interested in the lab." She cocked her head and studied him.

He shrugged. "Just wondering how it's related to the wolverines and the kidnapped girls."

Astrid picked up her glass and drank. "Why don't you tell me something about you? I know you've served in the military, but what about your childhood?"

"I'm an orphan too. I never knew my parents, but I had a twin brother." He smiled. "Donovan and I never felt alone since we had each other. After a bad foster home, we spent a lot of time living on the streets. Donovan died when we were just teenagers. I got my life together after that. I studied and took the GED so

I could join the military. When I got out, I started the nightclub." He splayed out his arms. "My life story in a nutshell."

"There are so many parts missing from that story." She watched him carefully. "You're going to tell me the rest, but first I'll say I'm sorry about your brother."

His chest ached. Donovan would have loved Astrid. An overwhelming longing for his brother swept over him.

Astrid gasped, all color leaking out of her face.

"What's wrong?" He put his arm around his shoulders.

"I'm fine," she said, catching her breath. "I just felt dizzy for a bit."

He tightened his hold. "Let's go find Irja so she can check you out."

Astrid pushed away from him. "No, I'm fine now. I don't want to take Irja away from the party. She so rarely allows herself any fun." She stood. "We should join in too. It's not every day there's a royal wedding." She must have caught Luke's clueless look. "Leif is our king, ordained by Odin. Ever since Naya became his *själsfrände*, she's been our queen."

Luke wasn't sure how much more crazy sauce he could digest. He decided to ignore the whole king-and-queen thing for now and concentrate on what he'd wondered earlier. "Are we supposed to have a hand-fasting ceremony?"

Astrid looked away. "I don't think it's required. We had one for Naya and Leif since she became our queen and as part of her Valkyrie initiation."

Luke wasn't buying her casual tone. Before he could say anything, his pocket buzzed. He fished out his phone and found a text message in code on the screen. Whalert.

"I have to go." He hated the disappointed look on Astrid's face. "I'm sorry, but this can't wait. It could determine my…the club's future."

Astrid waved him on. "Go. I'll be fine. You'll miss the best bonfire ever, but that's your loss."

He leaned in for a kiss, and she briefly touched her lips to his. He hesitated but didn't know what to say, so he just walked off to find Pekka. He wanted the guns and the switchblade back. At the tree line, he realized he'd need a ride back into town and turned back to ask Astrid.

Her eyes were closed as she reclined against the log, her legs curled up under her. Sipping her drink, she looked achingly beautiful and very alone. He was about to go back to her, but the phone buzzed again. Luke clenched his jaw. He had to make good on his promise to Donovan.

If he went back to Astrid, he'd want to stay with her. He'd ask Pekka for a ride.

# Chapter 22

ASTRID LEANED BACK ON THE GAME ROOM'S OVERSIZE couch. Her feet ached from dancing around the bonfire like a maniac. Her head was a little foggy from too much mead, and still she couldn't sleep. She kept mulling over the conversation with Luke. There was something off about it. He'd extracted a lot of information from her without giving much in return. Why was he so interested in the North Dakota lab? After hours of staring at the ceiling and not coming to any conclusions, she'd given up and gone to the game room in search of something to read.

Her old favorite, *The Lord of the Rings*, lay open on her lap, but she couldn't concentrate on Frodo's adventures. She was still pissed about Luke leaving. Like Henri, Luke put his work first. She wished he'd been a little more reluctant to leave. Maybe she hadn't properly explained how much the wedding meant to her and how important it was for him to be there. Maybe he wasn't interested in her outside of the bedroom.

She closed the book and abandoned the needy thoughts. She should concentrate on things she could control instead. The fertility lab had to be shut down before the wolverines ordered another load of abducted women. Since when did Loki's creatures have the intelligence to plan something like kidnapping and taking the victims across international borders? Someone else must be the brain behind the operation. Loki himself wasn't allowed in the mortal realm—the Norse gods' council forbid it. If the half god had gone against their rules, Odin and Freya would have noticed and told Leif. Wouldn't they? She rubbed her forehead.

The king had called a meeting for eight a.m. to discuss the plan for destroying the lab. She felt bad about Leif and Naya not getting more than a few hours of a wedding night. It seemed duty trumped everything. But that was their function. They'd had their regular lives as humans a long time ago. Now they were warriors on a mission from the gods. Things like vacations and honeymoons were not for them. How did Naya feel about giving up a normal human life without the reward of immortality? How would I like?

Although he worked all the time now anyway.

The door to the computer room opened, and Ulf stepped out. Astrid bristled. She still had unfinished business with him. He stopped dead in his tracks, eyes wide, when he noticed her on the couch.

"I thought everyone had gone to bed." He looked around as if hunting for an escape.

"You thought wrong."

He gave a half smile. "Great wedding, right?"

Oh no. They were not doing small talk. "I think you have something to say to me."

He ran a hand across his shorn hair. "Look, I didn't touch Holden. We may have had words, but—"

She held up her hand. "That's not what I'm talking about. You abandoned me on a mission."

His face twisted. "That was a shit move, I know. I'm sorry."

"Why did you?" She splayed out her hands. "I know we've never been close, and we've had this crazy rivalry for as long as I can remember, but are you now out to get me?"

"No, of course not." He sat down beside her. "I don't know what I was doing. I've had this idea you and I could…" He scowled. "Forget it."

"Could what?" she insisted.

"That we could be more than friends." He watched her intently.

Astrid looked down at the book in her lap. "I had no idea you felt that way."

"It was a stupid idea. One of the others mentioned that you and I bickered like an old couple. My mind extrapolated from there." A corner of his mouth lifted. "I was obviously way off the mark."

"Obviously, or I wouldn't have bonded with Luke."

Ulf's face clouded. "I've been digging on the Darknet all evening for chatter about the lab and the women we rescued. I found some disturbing information about Holden."

Astrid's heart beat faster, but she kept her poker face. "And?"

"There is this guy named Kraus. A really bad guy from Germany who's popped up in Pine Rapids. He's into everything: drugs, weapons, money laundering, and human cargo."

Alarm bells started tingling at the back of Astrid's mind. She knew that name from somewhere.

Ulf brushed something invisible off his knee. "Holden seem to be in business with this guy. They've met several times."

No, no, no. This couldn't be true. Luke wouldn't be in business with anyone who was involved in human trafficking. She knew his business touched the gray areas of what was strictly legal, but he wouldn't make money from human trade. Would he?

It finally came to her. Kraus had called Luke when she was at his apartment. She'd seen his name on the phone display. "How do you know this?" Her voice sounded desperate.

Ulf's face softened. "I was searching for footage on Kraus and came across a Denver PD video of him meeting with Holden. I then checked our local police department's surveillance archive and found more footage. They've met twice. As recently as this evening."

Astrid went numb. "Show me."

Ulf looked like he wanted to protest, but she headed straight for the computer room. He followed and gestured for her to sit in the chair next to his. Rows of data scrolled on three big monitors. She had no idea what it meant. Ulf clicked a few keys, and a grainy video popped open.

Two men sat at a table in what looked to be a diner. Despite the low resolution, she clearly recognized Luke. There was no sound, but the other man slid a folder and a thick envelope across the table to Luke. It was the right size for bills.

"That envelope is full of money," she whispered.

Ulf nodded. "But we don't know what kind of business they're doing."

"Doesn't matter. Luke would have researched this guy. He would have found out about the human trafficking, but he still decided to work with him." Her heart raced. Luke knew where Camila and the others were. He was the one who'd told them about the refugee organization. She stood. "I have to go."

Ulf grabbed her hand. "I'll come with you."

She shrugged him off. "This is something I have to do alone." It was better to be alone. That way, nobody could disappoint you. Hurt you.

She rushed out the door, ignoring Ulf shouting after her.

She'd told Luke why she related to Camila and the others after the rescue, and he had still gone into business with Kraus. Today when she'd told him all the sordid details of her life as a thrall, he'd seemed to understand. He even seemed angry. Had that been an act? How could he meet with that scum and take his money after what she'd told him about being someone's property?

—✺—

Luke's doorman was fast asleep behind his desk when Astrid ghosted by. She may not have Sten's ninja skills, but she could be quiet enough. The elevator took forever, but it gave her time to collect herself. She forced herself to breathe deeply.

Unfortunately, she couldn't calm her thoughts. She should have a plan before she barged in on Luke. Let him explain why he was meeting with Kraus. There could be a reasonable explanation… She laughed out loud at how desperate she was.

When had she become this stupid woman grasping for a reason to hold on to her lover? The only reason to be in business with scum like Kraus was that there was a lot of money to be made.

The doors dinged open. Striding toward Luke's door, she undid the safety of her gun but kept it holstered. She squared her shoulders and banged on the door. It took three more tries before she heard movement inside. Luke opened the door squinting. His hair stood on end, and he was wearing only a pair of navy boxer briefs.

"Hey." He rubbed his face and broke out into a smile. "I missed you but didn't want to call until morning. I figured you'd get to bed late because of the party."

She stepped past him. "I have some questions."

He closed the door. "Okay." His forehead furrowed. "About what?"

"About Kraus."

His face went blank and then hardened. "How do you know about him?"

Her heart sank. He wasn't trying to explain himself. "This time it's my turn to ask the questions." She pointed at him. "It's your turn to answer."

"Hey, calm down." Luke stepped toward her and she took a step back, hand reaching for her gun. His eyes widened. "You came here carrying heat? You're afraid of me?"

She shook her head. "I'm not afraid of you. Just cautious, now that I'm getting a better idea of who you are."

"Astrid, I—" His eyes softened, but she resisted their pull. He reached for her, and she took another step back. His face turned cold. "So you have decided I'm a low-life criminal."

"I have no idea who you are, but I know the people you do business with are among the lowest scum of Midgard."

"And that makes me scum too." It was a statement.

"If you say so." She had to swallow hard to get the big lump in her throat to go down.

He jammed his hands on his hips and looked down on the floor. A tic pulsed in his jaw. "Tell me how you found out about my meeting with Kraus."

"It's not important."

He looked up, eyes blazing. "It's extremely important. If you found out, others can too." He took a step toward her. "I'm not fucking around, Astrid. Tell me."

She pulled her Glock. "I'm not the one giving information tonight. You are."

Disbelief filled his eyes. "You're pulling a gun on me?"

She changed to a two-handed grip to keep her hands from shaking. "Tell me what your business with Kraus is. Did you tell him where Camila and the others are?"

He shook his head. "This is what you think of me? That I could hurt women, trade them like cattle to the highest bidder?"

She swallowed. "I don't know what to think anymore. But the truth is, I don't know you at all. You've given me nothing. I shared what had happened to me, and you still left the wedding to meet with that scum." To her horror, she felt tears well in her eyes. She blinked them away. "You obviously know Kraus deals in human trafficking, and you're still in business with him."

The tic in his jaw was back. "It's very complicated."

"Uncomplicate it for me."

"I can't. There's too much at risk. You have to trust me." He held his arms out. "Put the gun away. Tell me how you found out I was meeting with Kraus."

She kept the gun pointed at him. "Denver PD and the local precinct here in Pine Rapids have surveillance video of your meetings."

"Fuck. That's very bad." Holden seemed lost in thought. "I have to fix that."

This was an odd response. "Tell me what's going on." She lowered the gun but kept her double grip. "If this thing between us has any chance, you have to. I can't—" Her voice broke. She cleared her throat. "I can't be with someone who profits from slave trade."

Luke's gaze on her was sad. "Deep down you know I'm not that guy. Trust your instincts."

Her heart wanted to believe he wasn't capable of hurting Camila or the others, but her instincts obviously weren't worth shit. The facts were: Luke was in business with Kraus, a man who made money from abducting and selling women. And she knew nothing about Luke that would make her trust him implicitly. "Explain what's going on and maybe I'll believe you."

He shook his head. "People's lives depend on me keeping quiet."

She raised the gun again. "Right now, your life depends on you telling the truth."

"You wouldn't shoot me." His eyes flickered.

"It doesn't have to be a kill shot, but I can still make it hurt." Her heart thumped so loudly that she was sure he could hear her, but her hands were steady.

Luke scowled. "I'm going to humor you. Let's sit."

She gestured with the gun for him to walk ahead. They took their seats across from each other in his ridiculously soft leather couches. Her mind flicked through images of what had happened the last time they'd sat here, but she kept a tight rein on her thoughts before they went down that path. "Talk," she said.

"For Christ's sake. Lower your gun, Astrid." Luke shoved his hands through his hair. "I can't concentrate with that thing pointed at me."

She put the gun next to her on the couch. "Good. Then you can't make up any lies."

Glaring at her, he nodded. "Fine." He turned toward the windows, clenching his jaw. When he faced her again, his eyes flickered with something that looked like regret. "I'm an undercover FBI agent. I have been for the last eighteen months. I've been surveilling Naya, you, and now the others."

Something cold clamped down around her heart. "That's impossible. Naya worked for you. She would have checked you out. She would have figured out if you had a fake persona."

He gritted his teeth and leaned forward, elbows on his knees, but didn't look at her. "I work for a covert operation of the FBI. We operate completely in the dark, have our own IT infrastructure, our own procedures. Not even the FBI knows who I really am."

"What's your real name?" She had to know who he was. Who she'd shared a bed with.

He looked up. "It's still Luke, but my last name is Hager."

"All this time…" She sobbed but managed to turn it into a sad chuckle. "All this time you've targeted me. I was your in to get to Naya." Despair filled her. She'd led danger to the fortress door. How could she be bonded to someone who lied to her? What kind of cruel joke was Freya playing?

She couldn't breathe.

Luke moved forward, but she held up her hand to stop him. "Tell me why," she croaked. "Tell me why you went through all this trouble to get me to trust you." Her lips stretched in a bitter smile. "Tell me why you literally fucked me over."

He shoved a hand through his hair. "It wasn't like that. I didn't plan to sleep with you. That first time in the club, I didn't even know you were affiliated with Naya. I just about freaked when you walked into the club the day I was meeting with her."

Astrid remembered the meeting well. She'd freaked too. Luke was supposed to be just a one-night stand. A way to calm her berserker temporarily. "Why are you so interested in Naya?"

Luke stood, and she quickly drew the gun on him. Hurt flickered in his eyes, but she didn't give a shit. "I'm getting something to drink," he said. "Do you want anything?"

"I'm fine." He'd probably drug her. She watched him go to the kitchen area and return with a bottle of water. "Naya," she repeated.

With a sigh, he sat down again. "I knew Naya was somehow associated with the labs that are creating super soldiers. I just didn't know how. The goal of my mission is to take down those labs and the people responsible for them."

She looked down at the gun she was holding in her lap. "So you kept sleeping with me to get to Naya." She embraced the anger filling her chest. It was better than the cold lump forming around her heart. She looked him straight in the eye. "I took you to my house when you got sick. Endangered everyone I care about so you would get better." She laughed bitterly. "I'm such a fool. I gave you exactly what you wanted."

"You don't understand." He cleared his throat. "I grew up in a lab just like Naya's. I had a brother who couldn't take the treatments. My brother died."

Astrid sat back. This was not what she expected. She felt bad for his brother, but he had used her for weeks. All because of a brother who was already dead. "I get the need for revenge, but don't you care about who you hurt in the process?" People like her. She swallowed again. "Is every method justified to get your answers? Could you not have gotten close to me without screwing me?" She shook her head. "You must have pissed yourself laughing when I showed up here talking about handfasting and engagements."

The tic in Luke's jaw was back. "No," he mumbled. "I wasn't supposed to...like you as much as I did. I couldn't help myself. After that one night at the club, I couldn't stop thinking about you. I had to—"

"What about Denver?" She didn't want to hear what he had to do. "That wasn't really a fluke meeting, was it?"

He shook his head. "You have to understand. Nothing will stand in the way of bringing down the people who made my brother's life so miserable that he killed himself."

"So to you it's totally okay to lie to me, fuck me over, and make me a traitor to my people, all in the name of your dead brother?"

"I didn't think about it like that."

"How did you think about it?"

"I couldn't stay away from you. I needed you too much." His eyes burned with regret, but she steeled herself against it.

She stood. "Don't try to complicate things by pretending you had feelings for me." She holstered her gun. "We're done." She took the few steps leading to the door and opened it.

"Astrid, please understand—"

"I do understand. It's very simple really. Your dead brother is the most important person to you."

He hesitated but then nodded. And there it was. It was so simple when she broke it down. There would always be people more important than her. Nobody would ever put her first.

"I hope you find your revenge," Astrid said. "I'm sure your brother would be very proud of everything you've done."

She stepped through the door, and it swung closed behind her as she walked down the hallway. She really did understand. He'd only used her for his own gain. A thrall could earn her freedom, but that didn't make her important or valuable.

The elevator took too long, so she took the stairs instead. Through blurred vision, she raced down the steps, proud of the fact that she didn't spill a single tear until she got to the car. Once behind the tinted windows of the SUV, she allowed them to flow. As she drove off, she vowed that those were the last tears she'd shed for any man.

Especially Luke.

All that was left now was to confess to the king how she'd betrayed her people.

# Chapter 23

LUKE SCANNED THE DIVE BAR THAT WHALERT HAD reluctantly agreed to meet in. It was located across the border in Idaho. The decor looked like the interior designer couldn't decide between a hunting lodge and a biker bar. Harley-Davidson T-shirts and chrome hubcaps competed for wall space with antlers and various taxidermy.

It was early afternoon, but three patrons were already well on their way to half drunk at the bar. Judging by how well their asses fit the indentions on the stools they sat on, they were all regulars. Whalert were nowhere to be found, so Luke chose a booth far from the bar and sat down on the slightly sticky vinyl.

Christ, how had Whalert found this place?

A waitress appeared and asked what he wanted to drink. Her tight T-shirt showed off the bar's logo as well as her ample cleavage. She cocked her hip flirtatiously, but her heart wasn't in it. Her voice came out flat, and she didn't make eye contact. He asked for coffee, and she shuffled off toward the bar.

Luke scratched the twenty-four-hour stubble on his jaw. He hadn't been able to go back to sleep after his fight with Astrid. *Fight* was such a mild word for what had really happened. *Fucking disaster* fit better. He'd revealed who he truly was, completely blown his cover, and it didn't mean anything because he'd hurt her.

He would make things right with her. He would…

He would stop lying to himself. She didn't want anything to do with his sorry ass.

He'd fucked up her life. He would never forgive himself for that.

He needed to get his head back in the game though. If both Denver and Pine Rapids PDs had surveillance footage of him, they were most likely tailing him too. And if they were following him, they could be following Astrid. He didn't know how far the corruption reached, but the idea of whoever wanted his boss also knowing about Astrid made his stomach turn.

Whalert slid into the seat across the table, startling Luke. The door hadn't opened. "Where did you come from," he asked.

"Back door." Whalert aimed his thumb toward the innards of the bar. Luke didn't bother looking. "You look like shit," his former boss told him.

"Haven't slept much."

"You look like you have the flu or something."

Luke did feel like he was running a low-grade fever. His muscles ached and his skin was sensitive to touch, but there were too many other things to worry about right now. He looked Whalert over. His face was covered in a dingy beard, and his flannel shirt had completely lost whatever its original color was. "You don't look so well yourself."

Whalert smirked, the expression little more than a twitch in his tired face. "Haven't slept so good lately myself."

The waitress plopped down Luke's coffee, and Whalert asked for one as well. He was rewarded with

a big sigh and an eye roll. Whalert returned his gaze to
Luke. "Why are we meeting?"

Once Luke had figured out his boss was close by,
he'd insisted on a meeting instead of talking on the
phone. It was easier to persuade people in person.
"Denver PD and Pine Rapids PD have footage of me
meeting with Kraus."

"Fuck." Whalert slumped down in the booth. "I didn't
think about scrubbing police databases."

Luke stirred his coffee. It smelled like it had been on
the burner for a while. "I wouldn't have either. FBI must
have reached out to the police to keep tabs on Kraus. If you
hadn't had to run, we could have planned accordingly."

"We have to pull you," Whalert said. "You're compromised. I know it's an insult to ask, but you're sure
you weren't followed to this place?"

"I know how to shake a tail," Luke said. He'd been
followed from his apartment, but that detail was probably still watching his car parked outside the coffee
shop in which he'd changed clothes before sneaking out
the back way. He'd come to the bar on the Ducati bike
he kept in a storage unit, rented under yet another fake
identity. "I can't pull out though. We've come too far,
and I've taken money from Kraus." And now he owed
Astrid. He had to fix all this, or at least take out Kraus.

Whalert rubbed his forehead. "What's the alterna-
tive?"

"We have to retrieve the information from the local
PDs, see how far it's traveled up the chain in DTU and
FBI, and then erase all of it from their records."

Whalert barked out a laugh. "Sure, I'll get right on
that." He shook his head. "I think this is where we say

our good-byes. If you followed the advice I gave when you first joined my office, you have a few unused identities hidden in a safety deposit box somewhere. Now is a good time to use one of those."

Luke shook his head. "I'm not joking. I know someone who can do this for us. She did cybersecurity for the nightclub, and she can hack into anything."

"And if she gets caught?"

"She hasn't been so far." Luke was pretty sure Naya had rummaged through all kinds of government databases. As much credit as Whalert deserved for his efforts to keep the DTU division completely separate from FBI, it was still a small miracle she hadn't blown Luke's cover when she screened him as a client.

Whalert mulled that over for a moment and then nodded. "Set it up."

Luke fished out his phone and called Naya's number. She answered on the first ring.

"You have fifteen seconds to tell me what you've done to Astrid. She's not talking to any of us. Only Leif knows what's going on, and he's not sharing."

Luke cringed. "I'm a jerk, but that's not why I'm calling." Naya terminated the call. "Shit." Luke smacked the table.

Whalert leaned back in his seat. "Women troubles?"

Luke shot him a dark look. "It's not what you think." He tapped a text message to Naya: Pine Rapids PD is following Astrid and others. She may be in danger. A long minute later, his phone rang.

"Explain," Naya demanded.

He put her on speaker. "It's a very long story. We need to meet." He could hear her talking to someone in the background. Their voices became louder and then muffled, as if she put her hand over the speaker. Was she talking to Astrid? A useless twinge of hope rose in his chest. He clamped it down.

Naya came back on the line. "Picnic table at Bear Lake boat launch in two hours." She hung up.

Luke looked at Whalert, who nodded. "Got it," he said. "We'll drive separately."

—⁘—

Twenty miles north of Pine Rapids, Luke steered his motorcycle off the highway and onto the turnoff for the Bear Lake recreational area. The small, teardrop-shaped lake was popular with boaters and swimmers in the summer. This early in the spring, the park surrounding the lake was mostly empty. A single boat trailer sat in the parking lot, and he could see a lone fisherman out in the middle of the lake.

Luke lowered the kickstand of the Ducati and cut the engine. He removed his helmet and tugged off his gloves as he walked to the nearby picnic tables. He'd just sat down when a silver Porsche Boxster S pulled in next to his bike. Naya and Leif got out and approached the table. They slid in across from him. Naya's eyes blazed with anger.

Leif's glare was ice cold, his face an impenetrable mask. He put his cell phone on the table.

"So, you brought backup," Luke said to Naya, trying to break the ice. His own backup, Whalert, had parked half a mile up the highway and was making his way cross-country to the lake. Hopefully he'd be among the trees soon, covering Luke's ass with firepower.

"I didn't bring him," Naya said. "He insisted on coming." She glared at Leif, who ignored her.

Keeping his focus on Luke, the blond giant leaned back and crossed his arms. "Put your hands where I can see them."

Luke laid his hands on the table, palms down. "He doesn't really blend well." He aimed his words at Naya, avoiding Leif's icy stare. An itchy feeling on the back of his neck told him he was being watched.

"I've already explained that to him," she countered.

"Enough chitchat," Leif bit out. "Why are the police following Astrid?"

Luke debated how much to tell and how to spin it. Better to just lay it all out there. "I work for the government—"

Naya jerked back. Leif didn't look surprised, but he cursed under his breath. It came out as a growl.

Luke held up his hands, palms facing Leif. "We're just talking, right?" Luke's heart rate increased. His nostrils flared.

Leif's eyes widened. He looked at Naya, and an unspoken message passed between them.

"Which part of the government?" Naya asked.

"It's a covert operation within the FBI." He launched into an explanation of how DTU was operating under more freedom. He finished by describing their mission of taking down the covert genetic labs. "I know you were involved in taking down the North Dakota lab," he said to Naya. She nodded but didn't volunteer any details.

Leif's phone buzzed, and he turned it over to check his screen. "Is the guy in the woods with you?" he asked Luke. "Does he work for DTU as well?"

Damn it. How had they caught Whalert? The guy was a master in staying hidden. "Yes," Luke gritted out between clenched teeth. "He's my boss. My former boss." He rubbed his face. "It's a long story."

Leif tapped a few keys on his phone and then put it back down. "Sten's bringing him over."

"When you hired me to work on your club's security protocols, I thoroughly screened you. How did I not find your government connection?" Naya's forehead furrowed.

"Maybe you're not as good of a hacker as you think you are," Luke said. Leif growled again, and Luke hastily continued. "DTU is on a completely different IT infrastructure. We have access to FBI's information and databases, but they have no clue who we are. They think we're just another division."

Naya nodded, distracted. Her eyes glazed over as if she was figuring out how to break into the DTU system. Luke was okay with that. He'd probably ask her to do exactly that in a minute.

Whalert appeared at the edge of the woods and walked across the parking lot. The young blond who had heckled Ulf at the wedding followed close behind. He must be Sten. His face was much more serious and closed up than last time Luke saw him.

When they reached the table, Sten nodded to Leif and then walked over to lean against the Porsche.

Whalert looked at Sten, and then he turned to Leif. "What are you guys? SOG?"

Leif's eyebrows rose. "Something like that."

Naya snorted.

"What's SOG?" Luke asked.

"Special Operations Group," Whalert answered.

"It's a Swedish counterterrorism unit. They've only been operating since 2011 but are one of the most effective in the world. Think of them as a combination of Delta Force and Navy SEALs. They're one of the most secretive military units. Nobody knows how many troops they have or their organizational structure." He shook his head. "As soon as you told me you'd met Scandinavian military operating within the United States, I figured they must be SOG." His voice was laced with admiration.

Luke shot a look at Leif, who returned it with an ice-cold glare of his own. Luke decided that if the SOG explanation worked for Whalert, they should stick with that. The whole "immortal warrior sent on a mission by the gods" thing would just cause a lot of headaches. He wasn't sure he'd quite wrapped his mind around that himself.

Whalert sat down next to Luke. "What's your target?" he asked Leif.

Naya put her hand on Leif's arm. "To take down the genetic labs," she answered.

"That's ours too," Whalert said. Luke shot him a look. His boss never shared information, not even with his operatives. All of a sudden he was Chatty Cathy. "They're SOG," Whalert said to Luke, as if that justified giving away secrets.

Naya and Leif exchanged a look again. "Can we get back to why the police are targeting us?" Naya asked.

Luke explained how he'd been working undercover as a nightclub owner and how he'd lured in Kraus once it became clear he was involved with the genetic labs. He rubbed the back of his neck. The tingling feeling he got when someone had their sights on him wouldn't go away. "Does Astrid know you are undercover?" Naya asked.

"She does now." He avoided looking at Leif.

"You dick," she hissed. "Did you use her as part of your cover?"

"No," Luke exclaimed and then scratched his chin. "Yes, maybe. I don't know." He rubbed the back of his neck. "I didn't fake how I felt—feel—about her. I may not have told her the whole story, but everything that happened between us was real." He met Naya's eyes, imploring her to believe him. "I will fix this."

Leif shifted in his seat. "You have to." He glanced at Whalert. "For Astrid's sake." He must be talking about the berserker going into permanent battle fever. But didn't that just happen when one of the bonded people died? Luke grabbed Naya's hand, but dropped it when a low warning rumbled through Leif's chest, vibrating the whole table. "My brother and I grew up in a lab in Northern California. I never knew my parents. As far as I know, I may have been born in that lab."

Naya slowly shook her head. "You think you were born in a lab?"

Whalert grunted. "I knew there was a reason you were so gung ho about this mission."

Luke ignored him. "We escaped and stayed hidden, but my brother died. The chemicals they injected us with in the lab gave him horrible nightmares and hallucinations. He couldn't handle them. He committed suicide."

Naya's eyes filled with tears. "I'm so sorry," she whispered.

Leif studied Luke as if he was trying to figure out

whether Luke was lying. "You know that a sappy story about a dead brother would pull on Naya's sympathies. Before I believe you, tell us what the drugs did to you."

Whalert tensed next to Luke. "Yeah, what did they do to you?"

"I'm a little faster and stronger than the average guy."

"A little?" Whalert snorted. "I knew there was something weird about your skills. Your military service records are filled with incidents where you pulled off a last-minute miracle and saved the men of your unit. And you forgot to mention how your rifle always finds its target. Your shooting instructor at the academy wrote two pages in your evaluation about how he'd never seen anything like it."

Luke decided not to mention the wolverines he'd missed when he and Astrid rescued Scott. Up to that point, he'd always hit his target. But then, he'd never met anyone who moved as fast as those freaky creatures.

Naya watched him intently. "The head scientist at the North Dakota lab told me all the soldiers of my generation were dead."

Luke shrugged. "Well, here I am. Not dead." He started to smile but changed his mind when he caught Leif's icy stare. It said Luke's alive status could be downgraded very quickly.

"So, why this meeting?" Leif said. "What do you want from Naya?"

"I need someone to hack into the Denver and Pine Rapid PDs' systems and get rid of the video."

Naya straightened. "And we should pull any files they may have on you or Kraus." She fished out her phone and started tapping its keys. "I'll get Ulf to start right away."

Leif held his hand over hers to stop her typing. "Can we at least talk about this before you agree to help them?"

Naya shook her head. "They're working to bring down the labs. Of course we're going to help them." She shook off Leif's grip and focused on Whalert. "You should check the FBI and DTU records as well, in case the PDs have sent them information."

Whalert shifted in his seat. "That's going to be a problem. I'm not actually with the bureau right now." He told them about sending in the blood sample and the fallout from that.

Leif's gaze bore into Luke. "You sent Astrid's blood to the FBI lab for analysis." His voice was dangerously dark.

"I wanted to see if she was telling the truth about who she is."

"You wanted to see if *she* was telling the truth?"

Luke cringed.

Naya tapped faster on her phone. "We need to see what became of that sample and erase any records." She gave Whalert a quick smile. "And see who ordered the email to be deleted from your account."

"You can do all that?" Whalert asked. "Won't someone notice you dicking around in all of these databases?"

"They haven't so far." She shot him a cocky grin. She turned to Leif. "We should continue to unravel the money trail to this Kraus guy. If anyone is helping him financially, they're probably behind the fertility lab."

"Hold up," Luke interrupted. "What fertility lab?"

Leif sighed and rolled his eyes.

"What?" Naya asked. "He would have found out eventually anyway."

"How?" Leif threw out his hands. "They don't have access to any information. They're frozen out of their agency."

"Astrid would have told him," Naya countered. "After they made up and were back together." She shot Luke a smile.

The cold lump that had lodged in his chest ever since Astrid left his apartment thawed a little. If Naya thought he had a chance to make it right with Astrid, maybe there was hope.

Whalert leaned in over the table. "What about this fertility lab?"

"We found a warehouse by the railroad tracks that looks like it's an in vitro fertilization facility," Leif said.

Luke nodded. That explained the location marked on the map found on the tablet.

Naya picked up the thread. "The abducted women we rescued were probably destined for that warehouse. There were human-size cages inside. I'm certain Kraus is connected to both the lab and the abduction."

Luke swallowed. The thought of women imprisoned and used in genetic experiments turned his stomach. Anger rose in his chest. "Did Astrid see this lab?" She'd befriended one of the Mexican women, and knowing about the lab would have hit her hard.

"She's the one who discovered it." Leif's voice was quiet.

No wonder she'd been upset when she found out he had met with Kraus. She had the image of those cages in her head when she came to confront him.

"What's next on our action-item list?" Whalert asked. "What do you need from us?"

Naya looked at Leif expectantly and squeezed his arm.

He rolled his eyes but caressed her hand. "We've already started digging up information about Kraus. We know he's financing the lab here in Pine Rapids. We want to see if he has other investors. We don't have his address yet, but when we do, we'll…have a conversation with him."

"Who has jurisdiction once you arrest him?" Whalert asked. "Will he be extradited to Sweden?"

Leif turned and looked out over the lake. He gestured to the fisherman in the boat. "Sure," he mumbled. "We'll extradite him."

A chill ran down Luke's spine. Kraus would not stand trial anywhere. Once Leif and his warriors got their hands on him, he'd be exterminated, not extradited.

"I want in on the action," Luke said. "I want to be there when you take down the lab."

Leif quirked an eyebrow. "You've done enough, don't you think? I need my warriors in top shape, and having you in the group is going to distract them. All of them. It's not just Astrid who wants to kill you."

Luke gritted his teeth. "Kraus thinks I'm laundering his money through the club. If I call a meeting, he'll be there."

Leif watched him with cold eyes but nodded once. "I'll keep you posted."

Luke hid the triumphant smile about to break out on his lips. He was in.

The sound of a boat engine reached them, and Luke turned to watch the fisherman approach the boat launch.

"We better adjourn our meeting if we don't want this guy to overhear us." He frowned. There was something familiar about the guy.

"Yep, good plan," Leif said and stood. He walked over to the boat and caught the line the fisherman threw him. The guy then handed Leif the fishing rod and jumped ashore holding a rifle case. He nodded at Luke, who finally recognized him as one of the wedding guests. "Meet my marksman, Per," Leif said with a shit-eating grin.

That explained the itch on Luke's neck. The entire meeting had taken place with a long-range rifle aimed at his head.

Leif and his warriors were not to be underestimated. He'd better remember that.

# Chapter 24

ASTRID WATCHED THE DARK STREETS OF PINE RAPIDS pass by the window of the black Escalade as they rolled toward the warehouse district. She ignored the dull headache that had plagued her for the last three days, ever since she'd stormed out of Luke's apartment. Irja told her it was caused by Astrid's separation from her *själsfrände*. That was also why a low-grade fever racked Astrid's body. She pulled out a jar of ibuprofen and swallowed two pills with the help of a swig from her water bottle.

"That's not going to cure your problem," Naya said. The queen was sharing the backseat with Astrid, while Leif drove and Ulf rode shotgun. "You should talk to Luke."

"There's nothing to talk about." The bastard had lied to her. Used her. She closed her eyes to clamp down her restless berserker. The beast paced and shook its restraints. For the last twenty-four hours, her inner warrior had been close to the edge of running completely amok. Astrid was pretty sure the only reason she was allowed on this mission was because Leif was afraid of what would happen if he didn't keep an eye on her. Her berserker technically had to listen to the king's commands.

"He had a reason for what he was doing," Naya insisted. "His brother killed himself because of what had happened in a lab. Luke couldn't know you were on his side."

"He should have known by the time he left Denver," Astrid bit out.

"Did you know you could trust him by the time you left Denver?"

Astrid clenched her jaw to keep from snapping at the queen. Maybe she hadn't trusted Luke implicitly back then, but enough to sleep with him. Enough to believe his interest in her had been real and that he'd pursued her because he wanted to be with her. What he'd wanted was information and bonus sex. She'd been played the entire time. "I don't want to talk about Luke."

The queen ignored her. "Think about it. He didn't have to help you rescue Scott. He could have left you on your own in Denver and then made contact once you were back in Pine Rapids."

Astrid swallowed. "He wanted information from me and knew he had to get me to trust him. That's why he helped. It was all part of his game."

"On some level, you know that's not true." Naya's voice was gentle. "And even if you believe that, why did he help us place the abducted women where they could get counseling? He did that because he knew you cared about Camila and the others, that you related to their situation."

"Let's concentrate on tonight's mission." Astrid didn't have enough mental strength to process the Luke situation *and* prepare for battle with a jittery berserker.

The warriors had had the lab under surveillance ever since she and Ulf first discovered it. Tonight, Torvald and Pekka had been on duty, and they'd called in some

unusual activity. The warehouse was crawling with
wolverines unloading equipment and stock. Ulf and
Naya hadn't seen any news on the Darknet about more
human cargo making its way to Pine Rapids, but the
creatures were preparing for something. Unfortunately,
the building had some kind of jammer rigged so Leif's
team couldn't use satellite imaging to monitor the wolverines' heat signatures.

"I wish we had a little more time before we have to
storm the lab," Naya said. "I've tracked the main finan-
cial backing of this clinic, lab—whatever it is—to an
investment banker in New Mexico. It's a little too much
of a coincidence that the Vikings in New Mexico are
having trouble with these new wolverines and that's also
the state to which the money trail leads."

"You're worried the finance guys will go underground if we take down the lab tonight?"

"Not exactly. They have a legitimate front, so they'll
probably just get rid of the evidence and continue to operate as if they're a fully legal business." She turned and
gave Astrid a chilling smile. "But we don't really need
evidence to take them down. It's not like we're going
to bring them to trial." An ice-cold tickle trailed down
Astrid's back. The queen sounded downright bloodthirsty.
Astrid's berserker picked up on the mood and paced faster.

*Fight*, it whispered. *Blood*.

Naya's nostrils flared when her berserker felt Astrid's
inner warrior's restlessness. "You okay?" she asked.

"I'll be fine once the fighting starts." Maybe she'd
finally be able to sleep tonight if the berserker got
exhausted in battle. The problem was that sometimes a
good fight riled up the beast even more.

She got her head in the game. "So, we have Torvald and Pekka on-site. Sten and Harald have gone ahead on the Kawasakis to help survey the terrain. Is Per on the rooftop with his rifle?" Per had left the fortress with Irja earlier in the afternoon. Neither had come back before the rest of the warriors headed out. Astrid assumed Leif or Naya had been in contact with them via phone and they were meeting the rest of the team on-site.

Naya turned to look out the window. "Irja and Per are not participating in this mission."

That was unusual but not unheard of. Usually someone stayed behind at the fortress to prepare for any wounded being brought back. But tonight Scott was taking care of that duty, so Irja and Per could have joined them. "Are they okay?" she asked.

"Yeah," Naya said, still facing the window. "They're working on something else."

Leif glanced over his shoulder at Astrid. "They're backing up Holden."

She froze. "Why does Luke need backup?"

Naya faced Astrid again. "He's meeting with Kraus. We've narrowed down the government corruption to three possible candidates. Luke's going to see if he can trip up Kraus to give us the final clue." Naya watched her carefully.

Astrid forced her face to remain calm, but her heart raced. If Leif had sent Irja and Per as backup, he believed there was a threat to Luke.

As if he could read her thoughts, Leif shot her a quick look through the rearview mirror. "It's just a precaution. Luke's helping us out by meeting with Kraus. That means we have his back."

"Okay," Astrid said. "I wasn't worried."

"Liar," Naya said.

Astrid ignored her.

Leif slowed down the car as they got closer to the warehouse and turned off the headlights. They crept down the streets and then turned into an alley a block away from where Ulf and Astrid had first encountered the wolverines. All four of them exited the car and closed the doors with the softest of clicks. Ulf handed them their communication headsets.

Leif looped the set over his ear and waited for the others to do the same. He tapped the mic with his unique signal. After a short delay, a response sounded. Harald, Torvald, Pekka, and then Sten all signaled that they were connected. Naya tapped in her signal, and Astrid added hers before Ulf did the same. Everyone was set and raring to go.

Astrid closed her eyes and connected with her berserker. The beast threw its head back and roared. She sent it a command to calm, with minimal effect, but she was able to reach beyond her own inner warrior and search for the connection her beast had with the others. The invisible web glowed brightly in her mind. It was familiar but also more intense. Ever since the king's and queen's wedding, the connection she felt with the other warriors had increased in strength.

She followed the threads and identified each of her battle brothers and sisters. She could even detect Irja and Per, although they were dimmer because of their distance. Both emotionally and geographically.

Being on another mission meant their mental focus was not on a shared goal with Astrid. She startled when she noticed a third presence with Irja and Per. Something wasn't right about its essence. She tried to analyze why it felt off, but her own inner warrior grew agitated as she extended her senses.

*Go*, it roared. *Go now*.

Astrid severed the line with the odd connection, which infuriated her berserker. It howled out its frustration.

Someone grabbing her arm made her snap her eyes open. "Odin's eye," Leif said. "Are you okay? It felt like your berserker was on the verge of taking complete control."

"I'm good," Astrid said. "Just a little unused to the strong connection between us." Who was the third berserker with Irja and Per? She looked toward Naya. The queen had been a mortal—might still be a mortal—but she now had an inner warrior. Had Luke developed an inner warrior through the *själsfrände* bond?

"Astrid," Leif shook her.

"What?"

"Are you sure you're okay? You zoned out again, didn't hear a word I said." He frowned. "I think you should sit this one out."

"No," Astrid hissed. "I need this fight." Leif dropped his grip but still looked doubtful. The words rushed out of her. "It's the only thing that will calm the berserker. I'll take up the rear position and return to the car if I feel I'm about to lose control."

Leif hesitated, but then gave her a curt nod. "Fine. But any sign of trouble, and you get the hell out of here."

"Promise."

They fell into position with Leif and Ulf in the lead, shoulder to shoulder. Naya was just behind the men, and

Astrid took the rear as promised. They would go in the back door while Harald and Sten took the front. Torvald and Pekka were positioned by a smaller side door.

They reached the parking lot in the alley and crept along the walls of the building to stay in the shadows. Leif ghosted up the stairs of the loading dock, and the rest of them followed. He and Ulf positioned themselves on either side of the door while Naya and Astrid hung back.

Ulf grabbed the handle and twisted slowly. He made eye contact with the king and nodded once. The door was unlocked.

Leif tapped the ready signal on his mic. It was returned by each of the warriors.

Ulf tore open the door, and the four of them jogged down the hallway to the double doors at the end. Leif kicked them open, and the Viking team spilled into the warehouse.

Twenty or so wolverines milled around in the huge space, stocking the cabinets with supplies. They turned around and froze in place.

Harald and Sten entered on the opposite side of the room a few seconds later. The wolverines' heads swiveled in unison, and Astrid would have laughed if there weren't so many of the creatures.

Torvald and Pekka appeared behind Harald and Sten.

The whole gang was there, so let the fighting commence. The problem was that even if Irja and Per had joined them, they'd still be dealing with a two-to-one opponent ratio. Whatever had jammed the satellite imaging had also kept their berserkers from getting an exact count of the number of wolverines.

Advantage, wolverines.

"Fuck," Harald's voice said in the headset. "What are they waiting for?"

As if his voice had broken their enchantment, the wolverines threw down whatever they had in their hands and rushed the warriors. Astrid's group had only a few seconds to fan out into fighting formation. The wolverines moved impossibly fast. She tried to keep an eye on the two that seemed to be heading her way, but a third came out of nowhere and grabbed her braid from behind. It pulled back her head, exposing her throat. She jammed her elbow in its side and followed up with a back fist when the creature bowed forward.

It lost the grip on her hair, and she rotated her body just in time to avoid a jab from another creature, only to receive a flying punch to her temple from somewhere else. She'd completely lost perspective of where the suckers were. She dropped to the floor and rolled as her head rang from the impact of the punch. Through her headset, she heard the others' grunts and exclamations. They sounded like they were having as much trouble as she was.

She crawled under a counter to regroup, but one of the creatures caught her leg and pulled her out. Astrid twisted so she was facing the floor and pushed off with her palms. She twisted again midair and tried to execute a back kick to the creature's face, but her limited range of motion made the impact too weak to hurt. It was still enough for the wolverine to lose its grip, and she planted both feet on the floor again. Claws swiped along the full length of her back, but luckily her leather jacket held.

The strikes were coming so quickly that all she could

do was try to block and evade. There was no time to get in a kick or a punch of her own. She had no idea how many opponents she was fighting. Three, maybe four?

She opened her connection with the berserker wide. The beast roared alive, its essence expanding until it felt as though it physically existed inside her body, filling her limbs. She caught another jab in the shoulder. The impact threw her into the wall.

The berserker roared a battle cry through Astrid's throat and mouth. She heard answers from the other warriors. She had to dampen the connection with her inner beast to remain in control of her body. The berserker flailed and scratched at its bindings, but she held fast.

A movement out of the corner of her eye had her instinctively throwing a jab. It made solid contact with a creature's jaw. When the wolverine hit the floor, she stomped its throat and crushed its windpipe. She hadn't drawn her knives yet—there hadn't been time—but now she buried a dagger in the wolverine's carotid artery. The berserker screamed in triumph, and again there were answering cries from her battle brothers and Naya.

Her victory was short. A vicious kick to her back made her fall forward, and all the air rushed out of her lungs. She gasped and had the horrible realization that she was losing this battle.

*No!* the berserker screamed. *Fight.*

Claws pierced Astrid's shoulder through the leather. She swept out with her foot and knocked the creature down, but its claws scraped across her already abused back. The leather jacket was getting shredded. She grabbed the creature as it went down and sliced her knife across its throat. It wasn't one of her favorite moves, since it meant she'd be sprayed with blood, but at this point, survival was more important than style.

As she turned in search of another opponent, the lights went off. Curses went off in her headset, and her heart rate increased. The berserker, however, seemed eerily calm. Astrid slowly expanded her connection with it. In her mind's eye, she could "see" where they were in the room, but there was more. She knew where the wolverines were too.

Slowly she expanded her senses. The berserker had always been able to detect if wolverines were near, but not their exact location.

Now Astrid not only sensed the location of each creature, but if she focused on one of them, it was as if they moved in slow motion. She had time to prepare, block, and countermove. She immediately used her advantage to take down another monster and sever its throat.

"Open your senses," she shouted over the headset. "Let your inner warrior show you where the fuckers are."

The other warriors quieted down, but then the first exclamation of wonder came through, and then another. "Odin's ravens," Leif shouted. "I can work with this."

Astrid smiled in the darkness and concentrated on the wolverine closest to her. She hit it with a semicircular kick before burying one of her daggers in the nape of its neck. It went down without a sound, and she swiveled to meet the next attack.

All of a sudden, she heard a shot. When did the wolverines start carrying guns? She didn't feel a bullet's impact, but she sank to the floor as an excruciating pain bloomed in her chest and spread.

The connection with the other warriors faded away.

She could hear her berserker howling, but that too became muted. Her heart pumped slower and slower until it completely stopped. And then everything went blank.

—∿∿—

When she came to, the warehouse had disappeared, and instead she was lying in the grass with a brilliant sun shining from above. She sat up and looked around her. Silver birches surrounded the clearing, their leaves swaying gently in the wind.

This was Freya's meadow. Astrid had spent plenty of time here, around seven hundred years or so. Time passed differently in Asgard though, so counting in human years was futile. Back then, she'd trained with other Valkyries and the meadow was never empty. Where were Freya's maidens now? And why was she here? Had she died?

"No, my daughter. You are not yet departed," a voice said, startling Astrid. Freya sat right beside her in the space that had been empty a moment ago. Her long, straight, silver-blond hair cascaded down her shoulders and ended at her waist. Her white dress sparkled in the bright sunlight.

"Then why am I here?" Astrid stammered.

"To make a choice."

Astrid frowned. "A choice?"

Freya tilted her head. "Of your trust in me."

That didn't even make sense. "I always trust in you."

The goddess laughed. It sounded like silver bells playing in the wind. The birch trees seemed to answer her laughter. Their leaves rustled in time with the bell-like chimes. As quickly as it had started, the laughter stopped.

Freya slapped Astrid hard across the cheek. Her head whipped to the side, and she saw stars.

That was new.

"Then why do you doubt my choice of your *själs-frände*?" the goddess barked.

Astrid cradled her cheek and opened her mouth to answer.

"Don't be so insolent as to attempt a reply." Freya's eyes were deep pools of glittering darkness. "You were always an obstinate Valkyrie. I indulged you because you usually made me proud. Lately, you've done nothing but disappoint me."

Astrid swallowed hard and kept quiet.

"Think about your choices and your actions. From now on, I expect better of you." Freya lifted her hand, and Astrid flinched. Instead of the expected slap, a caress trailed down her cheek. In a blink, the goddess disappeared.

Astrid lay back in the grass and closed her eyes. Freya had chosen Luke for her.

She didn't blindly believe in the gods' will, but a direct order from the goddess was not something to argue with. Although, apparently that's exactly what she'd tried to do.

She moved her jaw. It was still sore. The Mother of Valkyries packed quite a punch. Astrid closed her eyes. How would she get back to Midgard?

She yawned and then winced when her jaw ached again. Drowsiness fell over her like a heavy blanket. She tried to open her eyes, but lost the struggle and sleep claimed her.

—◦◦◦—

Someone was shaking her shoulder. "Wake up, honey. You're safe now."

She struggled to open her eyes and stared into Irja's face bending over hers. "What happened?" she croaked.

Irja smiled. "You passed out in the warehouse. The others brought you home."

She pushed herself up to sit against the headboard. "There was a gunshot." She rubbed her chest, but the pain was gone. "Are the others okay?"

"All the warriors from the warehouse are back in one piece. We had a few claw marks and wounds, but none too serious. I gave everyone antidotes, but except for a slight fever in Torvald, there are no other signs of poison. Sten hit his head and has to be monitored for concussion, but there have been no signs so far. I expect—"

Astrid interrupted. "You're rambling. You only do that when you're nervous or have bad news."

Irja turned around, her eyes were sad. "It's Holden. He got shot."

Astrid rubbed her chest again. "I felt it," she said. "That's why I passed out in the warehouse. I felt his heart stop." She struggled to get up. "I have to go to him." She had to connect with his berserker, make him stay alive.

Irja pushed her back down. "He's not here. He lost too much blood, and I wasn't sure what our immortal blood would do to him. We took him to the hospital so he could get a transfusion using mortal blood."

"Then I'll go there." Astrid put her feet on the floor and stood. She swayed, and Irja caught her before she went down.

"You're not strong enough yet. You've been unconscious for almost twenty-four hours."

"I'll be fine. Just help me get dressed." *Luke had been shot. His heart had stopped.* Her breath hitched. "Irja, I have to go to him."

"There's nothing you can do for him. He's in intensive care. The doctors operated to repair the damage, and they managed to start his heart again." She swallowed. "He's in a coma. They don't know if he'll come back to us."

"He'll come back to me," Astrid said.

Sadness clouded Irja's face. "We don't know that."

"I do know," Astrid insisted. "Freya told me."

Irja hesitated but then nodded. "I'll drive you."

---

Astrid walked into Luke's room without Irja. The nurse at the station had said only two visitors at a time were allowed, and someone was already in there. The first thing she saw as she stepped through the door was Luke lying motionless in a hospital bed. He was hooked up to a heart monitor and an IV. She blinked furiously to dry the moisture in her eyes. She'd promised herself never to cry over Luke again.

Someone cleared their throat, and she looked up. Rex smiled at her gently from across the room. "They called me when he arrived," he said. "Apparently, I'm his emergency contact."

"How is he?"

The tall, dark man shook his head. "They say he could wake up any minute." He scratched his jaw. "Or never. Basically, they have no idea why he's not waking up."

Astrid walked up to the bed and put her hand over Luke's, the one that wasn't hooked up to the heart monitor. "It's my fault he got shot," she said. She tapped into her berserker and tried to get it to connect with Luke's. The beast ignored her but grunted contentedly as she stroked Luke's hand.

"Come again?" Rex asked. "Did you tell him to go meet criminals in the middle of the night without backup?"

"He did have backup."

"He didn't have me." His voice was laced with anger. "If he'd told me what he was up to, I could have covered his ass. Instead he left me to babysit the club."

"He had his reasons for keeping you out of it."

"Oh please, like I didn't know he was Mr. Undercover Cop. It was obvious his heart wasn't in the money laundering he supposedly used to finance the club. I saw the accounts. He was stupidly happy over making legal money. Anything dirty, he ferreted away and didn't touch. He couldn't pretend to break the law if his life depended on it."

"He pretended well enough for me," Astrid said quietly.

Rex rocked back on his heels. "I thought you were undercover too."

She smiled sadly. "Nope, I was the mark. I had no idea it was all pretend."

"If you think Luke's feelings for you were fake, you're seriously deluded. Ever since you first stepped into the club, he's never been able to keep his eyes off you." Rex chuckled. "Took him long enough to make his move, and then you disappeared. He was foul-tempered for months after that."

Hope rose in Astrid's chest. Freya had told her to trust in the goddess's choice. She'd basically bitch-slapped Astrid for not following her berserker's lead. "He was probably irritated because he didn't know how to find me and he needed to get close to me for his mission."

"Nope, that's not it. The guy had—has—it bad for you." Rex walked across the room to a chair in the corner and picked up a jacket. "Now that you're here, I'm going back to the club to make sure it keeps making money for him." He handed her a card. "Call me if you need me."

"Thanks, Rex." Astrid's smile was wobbly.

"Anytime." He left the room.

Astrid sank down in the chair next to the hospital bed. All she had to do now was will Luke to wake up so she could tell him what a dickhead he was. And then maybe she'd forgive him. She shook her head. No, she wanted them to start over with a clean slate. No forgiveness or guilt. Just the two of them getting to know each other without hidden agendas.

She lowered her head and prayed to Freya for a second chance.

# Chapter 25

THE NURSE CAME IN TO CHECK LUKE'S VITAL SIGNS, startling Astrid from her dozing. She sat up straight. Her neck creaked as she worked out the kinks. Two days in the chair was making her very stiff. The nurse gave her a small sympathetic smile, which Astrid returned. It felt more like a grimace though.

She looked over at Luke, who still looked like he was just sleeping. And maybe he was, but he'd been sleeping since his surgery three days ago. All vital signs were normal. The doctors assured her the operation had been a success, but they still didn't know why he wouldn't wake up.

She tapped into her berserker. The beast was happy and content as long as Astrid remained next to Luke. She tried to reach further, to connect with the other warriors and see if she could find the presence in the web that she thought might be Luke.

Her berserker didn't allow any access beyond the connection between it and Astrid. It remained completely focused on Luke in the real world and didn't give a shit about any of the other warriors. Stubborn beast.

A soft knock on the open door announced Ulf. "Hey." He smiled carefully.

Astrid hadn't seen him since the fight in the warehouse. Irja and Naya had both visited the hospital and kept her company, but the rest of the warriors had stayed away. They probably thought she was unstable with her *själsfrände* injured. She returned Ulf's smile. "Hey, yourself."

He held up a duffel bag. "Naya told me to bring you some clean clothes."

"That's great. Thanks." She grabbed the bag and put it in the corner.

Ulf wiped his hands on his jeans. "She would have come herself, but she and Leif are prepping Whalert. He testifies tomorrow." Naya and Ulf had hacked into enough records to figure out that the person who had manipulated DTU to put a kill order on Whalert was a federal prosecutor. They didn't know how deep the corruption went, but they had enough information to clear Whalert.

Unfortunately, that's as far as the trail went. The federal prosecutor had taken money to falsify documents that would get rid of Whalert, but he didn't know anything beyond that. And the person who had paid him was a fake persona no longer used. No leads to who had used the ID could be found.

Kraus was dead, so they couldn't extract any information from him. Per had put a bullet in his head as soon as Kraus shot Luke. Astrid rubbed her chest. "I'm sure Whalert will do well during his hearing."

Ulf smiled weakly and turned to look at Luke. "How is he?"

"The same. His vital signs are strong. There's no reason why he shouldn't come out of the coma. The doctor says it can happen any time, but also not to have hope, because it may *not* happen."

"Talk about mixed messages." Ulf rubbed his jaw. "Listen, I want to apologize for being a complete ass."

"You already apologized for that," Astrid said. "In the game room when you told me about Kraus and Luke."

Ulf grimaced. "About that." He pointed to the armchairs by the hospital bed. "Can I sit?"

"Sure." Astrid sat down in the chair closest to the wall, and Ulf took the other.

"I may have been a little overzealous in digging up dirt on Holden. I was very motivated after he showed up at the wedding."

"If you hadn't found that footage, Naya would have eventually. You did your job. Don't feel bad about it."

"I still could have handled the whole situation with your *själsfrände* with a little more grace and dignity." He glanced at Luke in the bed. "I went a little crazy."

Astrid shrugged. "It happens." She truly didn't have any hard feelings against Ulf. He'd been reckless and messed up. She'd been in that situation herself several times, especially during the first century she'd spent among the mortals. She had no right to judge.

"Leif is sending help to the Vikings in New Mexico. Scott and Pekka volunteered to go, and I'm joining them."

"You don't have to leave." Three warriors gone would seriously deplete their defenses. Plus, as much of a pain in the ass as Ulf was, she'd still miss him. Ulf had been part of her family for eighty years.

"I know, but I want to. I'd like to see more of Midgard than just Pine Rapids."

"It's going to be weird not having you to bicker with," she said.

He laughed. "Friends?"

"Friends." She leaned over and hugged him. Ulf stiffened at first, but then put his arms around her and held on for a while. Something loosened within Astrid. It felt like a click deep inside her body. Her berserker growled loudly. She withdrew from Ulf. He kept his arms around her in a loose embrace.

Astrid looked over at Luke.

He watched them intently, storm clouds brewing in his gunmetal eyes. "Get your hands off her," he croaked.

Ulf laughed again and squeezed Astrid one last time before letting go. "She's all yours." He stood and left the room.

Luke's eyes were blazing with anger as he watched him go.

"You're awake," Astrid whispered.

"Why are you making out with him?"

"That's your first question? You're in a coma for three days, and that's what you want to know first?" She rubbed her forehead. "I am seriously so happy to have two X chromosomes."

—⁓—

Even with bags under her eyes, Astrid was the most beautiful woman he'd seen. Luke tried to reach for her, but there were wires in his way. She noticed him struggling and came and sat on the bed next to him.

"What happened?" His throat felt like sandpaper.

Astrid handed him a cup of water with a straw. "You were shot." He remembered the meeting with Kraus. One of his questions must have tipped the guy, because all of a sudden he had a gun in his hand.

Luke struggled to sit up. Astrid helped, piling a bunch of pillows behind him. "I patted him down," he said. "He had no gun on him."

"It was taped under the table." So maybe the guy had been suspicious from the beginning.

"How long was I out?"

Astrid swallowed. "Your heart stopped, and you lost a lot of blood. The doctors operated on you for ten hours. That was three days ago."

"I've been an idiot."

"Yeah, you swept the place before the meeting and didn't check under the table. I'm surprised Irja and Per didn't double-check your sweep." She fiddled with his pillows again. "Rex is pissed you didn't bring him for backup. He says he would have found the gun."

"That's not what I meant. Although, I wouldn't let Irja and Per check the diner. I thought bringing strangers would tip Kraus off and told them to stay out of sight." He cleared his throat. "No, I've been an idiot about us."

"Yeah, that too." Astrid caressed his jaw, a small smile on her face. Was it possible that she would give him another chance?

"I will fix it though." He fingered one of her curls. "I love you. I think I've loved you since I first saw you."

She snorted. "Lust and love are not the same thing."

He grinned. If she was joking about the situation, there was still hope. "We can figure this out. Give me a chance to prove that I love you."

She tapped her index finger to her mouth. "I'll think about it."

He pulled on the curl he was holding until her lips met his. Calm poured into him from the contact, and something deep inside him purred as if he were a fucking cat. Startled, he let go of Astrid. "What the hell was that?"

Her eyes glittered with laughter. "We're going to have to test this, but I'm pretty sure you've somehow acquired a berserker."

That would take some time to get used to. "Let's test it right now. Kiss me again."

She pulled back. "On one condition."

He'd give her anything she wanted. "What?"

"Tell me why three days of me pleading with you to wake up were completely ineffective, but me hugging Ulf made you perk right up."

He paused. "I don't know what happened. I was dreaming about you and everything was peaceful, then all of a sudden all my instincts were on alert. It felt like a major threat. I opened my eyes and there he was, making out with you."

Astrid mumbled something under her breath. It sounded like "testosterone overload," but he didn't pay attention because she leaned down and kissed him again.

# Epilogue

*Three months later*

ASTRID PUT AWAY THE SWORD SHE'D POLISHED AND sharpened and walked into the training area. She reached for some tape to use on her hands while she pummeled the sandbag. She'd pretty much moved in with Luke. It didn't take much—he gave her some closet space and she was good to go. She still came back to the fortress to work out though. Luke's apartment building had a state-of-the-art gym, but it wasn't the same as working out with the equipment in the fortress. For starters, there were too many people in Luke's gym. She needed space to practice jabs and kicks on the sandbags. Plus, the mortals would freak out if she sweated it out at top capacity. And there was no sparring ring at the fancy gym. Not that she'd get a workout if she went up against humans, but a true gym needed space for sparring.

They'd had to come up with a new patrol schedule since Ulf and Pekka had left. Scott hadn't really participated in patrols, but he'd been in charge of the training schedules and the weapons. His absence was definitely noticeable.

If it wasn't for the fact that only sporadic wolverines showed up every now and then, they would have been in trouble with three men short. Things were so slow that Irja considered leaving on an extended medical rotation.

Although most other Viking warrior tribes had some kind of medical person among them, there weren't many with Irja's capabilities. She'd gone to modern medical school and conducted research on various medications for the Norse. Most recently, she'd figured out the antidote to the wolverine poisons. Other Viking tribes constantly requested that Irja come for a visit. Astrid worried about Irja. The Finnish Valkyrie seemed down, maybe because she missed her brother.

Astrid finished taping up her hands and started her warm-up. Since today was a light day, she didn't bother with gloves before attacking the sandbag. Her training was completely different now that the berserker wasn't always clamoring for control. She could focus on increasing her skills instead of going for complete exhaustion to sleep at night.

That problem no longer existed. Luke made sure she was tired before they went to sleep. Astrid smiled. They spent most of their days apart, she at the fortress and Luke at his office. Officially, he was still managing the nightclub, but Rex actually did most of those duties. Luke was the new liaison between DTU and the Norse warriors. Whalert had been reinstated as Luke's boss. He still thought Leif was the commanding officer of an SOG unit, which worked out well. The new partnership was only known by Whalert and Luke. Until they found out who in the government was in charge of the covert labs, DTU would remain a secret.

Astrid executed a semicircular kick and bounced on the balls of her feet as she prepared for a series of jabs and hooks. She paused when Per came running into the room. The younger Viking stopped to catch his breath.

"Hey," he wheezed. "I need your help."

"With what?"

"This thing outside in the glen." He ran out again.

That made no sense, but Astrid followed him to the clearing in the woods. She slowed as she drew nearer. Everyone was clustered around the big basalt rock at the end. She approached slowly.

"You're in workout clothes," Naya said when she saw Astrid.

"Yeah," Astrid drawled. "I was working out."

"Never mind." Irja took her hand. "Come here." She pushed Astrid in front of the group.

The warriors parted and formed a semicircle behind her. She turned around. "What's going on?"

Harald grabbed her shoulders and made her face the slab again.

Luke walked out of the trees, dressed in a charcoal tunic over pants in the same color. He wore a navy wool cloak fastened with a Norse silver brooch. He looked amazing.

When he reached her, he swung the cloak back across one shoulder and lowered himself on one knee.

"What are you doing?" she asked, her heart racing.

"Hush, *jänta*," Torvald said. "It'll be obvious in a moment."

Luke grabbed her left hand. He frowned at the tape but then shook his head. "Astrid," he said, looking up into her eyes. "I have loved you ever since that first moment I saw you and fell in lust with you."

Laughter bubbled up inside her. She threw back her head and let it escape.

Luke smiled, but the others looked at her like she'd

completely lost it. Considering how much trouble she had trying to stop laughing, they might not be wrong.

Luke tugged on her hand, and she calmed down.

*Listen*, the berserker demanded, which was ironic considering how rarely the beast listened to Astrid.

"You are the strongest, most courageous warrior I've known." He held up a thick gold ring with an oval, green jade stone. "This made me think of your amazing eyes. Would you give me the immense honor of becoming *min fru*?" His pronunciation was horrible, but she understood well enough.

Astrid couldn't draw in enough air to say anything. She nodded, and a cheer went up behind her. "Yes," she whispered when she was finally able to breathe. "*Ja*."

Luke tore off the tape on her left hand and pushed the ring onto her finger. It fit perfectly. She held out her hand to admire it.

The leaves of the ash trees rustled.

*Good choice*, Freya's voice whispered right next to Astrid's ear. She turned, but the goddess wasn't there.

"There's more," Naya shouted. Leif clamped his hand over her mouth, and whatever she was going to say next was lost in a series of furious mumbles.

Sten held out a roll of papers, which Luke grabbed. He motioned for Astrid to step up to the stone slab with him. She joined him and watched him roll out the papers on the flat surface. They were blueprints.

Astrid peered down on them, trying to make sense of the lines. "What are those?"

"Our new home," Luke said. "If you want it to be." He looked worried.

She looked closer at the drawings. "But that's the fortress."

"Yes." Luke put his finger on one area of the drawing. "But this is a part of the fortress that doesn't exist yet. An extension." He peeled off the top sheet. The new drawing was a blowup of what he'd pointed to before. "We'll have our own suite of rooms and a small kitchen." He grinned. "And a large shower with dual heads."

Astrid returned his grin. Her head spun. He was giving her a house, right here where her family lived. "Who's going to build this? Nobody can find this place unless they're in the car with one of us."

The king cleared his throat. "When the architect came to do the drawings, Naya convinced him that I'm an eccentric millionaire who only allows my vehicles, driven by my people, to come onto the property. I'd be willing to resume that role for a limited time with the builders."

Astrid giggled and the king threw her the evil eye, which made her laugh harder.

Luke pulled her in for a hug. "The warriors and I will do most of the work. We'll only need actual builders for the big jobs."

"I better help," Astrid said. "Have you seen how projects planned by only men have worked out around here?"

Luke grinned and gave her a quick kiss. "I know you're more than capable of building a house." His face turned serious. "But let me do this for you. Let me give you—give us—a proper home."

Astrid pressed her lips against his. "You already have," she whispered.

Luke let go of the drawings and pulled her into his embrace. He leaned her back against the rock slab and deepened the kiss.

"Time for everyone else to leave," Naya shouted to the others.

Astrid was dimly aware of the group leaving, but then she aimed her full attention on the man kissing her. He was her everything.

He was her home.

*Keep reading for an excerpt from the first in Asa Maria Bradley's Viking Warriors series*

# VIKING WARRIOR RISING

NAYA'S HANDS SHOOK AS SHE CLIPPED THE LAST ALLI-gator clamp over the electrical wires, short-circuiting the power and the security alarm.

"Get it together," she muttered to herself.

As she crouched and peered down the darkened corridor, her infrared goggles helped her see the contours of the barred doors. Her brother was behind one of those. Alone.

She jogged down the hallway to the only cell giving off a heat signature.

"Scott," she whispered through the bars of the cell door, but the man lying on the cot didn't move. Her fingers recoiled when she touched the cold metal, remembering how often she'd been trapped in a cell just like this. She had to get her brother out. He'd suffered enough at the hands of Dr. Trousil and the rest of the lab's scientists. They both had.

The door swung open silently and she entered the cell. She shook her brother's shoulder, keeping her hand hovering over his mouth in case he woke up screaming.

He remained lying limply on his side. When she turned him onto his back, his arm flopped over and dangled down the side of the cot.

Holding her breath, she leaned closer to his mouth. A weak puff of air fluttered against her cheek. Relief flooded her body. She joggled him again. "Scott, you need to wake up."

He still didn't react.

Naya hoisted him in a fireman's carry so that her much smaller frame could transport his six-foot body. Another five minutes and the security guards would return to patrol this end of the building. She'd figure out how to wake him later.

Her brother had weighed almost two hundred pounds when she last saw him. It had taken her eleven months and six days to return. Hanging across her shoulder now, his body barely slowed her down. She headed for the closest exit. The door closed softly behind her and she jogged across the field. When she reached the perimeter fence, Naya carefully lowered her brother to the ground and slid the bolt cutters out of her backpack.

"Hold on, Scott. Just a few snips and I'll have you out of here." She glanced down, trying for a hopeful smile, but her lips quivered. She remembered his nervous, yet excited, laugh as they raced toward this same fence that night almost a year ago. They had been so close to getting out together. He'd boosted her up on top of the fence, smacking her behind. "Let's finally get the hell out of here," he'd shouted.

She'd just reached down to help up Scott when the first shot rang out. The second pierced her brother's thigh and he fell screaming to the ground.

She blinked. *Can't think about the past now.* She couldn't fuck this up. There might never be another chance. Her sharp cutters snipped the wires like they were string instead of high-grade reinforced steel. A normal human wouldn't be able to bend back the serrated wire, but Naya was not normal. Ten years in the lab and weekly serum injections had created a super-soldier out of the twelve-year-old girl she had once been. Now she was the ultimate weapon. The ultimate freak.

She doubled over the folded metal to keep her brother from getting caught on any rough edges. Her baby brother. The only family she had left.

She slid Scott's unconscious body through the hole, hoisted him over her shoulder again, and then headed to the rental car parked in the woods. The smell of fresh pine permeated the air as her combat boots pounded the needle-covered ground. The crisp forest cleared her mind of things she no longer wanted to remember.

Now that Scott was out, she could build a life and never think about the years in the lab.

Soon, the dark-green Jeep glittered in the moonlight filtering through the trees. Without slowing, she punched a button on the key remote. Behind her, a powerful boom of an explosion drowned out the double beep of the doors unlocking. A kaleidoscope of red and orange illuminated the night sky. She heard shouts and commands carry through the woods from the compound. A bitter smile stretched her lips. That would keep them occupied for a while.

Growing up in the compound, she'd spent countless hours honing her combat skills, but the government-sponsored black ops program had also trained her in electronics, cyber technology, and weaponry—including explosives. "I used everything you taught me," she whispered at the flames.

She cradled Scott's head as she slid him into the backseat. His eyelids fluttered. For an instant, indigo-blue eyes so like hers focused on her. A slow smile spread across her brother's face before his eyelids fluttered closed again. "I knew you'd come for me, Neyney."

The childhood nickname pierced her heart. "I told you I would," she whispered. She kissed his forehead and brushed back his ink-black curls—the same color as her own spit-straight hair.

He mumbled something incomprehensible before his body fell limp against the seat. She clicked his seat belt in place and allowed herself to touch his face once more before she slid into the driver's seat. A glance in the rearview mirror told her the lab security forces were too busy fighting fires to come after her—for now. But they would eventually. And when they did, she'd better be ready for them. No way she'd let them imprison her brother, or her, again.

She threw the Jeep into four-wheel drive, hit the accelerator, and pushed the car as hard as she could down the rutted old logging road. Scott's head bobbed back and forth in the rearview mirror, but he didn't wake up. She swallowed the lump in her throat and pressed harder on the gas. Once they reached the main arterial, she eased off the pedal. No reason to attract attention.

She tuned the radio to the classical music station. Getting to Dr. Rosen's clinic in Colorado was the most important thing now. The doctor and his team had been sampling her blood for the last six months. Hopefully whatever he had learned would help Scott. Dr. Rosen was the best in his field. More importantly, he was her only hope for curing her brother. She settled in for the fifteen-hour drive from North Dakota to the exclusive medical facility.

---

Two days later, Naya struggled to keep her expression neutral as Dr. Rosen leaned forward in his chair, concern glimmering in his emerald eyes. He pushed up the rimless glasses perched on his nose and addressed her by the alias she'd given when they first met. "Ms. Driscoll, I'm afraid there has been no improvement in your brother since his intake."

"Maybe we need to give it a little longer before the drugs will work." She resented how her voice sounded. Pleading. She hated not being strong.

Dr. Rosen paused, his eyes kind. "I don't think waiting will help. I'm afraid we're going to have to try a different approach."

Naya's gaze drifted from the doctor's as she allowed his words to sink in. A bank of windows behind his desk revealed breathtaking views of snowcapped mountains. The clinic's exclusive clientele included media-shy movie stars and foreign dignitaries. It was the perfect place to hide her brother. She also needed it to be the perfect place to cure him.

"You said the modified formula your team developed based on my blood looked promising." All that research for nothing, but she refused to give up. There had to be a way to save her brother.

Dr. Rosen pushed up his glasses. "We had some promising nerve reactions after the first doses, but Scott reverted back to his vegetative state—"

"Don't say that." Naya burst out of the chair. "He's not a vegetable. He holds himself up, supports his body without help." She clenched her fists. "He spoke to me, damn it."

He held up his hands, palms facing her. "That may have been a temporary reprieve from his condition."

She slowly sat down again. "Are you saying he's getting worse?"

"At this point, I don't have a clear diagnosis. However, unresponsive and bedridden patients run a higher risk of infection, which can lead to respiratory complications, even organ failures. I can remedy that with antibiotics, but I'm not sure I can repair the extensive neurological damage Scott has sustained."

To avoid the pity in the doctor's eyes, Naya looked out over the mountains again. "Why are the drugs in Scott's blood shutting him down when I'm functioning just fine?" Better than fine, but the doctor didn't need to know that. He lived in the normal human world, blissfully ignorant of monsters and freaks like her.

"What do you propose?" Naya gripped the armrest of the chair and eased up when she heard the wood creaking. She had to rein in her emotions or she'd treat the doctor to a full freak show.

"We can continue to tweak the formula and hope for better results. I'd also like to explore your brother's vascular system and test how it differs from yours." He put his hands on the desk. "At this point, I must caution you about the high cost of therapy that may ultimately not produce the outcome you want."

"Let me worry about the money." Nothing was too costly if it helped Scott. Besides, she earned enough. As one of the best cybersecurity experts in the world, her services did not come cheap.

She stood. "I'd like to visit with my brother again before I leave."

The doctor rose as well. "Of course. He'll be well cared for until you come back."

"Until then, please keep me updated."

Dr. Rosen nodded. "I will personally send you a weekly report."

Naya thanked him before leaving the office.

She didn't want to leave her brother, but living near Scott in Colorado was too risky. If the handlers found her, they might also find him. Naya harbored no illusions about their outcome if the handlers caught them. They would be neutralized, or worse, returned to the lab for more experiments.

Naya wouldn't let that happen.

Her heavy boots beat a dull staccato as she strode down the hallway. Smells of antiseptics and disinfectant wafted through the air. Naya shivered. Those same scents had permeated the lab in which she had spent most of her life.

Taking a deep breath, she opened the door to her brother's room. He sat unmoving in a wheelchair, staring into space with empty eyes. "Scotty, it's me, Naya." She crouched before him, taking his limp hands in hers. His skin was dry and warm. He had spent the last two days sitting or lying, depending on which position the nurses put him, and always unnaturally still. He hadn't spoken to her again.

"I know you can hear me." She paused, waiting for a response. Naya touched her brother's cheek and hair, but he didn't react. She stood and averted her face to hide the tears about to spill. "Shall I read to you a little? How far did we get this morning?" She crossed the room and picked up the astronomy book she'd bought, his favorite subject. At least it had been when he still talked and walked and laughed.

She wouldn't let her thoughts continue down that depressing path, as if he was already beyond saving. Instead, she began reading to her brother about distant nebulas and galaxies. For another hour, she would pretend they were back in their childhood home, their parents still alive and watching TV while she read her little brother a bedtime story.

# Acknowledgments

I would need an infinite amount of pages to acknowledge everyone who deserves it, but I want to say thank-you to:

Sarah Elizabeth Younger, for being a friend and the best agent a writer could wish for. And to Nancy Yost and the rest of the NYLA team.

My editor, Cat Clyne, for her endless patience, support, and understanding. She has taught me so much. I love working with her.

The Sourcebooks team, with special shout-outs to Deb Werksman, Amelia Narigon, Beth Sochacki, Heather Hall, and Dawn Adams.

The Dreamweavers and Team Sarah. They help me through the challenges and are the first to celebrate my triumphs.

The Spokane Wild Women, especially Jere' and Ally, for being my biggest fans.

Cherry Adair, Virna DePaul, Sara Humphreys, Paige Tyler, Susanna Kearsley, Gina Conkle, Rebecca Zanetti, and Ilona Andrews, all authors who generously supported me.

The bloggers who showered the series with love, especially Elizabeth Haney, Jessie Smith, Phoebe Chase, and Sue Brown-Moore.

My readers for loving the Viking Warriors and for writing to tell me about it.

My Swedish, English, and Texan family. Especially my mom and my brother who live far from me but are always near my heart.

My husband for being my anchor, my best friend, and my very own Happily Ever After.

# About the Author

A double RITA finalist in 2016, Asa Maria Bradley grew up in Sweden surrounded by archaeology and history steeped in Norse mythology, which inspired the immortal Viking and Valkyries in the Viking Warriors series. She arrived in the United States as a high school exchange student and quickly became addicted to ranch dressing and cop TV shows. Asa holds an MFA in creative writing and an MS in medical physics. She lives on a lake deep in the pine forests of the Pacific Northwest with her British husband and a rescue dog of indeterminate breed. Visit her at AsaMariaBradley.com and follow her on Twitter @AsaMariaBradley.